I0823285

GILDED IN VENGEANCE

ALSO BY LYSSA MIA SMITH

REVELLE

GILDED IN VENGEANCE

LYSSA MIA SMITH

STORYTIDE
An Imprint of HarperCollins*Publishers*

HarperCollins Children's Books,
a division of HarperCollins Publishers,
195 Broadway, New York, NY 10007

HarperCollins Publishers, Macken House,
39/40 Mayor Street Upper, Dublin 1, D01 C9W8, Ireland

Storytide is an imprint of HarperCollins Publishers.

Gilded in Vengeance

harpercollins.com
Library of Congress Control Number: 2025940238
ISBN 978-0-06-323962-3
25 26 27 28 29 LBC 5 4 3 2 1
First Edition

For the girls who know the precise pain
of a friend's knife deep in their backs

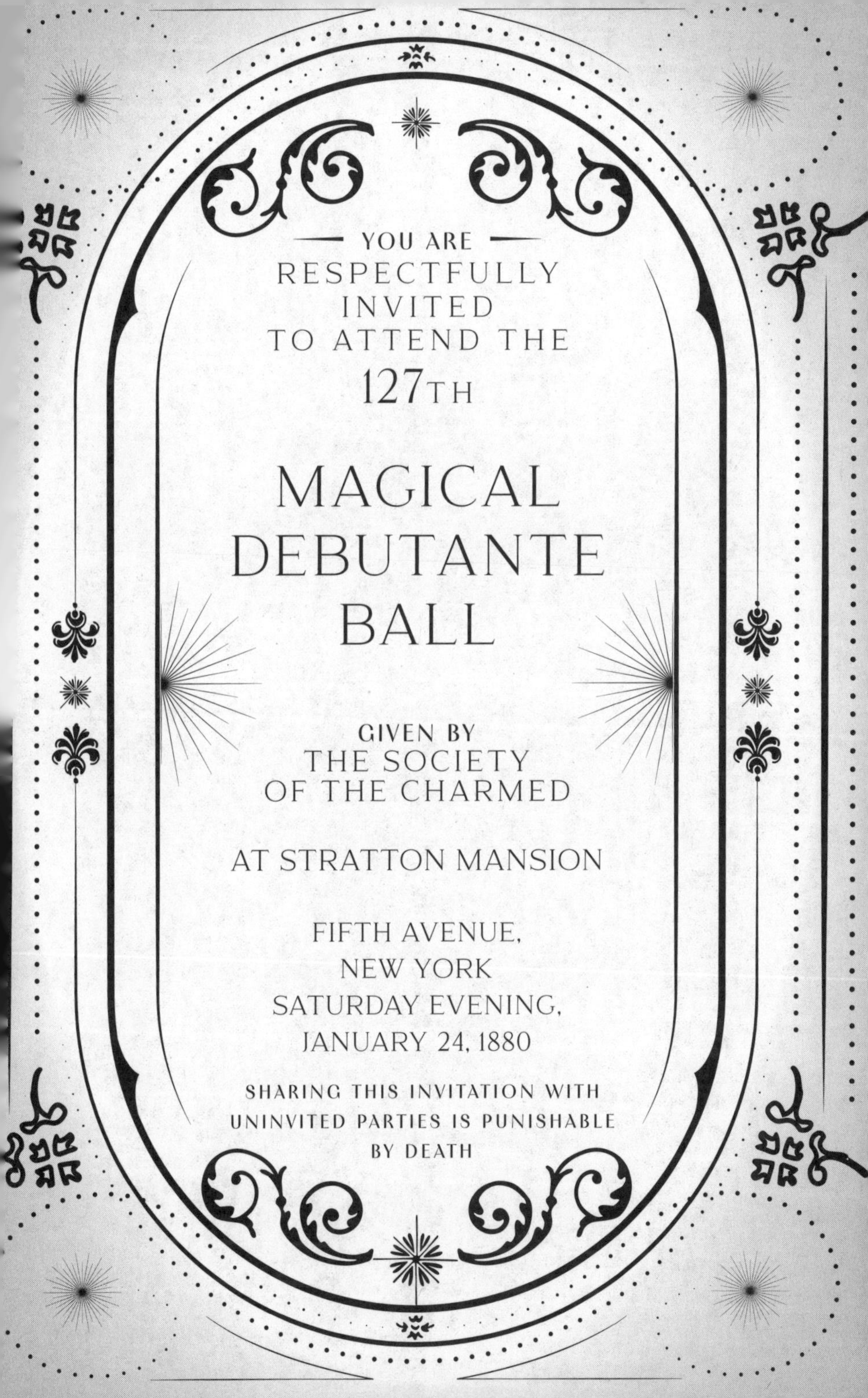
YOU ARE
RESPECTFULLY
INVITED
TO ATTEND THE
127TH
MAGICAL
DEBUTANTE
BALL
GIVEN BY
THE SOCIETY
OF THE CHARMED
AT STRATTON MANSION
FIFTH AVENUE,
NEW YORK
SATURDAY EVENING,
JANUARY 24, 1880
SHARING THIS INVITATION WITH
UNINVITED PARTIES IS PUNISHABLE
BY DEATH

PROLOGUE

TWO GIRLS ATTENDED A MAGICAL ball, but one was never seen again.

Their invitations arrived months in advance, whorls of black ink shimmering with eternal wetness. Hiding them beneath their floorboards, the girls dared to gaze upon them only late at night, when the ruckus of their tenement house had settled to a peaceful whisper. By day, they could not risk a glimpse.

Out of sight, but never out of mind.

They ought to practice their magic, Emmy insisted. To gain acceptance into the secretive Society of the Charmed, they needed to perfect their rare magical gifts.

They ought to practice their dancing, Grace always countered. For the girls to gain acceptance, the Society must deem them elegant young ladies, worthy of matches with their handsome sons.

Enchantments or etiquette? Magical laws or social ones? The same debate they'd had since they'd each discovered that the little girl across the hall also possessed magic. The world's oldest, most sacred secret, and they were both a part of it.

But never apart from each other.

Magic's existence was an invisible shield, safeguarding them from the mundane world of school and sewing, all of which they endured together. They had no thoughts they did not share. No dreams that went unspoken. Whenever Grace's mother disappeared into the beer cellars for weeks at a time, Grace wordlessly found her way to Emmy's flat. When the vile woman inevitably crawled home, Emmy's father still set an extra place at his kitchen table for Grace, and one at his candlelit magic lessons, too. He had one daughter of his blood, as he liked to say, but two of his heart.

And so, as the winter nights grew colder and the ball drew closer, Emmy timed how long she could endure magic's suffocating weight while Grace befriended a girl with the gift of fabric enchantment, then begged her to make their gowns. Emmy attempted to transform cheap metals into solid gold while Grace perfected her posture by balancing Emmy's books on her head.

Emmy dreamed of feeding her insatiable appetite for magical knowledge. For answers.

Grace dreamed of never feeling hungry again.

The night of the ball, Emmy and Grace draped cloaks over their gowns and hurried to the luxurious horse-drawn carriage. If any of their neighbors had looked too closely, they might have noticed that faint clouds meandered over Emmy's skirts while snowflakes careened over Grace's. Enchanted gowns, just like those in Emmy's fairy tale books.

Jimmy Li, the tallest and most handsome of the tenement boys, offered Emmy his hand as she teetered on the carriage step, unaccustomed to a proper gown's absurd weight. Their neighbors beamed at Emmy's father, whose gifts as a healer had saved many from the curse of unemployment and its bedfellow, destitution. Even without knowing of magic's existence, they knew a miracle worker lived among them, and they loved him for it.

As the horses trotted away, Emmy rubbed the hand Jimmy had touched, her high spirits fading. Truth be told, the girls knew little of the Society of the Charmed, save what Grace's father had disclosed during his rare visits. Merely accepting the invitation was to commit to one of two fates: That of Society servants, like the maids who harnessed wind to dust the great mansions or the gardeners who kept roses in bloom all winter long. Or that of protégés, debutantes of humble roots but extraordinary potential who received patronage from the Society's elite families so that they could join its upper ranks.

Both girls, Grace's father had said with pride, had what it took to become protégés. Emmy thought he'd meant they were unusually talented. Grace had thought it was because they were pretty. He'd died before they could ask. But two years later, their invitations had arrived like he'd promised.

Tonight was their only chance to prove their worth.

If the Society deemed them protégés, this would be the first of many balls they'd attend together. It was a future they'd envisioned for ages: Emmy losing time in libraries bursting with ancient magical texts, only to be dragged out by Grace, who'd have closets full of fashionable gowns waiting, courtesy of their generous stipends. The tutors who'd push their magic to new heights, ensuring that both girls remained beloved contributors to the Society. The culinary delights they'd taste together. The music, the dancing, the pageants and plays. And though Emmy vowed to return home often to amuse Papa with tales of life uptown, Grace swore she'd never set foot south of grimy Houston Street again.

Outside the carriage windows, regal brownstones replaced the ramshackle tenement houses. The streets grew quieter, the velvety evening sky free of chimney smoke and clotheslines and telegraph wires. As Emmy gazed at the first stars, an otherworldly calm swept through her, even as Grace trembled with unbidden anxiety. They both possessed unique gifts, which ought to set them apart from the debutantes with common elemental magic. Wearing such stunning gowns, they looked more like proper young belles than future maids. And most importantly, they had practiced and trained for as long as Emmy could remember. They were ready.

That tranquility stayed with Emmy as they entered the alley beside the grandiose manor and masked guards hurried them through a hidden door, their revolvers dark streaks against their pearl-white uniforms. As they stepped inside the majestic ballroom and were promptly separated from Papa. As they watched their fellow debutantes, also sixteen and wide-eyed, showcase their wondrous gifts. Rain making. Wind harnessing. And, most astounding, a scarlet-haired girl who disappeared from the stage, rendering herself invisible.

Despite the formidable showing, Emmy's cheeks ached from smiling. Until tonight, she'd seen only Grace's and Papa's gifts. There was still so much to learn, so much she did not understand about how magic worked. Its origins. Why a few possessed it but most didn't. And although she cheered for each debutante, she knew, in her heart, that her gift could outshine theirs.

Grace knew it, too. All too well.

Upon her turn, Emmy climbed onto the stage and faced the sea of masked strangers: the Society of the Charmed. If Grace was correct, some of the richest, most powerful people in New York were among its secret ranks. Beneath their white masks, their eyes appeared icy, but Emmy kept her gaze fixed on Papa, who stood in the back with the other debutante parents.

Emmy held a small toy soldier out to the crowd. Once they'd had ample chance to see how ordinary it was, she closed her fist around it and, with a ragged inhale, tugged on her power.

It answered her call immediately, the air cooling with the invisible mist that always accompanied magic. As she pulled it into her lungs, its heaviness spread over her until her muscles trembled from the effort. In her mind's eye, she envisioned the toy soldier in her palm. *Tin, tin, aluminum. Tin, tin, aluminum.* With a heaving breath, she forced her magic inside the figurine, making the metal denser. Richer. Exquisitely shiny, like the golden shimmer of Grace's hair in the sunlight. As strong as Papa's hands when he laid brick. As soft as his touch when he kissed her forehead before leaving for his shift.

It was risky, attempting a transformation she'd achieved only a few days earlier, but Emmy could not think of failure, not while the metal grew warm and slick in her hand. She hardened the gold—it *had* to be gold, not metal gunk, or even gilded tin.

When she could bear it no longer, Emmy released her magic and opened her palms.

A golden nugget glittered in the candlelight. Misshapen, yes, but shiny and pure.

On trembling legs, Emmy crossed the stage and dropped it onto the table occupied by three men. The triumvirate, Grace had called them. The leaders of the Society of the Charmed.

They snatched the gold she'd conjured, scrutinizing it as Emmy caught her breath. Their faces remained hidden, but their eyes were rapt with interest.

One by one, the triumvirate rose, their gazes fixed on Emmy.

One by one, they began to clap.

The audience surged to their feet, their cheers so thunderous, the stage vibrated beneath her. Papa beamed with the same pride that ballooned in Emmy's chest. She could have drowned in her happiness, in the exquisite satisfaction that she'd done it. She'd dazzled the Society of the Charmed by transforming cheap metal into solid gold.

So enraptured was Emmy, she did not notice the tuxedo-clad boy in the front row, gaping at her in unfathomable recognition. His eyes were as gray as rain, his mouth parted in shock.

So enraptured was Emmy, she did not notice the strain in Grace's smile as they embraced beside the stage. She did not even notice how Grace's hands shook as Grace showcased her own rare gift, imbuing a silk glove with the redhead's invisibility so that its wearer disappeared from sight. Bridging magic, her father had called it. Infusing objects with the magic of others.

But once Grace's standing ovation had finished—a hair less enthused than Emmy's, though both girls pretended not to notice—Grace never looked away from her oldest, dearest friend. Grace watched, her blue eyes wide with childlike innocence, as the triumvirate called Emmy back to the stage.

Grace watched, with bated breath, as they accused Emmy of fraudulent magic.

As Emmy tried to conjure gold again but found her power inexplicably gone.

As the guards slashed Emmy's gown from neck to hem.

As fool's gold tumbled out of Emmy's skirts, hidden there at Grace's request by her new friend, the enchanted dressmaker.

As Emmy was sentenced to rot in the Society's secret prison.

As her doting father was shot like a rabid dog when he tried to intervene.

Two girls attended a magical ball, but one was never seen again.

At least, that was what those who betrayed her believed.

ONE

EMMY VALLILLO HAD DEVELOPED AN affinity for screaming.

Ignoring the stabbing pain in her throat, she stood in front of her iron door and shrieked. *A vocal cord hemorrhage*, Papa would have called it. Sometimes she pictured him in the corner of her cell, hunched over his beloved anatomy book. The longer she spent in Grimsbane Tower, the less she trusted her eyes. Or her ears, for that matter. Or her heart.

Her naive, pathetic heart.

A welcome heat prickled her skin as Emmy screamed louder. Whenever she carried on like this, the guards eventually threatened to beat her to silence. Hollow words. Not once had they entered her cell. Not once, in eight hundred and twenty-eight days.

But at least they'd speak to her, which was all the opportunity she needed.

As if on cue, the pass-through window in the center of her door jiggled as a guard unlocked its metallic flap. With considerable effort, Emmy swallowed her excitement. The guards hated when she smiled.

The metal flap yawned open, revealing the male guard with the long face that resembled a horse's. "You're as dumb as rocks, aren't you, little princess?"

How they loved to tease her about the ruined ball gown she still wore. As if she had any choice in the matter. But the joke was on them, for the torn dress had served as a pillow and a bed mat for two years. And although the embroidered clouds no longer meandered across the once ivory satin, they were her constant companions, a permanent reminder of her foolishness.

Proper gowns weigh as much as horses, Grace had teased when Emmy had protested the bulky garb. *A gift from sweet Clara Claremont, whose magic enchants fabric patterns into motion.*

Lies. Nothing was free. The Claremont girl was far from sweet. And gowns were *not* supposed to weigh as much as horses. Not without fool's gold sewn into their hems.

"Bring me a book," Emmy rasped, "and I'll never make another peep."

There was no escaping Grimsbane. She'd never even left her cell. But today, she was determined to earn a distraction. No matter the cost.

"How many times have we told you? No one can hear you." With his usual sneer, the horse-faced guard patted the stone wall. "No sounds get in. No sounds get out."

Or so they claimed. Of course, there was some truth to his words. Emmy couldn't hear so much as the guards' approaching footsteps, let alone another prisoner. The only time she heard anything at all was when they unlocked her pass-through window. Still, some echo of her screams must have penetrated the magic in the walls, or they wouldn't bother to shut her up. "Bring me a newspaper. An advertisement. *Anything.*"

The guard stared as if she hadn't spoken.

There had been a time when Emmy had tried to reason with the guards, had protested her innocence night and day, shouting that she, Emilia Vallillo, was no fraud. That she possessed rare transformation magic. That, even without a patronage, she'd learned to turn water into wine, moth-bitten cotton into thick wool, even flimsy tin into bona fide gold. That she'd been framed.

They'd told Emmy to show them, knowing damn well she could not. Because her magic was gone. Ever since she'd tried to prove her innocence at that cursed ball, she hadn't felt a lick of it. No, her only taste of power now came from the guards. Just last week, Horse Face here had whipped a gale through her cell, pelting her with dirt and rocks.

"You know what?" he said abruptly. "I think I *will* bring you something special."

She highly doubted that, but the tiny door slammed shut, cloaking her in unyielding silence once again. For most of her life, she'd lived in a tenement house bursting with conversation in so many languages, Papa had called it the Tower of Babel. Now she was trapped in a quiet so suffocating, her mind filled it with a deep voice whispering, *Hold on, just a little longer.* Another hallucination, one she pretended was Papa. But he had died—no, been *murdered*. By the same vile man who'd declared her a fraud.

With a ragged inhale of stale air, Emmy huddled against her favorite wall, the one that was a smidge warmer than the rest. Weak daylight streamed through the tiny oval window opposite the door, far too high and too narrow to provide any hope for escape. It illuminated the faint tally she'd scratched into the stones, the jagged lines taunting her with their abundance. Seven hundred. Eight hundred. On and on and on. She tried not to keep track of the date—April 30, 1882—but her mind was rather fond of torturing her with it. Her mind was also fond of picturing what Grace might be doing on such a spring day. The magic she was learning. The parties she was attending.

Perhaps waiting for the guard's return *was* her punishment. A typical hour in the penitentiary felt like a year. Anticipation, however, stretched the afternoon to a century, the shadows creeping longer and longer until the darkness swallowed them whole. In her first months here, the nights she'd spent shivering in unyielding blackness had tortured her, but now, there was a strange comfort in the darkness. After all, it hadn't broken her.

After an eternity, the metallic flap creaked open once more. Unable to stop herself, Emmy hurried toward it, shielding her eyes from the abrupt light of the hall sconces.

"Hungry, little princess?" the horse-faced guard cooed. A feminine snicker rose behind him, and Emmy braced herself. Two guards meant trouble. Perhaps they'd hidden a decomposing rat in her gruel again. Or maybe when she reached for the tin, they'd hit her with the female guard's water magic.

Still, a visit from two guards was a rare novelty, one Emmy would not waste.

As Emmy drew closer, the sharp, pungent scent of urine flooded her nostrils. They'd pissed in her dinner. How original.

"Come now, little princess." The female guard's eyes were alight as Emmy feigned interest in the same grayish gruel that had sustained her for two long years. "Even rabid dogs get hungry, don't they?"

"We kept it warm for you." The male guard dangled the piss meal precariously over the edge. They usually avoided reaching into her cell, but their mischief had made them reckless.

Emmy sank her teeth into his fleshy arm.

The guard screeched and flailed, but Emmy only clamped down tighter. Such beastly cries he made, and yet *she* was the feral creature. He should have known better than to stick his arm in a dog's cage.

When he finally wriggled away, he did not laugh, but Emmy did.

This wild laughter took her sometimes, carrying her right to the edge of sanity. She could not afford to sink into delirium again, not when the guards were far from amused. Still, guffaws slipped between Emmy's chapped lips, even as the guard stuck her hand through the slot, muscles tensing with magic's grueling effort.

A deluge of water struck Emmy in the cheekbone like a brass-knuckled punch. She dove out of its path, but the guard angled her palm, soaking Emmy until the wet silk clung to her scrawny limbs.

It was the guards' turn to laugh now. Emmy glared at them as coldness convulsed through her, not giving them the satisfaction of—

A thunderous crash, loud enough to shake silt from the stone walls.

Emmy stilled, shivers and all.

The guards hurried away, the pass-through window slamming shut. Emmy lunged for it, and for once, they'd forgotten to lock it. With her forehead pressed against the cool metal, she searched the hall.

The male guard slammed against Emmy's door with a deafening *crack*.

Emmy scampered back, dropping the metal flap before she thrust it open again.

He was lying on the floor, his neck twisted at an impossible angle. Dead.

Emmy tried to blink away the hallucination. But he remained on the floor, the arm she'd bitten limp at his side.

The female guard backed into Emmy's line of vision, her hands raised. "Wait, Fontaine—"

A dark figure gripped her neck and snapped it.

The popping sound was much like a cracked knuckle—only louder.

Emmy must have gasped, for the dark figure whipped toward her. As she yanked her hand back, the pass-through slammed shut, but Emmy remained just behind it, her pulse hammering in her ears. Waiting.

The slot creaked open, revealing a pair of stormy gray eyes.

TWO

EMMY GAPED AT THE MAN on the other side. Dark tangles of greasy hair. Sun-starved skin as pale as her own. Youthful features but haggard, as if he'd already lived one hundred miserable lives.

He was a fellow prisoner, one who'd just killed two guards in hardly as many seconds, yet he was not even out of breath. More alarming, there was a sharpness to the gaze that held Emmy's, one that betrayed far more than a natural curiosity. He took in her tattered ball gown, her frail figure, the filth that marred her once pretty face—and he laughed.

Emmy crept backward across her cell, not letting the madman out of her sight. His laughter died as abruptly as it began, and he rattled her door as if testing its strength.

"If you come in here," she rasped, her heart in her throat, "I will tear off your limbs."

He tilted his head, a hawk contemplating a mouse. "Don't you want me to free you?"

Free. Even if he could open her door, there was something disturbing about his stare. Something not unlike her old alley cat after it had snagged a rat, carrying its corpse for days, not putting it down to eat or even sleep. *Monomaniacal*, Papa had called it. Singularly obsessed.

That was how the madman looked at her now. As though he'd found a prized rat.

He shook the door once more, the locks clanging against their iron restraints, and Emmy covered her ears. If he'd killed two charmed guards so easily, she did not stand a chance against him, no matter how well Jimmy Li had taught her to punch.

His lips curved. "You're that debutante, aren't you? The fraud."

"I'm no fraud," Emmy snarled.

"I was at your ball. You claimed to transform things, making gold from . . ." He waved a dismissive hand. "Something."

His silky voice was relaxed and casual, despite the bodies behind him.

"Very well," he sighed, rising to his feet. "You'd only slow me down."

As the slot slammed shut, Emmy stiffened, her indecision rooting her in place. He had no reason to help her. He'd just as soon kill her, if given the chance. But that cursed word sprouted roots in her mind: *free*.

"Wait," she rasped, her heart hammering against its cage.

But he was gone.

Emmy scrambled to her pass-through window. "Wait!"

He reappeared far too quickly, a slow smile spreading across his gaunt cheeks.

Free, free, free, she nearly begged, the sudden burst of hope dizzying. "She keeps the keys in her left pocket." Emmy motioned to the lifeless female guard.

"And what will you do for me?"

She glared at him. "You offered to free me."

With a furtive glance down the hall, he rose to his feet.

"I *can* make gold," Emmy called after him.

He shrugged as he strolled away.

Emmy racked her brain for something, anything to turn him around. "I can transform a guard to look like you. No one will know you've escaped."

He slowed to a stop, glancing over his shoulder. "You can do that?"

"Of course." The lie rolled off her tongue easily, though panic followed closely behind. Papa had been the one who excelled at transforming human cells, but he'd used his magic only to heal people, not to alter their appearance. Though he'd been Emmy's mentor, her specialty was transforming nonliving things, like buttons or— What did it matter? Her magic was gone.

The madman knelt beside the female guard's limp form, searching her pockets.

Treacherous, agonizing hope coursed through Emmy as he returned with the loop of keys. Metal scraped metal as he tried the first one in her lock. No luck.

Open, she pleaded as he tried the next key. Her lungs ceased working, her heart ceased beating.

Open. Another key jangled against the lock. If a guard heard it, or if this other prisoner decided Emmy wasn't worth the effort, she would be stuck in this cell forever—

The click echoed through her cell. Her door ground open.

Pushing past the other prisoner, Emmy rushed into the hall until her entire body was outside the cell. Not far enough. She lunged toward the stairs, but he caught her wet sleeve. She could have struggled, but she froze, hating the feel of his fingers against her emaciated bicep. Still, better that he thought her compliant. For now.

"Make him look like me." He glanced down the dark hall, frowning. "Quickly."

Her face must have betrayed her panic, because he thrust something at her.

Emmy shook free and backed away, pressing against the wall so that she could see him and the corridor doors at the same time.

"Take it." With a quick glance down the hall, he held out a strange metallic coin. "The Society blocked your power, didn't they? This will free it."

Emmy's magic was not blocked; it was *gone*. And any minute now, she'd be discovered out of her cell with two dead guards at her feet.

Hand still outstretched, he stepped toward her.

She pressed deeper against the wall, ready to bolt.

But he continued to stalk closer. Like Emmy, he wore bedraggled formal wear—a tuxedo, in his case, with torn coattails that fluttered in the cool draught—but unlike Emmy, he moved as though he'd been born wearing a silk tie and tailored pants. That was the confidence he oozed, despite his crumpled attire: the surety of the rich.

There was little Emmy trusted less than the rich.

Still, his confidence could be a weakness. He could underestimate her. And if she was discovered by the guards, his affinity for swift violence might come in handy.

With trembling fingers, Emmy plucked the coin from his palm, his skin shockingly warm. As she closed her fingers around the strange metal, the air chilled, ever so slightly.

A glutton for disappointment, Emmy reached for her power, but nothing happened. And of course it didn't. Ever since that cursed ball, she had not felt magic's ethereal mist.

And if this madman realized it, he'd snap her neck, too.

With an exasperated noise, he snatched the coin. "Step back."

"What are you going to do?"

He rubbed his thumb over his fingers, and a single black flame erupted from his hand.

Emmy gaped at the sudden magic. He'd conjured it more easily than Papa. More easily than even *her*, and she'd been the fastest of all the debutantes at that ball—by several seconds.

Moving quickly, he dragged the female guard into Emmy's cell and the male one into his, the door of which was nothing but melted metal. He raised his arms, and gray-black flames spread over the female guard, licking at her face until her skin was a patchwork of charred skin and ivory bone. With a dark smile, he spread his hands, and the black flames climbed the walls that had trapped Emmy for two long years. Shards of stone burst from the ceiling she'd memorized, crashing to the floor. His flames were straight out of hell, as black as night and deliciously destructive.

Swallowing the strange urge to laugh, Emmy watched her prison cell burn.

Every guard in Grimsbane Tower had to hear the commotion.

Shouting something over the inferno of flames and falling stone, the other prisoner sprinted down the hall, his coattails fluttering in his wake.

Madman or not, with magic like that, he was Emmy's best chance of escape.

Lifting her torn skirts, she ran after him.

THREE

ANY MOMENT NOW, GUARDS WOULD burst into the corridor and drag Emmy back to hell. The certainty of capture was almost preferable to the possibility of freedom dangling over her like a guillotine. They would be caught. It was only a matter of when.

And yet, in all her eighteen years, Emmy had never run so quickly.

As she reached for the stairwell door, the other prisoner yanked her into an empty cell. Emmy's instincts roared to life, and she made use of her sharp elbows, the fists Jimmy had taught her to wield. But the madman held her tightly against him, covering her mouth. What a damn fool she'd been, turning her back to him, even for a—

The hallway exploded with shouting as guards poured through the stairwell door. Emmy froze. One more second out there, and they would have run right into her.

How could he have heard them coming?

As the guards flooded the hallway, Emmy choked at the bitter taste of the madman's filthy hand. But the rush of guards ceased, though their shouting continued down the hall.

"When I say go," he murmured in her ear as he uncovered her mouth, "take these stairs to the bottom."

"You first." She would not be his bait.

His chest trembled as if he'd bitten back a laugh. "Get ready."

He released her, and Emmy shook out her arms, gathering her courage. Judging by the distant shouting, the hall had to be full of guards. If one of them turned away from the fire at the wrong moment, they'd be caught, that guillotine of dashed hopes delivering its final blow.

"Now."

He burst into the hall, and Emmy waited two agonizing seconds to ensure he hadn't been spotted before she followed. The commotion was louder here, but she did not spare a glance toward the guards, slipping into the stairwell as quickly as she could. Then the two of them were off, barreling down the steps, their dirty feet thundering against the uneven stone. Emmy was delirious with impatience, nearly tripping as they spun, spun down the spiral of the stairs.

Reaching the bottom first, the other prisoner lunged for the next door but staggered away, tugging Emmy into the darkness beneath the stairs. This time, she did not fight him, not even as he trapped her between his back and the wall.

The door swung open, unleashing a stampede of boots and a gust of air so fresh, Emmy nearly choked on it. She was so close. So painfully close.

The guards grumbled to each other as they took the stairs one at a time. If they noticed the shadows beneath the stairwell, or the drips Emmy's wet gown had left on the stairs, she would never set foot beneath the vast sky that beckoned just beyond that door.

After an eternity, the footsteps overhead quieted, then ceased.

"Let's go." Releasing her, the madman smoothed his tattered lapels and opened the door the guards hadn't bothered to lock. Before it could shut again, Emmy slipped through it.

She sprinted into the night, greedily inhaling the sudden scent of pine and spring and woodsmoke. The air was alive. *She* was alive, some dormant part of her roaring to life.

But not free. Not yet. It had been the middle of the night when they'd dragged her here, but she was fairly certain that Grimsbane Tower was hidden among the private buildings on Randall's Island, not far from the ordinary prison. To escape, she'd need to cross the Harlem River undetected.

The other prisoner half crouched, half ran along a crumbled stone wall before disappearing into a dark copse of trees. Emmy scampered after him, glancing over her shoulder every few seconds. Here, the darkness was nearly impenetrable. But her eyes adjusted quickly, courtesy of two years without so much as a candle.

"My friend is here with a boat," he whispered. "We just have to find it."

A dozen questions rose to her lips, most important among them *Are you prone to hallucinations?* But he was off, slipping between the trees.

She could follow him. After all, he'd gotten them this far without being caught, and he seemed to possess an uncanny sense of the guards' whereabouts. But even if the boat were real, it'd be far too easy to spot a vessel crossing the channel in the moonlight.

Hunched low to the ground, Emmy kept walking underneath the trees near the embankment, careful to make as little noise as possible. The river narrowed as she turned northward. Though the dark silhouette of trees still lined the opposite shore, flickering lamps broke the black night beyond them. Harlem, hardly two hundred yards away. All this time.

The novelty of the brisk spring air faded as Emmy slipped out of her decrepit ball gown, hiding the damned thing in the hollow roots of a weeping willow. Her underdress offered little protection from the wind, but at least it wouldn't drown her.

"Have something against boats?"

Emmy nearly slipped off the rocks by the river's edge.

Arms crossed, the other prisoner sauntered toward her like a disapproving prince rather than a filthy prisoner. He was tall—not as tall as Jimmy Li, but no one was as tall as Jimmy—with a broadness to his chest, despite his wiry limbs. He might have been thirteen or thirty; she hadn't the faintest idea. But he held her gaze with bone-chilling intensity. For someone who had freed her on a whim, he was far too invested in keeping her near.

He inched closer. "I'm not going to—"

Before he could grab her, she jumped.

Christ, it was shockingly cold—it took everything she had not to climb ashore. But she waded deeper, stifling her scream as the frigid waves splashed her bare thighs. The water was strangely slick with whatever waste had been dumped in it, and she hadn't an ounce of fat left on her to stave off hypothermia. Still, it was either the river or Grimsbane.

Gathering the last of her courage, Emmy dunked beneath the surface.

With numb limbs, she forced herself to keep swimming underwater, away from watchful eyes. Her pace slowed, her lungs screamed, and the need to turn around was all-consuming. But she had to keep going. All she needed was a distraction from the cold.

Grace.

If Emmy drowned in this filthy, freezing river, Grace would think she had fooled Emmy. She'd think she had won.

Grace had pretended to be horrified when the Society guards tore Emmy's ball gown to shreds onstage. She'd seemed as shocked as Emmy when fool's gold had spilled from Emmy's skirts. And for a few minutes, Emmy had fallen for her innocent facade, just like she'd fallen for a decade of phony friendship.

But as the guards had seized Emmy, as she'd gaped at her dearest friend, Grace had locked eyes with another young woman. The one who'd made their gowns. And Grace's lips had curved ever so slightly.

For most of Emmy's life, she'd been on the receiving end of that smile. It meant mischief. It meant secrets.

All Emmy had to do now was picture that little fucking smile, and she'd never stop swimming.

Something brushed against her legs, and she jerked, splashing far too loudly. But it was only seaweed. A few yards ahead, smooth rocks glistened in the faint moonlight.

Somehow, she'd made it.

Emmy pulled herself onto the muddy rocks, her arms collapsing beneath her. The breeze on her wet skin was even crueler than the river, and her teeth chattered so hard, she was going to break them. Walking would return a bit of feeling to her limbs—and give her time to determine where the hell to hide.

But she could not muster the strength to stand.

Something scraped the rocks, and Emmy flailed in a pathetic attempt at self-defense.

The other prisoner stood on the shore, pulling a rowboat with a young man. His . . . friend.

Emmy tried to stand but her legs ignored her orders, so she sat and watched him conjure his dark flames and reduce the boat to ash.

As he turned, something downriver snagged his gaze. "What is *that?*"

Emmy whirled. A strange white glow brightened in the distant sky. Far too brilliant to be gas lamps, yet too pale and smokeless to be fire.

"Arc lights. Broadway's full of them now." Seeing the other prisoner's blank expression, his friend added, "Electric lamps? I thought the first one was installed before you, ah, went away."

Emmy gaped at the strangely illuminated sky. Electric *lights*? What else had she missed?

"Arc lights. Right." With a dazed expression, the other prisoner flopped onto the frozen mud and stretched his dark flames over her.

The heat was both exquisite and brutal, sending painful prickles careening over her blue skin. As she thawed, she could not move, not only because she wasn't foolish enough to leave the heat, but because the black flames hovered mere inches over her. She was trapped.

"Flames in the open?" His friend motioned to where Harlem slept behind them. "Should we also ignite fireworks to signal your return?"

"Is anyone near?"

"How should I know? I exhausted my power locating the guards."

Another charmed person. Given his nice clothes and that he'd just broken his friend out of the Society of the Charmed's prison, he was likely a Society member.

Odds were he had carried enough money for ferry fare. She only needed to find it—and run.

The other prisoner tossed his friend the same strange coin he'd claimed would unblock Emmy's magic. His blanket of black fire extinguished, leaving her instantly cold.

With a gasp, his friend backed away from the coin. "As if I want that cursed thing!"

"Just have a listen. See if we can stay here until she can walk."

"She's not coming with us."

"*She* is right here." Damn her ruined voice for wavering. Still, Emmy glared at the newcomer. Neatly parted blond hair. Clean, trimmed fingernails. If it came to blows, she'd be able to take him down far more easily than the murderous one, as long as she landed a kick in precisely the right spot. And if she could knock the coins from his coat pocket . . .

"How ladylike," he sighed, plucking the coin from the mud. "She's thinking of kicking me in the groin and stealing my money."

Her mouth fell open. "How did you—"

"Caleb's gift is telepathy," the other prisoner explained. "He can hear people's thoughts and speak to them, mind to mind. That's how I knew the guards' positions earlier."

"Jack Henrick Fontaine, how dare you!" Caleb glared at the other prisoner.

Fontaine. The female guard had called him that before he'd killed her. Even stranger, the surname stirred a deeper memory, though Emmy could not place it. Not that it mattered. It was time to get as far from that prison—and the Society of the Charmed—as possible.

But where to hide? Her former flat on Baxter Street would be the first place they'd look for her. Leaving the city was far safer, but the guards might search the ferries—and she hadn't a nickel for a ticket. Still, she could not continue on with two potential members of the cursed Society, especially when one continued to watch her like she was his prized rat.

She darted into the shadow of the trees, but the other prisoner—Jack, apparently—hurried after her. "Where are you going?"

"Home." The lie struck her like a battering ram to the chest. *The body cannot distinguish between physical and emotional hurts,* Papa had always said. *The same pain receptors fire, no matter the cause.*

Emmy no longer had a home. She no longer had a family. Or friends. Not anymore.

The mind reader winced. Still eavesdropping on her thoughts, damn him.

"If you're spotted, there'll be a manhunt for us both." Jack caught up with her in the trees. "Come with us. Our friend has a carriage waiting."

"Our friend," muttered Caleb from behind. "That charmless bastard is not my friend."

Someone not charmed? Had they broken the most fundamental rule of magic: Its secrecy?

Row houses lined the road beyond the trees, their windows mercifully dark. Only a single carriage stood on the empty road, its driver but a broad silhouette. The enormous horses tethered to it certainly looked capable of delivering Emmy far away from here. But she could not trust anyone, not for a single second.

No, she had to continue alone.

"Suit yourself." With a knowing grin, the other prisoner jogged to the carriage, waving at the driver, who hooted and jumped from his seat. Two friends for Jack Fontaine. Two people willing to risk their necks to break him out of jail.

A long time ago, Emmy had yearned for that sort of ironclad friendship. Like the gang of girls who'd pal around the neighborhood together, or at the very least, a sibling. When Grace had moved in across the hall, Emmy had assumed God had answered her prayers. A girl precisely six years old, like Emmy. With *magic*, no less. The two of them were closer than sisters, everyone always said.

But closest friends wrought the deepest wounds.

"Emmy? Holy hell—it's *you*."

Her heart ceased beating. *It couldn't be.*

As the driver walked toward her, Emmy rubbed at her eyes. He had to be an illusion.

With a smile so familiar it cut like glass, Jimmy Li threw his arms around Emmy.

FOUR

ACCEPTING A STEAMING TEACUP FROM Jimmy, Emmy stared at him over the rim. Nothing about this moment felt real. Not the earthy, bitter scent of oolong, or the black flames in the hearth, and certainly not her former neighbor, who, sitting beside her, looked impossibly *clean*. His inky black hair was shiny and untangled, and his handsome face had matured to a young man's. Other than his wind-whipped cheeks, there was little sign he'd driven a carriage all night to this empty mansion somewhere in the country north of the city.

Not that Emmy could verify their whereabouts. No, she'd spent the journey in the carriage boot with the other prisoner, hiding beneath blankets. All night, as they'd bumped and jostled, she'd regretted letting Jimmy convince her to go with them. But she could not walk away from him, not when he had the answers she needed.

"You're getting a nasty shiner." His dark brown eyes were gentle as he appraised her. "Did the guards do that with their fists? Or with magic?"

Jimmy knew of magic's existence now. Even stranger, he was perfectly at ease in a grand sitting room nestled in an even grander, albeit dusty, mansion. "What are you doing here? With *them*?"

"You've lost your voice. Have some tea and then we'll talk."

She shook her head. No amount of tea would heal her damaged vocal cords.

"Glad to see you didn't lose your stubbornness along with all that weight." With a wry smile, Jimmy blew on his tea. "I work for Jack Fontaine now. Was fixing up a few things here at Mistfield when he got himself arrested."

Jimmy presented it as if it was perfectly normal for him, from whom Emmy, Papa, and Grace had carefully hidden magic's existence, to work for a charmed person. "And you trust him?"

"He's great." He flashed her the grin that had made her heart skip a beat a lifetime ago. She and Grace used to count Jimmy's smiles, tallying who received the most. "And the blond one, Caleb Alton? Think of him like a mouse. All squeak and no bite."

Of course he trusted them. Even when the little street thieves used to slide their nimble fingers into Jimmy's pockets, he'd merely laughed and tousled their hair.

Still staring at her, Jimmy shook his head. "I can't believe you're here. Last I saw you, you were climbing into that fancy carriage with Grace and San Rocco."

Papa's nickname used to fill her with pride, but now the sound of it echoed through her. San Rocco was the legendary priest of Basilicata who had cured his people of the plague. None of their neighbors had known of magic, but they'd had their own way of understanding Papa's lifesaving services. He'd been a miracle worker. A living saint.

"Have you spoken to Grace?" She could no longer hold back the burning question. Part of her never wanted to see Grace again. Part of her longed to hunt her down and curl back her fingernails like the peel of an orange. Ten nails for ten years of friendship.

"Not since she returned that night." His broad shoulders tensed as he stared at the fire. From the moment Jimmy had arrived at their tenement house to live with his wayward uncle, Papa had taken him under his wing. He'd vouched for him with the foremen, helping Jimmy make enough to send money home to his mother in China. Jimmy had loved Papa like a father. And Papa had loved Jimmy like a son.

"What did she say?"

"That you'd been arrested for stealing. And that your pa had interfered with your arrest."

For stealing. *Stealing*. Emmy swallowed a mouthful of boiling tea.

"You're no thief, Ems." Jimmy's eyes were so full of conviction, she looked away. The Emmy he knew never would've stolen a penny, yet a few hours ago, she'd wanted to empty his friend's pockets. "I tried to get the address of the ball, but by the time we'd brought your father's body inside, Grace was gone. Told Mrs. Feinstein she was moving in with her aunt uptown."

The scream in Emmy's chest swelled. Grace's mostly absent father had fancied himself an esteemed member of the Society of the Charmed. He'd taught Grace all about it, planting the seeds for the fervent obsession she'd shared with Emmy. He'd had a sister in the Society, too, one Grace had never met: Mrs. Eleanor Windsor. If Grace had moved in with the Windsors, she'd either joined their household staff or received an offer of patronage from them as a Society protégé. But Grace would have never stooped to cleaning her rich aunt's floors.

Her dream had come true. Her betrayal rewarded.

"Were you there?" Jimmy paused, clearing his throat. "When they shot him?"

Swallowing another mouthful of boiling tea, Emmy traced its burn down her throat. She had been there, all right. No farther than two arms' lengths away when that terrible man had killed Papa without a modicum of remorse. As if he'd just stomped on a cockroach and not ended the life of the gentlest father, one who healed his neighbors without accepting a penny, who sang while he cooked and hid silly notes for her to discover while he worked sixteen-hour shifts.

How Emmy had raged when they'd shot him. How she'd fought to reach him. But that vicious man had used his nightmarish magic to silence her pleas and freeze her movements. That was when she'd ruined her voice, straining to scream. To cry. To give Papa a single word of comfort as a halo of blood had spread around his head.

"I was with him," she finally said, suddenly tired. "Where did you . . ."

"Saint Ann's. We tried for the Transfiguration, but you know how they are."

Of course. The Irish priests wouldn't have let an Italian be buried on their grounds, even if it was his parish. "He always liked Saint Ann's."

Jimmy studied his teacup. "When Fontaine was arrested, and Caleb first snuck near Grimsbane to send him a message, he said Fontaine was all alone in his cell. That they never let him out, never gave him anything to do." He hesitated, carefully choosing his words. "Was it the same for you?"

Too exhausted to fight the knot in her throat, Emmy fixed her gaze on the black flames.

"So you watched your father die, then spent the last two years with nothing but your grief." Jimmy scrubbed at his jaw. "Jesus, Ems. How did you not go mad?"

In the end, those bouts of madness had been a reprieve, for a mad mind ceased praying to a silent God or begging the guards for something—anything—to distract her from the images burned into her retinas.

Papa's crimson halo. Grace's secret smile.

Emmy cleared her throat. "Does Grace visit Baxter Street? Is her mother still there?"

Jimmy raised his brows at her abrupt change of subject, but did not push her. "Not that I've heard. But I live here now, at Mistfield Manor."

"How did *that* happen?"

"I met Jack at San Rocco's funeral, actually."

She nearly spat out her tea. "He was at my father's funeral?"

"He and his sister stood out like sore thumbs." Jimmy chuckled to himself. "Figured they had to be the rich folks who had invited you and Grace to that ball. So I followed them. Demanded to know where you were, because you weren't in the Tombs or in any of the other jails. And they told me all about that ball. They were petitioning for your release when those bastards came after *him*—"

"He knew me?" Emmy could not keep the shrillness from her voice. "Before last night?"

Jimmy gave her a sideways look. "He didn't tell you?"

She replayed it in her mind, the way Jack had stared at her through her pass-through slot. How he'd laughed at her. Taunted her. Walked away and made her *beg* him to free her.

"Where are you going?"

By the time Jimmy got to his feet, Emmy was already in the hall.

Bloody hell, this place was enormous. Door after door, room after room fanned out around her. She kept walking, her head spinning at the unkempt extravagance. Portraits framed in dusty silver, crystal chandeliers cloaked in cobwebs. Twin staircases unfurling like ribbons, each punctuated with a crumbling alabaster bust.

"This is their *home*?" Emmy hissed, nearly tripping down the steps. "The Fontaines?"

He hesitated. "Only in the summers. The main house is in the city."

Emmy had to grip the banister to stop the three-story entrance hall from spinning. Her whole life, she'd been aware of the lavish lives of the rich. But that awareness had been a theoretical thing, much like how she believed in God and the existence of the Pacific Ocean, though she'd never seen either. But this mansion—occupied by a single family, and only in the summers—shattered all her preconceived notions of what it meant to be disgustingly wealthy.

"I don't like that look in your eyes." Jimmy touched her arm, and she flinched, which only deepened his frown. "Maybe you should rest."

Voices. Distant but unmistakable. Like a hound with a scent, Emmy wove through a series of darkened rooms with dust sheets draped over the furniture. Soon she stood in front of a pair of rustic French doors, behind which muffled voices spoke animatedly.

As she burst through the doors, the voices broke off.

Her bare feet sank into a soft rug, and she slowed, blinking hard. Not an illusion. The floor-to-ceiling bookshelves were real, as were the two young men staring at her.

She almost did not recognize Jack Fontaine without his dirt-streaked cheeks and splotchy beard. He looked younger, perhaps even her age. He'd cut his hair, too, his locks no longer tangled at his shoulders but freshly washed, the damp ends falling in chocolate waves over his forehead. Without all that filth, his face was entirely disarming. Angelic cheekbones and a full mouth gave him a hint of youthful innocence, yet there was a menacing air to the cut of his jaw, the dark brows illuminating those smoky eyes. It was the face of someone who reveled in his beauty. Who wielded it like a weapon.

"You knew who I was." She folded her arms, her dirty underdress suddenly far too thin.

Jack grinned with the smugness of someone playing a game—and winning.

"How about a little gratitude?" Caleb rose from the couch. "We got you out, didn't we?"

"Alton, Li, give us a moment?" Jack kept those gray eyes trained on Emmy.

With a reassuring clap on her shoulder, Jimmy slipped out the door before she could protest. As Caleb followed, he paused to glare at her. "I could have gotten him out months ago, but he insisted we make a plan that included you. Remember that."

A bald-faced lie. If Jack had spent even a single day in Grimsbane for a stranger, then he was a goddamn fool, and he did not strike her as one.

As soon as they were gone, Jack kicked his legs onto the desk. "Emilia Vallillo. Eighteen years old. Only child born to Matteo Vallillo, an Italian immigrant with a healing gift unknown to the Society of the Charmed, and the late Bridget Vallillo, nèe Fitzpatrick. Was your mother charmed, too?"

She hadn't been, but Emmy snapped her jaw shut. He was trying to unsettle her with what he'd learned from Jimmy, and she would not give him the satisfaction.

Jack steepled his fingers. "Your mother died of appendicitis when you were eight. Your father raised you himself, with a little help from your neighbor Mrs. Feinstein, for whom you sewed while he worked. You lived at 31 Baxter Street your entire life, on the fifth floor, second door on the right. Your father made sure you were educated in the basement of the mission school on Park Street. Your teachers must have been quite good, because you don't speak like you're from Five Points."

She let the insult simmer as she stared at him, unblinking. Papa had gone to great lengths to ensure that both she and Grace were not only well-read, but well-spoken.

"Conjury, your father taught you himself, usually after he finished his construction shifts with my dear friend Jimmy Li. Your father's gift worked only on living things, but you transform nonliving things. How am I doing thus far?"

Jimmy could not have told him about her and Grace's nightly magic lessons with Papa.

Emmy forced herself to breathe. To blink. "Don't you dare speak of my father's magic."

"The Society of the Charmed forbids us to use the word *magic* in case an ordinary person overhears it. Call it 'conjury.'"

So he *was* a Society member. From her periphery, Emmy glanced at the door. Ten paces.

"Let's continue. You spent most of your time with Grace Montgomery, who lived across the hall. You learned of the Society from her, and she learned of it from *her* father, the late Richard Montgomery, who came from a long line of charmed Montgomerys, every last one of them pricks. Mr. Montgomery mostly ignored his illegitimate daughter, but once he realized the two of you were talented conjurers, he put you both on the Society's list.

"Your father had his doubts about you mixing with people like Montgomery, but he was never particularly fond of telling you no, so he accompanied you and Grace to the ball. But neither of you knew what Grace had secretly learned: the Society would select only one protégé that year. Given that you were attempting to make literal gold, she set into motion an intricate plan with the help of two new friends she'd made. She tossed you to the vultures, then took your spot among my people while you were in hell for two years, three months, and seven days." He grinned at her gobsmacked expression. "Which brings us to yesterday."

She'd been right; he was a monomaniacal cat after all, and she was the decomposing rat. The magnitude of his research should have chilled her to the bone, but— "Only one protégé?"

Her question pleased him far too much. "A new rule, introduced that year to appease fears that the Society was growing too large."

And there it was. Grace had betrayed her. Emmy had known that from the moment she glimpsed her triumphant smile. But until now, she hadn't had the faintest idea *why*.

Grace had done the math. When the result wasn't in her favor, she'd tipped the scale.

For once, Emmy's raspy voice did not waver, as she asked, "Who helped her?"

"Oliver Stratton." The muscles in Jack's jaw ticked. Speaking that name cost him something. "And Clara Claremont. Either name ring a bell?"

Clara Claremont was the enchanted dressmaker. Grace had met her at etiquette lessons the Society provided for debutantes—at a steep fee, one Emmy had refused to even mention to Papa. Grace had paid the exorbitant cost with the entire sum she'd inherited after her father's death, and Emmy hadn't been shy about her disapproval. Learning to curtsy should not have cost two years' rent. But Grace, apparently, had made a strategic investment.

For protégés, the social rules matter far more than the magical ones, she'd said to Emmy, pulling her away from her studies. *We should be learning to waltz, not reading old books.*

"Grace mentioned Clara." If he thought her cooperative, perhaps he'd reveal more than he intended. "She said Clara's family already belonged to the Society, so she was not debuting. But she wanted to use the ball to advertise her enchanted dress enterprise."

A free gown in exchange for crediting its designer, an heiress aspiring to be an entrepreneur. It was an alluring trap, and Emmy had fallen for it. Hard.

"From what I've gathered, Miss Claremont sewed fool's gold into your gown so that when you were searched, they'd find 'proof' of your deceit."

Even now, the simplicity of it all filled her with fury. All her life, Emmy had prided herself on her sharp wit, her high marks at school. Yet when she'd questioned the shocking weight of her ball gown, she'd believed Grace's excuse that fancy dresses were always cumbersome.

Pathetic.

Kicking his legs off the desk, Jack straightened. "Oliver Stratton sealed off your power so you could not prove your innocence. That's his gift: conjury binding."

"But why?" Emmy's voice pitched. "I've never even met him."

"Grace did. Clara introduced them, and they became rather fond of each other."

"Fond?"

"Writing love letters. Meeting privately." He waved a casual hand. "A sordid love affair."

Emmy scoffed. "Grace would never do such a thing." *And*, Emmy longed to add, *she would have told me.* A ridiculous notion, given all that Grace had hidden from her. Still, Grace was far too savvy to risk her reputation by meeting with a man in secret, let alone kissing one. That was something her mother would have done, and Grace was obsessed with being seen as her father's daughter. A true Montgomery.

Something like pity crossed Jack's face, which was far worse than his smirk.

Emmy's patience was thoroughly depleted. "What do you want from me?"

"Your help." Gone was the humor in his voice. "Grace, Oliver—the people who had you wrongfully imprisoned also framed me. And I intend to make them pay."

So he'd spent time with Grace while Emmy was imprisoned. Unsettling, that Grace had lived entire chapters of her life after she'd ruined Emmy's. "What happened?"

"I'll tell you once you agree to work with me."

"Doing what, exactly?"

"Evening the score." His mouth curved. "I have a plan. One that requires your conjury."

Emmy remained rooted to the floor. He claimed he wanted revenge for being wrongly imprisoned, but he'd learned everything he could about her *before* he'd set foot in Grimsbane. "Why did you attend my father's funeral?"

"My father passed me the gold nugget you'd made. It seemed far realer than whatever had fallen out of your skirts." He leaned back in his tufted chair, a prince relaxing on his throne. "I went to your father's funeral to see if he was charmed. Because if he was, chances were that you'd inherited some version of his gift. And I was right."

"No one knew of my father's magic."

"His *conjury*. And he might not have told anyone about it, but person after person called him San Rocco, the Italian saint who performed healing miracles. Someone even claimed he'd made a dead heart beat again. Is that true?"

It had been a little boy, crushed in the railyard. His heart had stopped beating on their kitchen table for ninety seconds. But Emmy would protect Papa's secrets, even in death.

Ignoring her silence, Jack shrugged. "He transformed injuries. You transform tin soldiers."

"So that's what you want from me? Gold?"

"More than that." He was growing restless now, frowning as he studied her. "Don't you wish to avenge your father? Yourself?"

It didn't matter what she wanted. Emmy had no magic. No Papa. Nothing.

"I see." He rose from the desk and dug into his pockets. "Stratton binds the conjury of every prisoner in Grimsbane. But this amplified my power, allowing me to break through."

He flipped the strange coin to her, but Emmy kept her gaze fixed on him, not missing his wince as it hit the floor. Loath as she was to believe anything he said, he'd made an inferno without breaking a sweat. And when his friend had held the coin, he'd read her mind without so much as wincing.

Hope. Treacherous, fickle hope. "What is it?"

"It's called a relic." As he picked up the coin, a ribbon of dark fire danced between his fingers. "Had Grace Montgomery not stolen your patronage, you would have learned all about these amplifiers. Most of the time, they make someone marginally more powerful, but my sister made this one particularly . . . potent. I want you to use it to help me ruin four wicked lives."

"Four?" Thus far, he'd mentioned only Clara Claremont, Oliver Stratton, and Grace.

"Oliver's suppression abilities are a derivative of his father's power." Jack arched a brow. "You're familiar with Chancellor Stratton's suppression conjury. He shot your father."

Emmy stilled.

Stratton. The name of her father's murderer was Stratton.

"Sleep on it." Slipping the relic into his pocket, Jack strode toward the doors. "Caleb and I left two charred bodies floating in the Harlem River, one wearing the ball gown you hid near the riverbank. Once the Society realizes we're not dead in our cells, they'll think we're dead in the river."

Two more bodies. He'd killed four people yesterday and spoke of it without a morsel of regret. Emmy backed away as he passed. "Why should I believe a word you say?"

"You shouldn't." He flashed her a puckish smile.

As if her disdain was yet another amusement for him. Just like her suffering, in that cursed cell, had amused him. "And if I refuse to help you?"

"Then you're free to go. I'll even give you a horse."

Liar. She kept her glare pinned on him as he sauntered from the library.

Once his footsteps faded down the hall, Emmy sank to the floor and closed her eyes, trying to stop the room from spinning. Revenge. Magical amplifiers. Grace's alleged romance. Emmy was far too exhausted to think straight.

The picturesque library was still there when she opened her eyes, shelf after shelf climbing over her head. Plush sofas basked in the sunlight streaming through the windows. Through the budding trees, the Hudson River shimmered like an ever-shifting mirror.

She and Grace had spent years imagining what life might be like if they were selected as protégés, and Emmy had pictured a library just like this one.

Too good to be true, just like Jimmy's presence. Just like a coin that would rejuvenate her magic, making her impossibly strong. Too good, too good.

Emmy rubbed her tired eyes. Jack might have lured her into his mansion, but leaving right away would do her no good. She needed to be patient, to keep her wits about her so she could figure out what, exactly, to do about Jack Fontaine.

FIVE

ONCE EMMY HAD LOCKED HER door and dragged a leather chest in front of it, she took stock of her room. An enormous four-poster bed rested atop a sprawling rug. A stack of books waited beside a velvet armchair. The ensuite bathroom alone was bigger than her entire flat on Baxter Street. Jack Fontaine was trying to tempt her to stay, but she would not fall for a single luxury.

The bath, unfortunately, was exquisite.

Once she slipped into the steaming water, a groan escaped her lips. As she floated in the claw-foot tub, dark plumes of filth drifted away from her body, obscuring her shockingly thin legs. When the water lost its warmth, she let the drain slurp it all down in a satisfying gulp. Another turn of the knob, and clean water rushed over her once again, blissfully hot.

For indoor plumbing, she'd sell her soul to the devil. Or, perhaps, to Jack.

Jack Fontaine. Even his name carried an air of deceitfulness. *Jack*, like the haughty face card in a French deck. And *Fontaine* evoked a foreboding feeling she still could not place, no matter how many times she whispered it to herself.

After she'd scrubbed her body of its endless grime, she put on a simple wool dress she'd found hanging in the nearly empty wardrobe and examined herself in the full-length mirror.

A young woman stared back at her, far too wearied to have lived a mere eighteen years. Her towel-dried hair was the longest it had ever been, hanging to the top of her thighs. Its chestnut shade had darkened, too, or perhaps that was in contrast to the shock of white that was her once golden skin. She was nearly translucent now, save the deep bruise cradling her left eye. And though she'd never been curvy, the penitentiary had eroded her figure's softness, leaving her hip bones sharp and narrow, her face gaunt. Only her irises remained unchanged, their brown still the same. *Coffee with a dash of cream*, Papa liked to say. His had been the same shade.

Emmy covered the mirror with her damp towel.

The dress was thick and plain in a comforting way, but it was not hers. Her frocks back home, handsewn and well-worn, were gone. The miniature portrait of Mama, gone. Everything Emmy owned was gone. Because Papa was gone.

And now she knew the name of the man who'd killed him.

Emmy forced a comb through her damp hair. After she braided it, she slid her cold feet into a pair of soft slippers, moved her makeshift barricade, and set off in search of Jimmy. If Jack was keeping secrets, Jimmy was her best chance of discovering them.

Following a savory aroma, she found herself outside an enormous dining room. The long cherrywood table could have seated forty guests, but Jack, Jimmy, and Caleb sat together on the nearest end, the rest of the chairs hidden beneath dustcovers. There was a casualness to their postures, a familiarity that revealed many meals shared here.

"Venison again," Caleb grumbled. "Can't you shoot anything else, Li?"

Emmy paused in the doorway. Jimmy *hunted* now?

"You're welcome to try," Jimmy quipped, "though we both know how well that'll go."

With a pop, Jack uncorked a bottle of wine. "I'm surprised you didn't shoot each other while I was gone."

"I am a man of great restraint." Caleb peeked underneath the silver cloche, revealing a platter of juicy, steaming meat—

Emmy must have made a noise, for the three of them spun to face her, gawking long enough for heat to rise to her cheeks. Sure, she looked like a frail ghost, but there was no need to *stare*.

"Whenever I see your black eye," Jimmy grumbled, "I want to hit someone."

The muscles in Jack's jaw ticked. "Did Laurel's water conjury do that?"

"She told you her name?" The guards had never told her anything, let alone their names.

"And Nick was bleeding from his arm before I killed him. Your doing?"

He asked far more questions than he answered. Fiddling with her braid, Emmy shrugged. "I bit him."

Jack grinned.

"Lovely," Caleb sighed. "She shares your casual affinity for violence."

"Says the person who left two bodies floating in the water," Emmy countered.

"They were from the morgue! And unclaimed for several weeks. But if you'd prefer the Society to notice you're missing and come looking—"

"Can we *not* talk about those corpses?" With a grimace, Jimmy eyed the meat.

Jack motioned to the chair beside Jimmy. "Join us."

Part of Emmy longed to refuse, simply to deny Jack the impression that he could tell her what to do, but she was far too hungry. As Jimmy pulled out her chair, Jack filled her crystal wine glass and Caleb dished thick slices of venison onto her porcelain plate. When no one was looking, Emmy pocketed her steak knife.

"*Salute.*" Jimmy lifted his glass, unable to meet her eye as he repeated Papa's favorite toast. The others toasted, too, and as if in a trance, Emmy followed suit.

How she longed to grab the meat with her hands and shove it into her mouth. Cutting required far too much patience, but she had no choice but to retrieve the knife from her skirt.

"It's gamey," Caleb murmured.

It was the most delicious thing she'd ever tasted.

Beside her, Jack was devouring his meal with fervor. She hadn't a clue how long he'd been imprisoned, but he must have survived on the same revolting gruel as she had.

"I miss the kitchen staff," Caleb sighed, cutting his venison into tiny pieces. "We haven't had a proper vegetable in so long, it's a miracle I haven't contracted scurvy."

"You've been squatting in a manor, not lost at sea." Jack piled more venison on his plate. Without asking, he did the same to Emmy's. "Have you kept tabs on the Society?"

"Here and there. I'm too recognizable to get close. But they're still concerned that their conjury is weakening. Most people blame the immigrants. Too many people sharing the brume."

Brume? Weakening magic—because of *immigrants*? The Society of the Charmed was, apparently, full of elitist bigots.

"Broom?" Jimmy repeated between mouthfuls. "As in a witch's broomstick?"

Caleb shot him a look. "How many times have I told you? *Witch* is an insult."

"*Brume*, as in a thick fog." Jack took a long swig of wine. "That's what conjury feels like: a heavy, invisible mist. When we conjure, we draw from the brume. It's our power source. How much we can pull varies from person to person, along with the gifts we power by using it."

Emmy tried to appear nonplussed as her mind spun. Papa had spoken of magic as if it were something inside them. But it certainly *felt* like a strange fog, and calling to it had always reminded her of having something heavy draped over her.

Despite her efforts to appear disinterested, Jack grinned as if he saw right through her. "Agree to help me, and you'll have access to every book on conjury my family has amassed."

Exactly what she'd wanted from a patronage. But now, earning the opportunity to learn about a crucial part of herself seemed ridiculous. People like her and Papa had just as much of a right to understand their magic as members of the cursed Society.

"Ah, so you're still undecided. Perhaps it'll help if you know a little bit more about us." Jack stabbed yet another slice of meat. "Caleb here worked for my family."

"I was the personal attendant of Miss Rose Fontaine," Caleb announced, his voice tinged with pride, "Jack's elder and far superior sister. That's all you need to know."

"How helpful, Alton," Jack said dryly, rolling his sleeves to reveal forearms that were surprisingly muscular, though unnaturally pale, like hers. "As for me, I was born into the Society because my parents were members. In fact, my ancestors were among its founders over a century ago. Our main residence is in the city, but I've always summered here in Avalon-on-Hudson, where many Society families maintain estates. We like to take breaks from prying eyes."

Emmy glanced at the empty seats. "Does your family know we're here?"

"I can't be sure." The ghost of a smile teased Jack's lips. "Since they're all dead."

Surprised, Emmy glanced toward Jimmy for confirmation, but he and Caleb were studying their plates, all humor gone. "Is that why you're seeking revenge? Because of your family?"

"Agree to help me, and I'll tell you." He took a generous swig of his wine. "Now as to my plan, I've already told you that I have four targets in mind: Chancellor Stratton, Oliver Stratton, Grace Montgomery, and Clara Claremont."

"The Claremonts' daughter?" Caleb frowned. "She had nothing to do with the fire."

A fire? Stabbing her next mouthful, Emmy tucked that tidbit away.

"She assisted Grace Montgomery in framing Miss Vallillo here. And," Jack added as he poured himself a new glass, "I never liked her."

Emmy let her face reveal nothing, which seemed to disappoint him. Good.

"Despite the protection their money and status afford them, all four of our targets possess fatal flaws. The chancellor, for example, is power hungry, while his son is lazy and greedy. We'll capitalize on these weaknesses to exact our own personal form of justice."

"What sort of justice?" Emmy asked. "Death?"

Jimmy chuckled. "Fontaine isn't planning to kill anyone."

Else, she nearly added. "He speaks of justice. And my father's dead."

"But San Rocco wouldn't want you to—"

"I don't care if they rot in jail or die." Jack's voice remained casual, even amused, but his gray eyes had sharpened to something murderous. "As long as they suffer."

"You don't mean that," Jimmy insisted, and Emmy waited for guilt to gnaw at her. *Thou shall not kill.* It was quite literally etched in the front of her school. She'd run her finger along the stone every day for a decade. But her conscience, apparently, had abandoned her.

"In order to set these traps for them, we need to be respected members of the Society of the Charmed," Jack continued. "Preferably in the inner circle, trusted by the chancellor himself."

"Ah, yes," Caleb grumbled. "Why don't we befriend the queen of England, too?"

"I'm sure Fontaine has thought this through," Jimmy chastised.

"Do you ever grow tired of agreeing with him?"

"Do you ever grow tired of *disagreeing* with him?"

"You cannot imagine how much time I've had to plan this." Jack gave Caleb a hard look. "Emmy here will transform our appearances so we're completely unrecognizable to the Society. She'll also make us all the money we need for Mistfield to be ready to receive visitors by June."

Her laugh exploded from her so abruptly, she nearly choked. He was serious. Which was an even stronger indication of his lunacy, because even if he could somehow get her magic back, she'd never transformed a face in her life.

"June?" Jimmy set down his fork. "But that's only a few weeks from now."

"Four, to be precise." Jack's piercing gray eyes glanced about the table, marking each of them in turn. "At the start of the summer, just as New York's elite begins to flock to Newport, gossipmongers in tow, the Society of the Charmed sneaks away to Avalon-on-Hudson. For the month of June, it's exclusive party after party, ball after ball, without a single reporter in sight. You cannot imagine the elaborateness of these private events. No expense is spared. Although most reside in New York, members travel from all over the country to attend."

Emmy began piling more venison on her plate. At least when Jack kicked her out, she'd leave with a full stomach.

"Do you know who holds the inaugural ball each year?" Jack waited for Emmy to lift her gaze. "The Windsors."

The meat in Emmy's mouth turned to chalk. Grace's aunt and uncle.

"I have our new identities all sorted out, but we need new faces." Jack set his strange coin—his relic—in front of Emmy. This close, it was larger than a quarter, its surface covered in swirls of silver and gold, as if they'd resisted being smelted together.

"Don't touch it," Caleb hissed as she reached for it. "That thing is cursed."

Jack rolled his eyes. "Rose would be the first one to remind you that curses aren't real."

"Yes, but that abomination led to her ruin!"

Pushing his dark hair off his forehead, Jack turned to Emmy. "My sister, like my mother, could glimpse the future. But their visions were brief and mostly abstract. Never one to be deterred, Rose spent years scouring old grimoires in search of a way to increase how much brume she could pull at once. Relics are typically made with a specific cut of bone from a deceased family member's sternum, but Rose made this one . . . differently. And with it, her visions became much clearer."

"Differently?" Caleb scoffed. "She desecrated the grave of a centuries-old witch!"

Jimmy bit back a grin. "I thought we weren't supposed to say *witch*."

Prophetic magic. Carved bones from dead relatives. As tempted as Emmy was to eschew everything about the Society, a larger, traitorous part of her was bursting with curiosity.

"She borrowed a bone fragment from a long-dead charmed person with the gift of amplifying other people's power." Jack shrugged. "Didn't you help her dig up the grave?"

"Only because I didn't think it would work." Tight-lipped, Caleb glanced at Emmy. "The only time Rose used that relic, she drew our deaths. In vivid, unforgiving detail."

Emmy whipped toward Jimmy. "You've seen your own *death*?"

"Not me," Jimmy said quickly. "I don't think she knew me well enough to draw me."

Jack shrugged. "It's rather useful information. I knew I wouldn't die in Grimsbane."

"And yet here you are, formulating a diabolical plan that will put you back in danger."

"Caleb—"

"If you're so hellbent on making this girl help you, she should know the risks." Caleb's hard look bore into Emmy. "Oliver Stratton will drive a knife through Jack's throat."

"Caleb, enough."

"And judging by how young they both look in the drawing, it'll happen soon. Very soon."

Jack rolled his eyes. "Rose's visions were not written in stone."

"Name one that did not come true."

"How about all those pretty girls?" He grinned at Caleb. "I haven't kissed them yet."

So he was a rake. How unsurprising.

Caleb turned to Emmy. "If you walk away, he'll have to quit this madness."

"If she walks away, I'll go after Oliver looking like I do in the prophecy." Jack helped himself to more wine. "If you're so worried about me, let Emmy here transform my face."

"Are you determined to drink yourself to death, too? You've had three glasses already."

"Now who is the one doubting Rosie's visions?" Jack lifted his goblet in a mock toast, and Jimmy hid his amusement behind another bite.

Caleb burst from his seat. "Rose would hate this. Your life matters more than avenging her death."

"Nothing matters more than that. *Nothing.*" Vicious pain swept across Jack's face, so acute, Emmy flinched.

So Jack Fontaine did have a heart. And for his sister, it bled.

Was her death somehow related to his arrest? And if so, what did that have to do with Grace? How Emmy longed to ask, but he would not answer, not unless she agreed to help him.

"I've heard enough." Folding his napkin with more fury than Emmy would have thought possible, Caleb stormed out of the dining room.

"It's Rose. He still can't talk about her." With a quiet sigh, Jimmy pushed away from the table. "You know I trust you, Fontaine, but this all sounds really far-fetched. Even for you."

"Et tu, Li?" Jack's slow smile was entirely unsettling. "I thought you wanted Emmy to clear her name, so she doesn't have to hide for the rest of her life."

"I want *both* of your names cleared, but this is dangerous."

"What if Emmy decides to stay?"

Emmy bit back her protest. Neither of them was even looking at her.

"I go where she goes." Jimmy shrugged as if it were the simplest thing in the world. "I owe it to her father. Hell, I owe it to *you*, Ems. We're family."

He meant his words. And for Jimmy, who'd worked himself to the bone to send money back home, there was nothing more important than family. Even if he was the bait Jack had used to lure her to Mistfield, she was foolishly relieved to have Jimmy here.

Jack's gaze flitted between them, his expression guarded. "Understood."

Once the door swung closed behind Jimmy, Emmy shifted in her seat. Back home, she'd been alone with young men plenty of times, whether in the coal cellar or in her flat while they waited for Papa. But Jack unsettled her. And for good reason. He was the sort of person who saw someone at their worst—like her in Grimsbane—and toyed with them.

Fortunately, Jack did not attempt to engage her further, instead seizing Caleb's and Jimmy's plates and dumping the remaining venison on both his and Emmy's. As he abandoned his utensils, she did, too, her ravenous appetite overriding her self-consciousness.

When every last scrap was gone, Emmy pushed her plate out of reach. "Your plan hinges on my magic." She stopped herself from adding *And it's gone.*

After wiping his mouth with a napkin, he set it down. "Give me your hand."

Emmy did not move.

"I don't bite. Unlike you," he added, those gray eyes alight. "Come on; I'll show you."

Eyeing him warily, she reached her arm across the table, palm up. He pressed the relic into it and closed her fingers around it, keeping his hand over hers.

He was so warm, she gasped, but before she could pull away, she felt—something.

Emmy stilled, holding her breath.

It was a tendril of that cool, otherworldly feeling. A slight heaviness to the air, though when she reached for it—for the brume, as Jack had called it—she could not touch it. Something was still blocking her, but she could *feel* magic again. And it was thrilling.

Leaning back in his seat, Jack grinned like a child who'd just acquired a new toy. "Many Society members wear ordinary relics, but those are mere candles, while this one is an inferno. We have to keep it hidden. They can never know."

As if Emmy had anyone to tell. Her hand tightened around the strange coin. "If I help you, this relic stays with me for as long as I'm here."

A bluff. Even if Emmy could transform faces—which she couldn't—she could not fathom fooling the Society of the Charmed. In a matter of weeks, no less. But with this relic, she just might get her magic back before Jack kicked her out.

Jack leaned so close, Emmy glimpsed silver flecks in his bloodshot eyes. "I'll let you in on a little secret, Emmy. Can I call you Emmy?"

"No." Truthfully, she did not care, but each concession was a slippery slope.

"Caleb was right about my sister's prophecies: they were never wrong." His voice was quiet, almost wistful. "And if Oliver gets me before I can get him, the relic should be with someone who will see our vendetta through. So you can have it. Even when I'm gone."

Jack held out his hand, offering her a gentleman's handshake.

She trusted that as much as she trusted his supposed plans for vengeance: not one bit. Still, Emmy could not walk away, not when there was a sliver of hope for her magic.

Emmy shook his hand. The heat of his skin prickled her palm, and a strange excitement stirred in her like a shifting tide, even as she was careful to reveal nothing. "I will not be a pawn in your chess game, Jack Fontaine."

"Never." His lips curved into a dark smile. "You'll be the knights, the rooks, and the queen, combined."

SIX

WITH THE RELIC IN HAND and magic's whisper in the air, Emmy had nearly convinced herself that she could become the weapon Jack envisioned. One whose power punched through Oliver Stratton's block on it. Who transformed herself and the others beyond recognition, and conjured all the riches they needed to outdo the Society of the Charmed.

One clever enough to beat Grace Montgomery at her own game.

But no matter how many times Emmy called to her magic, it did not answer.

"The first ball is in four weeks," Jack reminded her as she sat in the south wing the next morning, keeping Jimmy company as he hammered wooden planks for the new walls.

Emmy shot him a hard look. His shirt was unevenly buttoned, and he carried an opened bottle of wine, though it was not even noon. "You told me I'd have full access to your books on magic, but I couldn't find any in the library."

"*Conjury.* To blend in with the Society, you need to use the proper terms. And, small problem: the triumvirate seized my family's books on conjury when I was arrested, but we'll get them back." He leaned against an austere column. "Do I need to explain who the triumvirate is?"

Grace had told her about the three men who spearheaded the Society, each with equal authority: the chancellor, who led the ceremonies and made executive decisions regarding its laws; the commander, who led the Society's magical militia; and the keeper, who oversaw the Society's lofty budget, deciding which pursuits were funded and which were not.

The chancellor was Papa's murderer. The keeper was Mr. Windsor, Grace's uncle, who before the ball had never met his bastard niece. And who the commander was, Emmy hadn't the faintest idea, but she would not give Jack the satisfaction of asking. "They'll just let us in?"

"There are three ways to join the Society: through birth, through the debutante ball—which is mostly used to recruit servants and the occasional protégé, like good old Grace—and through a referral from a member who can vouch for one's good breeding. With a referral, we'll be granted temporary membership."

Emmy shivered at the thought. "Who would refer us?"

"I'll tell you once I have my new face." He grinned, his smile as crooked as his shirt, though his teeth were infuriatingly straight. "You did tell me you can transform appearances."

Her fists curled at the mention of their encounter at Grimsbane. "And if I cannot?"

"Li, you didn't tell me your girl was a quitter."

"She survived longer than you did in that hellhole," Jimmy shot back, still hammering.

Studying her, Jack ran a thumb along his insufferably chiseled jaw. "You both need to learn the Society's laws and regulations. And ballroom dancing. And table manners."

Jimmy wrinkled his nose. "About that. What if I'm just your contractor? That way, I can focus on renovations and not on waltzing."

Jack frowned. "You don't want to be an aristocrat?"

"Not if I can help it." Jimmy shuddered. "Anyway, Caleb says there's hardly any contractors who know about magic, and plenty of rich folks up here who want work done. Maybe I could fill that gap."

Surprised, Emmy blinked at him. For as long as she could remember, Papa and Jimmy had dreamed of starting their own construction company, one that could give the padrones a run for their money. But the Society shot men like Papa without repercussions. If Jimmy did business with them when he wasn't even supposed to know about magic, he'd be in constant danger.

But Jack appeared to be considering it. "I could introduce you as my 'building design specialist'—an exorbitantly expensive one, with a charmed family in China, though you didn't inherit conjury of your own. You'd still need a new face so Grace doesn't recognize you. But as my esteemed guest, you could attend parties without being expected to know our dances."

"Sounds perfect." Jimmy grinned, and the two of them engaged in a complicated handshake that left them laughing and Emmy feeling entirely out of place.

"You'll get your conjury back," Jimmy said once Jack had disappeared through the maze of support beams. "You just need more sleep, is all."

Lovely; even Jimmy was saying *conjury*. Emmy rubbed at her tired eyes, wincing as she touched her bruise. Jack was probably hiding behind some planks, eavesdropping. "I don't trust him."

Jimmy paused his hammering. "After what Grace did, I don't blame you."

"It's more than that. He's always staring." Even now, she could practically sense him nearby.

"He's curious. Before his arrest, I talked about you nonstop: your hobbies, your study habits, the way you and Grace were always racing through the halls, getting into all sorts of trouble. And, no offense, Ems, but that prison did a number on both of your, ah . . . sociability?" He flashed her a guilty grin before returning to his hammering.

Emmy fiddled with a crooked nail, trying to recall its chemical composition, to envision the bent steel straight and useful once more. Just before the ball, she'd taught herself to turn tin to solid gold, yet now she couldn't even straighten a scrap of steel. "Are you sure you want to do business with these people?"

"It's risky," he admitted, holding out his palm for another nail, which she obliged. "At first, I only took this job because Fontaine was my best chance of getting you out. But I like working for myself. And I *really* like how well he's paying me. With what I've been sending home, my mother's the envy of Guangdong Province."

Jimmy's smile was almost enough to coax one from Emmy. "Does that mean you've finally saved enough to visit her?"

His hammering stopped.

"Is she okay?" Emmy ought to have asked him about his family straightaway.

"She is, but . . . they passed a new law. Chinese people can't come here anymore. And if we leave, we can't return. I'm fine," he added as she rose, though he looked far from it.

"Just Chinese people?" Emmy hissed. "That's absurd!"

He tried to smile, but his eyes were sad. "Nothing I can do except wait it out."

That had always been his mantra. *Work hard. Prove them wrong*. But the foremen had paid him less than Papa, who they'd paid less than the Irish. *Utter insanity*, Papa had grumbled.

But Jimmy, clearly, did not wish to discuss the law any further. "Don't worry about me, Ems. Worry about that magic of yours."

Swallowing her groan, Emmy ran her thumb over the relic. The strange coin's subtle chill wrought bitter memories of Grace. Like her father, Grace could enchant ordinary objects with people's gifts, like bandages that, once imbued with Papa's magic, healed cuts and bruises. All of Grace's creations were ice cold, far colder than the relic. Still, whenever Emmy held it, she had to bat away thoughts of Grace.

"What happened here anyway?" She fiddled with a burnt wood scrap. "With the fire?"

Setting down his hammer, Jimmy wiped his damp brow on his undershirt. "Why don't you ask Fontaine? It's his story to tell."

Emmy would have rather swallowed a fistful of these rusted nails.

The days bled into one another, an endless cycle of failed magic. By night, Emmy barricaded her door and cuddled her knife. By day, she wandered the cobwebbed mansion, trying to conjure her lost power where no one could witness her failure. Not that anyone was watching. With the south wing still in disrepair, Jimmy had cajoled Caleb into helping him. She saw no signs of Jack in any of the dark, dusty rooms she visited, though he ventured into her room once, leaving behind a faint whiff of wine and fire smoke, along with some sort of introductory brochure about the Society of the Charmed.

The purpose of the Society of the Charmed is to ensure the survival of charmed persons, the pamphlet began, and Emmy nearly chucked the damn thing across the room.

Throughout history, ordinaries have turned on the charmed, blaming us for all manner of suffering. Centuries of "witch hunts" have nearly decimated our numbers.

Had Emmy not seen their leader murder Papa in cold blood, she might have bought their claims of protection. After a cursory flip through the other Society prerogatives—safety, education, and "furthering charmed bloodlines," which encouraged Society members to marry other members—she'd consumed all the propaganda she could stomach for a day.

Each night, at Jack's behest, all four of them ate together in the dining room. While the others usually fell into rapid conversation, Emmy stalked every crumb on her plate, swallowing her own opinions. She was not here to make friends; she was here to get her magic back. And Jack hardly seemed like a brilliant schemer. He even fell asleep at the table one night, drunkenly slamming his head into his plate.

"His father called him 'the harbinger of ruin,'" Caleb sighed, stabbing at his food—smoked venison. "I always thought that was rather unfair of Mr. Fontaine, but Rose drew it: Jack surrounded by the family headstones, the ground littered with wine bottles."

"Leave him alone," Jimmy warned. "He's grieving."

"She also drew him kissing several girls." Caleb pinned Emmy with a grave look. "Even if he manages to live past June, I wouldn't get too attached."

A prickling heat coursed through her. As if she cared how many girls Jack kissed. "What did Rose draw for your death?"

Caleb's cheeks darkened to the same burgundy as the wine. "That's personal!"

Emmy exchanged a look with Jimmy, who shrugged. Caleb had his secrets, too.

After another week of trying—and failing—to unblock her magic in the library, Emmy mustered the courage to venture outside, where a search party of Grimsbane's guards might surround her with ease. Spring had painted the landscape verdant green, so bright, it seemed impossible that such a shade was real. Leaves had burst into existence, seemingly overnight. A morning mist gathered over a meadow just north of the manor. To the west was the woods, cut with well-trodden dirt paths, all of which wove toward the cliffs overlooking the Hudson.

Emmy followed one of those paths now, remaining vigilant as she savored the stickiness of each step in the mud. Growing up, she had rarely spent time in the woods. She'd almost never left lower Manhattan until the el had opened and Grace had begged her to ride it uptown to people watch. Though Emmy hated the noisy train, she had always liked the old trees of Central Park, the way their branches stretched unapologetically in every direction, taking up as much space as they pleased. But those sprawling elms did not hold a candle to Mistfield's wilderness. There was not another home in sight, no matter which direction she walked.

Such privacy was a blessing and a curse. Scream in the tenements, and a dozen neighbors ran to your aid. Scream here, and not a soul would hear her, save the birds.

"The first ball's in eighteen days, Vallillo."

With a yelp, Emmy staggered back as Jack emerged from the thicket. "Were you spying on me?"

"Were you spying on *me*?" He carried his usual bottle of wine and wore his usual smirk. Even slightly disheveled, he was still alluring, with his bright eyes and unyielding posture. Snobbish and handsome. Just Grace's type.

"Shouldn't you be helping the others?"

"Li told me to stay away."

"Because you're always drunk."

"My father spent his life collecting wine he didn't live to enjoy. I'm learning from his mistakes." He held the bottle out to her. When she refused, he took a generous swig. "The triumvirate is already interviewing new referrals. We need new faces as soon as possible."

A tendril of panic skittered down her neck. His far-fetched revenge scheme was likely the only thing holding him together—and it was based on magic she did not possess.

"C'mon, Vallillo. Oliver conjure-bound me as well, but I broke free of it in two weeks."

"Congratulations," she muttered. He was probably exaggerating, but her competitive streak had not, apparently, withered away with the rest of her.

His piercing gaze swept over her. "Can I try something?"

"No."

"The chancellor suppressed your voice and movements when they arrested you. Your conjury failed you then, so maybe those memories are keeping it locked away now." He tossed his empty wine bottle into the brush. "I want to re-create that moment."

His words hit like a punch. She would not be re-creating a damn thing about that night.

"My father used to do it with guards who'd been conjure-bound while sparring with a Stratton." Seeing her skepticism, he added, "My father served as commander for many years, and his father before him. I was supposed to be next."

Emmy staggered back, absorbing the words. *Commander Fontaine.* That was why she'd recognized Jack's surname. His father had been the third member of the triumvirate.

No wonder he knew the guards' names. No wonder he was cocky enough to believe he could infiltrate the chancellor's inner circles. He *was* the inner circle.

"Can you trust me for a moment?" He stepped closer.

She stepped backward, farther down the path. "You just told me your father was in charge of the guards who made my life hell."

He drew closer, hands raised. "I'm going to restrict your movements. Use the relic to fight back and free yourself."

"Absolutely not." She stepped back, two paces to match his.

With a long sigh, he scrubbed a hand through his hair. "You'd rather be blocked forever?"

No part of her wanted to experience that paralyzed, helpless feeling again, but—he'd gotten his magic back in two weeks. Unless, of course, he was lying. "Fine. Make it quick."

He wasted no time positioning himself behind her. "Ready?"

Every instinct she'd honed urged her not to leave her back exposed, but she nodded.

He wrapped his arms around her, pinning hers to her sides.

A laugh burst from her. Her movement was restricted, yes, but she'd expected something far more nefarious from someone who'd trained to be commander of a magical militia. "And this worked on your father's guards?"

"Sometimes." His breath was warm on her neck, and she shivered, her laughter dying.

For two years, no one had touched her, yet Jack Fontaine's knees were now pressed against the backs of her thighs, and his chin brushed the top of her head. "That's enough."

"Then use your conjury to get rid of me."

"How?" The more she wriggled, the tighter he held her to his chest. He smelled of wine and freshly struck matches, far too pleasant. "This is inappropriate. Now let go."

"You're an escaped convict who is living, unsupervised, with three strapping young men. We're far beyond the bounds of propriety by now."

She sighed, which was a mistake; the curve of her small chest pressed against his arms, and she blushed something awful. Squeezing the relic, she searched for something to transform into a weapon, but it didn't matter. That ethereal mist remained out of reach. "It didn't work."

"What happened to the girl who bit the guard?" His low taunt warmed her ear, stealing her breath. "Why do you fold so easily now?"

Her temper rose but she resisted its pull. "I'm not going to fight you."

"Then I suppose we'll stay like this all night." His grip on her tightened. "It's not like either of us sleeps, anyway."

Her throat felt as if it were swelling shut, just as it had in Grimsbane, when she'd screamed and screamed. She tried to pull the coolness of the brume toward her, tried to call to it like a rod attracting lightning, but it stayed out of reach. "I mean it, Jack." She hated the tremor in her voice. Even worse, his arms tightened again in response. He didn't care.

She hardly knew him, and she'd let him trap her, just as she'd been trapped by guards who had been led by *his* father. She tried to push him off her, but his grip was suffocating. She could not move, could not breathe, could not do a damn thing as Chancellor Stratton lifted his revolver and aimed it at Papa's forehead.

As Papa jerked backward.

She hadn't been able to warn him. Had not been able to unleash a single wail, and that anguish boiled over inside her, scalding her from the inside out, trapped.

As Papa fell to the floor, his head snapping against the marble.

His blood oozing over the tiles as the masked strangers watched, utterly impassive.

As Grace smiled.

A heavy presence jolted through Emmy. Pushing at the guard's arms, she tried to free herself, but they remained stubbornly in place. She tried to scratch at him, but her nails were brittle. *She* was brittle, not able to conjure even a lick of magic, to transform a weapon, like fingernails into solid iron, that ancient, unyielding metal—

The restraints disappeared.

She blinked, power retreating as if sucked down some mythical drain.

In a daze, the woods came back into focus. The noisy caws of watchful crows. The warm breeze tickling her cheeks. Jack gripping his bleeding arm, marred with parallel streaks of crimson.

Her hands shook as she raised them. Each fingernail ended in a glinting, bloodstained dagger.

"Jesus Christ," she breathed, gaping at her weaponed fingers. "How is this possible?"

"Because my sister was a genius."

"Yes, but—I've never transformed anything *alive* before." The confession slipped from her lips before she could stop it.

"Don't worry, Vallillo. I knew you were lying back in Grimsbane." A slow grin spread over his face. "But I had a feeling your gift had *some* overlap with your father's, even if it's imperceptible. With the help of a bone fragment from a bona fide amplifier, that ability is magnified."

"That's an understatement." Never before had Emmy felt a rush of power like that. She called to the brume again, and the ancient mist crashed over her in a torrent of magic. No sooner had she pictured her bony hands than they shifted, her fingers once again pale and ordinary.

This time, when she glimpsed Jack's wicked smile, her lips curved in return.

"We need new faces as soon as possible," Jack said as he strolled backward through Mistfield's halls. "That way we can meet with the triumvirate and hire staff before the ball."

As if it were that simple. "It worked on fingers. Who knows if I can change faces?"

But even now, as she held Rose's relic, that mystical heaviness lingered, and Emmy had to resist the urge to transform everything in sight. With nothing but Papa's guidance, she'd learned to transform tin to gold. Just what might she do with a relic?

"No more moping around Mistfield, practicing in safe little nooks." Still walking backward, he turned the corner without missing a beat. "You need real danger. Real stakes."

Today was the first day she'd even ventured outside. And she still hadn't slept a full night, not even with her door barricaded. Danger was, perhaps, the last thing she needed.

When they reached her bedroom door, Jack leaned against the frame, practically thrumming with boyish excitement. "The Society keeps records of every known charmed family. Given my flames, we'll have to pose as distant Fontaines. Tomorrow, you can transform my family tree so we're already on it."

Transforming ink on paper seemed simple enough, but nothing Jack asked was ever simple. "And where does the Society keep these records?"

His eyes glittered. "In their headquarters, of course."

SEVEN

"WE'RE HERE," JACK WHISPERED AS he crouched beside Emmy, his eyes fixed on the dark field.

Emmy followed his gaze. After a four-mile trek through the woods, her feet ached, and she was embarrassingly winded, but they'd finally arrived at the headquarters of the Society of the Charmed. Allegedly.

She exchanged a glance with Jimmy, who looked equally confused. "Where is it?"

"It's hidden behind an illusion enchantment," Caleb murmured, "but it's there."

Illusory magic? Emmy studied the darkness with renewed interest.

"The Villadom family has the gift of illusions," Jack explained quietly. "A Villadom used to have to fortify it every few days, but the guards commissioned Grace to imbue stones around the perimeter with the illusion, giving the Villadoms a much-needed break."

"How useful," Emmy muttered. The Society was making the most of their darling protégé.

Jack kept his gaze trained on the dark field. "We enter through the basement, add our names to the books, then get the hell out."

"And if they see us?" Headquarters was always guarded, Jack had said, though only two guards were stationed here in the offseason, on a rotating basis.

Jack lifted a taunting brow. "You could transform our faces so they won't recognize us."

"I'm not ready yet." Emmy had to be careful. Unlike fingernails, faces were close to a crucial organ. One wrong move, and she might accidentally transform their brains to mush.

Jack, of course, disagreed.

"Are we sure this is a good idea?" Caleb asked in a hushed voice. "You two were exhausted just from walking. Perhaps I should do it. Or even Jimmy."

"It can't be a forgery," Jack insisted. "Only Vallillo can transform the handwriting and the ink to match precisely. It has to be her."

All day, she'd practiced with Jack. It was a simple transformation, one she could probably manage without the relic now that her magic was unbound. The quickest way was to scribble the words in her own hand, then transform them to match the original handwriting.

Jack passed her a crumpled sheet of paper. "Here are our new identities."

"'Nathaniel and Winifred Fontaine,'" she read, "siblings, and second cousins once removed to Jack and Rose Fontaine. You will still have the Fontaine flames, but I'll have inherited my mother's . . ." She glanced up from the paper. "Earth conjury?"

He shrugged. "You can transform plants to bigger plants."

Emmy swallowed her disappointment. Plant magic was better suited for gardeners.

"Oh, c'mon." Jimmy could hardly contain his mirth. "Plants are . . . exciting."

"We draw less attention with elemental conjury." The long walk had brought a rosy tint to Jack's cheeks, though he, too, seemed winded. "Besides, Mrs. Windsor herself has earth conjury. Exotic gardening is all the rage."

Peering over Emmy's shoulder, Caleb frowned. "You're adding *me* to the list of Society-approved servants?"

"The steward of Mistfield Manor." Jack clapped Caleb on the back. "A promotion."

"You think I broke you out of prison and helped you track down a girl who can transform us into whomever we please, all for a *promotion?*"

Jack blinked. "Steward is the highest-ranked position, yes?"

"You absolute snob!" Snatching the paper from Emmy, Caleb licked his finger and smudged the ink. "Jack will still be Nathaniel Fontaine but I will pose as Emmy's brother and chaperone, visiting New York to find her a respectable charmed husband."

"A *husband?*" Emmy hissed. As if this could get any worse.

Caleb rolled his eyes. "I won't actually marry you off, but the Society must *think* you're looking to wed—and that you'll inherit millions once you do."

"Fine." Jack snatched back the paper and began scribbling. "You two will pose as Winifred and Paxton Fairchild, distant Fontaine cousins whose surname should already be recorded by the Society. You're helping me settle into Mistfield this summer. And Jimmy is a building design prodigy from the far east, where the Society has no records. Now can we go?"

Unease swept over Emmy. Breaking into the Society's headquarters was about as wise as a girl from Five Points posing as an heiress. But Jack was already inching toward the tree line.

"Caleb and I will keep watch," Jimmy whispered. "He'll do his strange mind talking if you're in any danger."

"You know I can hear you," Caleb grumbled, though he gave Emmy a curt nod.

A rare kindness. That was suspicious, given how vocal he'd been about despising Jack's schemes. Maybe he *wanted* her to fail.

"Stay low," Jack whispered as she joined him at the edge of the clearing, her heart pounding. "We can't see them, but if they're paying attention, they can spot us. When we cross the illusion, you'll feel a popping sensation. Then we'll wait for the guard to circle round the building."

Her palms were clammy. Had she ever done something this

reckless? She ought to have been hiding from the Society guards, but here she was, heading *toward* them.

Jack began dragging himself through the overgrown grass on his forearms. Emmy followed, regretting her wool dress as it caught on the uneven ground. They made slow, grueling progress, keeping their heads down, their bodies low. So focused was Emmy on not panting too loudly, she almost missed the moment her ears popped.

The Society's headquarters blinked into existence hardly twenty yards away.

Emmy stared at the formidable building: three stories of pale stone, with black shutters framing the square windows. Manicured hedges lined the long path to the black front doors, and a front porch wrapped itself around the sides of the building before disappearing from sight.

They waited, unmoving, for a guard to make rounds. After an eternity, the front door swung open and an enormous man strode onto the porch, his golden lantern held high.

Emmy held her breath. Not a lantern, but fire magic, though his flames were not black.

Neither Emmy nor Jack so much as blinked as the guard peered into the darkness. He was supposed to walk the perimeter of the building, but after a minute, he went back indoors.

Thirty minutes before the next round. Jack resumed his crawling, more quickly this time, and Emmy struggled not to lose him in the grass. Finally, they reached the basement window on the southern wall. "It's locked," Jack whispered.

"You said it'd be open!"

"It will be." He grinned wickedly. "When you use your conjury to open it."

Emmy gaped at him. "I didn't prepare for this."

"You quite literally transformed your fingernails into knives yesterday. You have tremendous power." He poked at her hand that gripped the relic. "Use it."

She nearly made daggers again, just to make him bleed. He never gave her a bit of leeway, not even for a moment.

Pressing her free hand against the cool pane, Emmy tried to picture the glass molecules. Sand? Oxygen? The brume gathered around her, courtesy of the relic. But what should she transform? If she broke the glass, the Society would know someone had entered. She could alter the interior lock to something easy to push past, but she couldn't even see what it looked like.

"Must you overthink even the smallest of tasks?"

"Must you speak incessantly?" He was a terrible magic teacher, not at all patient like Papa.

But Emmy would never have another lesson with Papa, would never hear his voice again.

With her palm on the glass, Emmy envisioned the pane as thin as the newspapers that left ink on the pads of Papa's fingers. The brume rushed through her in a cool torrent, and the glass softened to a sheet of paper that tore silently in her hands. She'd done it.

Reaching through the window, Jack undid the latch and slid it open. "Ladies first."

"Absolutely not."

With a soft thud, Jack disappeared inside the basement. After a moment, she followed.

There were no candles down here, and certainly no gas lamps, but Jack stood a few feet away, his forehead creased in concentration as a small, shadowy flame appeared in his palm. Without the relic, his magic was arduous. Good.

"In and out," Jack murmured. "Let's find the records."

They'd landed in some sort of storage room, cluttered with columns of crates and old furniture. There were far too many bookshelves, each spilling with a random assortment of knickknacks and tomes. Leather-bound books were strewn beside a crate of pearl napkin holders. Plenty of others were stacked in perilously high piles, blocking the tomes behind them.

"I thought you said the Society is organized," Emmy whispered.

"The records will be. In the next room." He led her to a formidable-looking door. Removing a skeleton key from his pocket, he pressed it to his lips before sliding it in the keyhole. With any luck, the locks hadn't been changed since Jack's father was commander.

Mercifully, it clicked open, though it creaked in protest.

She stayed close to Jack's flame as he crept into the records room. Here, neat shelves were labeled with thick black letters. *Elemental. Alchemical. Sensile. Charmlinking.*

"Types of conjury," Jack whispered, his dim light illuminating the old bindings.

She considered the four categories. "Which one am I?"

"Alchemical. You use the brume only to power your transformations. Once you're done, you don't need it to maintain the change, because you've permanently altered the chemistry."

She nearly smiled. It was one of the ways Emmy's magic had bested Grace's: Emmy's transformations lasted forever, while Grace's bridged objects lost their strength with use. Part of her longed to ask Jack which type of conjury Grace possessed, but she tucked away the thought, instead taking in the treasure trove of ancient texts, each one begging to be read. There were grimoires, too—thick old books stuffed with handwritten notes from long ago. How she longed to pull them off their shelves, but touching them risked triggering some sort of protective charm, especially if the Society had used Grace's bridging magic inside as well.

They needed to hurry. Emmy moved from shelf to shelf, scanning their contents, but she soon came across a locked armoire. Through the glass, trophies glittered in Jack's dim light.

"The summer pageant trophies," Jack murmured, raising his dying flame. "I forgot they're stored here in the offseason. Each year, the Society commissions a trophy to demonstrate the winner's gift when touched. Grace's father enchanted most of them, but that's her job now."

Emmy stared at the gilded chalices. Never before had she been so tempted to smash something to pieces. But she continued walking to the next aisle.

Unlike those on the other shelves, these books were uniform in size and color: white, with their spines painted in thick, swirling black ink. Stretching onto her tippy-toes, Emmy trailed her finger over the alphabetized spines until she came across F. Her pulse quickened as she lifted the Fontaine book and spread the pages, the dry leather binding cracking.

1 OCTOBER 1517 HENRICK FONTAINE, FYRE MAGICK . . .

"Found it." Line upon line named the Fontaines throughout history, along with their dates of birth, living relatives, occupations, incomes, and other intimate details. Emmy flipped through the pages until she came to a list in the back.

DEATHS OF NOTE

HELENA FONTAINE (NÉE BEAUCHAMP), DIED IN CHILDBIRTH, 11 OCTOBER 1861

HENRICK FONTAINE, COMMANDER OF THE GUARD, DIED OF ANGINA PECTORIS, 14 APRIL 1881

ROSE OPHELIA FONTAINE, DIED IN FIRE, 28 MAY 1881

JACK HENRICK FONTAINE, DIED IN PRISON, 30 APRIL 1882

"Well, look at that," Jack murmured. "Not only am I dead, but my death is 'of note.'"

She searched for a glimmer of sadness in Jack's smirk. His sister's death was hardly a month after his father's. He *had* to be hurting.

He pointed to his own name. "Rather compelling evidence they're not looking for us."

A silver lining, at least.

Without wasting any more time, Emmy scanned the pages until she found Jack's great-grandfather, whose brother had lived abroad and had fathered one child. Although the man bore no children, Emmy extended the familial line, giving him a son, a grandson, and a great-grandson: Nathaniel. She could not close her eyes while conjuring, instead focusing on getting the ink *just* right.

"Your family tree is almost completely empty," she murmured as she shifted the swirling cursive. "More than half your relatives did not bear children."

"That's common. The charmed are far less fertile than ordinaries."

Less fertile? She glanced at him. "Why?"

"Who knows?" He leaned closer to scrutinize her work, close enough to feel the heat of him through her wool dress. "According to the Society, it's evidence that we're a dying breed. But maybe God just doesn't want us to outnumber the ordinaries."

Had her parents known that, when she was a little girl wishing for a sister? What other information about charmed folks did the Society hoard for themselves?

"With a bona fide sibling, you'll be even more of a catch this summer. The marriage frenzy is—" He stilled, his gaze darting to the stairs.

Emmy? Jack?

Emmy froze. The voice—the voice had been in her head. "Caleb?"

A carriage full of guards is heading toward you.

EIGHT

JACK REACHED FOR THE RELIC, but Emmy turned away, sliding the book back onto its shelf. The Fairchild tome was only a few to the left, and she quickly added Paxton and Winifred, millionaires whose maternal great-grandmother married the eldest Fontaine Emmy had invented. No sooner had she placed it back on the shelf than Jack grabbed her arm and pulled her through the door, his hands shaking as he fumbled with the key. As soon as the lock clicked into place, they sprinted toward the window. He threaded his fingers to give her a boost—

Voices flooded the stairwell, followed by footsteps.

Cursing under his breath, Jack tried to pull her away, but Emmy freed her hand, quickly transforming the torn paper back to solid glass. Jack's tugging on her arm became more insistent, and Emmy let him nudge her into the narrow, cobweb-ridden space between a bookshelf and the wall. He squeezed in beside her, his hard gaze locked on the staircase.

Men flooded the basement, one after the other, and Emmy could not breathe, could not trust herself to take one goddamn inhale, because there were three, four, five, six of them.

"Get the tables, gents." A white-uniformed guard rubbed his palms together. Even in the dim light, he carried himself with authority, though he was as young as the rest of them. Handsome, too, with dark hair and darker eyes, striking against his fair skin.

Beside her, Jack went lethally still.

Golden lantern light flooded the basement, bleeding into the gaps between books. She squeezed her eyes shut, as if they could not see her if she could not see them. But they could—if they glimpsed between the books.

A few guards dragged a table to the center of the floor, along with several chairs. The one barking orders slid into a seat, a cigar dangling between his lips.

For weeks, the only emotion Emmy had sensed from Jack was that vexing amusement. But as he stared at the handsome leader, he hardly blinked, his gray eyes burning with hate. *This* was the prisoner she'd met in Grimsbane, the one who snapped necks without so much as flinching.

These guards were their age. Jack had to know them.

"I heard you quit gambling."

"I swore off the pool halls." The leader grinned. "But what's a game between friends?"

A deck of cards appeared, along with an amber bottle of whiskey. Soon the basement reeked of cigars, and Emmy's throat burned with the need to cough.

Jack's warm hand found hers, and relief flooded her. For so long, she'd been alone in her paralyzing fear. But as she came to her senses, she quietly smacked him away. She didn't need comfort, she needed him to be ready to fight.

He squeezed her hand more insistently. Not intended to comfort, but a request. The relic.

If she gave it to him, she'd be defenseless—and he might burn these men to a crisp. Emmy waited for her conscience once again, but it remained silent. The past two years had taught her well: if it came to her life or theirs, she'd choose herself without hesitation.

Dragging her hand over the bookshelf, Emmy envisioned the discarded books plumper and taller, slowly filling every crack until no light shone through the gaps. Once they were completely out of view, she pressed the relic into Jack's fingers. As soon as it was out of her hands, the ethereal mist vanished. She still had her ordinary magic, but without the relic, it would be too slow and weak to keep her safe.

The bookshelf creaked as Jack shifted, but the guards' boisterous conversation continued. He pressed his free hand against the wall, and black flames seeped between his fingers.

"All right, boys," said the leader. "What'll it be? Stud poker?"

Jack swept his hand in an arc along the wall, a trail of red-hot stone blazing in its wake.

"You win with suspicious frequency, Stratton."

Stratton. The leader was Oliver Stratton.

How Emmy longed for another look at the man Grace had kissed. The man who, according to Jack, had blocked Emmy's magic, preventing her from proving her innocence.

"I suppress everyone's conjury so no one can cheat," Oliver insisted.

"Except you."

"Except me." She could hear his grin, could feel the guards' sycophantic laughter vibrating through her clenched teeth.

Jack completed his fiery circle and, with two hands, shoved the center of it. Stone scraped stone, though the noise was drowned out by the guards' chatter. Then, as night air poured through the hole he'd made, the scraping ceased for a terrifying moment—and in that cursed millisecond, the guards' voices quieted, an ill-timed lull in conversation. No matter how tightly Emmy shut her eyes, no matter how much she wished for more boisterous laughter, the silence persisted.

The stone circle crashed onto the ground outside.

Chairs screeched against the floor, and through the cries of "Did you hear that?" and "Over there!" came Oliver Stratton's unmistakable command. "Find out what that was. Now."

Snatching the relic back, Emmy squeezed through the hole in the wall, Jack on her heels. The guards were already moving the bookshelf, their shouts growing louder—

Emmy could not go back to Grimsbane.

Pressing both palms to the wall, she imagined it whole. It could not be scarred like her, or damaged like her, or hollowed or broken like her—

The stones knit back together seamlessly. Jack gaped, his surprise a mirror of her own. He made to run away, but the stone circle still lay on the ground, its edges charred. Slamming her palms against it, Emmy reduced it to nothing but dust; nothing, like her cell in Grimsbane, her life within its walls.

The stone was gone, and Jack was pulling at her, running—

"Hey! Stop!"

The voice was behind them, and Emmy had no time to think, her hands acting on pure impulse alone as she pressed her palm to Jack's face, imagining the handsome sneer of Oliver Stratton, that uniform of ivory instead of Jack's coat of midnight black.

"You're him," she whispered as the guard's lantern illuminated them.

"Where do you think you're— Oh, my apologies, Commander Stratton." In the darkness, the guard managed to look contrite. "Didn't see you had company."

Jack opened his mouth. Closed it again, before he threw an arm around Emmy. "Stand guard, Holtz," he sneered, his voice so much like Oliver's, Emmy's skin crawled. "I shouldn't be long."

The guard tipped his cap before turning back around.

"Keep walking," Jack gritted through the corner of his mouth.

Every instinct in Emmy roared against leaving her back exposed. How long until the guard realized he'd been tricked and they all came after them?

Her ears popped as they passed through the illusion again, but still, they walked. As soon as they reached the shadow of the trees, Emmy broke free of Jack and sprinted into the woods. Stumps and branches tripped her in the dark, making cuts all over her arms, her legs. Still, she ran. Her muscles screamed at her, and her lungs begged for air, but Emmy did not slow down until she was about to collapse. Finally, she stopped, hands clenching her knees as she tried to quell the nausea ratcheting up her throat, the jagged ache in her pitiful lungs.

Jack skidded to a stop beside her, gasping just as heavily. This close, the shape of his face was alarmingly incongruent, like one of his poorly buttoned shirts. If the guard had so much as lifted his lantern, they would have been caught.

He tried to speak but could not catch his breath, instead throwing himself on the forest ground, limbs splayed. Lifting a finger, he tried to speak once again but couldn't.

A laugh bubbled in her chest. She tried to contain it, but he looked so . . . ridiculous.

They ought to have kept zigzagging through the trees. Emmy tried, but that potent laugh sparked as soon as she looked at Jack again. Half Oliver, half himself. Though both were handsome, he looked positively terrible.

The laughter won. She wheezed with it, guffaws spilling from her like water past a dam. Whenever she tried to stop, she glimpsed the confusion in Jack's bizarre face, and she was a goner.

"What is it?'

"Your face," she managed to say.

He looked offended. "My face?"

Oh, this was the epitome of foolishness, letting herself lose her damn mind when the guards could be coming for them. Pressing her hand to his cheek, she summoned her magic. Humor still twitched his full lips, though his smile was no longer grotesque. Far from it, in fact. His true face was much nicer than Oliver's, and certainly more so than that terrible half transformation she'd done. With such good looks, he'd probably gotten away with all sorts of awful things as a little boy, never experiencing a single consequence. It certainly explained his arrogance.

When he was once again Jack, he grinned up at her. "Like I said: when you finally stopped overthinking your magic, it worked just fine."

"And yet you still haven't stopped talking."

A twig snapped in the darkness.

Jack moved with more speed than she would have thought possible. Snatching the relic from her hand, he jumped in front of her, igniting a dark flame on his palm.

"It's us," Jimmy called, Jack's flame illuminating their sweat-sheened faces.

Caleb's gaze swept over Emmy, his expression so bewildered, she glanced down at herself. Branches and twigs were tangled in her dress. Her hair had come loose while she ran for her life, and a few leaves had lodged themselves in what remained of her braid. Feral indeed.

"She did it." Jack's smile was devilishly alive. It was as if their close call had eroded away a bit of the mask he wore. This quest for vengeance—he reveled in it.

Perhaps something in her had eroded away, too, for she could not wipe the smile from her face. With the relic, she'd transformed a human face. Twice. She'd forged the Society's records right under their noses. For the first time in a long time, Emmy felt like an asset. A weapon.

And she rather liked it.

NINE

JACK HELD OPEN THE ATTIC window proudly. "Welcome to my favorite corner of Mistfield."

He'd brought them to the roof atop the ballroom, at least five stories from the ground. As she crawled out the window, she tried to keep her eyes on the roof tiles—and not on the sunset staining the sky or the ground far below. One misstep, and gravity would yank her to her demise.

"There's chimney smoke over there." Caleb squinted into the fading light. "Clarity Hall?"

Emmy's head whipped toward the distant plume. Clarity Hall was the Windsors' summer estate. Grace might already be in town. Here, in Avalon-on-Hudson.

After their successful break-in at Society headquarters last week, Jack had insisted Emmy begin to learn ballroom dancing. All week, Jimmy had driven her to private lessons north of Avalon-on-Hudson, their carriage the only one in sight. But this afternoon, they'd seen several.

"The servants are readying the estates for the arrival of the Society families." Jumping to his feet, Jack meandered toward the edge. "From now on, we must be extraordinarily cautious. Curtains drawn. Voices low. The Strattons have a footman with augmented hearing who eavesdrops on their supposed friends. And Grace has a lady's maid with the gift of invisibility."

A girl with invisibility conjury had debuted with her and Grace. When she'd disappeared, Emmy had been awestruck while Grace had only shrugged. *The magic of a spy*, she'd said, *not a lady*. Yet Grace had, apparently, been impressed enough to hire her.

Such a tiny deceit should not have stung as much as it did.

"So are you finally ready to tell us this plan of yours?" Jimmy asked.

Settling onto the roof, Jack stretched his long legs in front of him. "First thing tomorrow, Alton and I will go to the city to request an appointment with the triumvirate. If we make a strong enough impression, they might not ask to interview Vallillo."

Ladies who are referred to the Society require a male relative to vouch for their character, the Society pamphlet had said. Fine by Emmy. She was not ready to play nice with Papa's killer.

Stiffly, Caleb lowered himself to sit beside Jimmy. "And who referred us?"

"My dead father." Jack proudly held up a piece of thick paper. "With Vallillo's help, I have a letter in his precise handwriting that he sent to Nathaniel before his death. Society members aren't supposed to reveal anything to the charmed people they refer until *after* they're in, but they can't exactly punish the dead. It should at least earn us interviews."

She'd written the letter with him earlier, encouraging Nathaniel to forgo his world travels for a summer to experience a season with the Society of the Charmed.

"And while we're gone, Vallillo will continue to learn ballroom dancing." Jack grinned at her. "You're booked for every day until the ball, six hours a day."

The ball was ten days away. He was waiting for her to point out that her feet were going to fall off, but—Grace believed that a lady's character could be inferred from her dancing. That was her excuse for paying that exorbitant fee for lessons at the Society's favorite finishing school. *To be taken seriously, protégés need more than strong magic. They need to be flawless.*

Emmy, as Winnie Fairchild, also needed to be flawless.

"Assuming the triumvirate grants us trial membership," Jack continued, "we'll be on the guest lists from the first ball, the Inaugural

Splendor, to the last one, the Golden Gala. We only have a month to get chummy with our targets, learning as much as we can about them. Starting with Oliver. Based on his display at Society headquarters, he still loves to gamble."

"He said he quit the pool halls," Emmy reminded him.

But Jack waved a dismissive hand. "That won't last a week. He *lives* for cards. And he's a rotten cheater. If I can befriend him, as Nathaniel, we'll make sure he's caught."

"So he gets roughed up by card sharks?" Caleb scoffed. "That's hardly enough."

For once, Emmy agreed with him.

"We'll get him arrested and thrown in ordinary jail, where his conjury will be useless."

"But his father's money won't. He'll be out in no time."

"Unless the Stratton name is already ruined, and his father is already in Grimsbane." The corner of Jack's mouth lifted. "And while they're both in jail, with their reputations shattered, we'll bring their true crimes to light, clearing my and Emmy's names."

"But you haven't said *how* we'll ruin the chancellor," Caleb pointed out.

Or Clara. Or, most importantly, Grace.

"I'm getting there." Jack leaned back on his hands, so close to the edge, even Jimmy winced. "Clara Claremont is obsessed with her business. Despite misgivings about a young woman owning a modiste instead of furthering her family's bloodline, the Society adores her enchanted gowns. If we ruin her business, we ruin her."

Emmy's temperature rose at the mere thought of Clara's dreams coming true. "How?"

"To be determined. But I made you an appointment in her shop for next week."

"Have you lost your mind?" Emmy was far from ready to face the conniving heiress.

"Surely the great Emilia Vallillo can handle one charmed girl." He lifted a casual shoulder. "You need enchanted gowns—and we need to learn more about her business."

Against her better judgment, Emmy managed a tight nod. At some point between forging the Society's records and running for her life, Jack's obsession had begun to infect her. She'd fallen asleep picturing Grace's perfect new life in ruins, and she'd woken to visions of Grace's tear-stained face as she expressed how deeply she regretted turning on her one true friend.

Emmy wanted it, too. Vengeance.

"And next, of course, is Grace."

Emmy felt Jimmy studying her but she kept her eyes trained on Jack. Waiting.

"First, Emmy's going to befriend Grace, as Winnie."

"She'll see right through me." Grace possessed many flaws, but gullibility was not among them. In no time, she'd know that Winnie Fairchild was not who she claimed.

"Give yourself some credit. You're far cleverer than her." Jumping to his feet, Jack balanced on the steep pitch as he walked closer to Emmy. "All season, you'll push her buttons. Starting with Oliver."

"You can't be serious." It was laughable, really, that the Stratton heir would pay her any mind. Most of the time when boys had spoken to Emmy, it was to ask about Grace.

"It'll work—if you stop bristling every time a man is near." He squatted in front of her, invading her space to prove his point.

And damn him, she could not help but blush at his nearness. "So this is your big plan for Grace? We'll aggravate her?"

"Grace will do anything—*anything*—to be the Society's darling. In the year before my arrest, I watched her rise quicker than any protégé ever had. The Society commissions her conjury for all sorts of purposes. The Windsors practically consider her a daughter. And in her first season, she had three marriage proposals, all of which she graciously turned down."

Each detail was a stick of dynamite inside her, ready to explode.

"Talk about rags to riches," Jimmy murmured. "Why did she turn them down?"

"Because she has her sights set on the richest bachelor of all: Oliver Stratton."

Out of love? Or because she wanted his fortune to be hers one day?

"Grace didn't get this far by virtue alone. If we expose one of her secrets, the Society will spit her out like the trash she is." He kept his gaze on Emmy, waiting for her approval, for once.

"I'm glad she climbed so high." Emmy's voice remained even, for once. "Because now she has quite the distance to fall."

They stared at each other, Jack's slow grin practically glowing in the dying light. For better or for worse, Jack understood what it was like to hate someone with his whole heart.

"Fontaine?" Caleb cleared his throat. "The chancellor?"

"Yes, right. The chancellor." Jack stepped away from Emmy, and she sucked in a much-needed breath. "Given that the greedy bastard managed to get his son appointed to *my* position as commander, the Strattons now control two of the three triumvirate positions."

Commander Stratton. That was how the guard had referred to Oliver.

"I have no doubt the third member, Keeper Windsor, is a thorn in the chancellor's side. If we convince the chancellor that Windsor is conspiring against *him*, he'll go after Windsor in his usual vile, underhanded way. And we'll catch him."

Jimmy lifted a brow. "He'll risk it all on rumors started by folks he only just met?"

"No," Jack agreed. "If he's going to trust us, we need to give him good reason."

Emmy was learning to dread this particular smile of Jack's, but fortunately, it was aimed at Caleb.

"Oh no." Caleb rose, shaking his head. "Don't even think about it."

"When he interviews us, we'll ask to keep your gift a secret so others are comfortable in your presence. He'll be thrilled to have a mind reader all to himself. And when you help him—"

"Help him!" Caleb's face turned a furious shade of maroon. "The man did not so much as investigate Rose's death—"

"We need him to trust you." Jack shrugged. "It's the only way to get close to him."

"He threw you in jail! No trial, no sentencing, nothing. All to protect his rotten son."

Emmy froze. Jack still had not told her what had happened to get him arrested in the first place, but she was beginning to gather the pieces.

A fire. His sister's untimely death. And now: the chancellor jailing Jack to protect Oliver.

Caleb folded his arms. "You're supposed to keep my family's gift a secret. Just like your parents did, and their parents before them."

"It'll still be a secret." Jack looked entirely nonplussed. "He'll think you're Paxton Fairchild, affluent college student visiting the States for the summer."

"I can't believe how selfish you're being!"

"Is it selfish to want my sister's murderers to pay for what they've done?"

Caleb's hands fell to his sides. "In four days, Rose will have been gone a year."

Jack's perennial smile wavered, just a smidge. "And?"

"For once, I'm relieved she isn't here, so she doesn't have to watch you destroy the Fontaine legacy. Just as we all knew you would."

Jack's wince was so brief, Emmy might have missed it, had she not been watching Caleb storm past him. A moment too late, Jack chased after him, disappearing through the door.

Jimmy sighed. "We *almost* made it a whole day without them arguing."

"Were they always like this?"

"Hard to say. Everything was different when Rose was here." In the fading light, he managed a smile. "How are you feeling about all this?"

She considered telling Jimmy the truth—that she hardly felt anything at all, save the fear of capture that still plagued her most nights, and a budding hope that Jack's plans were not as far-fetched as they seemed. "I'm willing to give it a try. But even if they let us in, a month hardly seems like enough time to ruin four lives."

"If it gets too dangerous, say the word, and we'll leave, yeah?" His face was grim. "Jack says this is the only known community of charmed people. It'll be easier to avoid them if we hide out West, away from New York."

But if they left, Jimmy would lose his shot at his own business. And every day Emmy spent in hiding was another day Grace won.

They wove their way back through Mistfield's attic, the staffs' quarters eerily abandoned. Usually, Emmy had a sixth sense for Jack's whereabouts, but there was no sign of him or Caleb in the main hall, so she and Jimmy settled into the library, where Emmy continued sifting through illustrated books for inspiration. If Jack was leaving for the city tomorrow, he'd want his new appearance tonight. For the three boys, she'd already found fairy-tale princes and pirates, but her own face was much harder to design.

But Jack never came to the library. Nor did he come to her room, though as usual, Emmy spent most of the night lying awake, steak knife ready. At dawn, she abandoned all hopes of sleep and ventured into the hall. If he was late because of her, she'd never hear the end of it.

The door to Jack's room was ajar but his bed was empty. If he'd gotten drunk and passed out in the driveway, better that she find him, rather than the Society guards.

He was not in the driveway, mercifully. He wasn't in the wine cellar, either, though she nearly slipped on muddy footprints. A tendril of unease nagged at her, but perhaps Jack had gone in and out for more wine. Unless Grimsbane's guards— No, she could not think of them.

She had Rose's relic. With it, she was far from defenseless.

A heavy morning mist hung low over the dew-kissed woods. Hugging herself for warmth, Emmy followed the footprints down one of the winding trails, until they disappeared in a field with grass so tall, she nearly missed the headstones. There were at least a dozen of them, though only the newest-looking one had a bouquet of dead wildflowers atop it.

Jack was curled against it. Asleep, though his fingers still gripped an empty wine bottle. His jacket was haphazardly spread over him like a makeshift blanket. He'd probably done that for warmth in Grimsbane.

"Jack?" When he did not stir, she raised her raspy voice. "Jack, wake up."

The mist was steadily becoming a faint rain, but Jack did not stir. Was he dead?

Careful not to touch the headstones, Emmy crouched beside Jack and shook him.

With a yell, he startled, his bloodshot eyes darting about wildly.

"It's me," she said quickly, jerking her hand back from his shoulder.

His eyes were unfocused as they settled on her. "She hated being alone," he mumbled, his words heavy with sleep.

Emmy's heart sank. Perhaps this was the scene from the picture Caleb had mentioned: the harbinger of ruin. Which was unfair, really, because Jack was hurting underneath those smirks.

Ugh. Jack Fontaine was growing on her. Like a fungus.

As he tried to slip on his jacket, Emmy could not help but feel a pinch of sorrow for Jack, who had lost so much, so quickly. Perhaps that was why he spoke of death like an old friend rather than the thief it was.

"I know what you're thinking," he muttered, "but I'm fine."

"It might be better if we take more time to prepare. Maybe in a few months—"

"No," he said firmly. "By July, half the Society will be back in the city while the other will be in Newport. Either way, Mrs. Astor reigns over every guest list. Even if we won her favor in record time, the newspapers would scour for dirt on us. They'd eventually discover we don't exist. Besides," he added, flashing her a weak imitation of his usual smirk, "if Rose was right, I'll be long dead by winter."

But his cavalier words no longer fooled her. Death haunted him, too.

"You need to stop drinking. I mean it, Jack." She pried the empty wine bottle from where it was half buried in the grass. "You could have been seen last night."

"If you'd give me my new face already, it wouldn't matter if I'm seen." He was impossible, grinning as though he'd said something profound.

"Fine. Come here."

That took him by surprise. "You'll do it? Right now?"

Relic in hand, she motioned for him to scoot closer. If he wanted to treat his family's cemetery like a perfectly normal place to lounge, so be it.

"Make me irresistible. And try to remember what I look like." He shivered as she touched his cheek. "Once we clear our names, I'd like to be me again."

Emmy made a noncommittal noise, but she studied his face. Jack was not perfect. No, he had a little scar cut into his right brow, partially obscured by his chocolate waves. And his dark lashes were a bit too long, too innocent against those gray irises, which sparkled with a dozen shades of mischief, each more infuriating than the last. He was the love child of an angel and a devil, equal parts alluring and ruthless. It'd be easier to tolerate him once he had a new face.

As soon as she focused on the relic, that ethereal mist mixed with the faint rain, cool and soft as it flooded her. Tentatively, she touched his still gaunt cheeks. Power rushed to her fingertips, transforming them just as she'd envisioned. Moving to his nose, she pictured the straight one of the fairy-tale prince she'd found in the library books, and his nose shifted. His skin was warm and soft and far more distracting than any object she'd transformed. As her fingers grazed his jawline, she forgot what, precisely, she was about to alter.

"What is it?" He eyed her suspiciously. "Are you cross with me, too?"

A flush swept through her. "Tell me again how relics work."

His gaze flitted to Rose's headstone. "She made it in secret, following steps she found in an old book—the Fontaine grimoire, Caleb thinks. An ordinary relic is an entirely different creation. It wields the power of an ancestor, but only if their conjury is the same. If my father hadn't insisted on cremation, for example, I could have created a relic to add his brume access to mine, doubling my flames' strength. But Rose found a way to activate the dead witch's amplifying conjury. Even though she's not our relative and we're not amplifiers."

And the power coursing through Emmy was far more than double her ordinary strength. She was performing magic that was impossible on her own. Easily. Though she was not above using a bone from a dead charmed person, she'd prefer to know how, exactly, it worked. "I'd like to see that book."

"Then I'll get it for you." Their eyes met, and for a moment, he looked at her with the same disarming intensity that he had at Grimsbane. She nearly asked him what he was thinking, but he glanced away.

Soon Emmy fell into the rhythm of her work, her fingers growing bolder as she erased his handsome features. Rose's relic operated on instinct, anticipating Emmy's intentions the moment they took shape. His faint scars, the pale sheen a month of daylight hadn't shaken—with a caress of her fingers they were gone. She tamed his unruly waves and lightened them until they were fawn brown. In all the family portraits, the Fontaines shared Jack's striking gray eyes, so she kept those but brightened his irises until they glittered like the metal of a gun.

"Done." She leaned back to examine her work, nearly bumping into a nearby headstone.

Jack prodded his face with his fingertips. "Well? Am I infuriatingly handsome?"

Still handsome. But Nathaniel's face was tamer, somehow. Less intimidating.

With his back to her, Jack began picking up the empty wine bottles.

"Jack?"

He turned, brows raised. "It must be serious. You rarely call me my given name."

"Caleb said that the chancellor arrested you to protect Oliver." She waited for him to confirm, but of course he didn't. "What did Oliver and Grace do?"

"The same thing they did to you."

Her temper flared. This sort of purposeful evasion was precisely why she hadn't bothered to ask. "Why do you keep so many secrets?"

"And you're the epitome of trusting?" Despite the strangeness of his new face, his steely gray eyes glimmered with a familiar taunt. "We'll be back in a week. Try not to miss me."

"I'll survive somehow." A week without Jack and Caleb would have been much more appealing if it weren't full of dance lessons.

And if she didn't have to face Grace's darling friend Clara Claremont.

TEN

AS EMMY APPROACHED CLAREMONT ORIGINALS with Jimmy, she felt a strange camaraderie with the headless mannequins in the front windows. She, too, wore a luxurious summer gown. She, too, was mindlessly executing someone else's vision.

And if she wasn't careful, she, too, might lose her head.

"I'll be right here," Jimmy murmured as they stood just outside the shop. "If you change your mind, come on out. Fontaine will figure out a new plan."

She tried to smile at him, but his familiar voice coming from a stranger's face only further unsettled her. All week, she'd put off transforming him, but with Avalon-on-Hudson growing more crowded by the day, she could not wait any longer. He was now Zhao Rui, building design specialist. Still ridiculously tall and handsome, but his face was broader now, his eyes more wide set, and his hair thick and shiny. "You can change your mind, too," she told him. "Just say the word and I'll change you back."

"Maybe after I make my first million." His easy smile faded at whatever he glimpsed in her face. "You've got this."

"It's only a dress shop." The raspiness of her voice did little to quell her jitters. At least her shredded vocal cords were an asset now, completing her disguise.

"And she's only a rich girl. Probably doesn't even know how to punch." With a wink, he opened the door.

A bell tinkled as Emmy entered, and a young woman peered up from the front desk. Not Clara. "May I help you?"

"I have an appointment with Miss Claremont?" Damn the inflection in her voice. A true-born heiress would sound self-assured.

But the girl smiled affably. "And what is your name?"

"Winifred Fairchild."

Emmy waited for the girl to scream "liar" or for the pits of hell to yawn open right beneath her, but, of course, nothing happened, save the girl scanning her appointment book for Winifred's name. "Ah, there you are. Please follow me to our *special* selection, in the back."

The receptionist led her through rows of ordinary gowns, perhaps in case ordinary people entered the shop. Producing a key, she unlocked a door in the back of the store. "After you."

She'd fooled the receptionist. That was a start. Emmy nearly told the girl to walk in herself, in case it was a trap, but she did as she was told, entering a large, elegant office.

"Miss Claremont will be right with you. In the meantime, can I fetch you anything?"

Did proper girls require tea, or champagne, or a glass of water? What would Grace request? But a shake of Emmy's head seemed to do the trick, and the receptionist padded away.

Clara Claremont was about to walk through that door. And Emmy was about to vomit all over her office.

Certain she was sweating through her violet day gown, Emmy sat in one of the upholstered chairs and glanced at a rococo-style mirror above the desk. Her new reflection was still a shock to her, though she'd practiced conjuring it for days, along with the plainer disguise she'd used for her grueling dance lessons. But there was nothing plain about Winnie Fairchild. All the marks Grimsbane had etched into Emmy—her scars, her broken blood vessels, her perennially chapped lips—were gone. Her mousy brown hair was now a thick, shiny mahogany, one that revealed the subtlest bits of red when it caught the sunlight. Her pallid skin was a light gold. Her eyes larger and almond shaped, her irises the glittering hue of emeralds. Once she'd infused her cheeks with a rosy pink and thickened her dark lashes, she was beautiful beyond recognition.

Winnie Fairchild was flawless. Like a blade.

The door swung open, and Emmy hurried to her feet just as an elegant young woman entered, her scrutinizing gaze sweeping over Emmy. "You must be Miss Fairchild."

Clara Claremont was curtsying to her. And Emmy was absolutely frozen in place.

For two years, she'd tried to envision this very girl. Her umber curls Emmy had recalled, though they were now adorned with a stylish floral bonnet rather than with diamonds. Her cheeks were round and, though not as flushed with excitement as they'd been at the ball, pleasantly pink. But her hazel eyes possessed the same sharpness they had that terrible night.

Clara glanced behind her. "Where is your maid?"

A bit delayed, Emmy managed to copy Clara's subtle curtsy. "I, ah, don't have one."

"You don't have a lady's maid?"

"I don't have one *yet*. She stayed behind in Paris." Emmy would need to impart this supposed Parisian maid to Jack and Caleb when they returned.

"Not to worry. I have plenty of girls to help." Opening the top desk drawer, Clara produced a swath of crimson fabric. "Now, before we proceed, please remove your gloves and hold this."

Emmy eyed the fabric warily.

"You're rather careful, aren't you?" Amusement danced in Clara's eyes. "I verified your identity with the triumvirate, but one can never be too careful."

They'd met hardly five minutes ago, and Clara was already laughing at her. If only Emmy could bolt from the dress shop before she embarrassed herself further. But Jack's plan had, apparently, worked, and the chancellor had approved their temporary membership.

Unless Clara was lying and this was a trap.

Emmy studied the swath of fabric. An embroidered snake was coiled at the bottom of it, poised to strike. A piece of cloth could not reveal her true identity, could it?

Peeling the glove off her right hand, one finger at a time, Emmy took the swath.

The embroidered snake began to slither along the fabric, its narrow body curving and twisting underneath the candlelight. Enchanted, just like the clouds on Emmy's debutante gown.

"Looks like you passed." Clara tucked the serpentine fabric in the drawer. "It only moves for a charmed person. Can't have the ordinaries running around in enchanted dresses."

Emmy managed to meet Clara's too-clever eyes. "How lovely."

"My dresses are one thing," Clara drawled as she led Emmy down a new hall, nodding to a waiting attendant. "But this space is my favorite creation of all. I consider it a parlor for Society ladies, one where we can speak freely, laugh freely, and, of course, shop freely. With everyone arriving for the start of the season, it's nice and full today."

"Full?" Emmy squeaked. "I can come back—"

"Nonsense. A newcomer is just what we need." With a self-satisfied smirk, Clara pressed her palm to the wall at the end of the hall, and a door shimmered into existence. Emmy had no choice but to follow.

Once she stepped inside, she gasped.

Several chandeliers floated above the vast space, which was filled with ladies in colorful dresses lounging on plush chaises with champagne flutes. Mirrors lined the far walls, zigzagging so as to double, triple, quadruple the reflections of the girls who modeled gowns in front of them. Downright horrifying, to be surrounded by so many people. *Charmed* people.

Even more alarming: Grace might be here. In this very room.

"Ladies," Clara crooned, "please welcome Miss Winifred Fairchild."

All heads whipped toward Emmy, their reflections following suit like an obedient army.

Surely the great Emilia Vallillo can handle one charmed girl, Jack had said. Yet here were more charmed ladies than she could count. Forget Rose's prophecy. *She* was going to slit his throat.

"Is she allowed back here?" someone asked.

And after slitting Jack's throat, she'd hang him upside down like a calf for slaughter.

"Of course, Mrs. Villadom. The triumvirate granted her temporary status just yesterday."

That only raised more brows. With a knowing smile, Clara wove her arm through Emmy's and led her through the salon. She paused occasionally to point out the gowns fastened to the headless mannequins, but Emmy was no fool. *She* was the spectacle.

Focus. Emmy tried to make the appropriate expressions of delight as Clara led her through rows of beautiful dresses, the embroidery of each thrumming with life. On a silk gown as navy as twilight, gold-threaded stars careened across the sky. The floral petals of a rosy tea dress drifted in a phantom wind. "Touch activates the enchantment," Clara explained. "But only charmed touch. We're forbidden to wear them in public, of course."

Loath as Emmy was to admit it, Clara's gift was impressive. According to Grace, their debutante ball gowns had taken Clara weeks of back-breaking conjury. And there were *hundreds* of gowns in this shop.

Clara launched into a monologue about her summer line, her flagship location on Fifth Avenue, and her popularity among "all the *right* people," dropping surnames that might have impressed Emmy, had she followed the papers. Still, Emmy made an effort to nod and smile.

Just what had Grace said to convince Clara to sew rocks into Emmy's hem?

Emmy's whole life, she and Grace had known all the same people. They'd played stickball with the same neighborhood kids, sewed for the same lady on the first floor. Until Clara. It wasn't that Emmy had been jealous when Grace had begun to gush about the well-heeled girl she'd befriended at dance lessons; Emmy was more perplexed that Grace hadn't introduced them. That hadn't stopped Grace from imparting Clara's opinions on practically everything. *Clara says frills are so last season. Clara says the Society boys find elemental gifts unbecoming of a lady.* Each time, the slightest tension had sparked between Emmy and Grace, a brush catching a tangle in otherwise silken hair. But Emmy had reasoned it away. After all, she was unaccustomed to sharing Grace with anyone, let alone a girl from the elusive Society.

As Clara continued to explain this season's in-vogue patterns, Emmy stared at her.

This was the girl who'd sewn fool's gold into her gown.

This was the girl who had let her rot in jail for a crime she did not commit.

"If you're here for the season, you'll need an enchanted gown for each event, at minimum. Every lady with fashion sense will be wearing a Claremont original. Trust me."

"How long do the enchantments last?" Emmy's clouds had ceased moving in the first hours of her imprisonment, robbing her of her only distraction.

With a wink, Clara leaned closer. "They'll outlast us all."

Surely Clara wasn't foolish enough to lie to her customers. "How?"

"Hard work, Miss Fairchild. As a young entrepreneur, I never rest." Clara flourished her hand over the rows of fabric and mannequins. "Well? Which of my lovelies catches your eye?"

They were all gorgeous, and Jack would be furious if she didn't purchase at least one, but Emmy could not bring herself to please the dressmaker. Not yet. "Do you have anything else?"

Clara's smile tightened. "Picky, are we? Not to worry; I have plenty more."

As Clara sauntered away, Emmy tried to quell the fire in her chest. It'd be far easier to play nice if there weren't so many damn people watching her. The same people who had watched when she'd been up on that stage, trying desperately to prove her innocence.

The same people who'd watched, unflinching, as her beautiful gown was slashed open.

As Papa was shot.

"Miss Fairchild?"

To hell with Jack. Emmy would not give a cent to Clara Claremont.

"Excuse me, Miss Fairchild?"

Emmy nearly choked on her own spit. She knew that voice. Knew it as well as her own.

It was woven into all her memories, a thread tethered to the very core of who Emmy was. It was the voice she'd heard after her mother had died: *It's all right, let her go, it's all right*. The voice that had filled endless hours of chores, keeping Emmy entertained with dreams of balls and magic and secret societies.

Heart in her throat, Emmy turned to face Grace Eloise Montgomery.

"Pardon my intrusion, but I wanted to introduce myself." Dipping into an elegant curtsy, Grace offered Emmy a brilliant smile. "I'm Grace Montgomery, niece of Mr. and Mrs. Duncan Windsor."

Emmy opened her mouth. Closed it again.

This was Grace, *her* Grace, but her features were more elegant, her petite figure softer. She stood with impeccable posture. Her cheekbones, though still as round and rosy as apples, were high and proud. Never before had they been apart long enough for Emmy to notice the passage of time in Grace's face. But Grace had aged, ever so slightly.

"It's such a treat to have newcomers," Grace continued, and her voice was the falsetto singsong she'd used with teachers and nuns alike. "Just in time for the season."

Grace used to consult Emmy before she so much as combed her hair differently, but now she'd adorned her curls with a floral fascinator Emmy had never seen, soaked herself in a sweet perfume Emmy had never smelled. And the end result was exquisite: while Emmy had withered away, Grace's beauty had unfurled like a delicate bloom.

And she was looking at Emmy expectantly. "We were hoping to arrive before the season began." She hated how her voice trembled, hated the polite patience of Grace's smile.

"We?"

"My, um, brother." Every fact Jack had insisted she memorize vanished as she stared at Grace. *Her* Grace, but different. Refined. Elegant.

"A brother! Well, if he's as fair as you, the girls will be beside themselves."

"We're with our cousin, too," Emmy continued, her voice still wavering. "A distant one, but he's also . . . nice looking."

"How lucky for us." Grace uttered the words as if she were the queen of benevolence, gifting Emmy her polite conversation. "I do hope I'll be seeing more of you, Miss Fairchild."

And then she was off, the other girls whispering fiercely as she rejoined them on a settee. Her blonde hair was a darker golden. She'd grown, too, perhaps an inch. And she looked healthier, somehow. Every subtle change was a razor blade to Emmy's heart.

Worse, Grace was being kind to her, kinder than anyone else here. And worse still, Emmy's eyes burned as though someone had poured acid in them, and her chest felt as if a guard's heavy boot were pressing against her rib cage, the pain worsening the longer she stared at Grace.

The body cannot distinguish between physical and emotional hurts.

Far too late, Emmy recognized the burning behind her eyes as tears. Ducking her head, she wove through the gowns, searching for the blasted exit in this maze of beheaded mannequins. But she was lost in the sea of luxurious fabrics, unmoored in the memories of a friendship gone wrong. A terrible longing drowned her, wave after wave. For what once was. For what might have been.

For what could never, ever be again.

A back door. Shoving her voluptuous skirt through it, Emmy gasped the fresh air. Squeezing her eyes shut, she hunched on the ground and willed herself not to cry.

She'd gouge out her own eyes before she shed another tear over Grace Montgomery.

Someone sniffled, and Emmy reached for the knife she'd foolishly left at home.

A maid peered around a crate, her splotchy cheeks as crimson as her hair. "I'm sorry to bother you, miss." She hurried to her feet, but she, too, was crying.

"No, you stay." The entire modiste was probably gossiping over Winnie Fairchild's abrupt exit. No part of Emmy wanted to return, but the only way out was through the shop.

As Emmy rose to her feet and smoothed her gown, she stole glances at the maid. There was something familiar about her, though Emmy could not place it.

"If you don't mind me saying, miss, you may want to wait." The girl winced. "Your eyes are still red, and it'll be a lot worse if they know you've been crying."

"Thank you." Emmy tried to smile at her, all the while her pride shriveled like a raisin. If this maid knew Winnie Fairchild had been crying, then soon, *all* the maids would know.

With her watching, Emmy couldn't conjure away any evidence of her tears, so she lingered on the patio, trying not to think about Grace. Not the one standing inside, but *her* Grace.

It would've been easier if she were dead.

The door burst open again, and Emmy jumped to her feet as an elegant woman stepped outside. Wonderful; even more witnesses to Winnie Fairchild's demise.

The woman stilled, frowning at the maid. "Is everything all right, Mary?"

"Of course!" The maid—Mary, apparently—squeaked. "I was just . . ."

"She was just helping me get a bit of air," Emmy supplied.

"Ah." The lady offered Emmy a smile tinged with sorrow. "Looks like we had the same idea."

Emmy took in her pallid face, her blotchy cheeks, and her gown of mourning black. She was grieving.

For a few minutes, they remained in uncomfortable silence as Emmy tried to wish away all evidence of her tears. The grieving woman appeared to be doing the same. When Emmy finally reached for the door, the woman dabbed her eyes and straightened her back. "Shall we return together?"

It was a small kindness, one Emmy readily accepted. Better not to return alone.

The maid held open the door, offering Emmy a brief smile before she schooled her features.

As they trekked the narrow hall back toward the excited ladies' voices, the woman considered Emmy. "Forgive me, but I'm terrible with names these days. Have we met?"

"No, ma'am, I'm Winifred Fairchild." The lie was growing easier the more she repeated it. "I'm visiting for the summer with my brother and cousin."

"Ah, so *you're* one of the late additions to the Inaugural Splendor on Saturday." Genuine pride strengthened her fragile smile. "We host it every summer—except last, of course. My niece is determined to make this one the grandest yet."

Emmy nearly tripped over the doorway. The ball. Her . . . niece. "You're Mrs. Windsor."

"I am indeed."

So this was Grace's aunt, the one who had never visited. Her smile was so kind, it was hard to imagine her shunning a niece born out of wedlock.

"Where are you staying, dear?" Mrs. Windsor raised her voice over the chatter of the shop. "I'll have my footman deliver a proper invitation."

"Mistfield Manor." A surprising surge of pride accompanied Emmy's words. Despite herself, Jack's dusty mansion was growing on her.

Mrs. Windsor came to a stop. "What did you say?"

"Mistfield Manor." Emmy glanced around. The parlor had fallen quiet. "My cousin has been fixing it up. Because of the fire."

Judging by the rush of whispers, they all knew about the fire.

Mrs. Windsor had turned a ghastly shade of white. "Who is your cousin?"

"Nathaniel Fontaine?"

"You're a *Fontaine?*" Mrs. Windsor's hands flew to her chest as she gaped at Emmy.

Then crumpled to the floor.

Gasps and squeals erupted as Emmy surged forward to catch Grace's aunt, but Grace beat her to it, swatting Emmy away. Someone rushed for water, while another woman cried out for a doctor. All the while, Emmy stood there helplessly, trying not to melt under the unabashed stares aimed her way. "Is she all right?"

"How could she be?" Grace whipped toward Emmy, her sky-blue eyes sharp with accusation. "Your family killed her daughter."

ELEVEN

YOUR FAMILY KILLED HER DAUGHTER.

Emmy twirled about the Mistfield ballroom, the cobwebs on the chandeliers swaying in her wake. Hastening her pace, she replayed each shrill order her dance instructor had barked at her, from where to position her hand to where to look. Sweat glistened on her forehead, and her blistered feet begged to be free of her stiff ballroom slippers, but still, she spun.

Your family killed her daughter. How Grace's proclamation had delighted the dress shop. How quickly they'd humiliated Winnie Fairchild in her first hour of existing.

One, two, three. One, two. She stomped her screaming feet, sending dust motes whirling as she tried to recall the Grand March, tried to drown out all thoughts of yesterday's failure.

The ballroom doors burst open, and in sauntered the fairy-tale prince Emmy had designed: neat chestnut hair, straight nose, strong jaw. Jack, as Nathaniel.

"Did you miss me, Vallill— Oh." Jack froze, his foot dangling. Pure shock flooded in his widened eyes as he stared at Emmy's face—or rather, Winnie Fairchild's.

"'A simple dress appointment.'" She mimicked his debonair drawl.

He opened his mouth, then closed it again. Speechless, for once.

"Yes, I'm Winnie now, but we have more important matters to discuss." She folded her arms over her chest. "Yesterday, I was practically chased out of Clara's shop."

His Nathaniel complexion was paling by the second. "What . . . what happened?"

"I made a fool of myself." The understatement of the century.

He stopped gaping at her long enough to pull the ballroom doors shut. "Tell me."

"Mrs. Windsor discovered that Miss Fairchild is related to you and *fainted in horror.*"

He didn't look surprised, exactly.

Chest heaving, she studied him. "They all believe your family murdered her daughter."

"I'm aware." Averting his gaze, he raked his fingers through his hair.

"Clara had her receptionist escort me to the curb." And if that hadn't been humiliating enough, Grace had treated Emmy as if she'd physically assaulted her aunt. One tiptoe into the Society, and Emmy was already a pariah.

Jack began to pace, his expression unreadable. "I'd hoped that if you met them before the Inaugural Splendor, it would smooth things over a bit."

Them. Emmy stared at him. "You *knew* others would be there?"

He stopped pacing.

Deny it, she wished fiercely. She could not be the naive fool again.

"If I'd told you," he said carefully, "you wouldn't have been surprised when Clara threw you to the wolves."

The jolt of betrayal was all too familiar. He'd known. He'd known and he'd lied.

"If it had seemed like you were there to ingratiate yourself, they would have seen right through it." He shrugged. "This way, you couldn't overthink it."

The audacity of him, to use her emotions to further his plans. "Grace was there."

His brows disappeared beneath his now ruined hair. So he hadn't planned for that part. But he lifted a casual shoulder. "And you're still standing."

Callous words from a callous man. Shame on her, really, for expecting anything else. He'd never hidden his intention to use her like a weapon. This was what it felt like to be used.

Head high, she met those piercing gray eyes. An emotion she couldn't place flashed in them. Something raw, something heavy enough to heat her skin.

"Caleb was right." She still held his gaze. "You truly are selfish."

"Wait," he called after her, but she was done letting the puppet master tug on her strings.

Even with her door shut, the house buzzed with the charmed staff Jack and Caleb had hired off the Society's list. A steward. Two valets. A butler. Underbutlers. A cook. Footmen. Underfootmen. Gardeners. Coachmen. Grooms. Pages and stable boys. Housekeepers and housemaids and laundry maids and scullery maids and more possible spies than Emmy could count. Charmed people destined to wait on other charmed people who had accomplished the admirable feat of being born rich. The entire system was infuriating.

And maybe Emmy was a little bit mad at herself, too.

Grace had played the part of the benevolent young lady, sweet enough to welcome the newcomer while others kept their distance. Yet at the first opportunity, she had held Winnie responsible for the sins of all Fontaines. Loudly. She'd embarrassed a stranger who did not know a single soul there. And anyone present could easily dismiss Grace's cruelty, for the poor girl was only defending her grieving aunt.

Without even knowing Winnie was Emmy, Grace had outplayed her. Again.

"Winnie?" Caleb knocked on her door. "We're waiting on you for dinner."

Emmy nestled deeper in her bed. The only person she wanted to see was Jimmy, but now that they had a full house, he could not enter Emmy's room without causing an uproar.

"Come on, sister." Caleb's knocking grew more insistent. "Open the door."

With a groan, Emmy yanked off her covers and threw open her door.

As he took in her new face, Caleb's jaw nearly unhinged. He pressed his hands to his mouth as if lost for words, and Emmy readied herself for a much-needed compliment.

Caleb laughed. And laughed some more.

Her cheeks blazed. "If you think this is helping—"

"I'm sorry." Still, he could not tame his bemused smile. "You look marvelous. And we really do look like siblings." He motioned to the mahogany hair she'd given him, the shade identical to hers. His eyes were now green, like hers, and his skin was golden and freckle-free.

He shut her door, his lingering amusement a tad contrite. "The Windsors' Inaugural Splendor is tomorrow. We should practice being 'ourselves' at dinner, in front of the legion of footmen."

"I'm not coming." Emmy's traitorous stomach grumbled.

With a glance toward the door, Caleb lowered his voice. "He never lets anyone know what he's truly thinking. It used to drive Rose mad."

"I saw Grace." She hated that the words were spilling from her like a confession, especially to Caleb, of all people. "I had to hide so she wouldn't see me . . . ruffled."

As if Caleb gave a damn about her. As if he cared at all that she'd faced Grace too soon, that she could not close her eyes without seeing how beautiful she had become, could not breathe without feeling her betrayal slice through her heart.

"Did you know I was born here, at Mistfield?"

Emmy's jaw snapped shut. Caleb never spoke about himself. At least not to her.

"My mother was nurse to Rose and me, and the Fontaines were kind enough to let me stay in the nursery while my mother was working. My father was Mr. Fontaine's butler, and they were very good to my family. And to me." He tugged on his lapels, looking uncomfortable. "All this to say that I have known Jack longer than anyone. He has many flaws—keeping secrets highest among them—but he is never purposefully cruel."

She did not want to hear anything nice about Jack, but it had cost Caleb something to share this with her. Emmy fiddled with a loose thread. "You and Rose must have been close."

"It was not romantic between us, if that's what you mean." He smiled faintly. "But I knew all her thoughts, and she knew mine."

Emmy had certainly shared all her thoughts with Grace. Her ambitions, her aspirations, even her fears. But Grace had kept hers to herself.

"Did you ever want to be a protégé?" Emmy asked. "With your gift, plenty of families—"

But Caleb shook his head. "The debutante ball is a way to recruit outsiders with the right pedigrees. I was born into my place in the Society. Which was fine by me, because I wouldn't have wanted a life where everyone knew my gift and avoided me like the plague. Instead, I was paid handsomely to spend my days with Rose."

And yet he'd chosen to be Paxton Fairchild rather than a staff member. Caleb might have enjoyed his life as Rose's attendant, but he still had ambitions of his own.

"You know what?" Caleb straightened. "I'll have one of the millions of maids bring you up a plate, and we'll let Jack come up with some explanation for your absence."

"Really?" Her voice pitched.

"And while you're fuming, remember Rose's prophecy. Jack won't bother us for long."

Emmy's jaw slackened.

"Kidding. That was far funnier in my head." Blushing, Caleb turned toward her door.

"Caleb?" She waited until he looked at her, embarrassment still painting his cheeks. "What did Rose draw for your, ah, death?"

"Nice try." With a dark laugh, he slipped out her door, letting in the strange new sounds of the busy mansion.

The house had long ago quieted, but there was no way Emmy would sleep a wink with so many people nearby. Instead she lay in bed, replaying the thinly veiled excitement in Grace's eyes as horror had spread through the dress shop.

An earsplitting crash jolted Emmy upright.

Her wall exploded. Plaster and wood shot into her room, followed by thick smoke. Emmy was on her feet in an instant, narrowly missing the falling chunks. Before she could reach her knife under her pillow, Jack poked his head through the hole. "That took me nearly an hour."

Emmy gaped at him—at the mess he'd created. The giant hole between their rooms was blackened and smoky at the edges. "You couldn't just knock?"

"And ruin Winnie Fairchild's reputation? I think not." He tossed an enormous leather book onto her bed, then held out a pink envelope, its black seal loosened.

Keeping a wary eye on him, Emmy took the envelope.

Inside was a square of black paper fastened to fuchsia velvet by sparkling rhinestone pins. Its edges glittered with the suits of a Parisian playing deck: fuchsia diamonds and hearts, interspersed with onyx spades and clubs. The calligraphy at the center swirled like white smoke.

THE WINDSORS CORDIALLY INVITE YOU TO ATTEND

THE INAUGURAL SPLENDOR

AT CLARITY HALL

AVALON-ON-HUDSON, NEW YORK

SATURDAY EVENING, THE THIRD OF JUNE 1882

THIS YEAR'S THEME IS DANGEROUS GAMES.

PLEASE DRESS ACCORDINGLY.

"It arrived during dinner." Jack flopped onto the bed on the other side of the book he'd brought. "I thought you might like ample warning before you see Grace again."

So Mrs. Windsor was too polite to renege on her promise to send an invitation.

Sixteen hours from now, they'd be at Grace's ball.

"I have another gift." Digging into his pocket, he held out a silver chain. "If we affix Rose's relic to this, it'll lie flat against you, and you can use it whenever you please."

Snatching it from him, Emmy did not give him the satisfaction of testing if the coin would fit in the setting. "This doesn't change anything."

"No, but it makes you far less likely to lose my sister's relic." Kicking out his long legs, he reclined against her pillows as if he hadn't a care in the world.

She pointed to the hole she'd now have to repair. "Out."

"Gift number three." He patted the leather book. "Aren't you curious?"

"Out."

With a yawn, he nestled deeper into her pillows. "I used to be afraid of the dark."

"Out."

"Absolutely terrified. I couldn't be alone in the nursery without running out, screaming for my nanny. Do you know how I overcame it?"

He still wore his dinner jacket, though it had to be well after midnight. And despite her handiwork, dark circles had re-formed underneath his eyes. She'd made him into a beautiful new tapestry, one that was already fraying along the edges.

But he was not her concern.

"My father removed all the light from the nursery and locked me inside. I couldn't conjure for more than a few seconds, so I screamed *awful* things at him." His smile was a ghost on his lips. "But he was right. I could not be the future commander if I was afraid of the dark. By the third night, I was content to sit in the pitch-black nursery."

"What a cruel thing to do to a child." Papa would have never used her fears against her. Still, Emmy could not let Jack prey on her sympathies. "And in this allegory, I am the meek child afraid of the dark, and you're the cunning father who thrusts me into it?"

"My father taught me to think like a future commander. To eliminate guards' fears and hone their strengths." His gaze drifted to hers. "When I sent you to the dress shop, I was thinking like him, and not like a . . . friend."

"We are *not* friends."

"You have a gift for anger, you know that?" He scrubbed at his face. "I cannot think straight when you're upset with me. It's entirely too distracting. I couldn't even enjoy the first good meal I've had in a long time—and it was hanger steak, my favorite! So will you release me from this torture and forgive me already?"

He was quite literally pouting. With his mussed hair standing in every direction and his eyes wide and desperate, he was the picture of contrition. An infuriatingly handsome picture.

She pinned him with a glare. "This is a terrible apology."

"I made you a necklace." His lips quirked. "That must count for something."

"You haven't even said the words!" She pushed away from the bed, putting a good distance between them. "You want forgiveness, but you don't even regret what you've done."

He rose, too, stepping toward her.

She stepped back, nearly tripping on the edge of the hearth.

With a knowing smile, he approached once more, leaving her two options: risk his proximity or run away, just like he'd accused her of doing around men.

She would not give him the satisfaction of being right.

"I'm sorry, Emilia Vallillo," he murmured with taunting sincerity. "Caleb was right. I'm a selfish cad."

Curse him for wielding his proximity like a weapon. Already her heart was quickening, her body attuned to the shrinking space between them. It ought to have been easier to be near him, now that he was Nathaniel, but Nathaniel was attractive by design.

How many times would she have to be hurt, or used, or cast aside, before she'd learn? He'd lied to her. He'd *laughed* at her in Grimsbane.

She was in far too deep to quit their schemes, but she could never trust Jack Fontaine.

Propriety required one of them to move, but Jack had been right; Winnie Fairchild could not bristle each time a young man drew near. She needed to be the opposite of the sort of girl who cried behind a dress shop.

She needed to be brave.

Though there was hardly a foot between them, Emmy leaned closer. And it worked. Jack's pupils widened, his smug expression melting away. For the first time since Grimsbane, Emmy held the edge.

"For the sake of our plans," she said quietly, "we can consider this matter closed."

He turned away, unable to look at her, and Emmy smiled victoriously. Being beautiful was going to be fun.

Retreating across the room, he opened the leather book. "I thought you'd want to see these."

It was a portfolio of sorts, one with black-and-white drawings protruding from its edges. As he pulled out a picture, Emmy had no choice but to come closer.

The background was a blur of shadows, but the foreground was a remarkably realistic rendering of Jack's true face as he knelt in front of Oliver Stratton. Both boys were wearing formalwear, though as usual, Jack's top button had come undone and a lock of hair tumbled over his forehead. His face was either shadowed or bruised, it was hard to tell. He gazed beyond the drawing, his smile uncharacteristically sad.

As Oliver Stratton slashed his throat with a knife.

"Oliver spent a great deal of time here at Mistfield, where he could avoid his prick of a father. We were friends, I guess you could say. If our lives had gone according to plan, once our fathers retired, we would have taken their positions and joined the triumvirate together."

Emmy could not stop staring at the thick droplets of black ink spilling from Jack's neck. With a healer for a father, she was no stranger to knife fights. Usually, people aimed for the heart, though it was protected by its cage of bone. The neck, however, held several crucial connections—between the head and the heart, the lungs and air, the stomach and nourishment—yet all that protected it was soft flesh. And if Rose's prophecy was to be believed, Oliver's knife would slit Jack's like butter. More unnerving, Jack was on his knees, not even fighting back.

"To understand what happened, you need to see this, too." He set a second drawing in front of Emmy. Like the first, it contained no color, only thick black strokes that shone in the candlelight. Fire engulfed the beautiful girl at the center, who lay in a four-poster bed, eyes wide and lifeless. Rose Fontaine, surrounded by black flames.

A pit formed in Emmy's stomach. "She drew her own death."

"It was unsettling, to say the least. Rose tried to make light of it, but we changed all the candles in the house to ordinary flames, just in case." Jack studied a splinter on the mantel. "A few weeks after she drew this, I stumbled home so drunk, I fell asleep in my suit. Sometime before dawn, I woke to Mistfield on fire—with my black flames. But I couldn't move an inch, not even to turn my head."

She knew that frozen feeling all too well. "So Oliver can suppress movements, too. Like his father."

"He can, but that night, he had a little help." The muscle of his jaw ticked. "There was a blanket over me, one that Grace had bridged with his conjury. She was with him, searching Rose's room for the relic. I don't know how they knew about it. But they came for it."

Emmy's heart slowed, her hand closing around the cool, ancient coin. It had been amplifying her conjury for only a few weeks, but already, she could not fathom parting with it.

Especially to Grace.

"Thanks to Caleb's conjury, we know that Grace was the one who found the relic in Rose's room. Like me, Rose was trapped in her bed. With her bridging conjury amplified, Grace was able to use *my* conjury without laying a finger on me. She took my flames from a room away. Within seconds, Rose's room was on fire."

Grace, able to steal other people's gifts and wield them as her own. A lick of something unpleasant, something just south of envy, struck Emmy. "How did you escape?"

"My own flames can't burn me, but they burned through everything around me, including the blanket. Once I was free of it, I ran like hell, following the trail of destruction they'd left. But Fontaine fire burns far hotter and faster than ordinary flames. Rose never stood a chance." His voice remained even, but he could not meet Emmy's gaze. "I found them mounting Oliver's horse in the woods, near the cliff overlooking the Hudson. When I pushed him off his mount, Rose's relic fell from his grasp. He tackled me and tried to wrestle it back, but I pretended to drop it over the edge, which made him murderous enough to try and drag me over the edge. When the guards arrived, they had to pull us apart. And when his father interrogated us, neither of us mentioned Rose's relic. Caleb confirmed it later: Oliver and Grace never told a soul."

"Why?" A powerful amplifier seemed like the sort of thing the Society would celebrate.

"Maybe they feared the Society would take it from them, and they didn't want to share. Maybe Oliver wanted to impress his father with exponentially stronger power. Or maybe they wanted to find out how Rose had tapped into the gift of a long-dead charmed person so they could go from grave to grave making all sorts of relics from old witches. Which, fortunately for us, they can't do." A bit of pride added much-needed light to his gray eyes. "Because relics must be forged with Fontaine fire, and I'm the only wielder left."

So his strange flames had a purpose, other than being downright morbid. "But you were able to hide the relic from them."

"He had the river searched for months. And in Grimsbane, he had me searched, too, but I had my ways of hiding it." He grinned as if daring her to ask.

Better that she didn't. "And the chancellor arrested *you*? Surely it was suspicious that Oliver and Grace were here in the middle of the night."

"Ah, but your dear old friend wove a clever tale for that." Folding his arms, he leaned against her bed post. "With tears in her eyes, Grace bemoaned how I'd seduced her cousin Elizabeth Windsor. Oliver was a knight in shining armor, arriving in the middle of the night to protect Elizabeth's virtue. And, as you learned at the dress shop, Elizabeth could not deny it."

He removed a third drawing from the portfolio. Grace was burning alive, eyes wide, and Emmy let out a strangled noise, unable to look away—

But it was not Grace. They had the same light hair and wide, innocent eyes, but this was a different girl. "This is Elizabeth Windsor."

"Grace's cousin," Jack confirmed. "And Rose's friend. I don't know if Grace sought to ruin Elizabeth's reputation by putting her in my bed, or if Elizabeth had tried to stop them, but she was also trapped underneath that charmed blanket. With my movements suppressed, I couldn't even look anywhere but straight ahead." His teeth ground together as he studied his knuckles. "I never even saw her."

His guilt was plain, though he was expertly avoiding it.

Emmy stared at the macabre drawings strewn across her bedsheets. Unnerving, to say the least, especially given that all but one of these prophecies had already come true. "So the chancellor arrested you for their deaths, letting his son off the hook."

"It was their word against mine. Two great houses—three, if you consider Grace a Windsor—but no one in their right mind believed I'd harm my own sister."

And yet he'd been arrested. "So what happened?"

He brushed an invisible piece of dust off his sleeve. "Just as the chancellor was leaving, I may or may not have tried to knock Oliver off the cliff. With my fists."

"You struck him?" Emmy gaped at him. "While trying to prove your innocence?"

He shrugged. "Oliver has a face that just *begs* to be punched."

Of all the senseless reasons to be arrested. Stifling the urge to berate him, Emmy turned back to the nightmarish artwork. Caleb had a point. Jack was safer in disguise.

Gathering the drawings, he tucked them back inside the portfolio. "Now that you know everything, do you feel more prepared?"

Emmy would face Grace—at Grace's new home, no less—in a matter of hours. "I suppose."

"She may have had more time here, but you're smarter than her." Jack gave her a hard look. "Study how the Society acts. Learn the unwritten rules."

If only she felt a modicum of the confidence he had in her. "How can you be so sure?"

"Because Jimmy's been boasting about you for years. How high your marks in school were, how hard you worked at anything and everything." Stifling a yawn, he set the portfolio on her night table. "Either we both lie awake, listening for Grimsbane's guards, or we spend the night reviewing everyone who will be at the Inaugural Splendor. What do you say?"

She ought to have kicked him out, after the way he'd lied to her about the dress shop, but—the ball was mere hours away.

Crossing her room, Emmy healed the hole in her wall and transformed the debris until it was nothing but dust. Returning to bed, she settled opposite Jack and smoothed her nightgown over her bare legs. "Tell me everything."

TWELVE

FOR THE SECOND TIME IN her life, Emmy rode in an opulent carriage destined for the Society of the Charmed, only this time, she was not imagining her dreams coming true while sitting beside the girl conspiring to ruin them. This time, she would not trust a soul.

At Jack's insistence, Emmy had spent the day conjuring their formal wear to match the theme. He, Caleb, and Jimmy wore black tailcoats and vests, with their cuffs and ascots checkered like game boards. For her part, Emmy had drawn inspiration from the queen of hearts: playing cards hemmed her full onyx skirt, which fell in waves from the tight bodice. Magenta silk folds draped over her hips, held in place by heart-shaped opal pins. Rose's relic hung from its new chain, hidden deep in the gown's bodice. Safely out of sight.

Jack flexed and unflexed his hands. No gloves, so he could flaunt his Fontaine flames. "Almost there. Let's review the plan."

Caleb drummed his fingers on the top hat in his lap. "After our meeting in the city, the chancellor knows I'm a mind reader. Given that he registered me as a nugat, he's willing to lie about my gift. But I need him to want me to be *his* mind reader, so tonight I'll try to earn his trust by helping him win in cards or something."

A nugat, the magicless offspring of a charmed bloodline. Jimmy was posing as one too. If Emmy tripped on Society slang all night, they'd sniff her out as a fraud in no time.

Jack glanced out the window for the umpteenth time. "And your goal, Vallillo?"

"Not making a fool of myself." *Again*, she nearly added.

"Your *other* goal?"

She felt rather silly, saying it aloud. "Oliver Stratton."

Jack leaned forward. "You will use your looks and, more importantly, your wealth, to catch his eye. The more Grace feels like you might ruin her hopes of Oliver proposing this summer, the more reckless she'll become."

It would never work, but she'd agreed to try, at least tonight.

"And I'll keep my ear to the ground. You'd be surprised what people will say when they assume I don't speak English." Jimmy tugged at his suit as he glanced out the window, his perennial smile tensing.

The carriage turned off the main road, and Caleb's lips thinned. "We're here."

With a pit in her stomach, Emmy pressed her forehead against the glass. Trees, trees, and more trees. The driver was racing toward them, a head-on collision with the thick trunks—

Her ears popped. The carriage slowed. The woods disappeared.

A nervous laugh burst from Emmy as they passed through the illusion, the temperature dropping with magic's signature coolness. Caleb and Jimmy exchanged tight smiles. Only Jack managed to look unaffected as he grinned at the distant Clarity Hall.

Grace's aunt and uncle had built a mansion hugging the edge of the Hudson. The lowermost rooms were cradled by the rugged cliffs, framed by sprawling terraces with panoramic views of the river below. But the mansion stretched high above the bluffs, higher even than the stately oak trees lining the long driveway, which was filled with waiting carriages.

Someone shouted, and the carriage came to an abrupt stop.

"A routine check," Jack murmured, though his knuckles whitened as Society guards surrounded the carriage. Their eyes met, and somehow Emmy knew that he was also thinking of Grimsbane.

They could not return there. Ever.

Lanterns lifted, the guards peered in their windows. Emmy tried her best to not look rattled. She had a relic of unfathomable strength. If they tried to lock her away again, she'd make herself into a weapon.

After an eternity, the guards waved them forward, and Emmy could once again breathe.

"Stay close," Jack murmured as they disembarked in front of the celestial mansion. She took his waiting arm, Jimmy and Caleb close behind. More guards were stationed here, and Emmy's skin prickled with their unabashed stares.

They followed the other guests down a walkway covered with a fuchsia runner, its edges also checkered like a game board—but the black squares flickered to white, and the white to black. Clara's fabric enchantment, yet again. The surrounding hedges were cut like chess pieces, their needles as black as night or as white as snow. Earth conjury, perhaps. As they walked past them, the little pawns shot water in high arcs over their heads. Water conjury, bridged by Grace.

"They expect us to look impressed," Jack whispered. "Since this is the only known community for charmed folks, most newcomers have never seen conjury out in the open."

Emmy wasn't simply impressed; she was enthralled. How she longed to examine each bit of conjury, to puzzle out what sort of gift made it work. But she continued along the path, descending the torch-lit staircase that hugged the cliffs without a railing in sight.

"Do the Windsors have a death wish?" she murmured, tightening her grip on Jack's arm.

"Miss Montgomery probably imbued the edge with air conjury. Anyone who falls will be pushed back." He stopped walking. "Should we test it?"

Before she could stop him, Jack dipped her over the edge.

Her scream was ear-piercing, and she clung to him, digging her nails into his back. But the devil only grinned. "Good. Now you look alive."

She glared at him. Once again, she'd let her guard down. And once again, she'd paid the price for it. "You're a real bastard, you know that?"

"And you're a beautiful, confident heiress. Act like it."

"Way to make a scene," Caleb muttered. "All eyes are on us now."

Judging by Jack's smug smile, that had been his plan.

"Mr. Nathaniel Fontaine and Miss Winifred Fairchild," the butler announced as they stepped onto the terrace. "Mr. Paxton Fairchild and Mr. Rui Zhao."

One hundred pairs of eyes burned into them as they greeted the hosts: Mrs. Windsor, a round-faced man who had to be Keeper Windsor, and, looking positively radiant, Grace.

She was hardly three feet away, and she was staring directly at Emmy. Dipping into a deep curtsy, Emmy cast her gaze to the ground.

"We're honored by your hospitality," Jack began in his flawless Nathaniel accent, and Emmy had to swallow her surprise at how different he sounded. "Thank you for having us."

"The Society sets the guest list, not us." Keeper Windsor shook his hand brusquely. "Though, out of respect for the ladies, might I ask you to refrain from conjuring this evening?"

"Of course." Jack's easy smile deflected the insult.

"He's worried I'll faint again," Mrs. Windsor said softly, squeezing Emmy's hand. "I feel terrible about the other day."

It was easy to return her sincere smile. "I feel terrible, too, after the shock I gave you."

"Still, it was not right that Miss Claremont asked you to leave. My niece has spoken to her about that. Isn't that right, Grace?"

Perhaps one day Emmy might be able to look at Grace without hurting, but not tonight.

If Emmy was the queen of hearts, then Grace was the ace of spades.

Black lace floated over her orchid-pink gown, with spade appliqués dancing across the enchanted skirt. The lace continued over her arms, hinting at the creamy skin underneath, before gathering into ruffles at her wrists. The ace was pinned to her hair along with a glittering headpiece of diamonds and a black veil. A minuscule pink heart had been painted on her cheek like a birthmark.

Though her aunt had addressed her, Grace was smiling at Jack as he reverently kissed her hand. Jack claimed to hate Grace, yet his eyes lingered on her pretty face after he released her. Emmy swallowed her frustration. Even he was not impervious to her charms.

"Grace?" Mrs. Windsor repeated, and finally, her niece's eyes slid back to Emmy.

"Oh, Miss Fairchild!" Grace kissed the air between them. "How glad I am to see you."

"I, ah, was very glad to have been invited." Spoken like a nervous, blithering fool. Emmy could hardly glance at Grace's familiar face without that sledgehammer taking aim at her chest again.

"I do hope you'll forgive me for my outburst the other day. My grief can be heavy at times, but I should not have let it get the best of me." Grace let her gaze fall to the floor, her expression so sorrowful that Mrs. Windsor wrapped an arm around her.

Did Grace truly grieve her cousin, who she'd known a year—whose death she'd caused, or at least been complicit in? Did she even know Emmy was supposedly dead?

"Consider it forgiven." Emmy managed a smile, one far too weak for Winnie Fairchild.

Dismissed, Emmy stole a look at Jimmy, but if seeing Grace in her new life ruffled him, his face betrayed nothing.

"Well, this is nice," Caleb muttered, eyeing the uninterrupted views of the Hudson. Over their heads, silver candelabras floated just out of reach, bathing the terrace in golden light. Guests meandered between game tables draped in black and fuchsia. Carnival games. Board games. Card games. Games Emmy had never seen. The guests drifted between them, dressed on theme: checkered gowns, playing cards sewn to top hats, even a swirling skirt of glittering carousel horses. But the patterns on their gowns shifted playfully. Enchanted fabric. Scores of it.

The sheer quantity of Clara's creations was infuriating. According to Grace, each cloud on Emmy's debutante gown had taken hours to properly enchant. Either Grace had been exaggerating, or Clara had help somehow.

As the Society stared at Emmy, she stared back. A few people had relics exposed on their necks, their shapes and sizes varying, though the gold and silver swirls were the same. Gilded bone fragments from deceased family members, worn like prized pieces of jewelry.

With Emmy's arm tucked in his, Jack changed direction suddenly, weaving through the tables. Even those immersed in their games paused to watch them pass.

He came to a stop in front of a regal-looking couple dressed like the white king and queen pieces of a chess set. "Chancellor Stratton. How lovely to see you again."

Emmy gaped at Papa's killer.

In his costume, she nearly hadn't recognized the man who'd sentenced her to endless imprisonment. But she would never forget that stern, pale face. His icy blue eyes flitted over her, utterly impassive as they moved to Caleb and narrowed. He might have helped them gain entry to the Society for the summer, but he did not trust the telepath.

"This is my cousin." Jack inclined his head toward Emmy. "Miss Winifred Fairchild."

With fire in her heart, Emmy curtsied to the vile man.

But the chancellor hardly even looked at her. "And this is my wife."

"Mrs. Stratton, what a pleasure." Jack kissed her gloved hand and introduced Caleb and Jimmy. Unlike her husband, Mrs. Stratton was rather chatty, asking about their lineage, the repairs at Mistfield, and their plans for the summer. As the boys supplied their rehearsed answers, Emmy stole glimpses at the chancellor, who watched the party like a sentinel. Judging by the deep-set lines around his scowl, there was about as much warmth in this man as there was in a glacier. To win him over, Caleb was better off using an ice pick.

"Come closer, dear. Let me have a look at you."

With an encouraging nod from Jack, Emmy drew nearer to Mrs. Stratton.

"Such lovely bone structure." Mrs. Stratton examined Emmy's face as if it were artwork to be judged. "Your green eyes are exquisite. Tell me, what does your father do?"

"He's in the gold business," Caleb supplied. That was their story: their world-traveling parents were busy overseas, trusting Paxton to accompany Winnie to New York to find a husband. "His mines are mostly abroad—"

"I believe I asked your sister." Despite her chastising tone, Mrs. Stratton's practiced smile did not waver as she turned back to Emmy. "Are the men in your family always this pushy?"

Emmy glanced toward Jack, remembering how he'd trapped her in his arms to unlock her conjury. The break-in at headquarters. The dress shop lies. "Usually, they're even worse."

Mrs. Stratton's lips quirked. "Give me your dance card, dear. My son is a lovely dancer."

Emmy could practically feel Jack's excitement as she removed the small card from her wrist. Once Mrs. Stratton handed it back, they were dismissed.

She'd expected Jack to snatch the card right away, but he stared at the crowd with his eyes unfocused. "Hey." Emmy nudged him, but he hardly heard her. "*Hey.*"

His gaze snapped to hers, and for the briefest of moments, she glimpsed his raw anger. His pain. But with a shake of his head, the mask snapped back into place. "Nice work."

Mrs. Stratton had seemed to like her well enough. Mrs. Windsor, too, despite their earlier meeting. If only middle-aged women were her targets.

With renewed swagger, Jack meandered from table to table, brokering introductions and making small talk with the people he'd known his entire life. As Nathaniel, he was the perfect mix of confidence and affability. Emmy tried to emulate his airs, all the while ignoring the lemon-size knot in her throat. Her new appearance seemed to be working, at least, and by the end of the cocktail hour, her dance card was nearly full. Nine dances, though she'd learned only six—and badly. She'd need to fake an injury or, preferably, disappear.

Much too soon, the orchestra began to play the opening notes of a waltz. Her first dance partner arrived—a boy named Richard Hamilton who hardly looked old enough to attend a ball, let alone drink champagne—but before Emmy could conjure a single good excuse, she was on the dance floor, her gloves saving her the humiliation of sweaty palms.

The waltz began.

Emmy could not think about her tattered nerves, not while counting *one, two, three* over and over. Richard tried to engage her in polite conversation, but Emmy had to focus on her feet. Richard was surprisingly graceful, and he smiled often, as if he could calm her nerves. She could have done much worse for a first partner.

Emboldened, Emmy stole a glance at the other couples. She could practically sense Jack to her left, wielding that roguish smile on a girl who looked positively hypnotized. Behind him, Caleb was waltzing with a young lady Emmy didn't recognize, and judging by his elegance, Rose had taught him to dance as well as he'd claimed. And beside him—

Grace. Dancing with Oliver, who wore his ivory uniform. Just like Grimsbane's guards.

A jolt of tension shot through Emmy as she watched them. Their locked gazes revealed unmistakable intimacy, the sort earned through stolen kisses and jailed friends and fires that burned innocent girls in bed. They were in love. And, if Jack's timeline was correct, they had been for years. Yet Grace had kept him from Emmy, had lied by omission through countless conversations about the boys they might meet in the Society. But Grace had told Oliver about *her*, given that he'd helped her schemes by conjure-binding Emmy. They trusted each other.

It was enough to make Emmy sick.

Poor Richard Hamilton was still talking amiably, but Emmy could not hear a word he said, not when she had a front-row seat to Grace's new life. Grace danced effortlessly, as if she'd been born a golden-slippered ballerina and not the bastard daughter of a rake and a wayward drunk. This life suited her. She seemed far more at ease here than she'd ever been back home. But Emmy would *never* belong here. She'd always be out of place with these people, no matter how much she practiced her curtsies or how pretty she made her face or how powerful her conjury. There was an unmistakable air to the elite. Grace had always possessed it, even in their tenement house. And Emmy did not.

Emmy stepped on Richard's toes, and he winced. "I'm so sorry!" Emmy exclaimed.

At his reassuring smile, Emmy relaxed—but someone snickered.

A glutton for punishment, Emmy glanced at the source. Clara Claremont was huddled with three other girls about their age, pointing at Emmy. They quickly turned away, but not fast enough to hide their amusement.

Heat rushed to Emmy's cheeks. She turned her attention back to

Richard, determined not to make another mistake. Somehow, she made it through the rest of the waltz without further embarrassment, but her next partner found her before she could hide.

Polkas were supposed to be fun, with spinning skirts and circling couples, but Emmy could hardly keep up her smile while she stepped on her partner's foot five bloody times—once hard enough for him to grab his toes while hissing in pain. The snickers grew louder, and humiliation scorched her face like a blistering sunburn. If the quality of her dancing was a testament to her character, then Winnie Fairchild was thoroughly depraved. It took everything she had not to run off the dance floor after the polka finally ended.

As Emmy picked up her skirts, Oliver Stratton stepped into her path. "My mother informs me that I have the honor of your next dance." He looked far from pleased.

A string of vile curses rose to Emmy's lips. She could not dance with Oliver, not without abandoning all hopes of impressing him. "I don't suppose we could . . . play cards instead?"

His sour expression brightened. "Some friends just sat for stud poker. Shall we join?"

Oh, sweet relief. Stud poker was a Baxter Street tradition. She was practically a shark.

Emmy flashed her first genuine smile of the evening. "Lead the way."

THIRTEEN

AS OLIVER LED EMMY THROUGH the velvet-draped tables, she winced at his uniform, the surface shimmering and rolling like trapped smoke. Even the guards now wore Clara's enchanted fabric.

"Here we are." Letting go of Emmy's arm, he motioned toward Clara and Grace, who were huddled together at a table. The urge to scream was strong and swift, but Emmy had no choice but to choke it down. She was to play cards with the three people who'd conspired to ruin her life, and there was no getting out of it.

"Miss Fairchild!" Grace patted the seat beside her with surprising vigor. "I'm glad Ollie saved your poor feet from yet another dance."

A snicker burst from Clara, and Emmy waited for humiliation to scald her cheeks, but for once, they remained cool. In a way, it was easier to face this version of Grace than the one who'd played the perfect hostess in front of her aunt. This Grace had a sharpness to her smile upon seeing Emmy with her "Ollie." Which meant that Emmy—or, rather, Winnie Fairchild—was getting under her skin.

As an attendant helped Emmy into her chair, Clara pinched the pink folds of Emmy's skirt. "You may be the only girl here not wearing enchanted silk."

Oliver groaned. "Can you drop the sales pitch for one night?"

"But Miss Fairchild didn't get a chance to place an order!" Clara smoothed the silk of her own gown, where black and white chess pieces danced across a chess board.

The wise course of action would be to buy a dress to study the conjury. Emmy tried to choke out the words, she truly did—but Clara was looking *so* smug. "I already own too many gowns."

"You don't feel dull, being the only girl here wearing ordinary fabric?"

"Not at all." Smiling in their presence was becoming easier with every barb.

"And what is your gift?" Clara pressed. "Something with dirt, I've heard?"

"Leave her be." Grace turned to Emmy, batting her lashes with an innocence she'd probably practiced in her mirror. "Do you know stud poker?"

"I taught Miss Montgomery a few years back," Oliver said. "I can teach you, too."

Emmy and Grace had played countless times—but Grace must have feigned ignorance so Oliver could explain it to her. Winnie could do the same.

Emmy smiled shyly at him. "I'd like that."

As Emmy pretended to listen to Oliver explain the rules, Grace spoke quietly with Clara, occasionally reaching for the drink her lady's maid held for her, the same one who'd been crying behind the dress shop. The girl's eyes met Emmy's, but the maid quickly looked away.

Wonderful; even the dealer's suit was swirling with enchantment. With his face drawn from the strain of conjury, he threw the cards in the air, shuffling them over their heads. He repeated the trick again, and Emmy could not help but feel awestruck as the cards danced about.

As they returned to the dealer's hands, he faltered, cards raining over them.

"Damnit!" Oliver jumped to his feet. "What the hell is wrong with you?"

"I'm sorry, sir!" The dealer wiped his brow. "Normally I can do it for several minutes."

"Well, you dumped cards all over the ladies! Now pick them up."

Hands shaking, the dealer hurried to gather the cards, and Emmy sat on her hands to resist helping him.

"Room for a fifth?" Jack stood behind Emmy, his hand on the back of her chair, Nathaniel's easy smile pinned to his princely face.

As introductions were made, Emmy's nerves settled just a smidge. Facing her enemies was far easier with an ally—and sometime over the last month, Jack Fontaine had become her ally.

The dealer began distributing the cards—in his hands, the ordinary way—and Emmy sat taller. How she loved the anticipation of stud poker, especially the first card, which each player received face down so only they could see it. The second card, and eventually the other three, was dealt face up, for all to see.

"Your card is the lowest, Miss Fairchild," Oliver said. "The first bet falls to you."

Emmy cleared her throat. "Are there limits to how much we bet?"

"Oh, we don't bet *money*," Clara said, her eyes alight. "We play for masks."

She motioned toward a black curtain strung beside the table. A series of macabre animal masks were pinned to it. A rabbit with frighteningly large teeth. A Canadian goose with a razor-sharp beak. A pig with a snout so realistic, Emmy searched its seams for blood.

"What do you say, Fontaine?" Oliver said. "Do you like games as much as Mistfield's predecessors?"

"I like them plenty." Jack's voice remained casual, even amused. "But I don't play them until I know the stakes."

"They're rather simple. The losers wear those masks."

"Easy enough. I'm in."

"And you, Miss Fairchild?" Clara turned that barbed smile on Emmy. "Or do you prefer your bets as boring as your dresses?"

"Clara," Grace admonished, though the corner of her mouth quirked.

But Emmy didn't mind Clara's overt aggression. The dressmaker had revealed a weakness, one they could exploit: she was terribly proud.

"Well?" Oliver reclined in his chair. "What do you say?"

Grace waited for Emmy's response. Clara, too, watched her patiently. *Too* patiently.

"What's the catch?" Emmy asked.

Clara's smile withered. "Why must there be a catch?"

"The masks are conjured," Oliver explained. "Once they touch your skin, your face will take their form. Here, I'll show you. Milton?"

A young man in uniform stepped away from the line of waiting attendants.

"Pick one." Oliver motioned toward the masks.

The attendant hesitated. "Will it be stuck on me forever?"

"Did I give you the impression this is optional?" Oliver snapped. "Mask. Now."

With a trembling hand, the attendant reached for the goose mask. As soon as his fingers grazed it, feathers shot from his cheeks, his eyes widened to inhuman black orbs, and his mouth stretched into a razor-sharp beak. He did not simply wear the terrible mask; he *became* the mask, his bone structure altering as if it had always been avian.

Clara clapped exuberantly. "Oh, how I love your magic, Grace!"

Grace smiled demurely. At her side, her red-headed maid took a wary step backward.

Somehow, the mask had transformed the attendant's face. But as far as Emmy knew, only *she* had the gift of transformation, though she'd never transformed a living thing without the relic.

Grace had bridged Emmy's magic countless times. With practice, she'd learned to infuse an object to make a particular transformation, like a jar that, when a pebble was placed inside, turned it into a button. She could also imbue the object with the gift of transformation itself, wielding it as if it were her own—for a short while. But Emmy's conjury didn't work on living things. Not without Rose's relic.

Something deep inside Emmy—something dark, something bitter—snapped.

Grace didn't make those masks with fragments of Emmy's conjury she'd saved for herself. She used fragments of Papa's.

"You can avoid the mask by folding," Oliver explained with agonizing calm, as if his poor attendant were not whimpering through a grotesque beak. "Or by winning."

Emmy forced herself to breathe. "Very well."

As the dealer dealt their third cards—a ten of hearts for Emmy—Grace leaned over to Oliver to whisper something. Emmy would have rolled her eyes, but something glittered deep in Grace's neckline. A coin of melded silver and gold, not at all on theme.

A relic. Circular, like Rose's, only a little smaller.

Seeing Emmy staring, Grace tucked it beneath her neckline. "My father gave it to me."

"The *only* thing that damn man gave you," Clara mused. Seeing Grace's look, she sighed. "Right, we're not supposed to speak ill of the dead."

"Even if they deserve it," Oliver muttered.

Emmy's head spun. Had Grace received the relic when he died a few years back, hiding it from Emmy? Or had the Windsors kept it until she became their protégé?

Even more unsettling: everyone else wore theirs proudly, yet Grace kept hers hidden.

Their fourth cards floated to them, and Emmy forced herself to focus. Oliver had a pair of kings, the strongest hand showing. Emmy, meanwhile, was showing the eight, nine, and ten of hearts. Utterly useless with her downturned three of clubs, but as far as anyone knew, she was chasing a straight flush.

The final cards fluttered to the table. The jack of hearts for Emmy. Nearly a straight flush on top—but worthless, given her downturned card.

"It takes a lot for me to fold, but those masks are downright horrifying." Jack pushed back from the table.

"I rather like them," Clara murmured as she peeked at her bottom card. The best hand she could possess was a high pair, and even that could not beat Oliver's kings. "I'm in."

The pig mask was the worst of them all. Emmy would enjoy Clara wearing it.

Like Emmy, Grace's four cards were of the same suit. A potential flush, but without the straight draw. "I'm in, too. What about you, Miss Fairchild?"

No fidgeting. No rapid blinking like an innocent little doe. She had the flush. Or perhaps she'd gotten better at bluffing. After all, she'd bluffed her way through a decade of friendship.

With that cursed club, Emmy's hand was even more worthless than Clara's. But she could not bring herself to fold. "I'm in, too."

Grace froze, her eyes widening ever so slightly.

Oliver chuckled. "Well, let's flip them over, ladies."

Clara, as expected, had nothing. For a self-appointed fashion expert, she laughed it off, as if wearing an animal's face for the rest of the evening was no bother at all.

Oliver showed two pair, just as Emmy expected. And Grace flourished her spade flush, a perfect match to her gown. *Quite* the coincidence.

Emmy was going to lose. Judging by the warning look Jack shot her, he knew it, too.

The relic's power was cool against her sternum as Emmy flipped over her final card, transforming her useless three of clubs to the queen of hearts. "Is this good?"

Grace's pretty little smile rotted away.

Oliver opened and closed his mouth. Twice. Speechless, because though her upturned cards were stronger than Grace's, he hadn't expected her to win. Grace was supposed to win. But Emmy had out-cheated her.

The nearby tables of partygoers paused their games to watch Oliver, Grace, and Clara pick out their masks: a deer with enormous antlers for Oliver, the pig for Clara, and a squirrel with lifelike fur for Grace.

"Nice hand, *Winnie*," Jack murmured.

Emmy refused to look at him. He'd forgive the risk when these three looked like animals the rest of the night.

Grace held her mask by its ribbons, careful not to touch it. "A gift for you, Mary."

Before Emmy could protest, Grace dropped the mask into Mary's hands, and the poor girl's face grew wide and furry, her eyes blackening.

"You're supposed to wear it yourself!" Emmy exclaimed.

"You thought *we'd* wear them?" Clara laughed as she held her pig's mask to the face of her own attendant, who tried to squirm away. As soon as it touched her, the maid's skin morphed to a lifeless pink and her nose swelled to a snout.

"This is for dropping the cards." Oliver tossed the stag mask to the dealer, who could not dodge it in time. As soon as it touched him, he yelped, and antlers sprouted from his temples.

The line of watching attendants shifted on their feet.

And Emmy's blood boiled. "You said, 'Only the winner avoids the mask.'"

If she'd lost, she would have been stuck in a mask. No one would have told her otherwise.

"Oh dear." Grace exchanged an amused look with Oliver before offering Emmy a consolatory smile. "We should have been clearer. In the Society of the Charmed, servants' bets are as good as our own."

That slippery little wretch. Emmy glared as Grace patted the arm of her squirrel-faced lady's maid, but Mary disappeared, vanishing without a trace. The onlookers screamed in delight, searching for the invisible maid as if it were another game.

"Care for another round?" Clara purred. Behind her, Grace and Oliver pranced about, arms wide as they searched for the poor maid.

"Maybe later." With a dip of his top hat, Jack excused himself, pulling Emmy's arm. "Turn around and curtsy to them," he said through his teeth.

"Absolutely not," she hissed.

"You're making a scene."

The other guests had paused their games to laugh at the staff whose faces had morphed into grisly, human-size animals'. Three innocent bystanders. No, worse: three people who depended on the Society to make their living. The wrongness of it stoked that fire in her chest. The more they laughed, the more Emmy burned.

"Miss Fairchild!" Clara called.

Halting her feet, Emmy tried to wipe the fury from her face before turning around. Clara was hurrying toward her. "Here's my card. In case you change your mind about your wardrobe."

Oh, she'd visit Clara's dress shop again, to find out exactly how Clara was making so many enchanted gowns.

As Emmy glanced at the card, something brushed her face, and she jumped back, swatting. But she was too late; an otherworldly chill was already spreading over her cheeks.

She knew that prickling sensation of ice seeping into her bones: Grace's gift.

Clara's delighted smile doubled, tripled, as Emmy swayed on her feet. "A rabbit's fitting for someone with dirt conjury, wouldn't you agree?"

The nearby laughter swelled as Emmy tried to pull off the mask, but it had *become* her. Bits of fur thrust from her pristine skin, and whiskers, oh God, *whiskers*—

The laughter crested as Emmy huddled on the ground, trying to hide her face from the delighted crowd. Jack was beside her, his shouts deafening to her too-large ears. She let him pull her to her feet, let him hide her ice-cold face against his chest. She was back at her debutante ball, half-naked in her torn gown. Outplayed by Clara and Grace, once again. How many times could she underestimate their cruelty? No matter the face she wore, Emmy was naive and pathetic and—

No. Winnie Fairchild would not be the jester of their terrible court.

With her face still hidden against Jack, Emmy let the brume surround her, let her power gather like a tempest. She pictured Winnie's face as she'd practiced it so many times in the mirror: breathtaking and alluring and closer to perfection than anyone ought to be.

Letting go of Jack, Emmy faced those who'd gathered to ridicule her, the newcomer in their sick, twisted games. As their laughter died, she tossed the mask on the ground at Grace's feet. "Such weak conjury. It hardly lasted a minute."

Grace's merriment vanished, and she glowered at Emmy, who glared right back. There wasn't a word in existence strong enough to capture how fervently—how deeply—she hated Grace Montgomery.

Before Emmy did something truly unhinged, she stormed away, weaving through the other games, past the dance floor, up the treacherous stairway beside the cliffs. With each step, her bravery threatened to abandon her, but she could not return. Even if she'd ruined her brand-new reputation, she would never, ever allow the Society to laugh at her again.

Movement flickered at the edge of the trees, just beyond the driveway. Grace's lady's maid blinked into existence, her furry face monstrous in the silvery moonlight. The poor girl.

With a covert glance at the guards stationed by the door, Emmy hurried toward the trees. A sob rattled through the maid as she clawed and clawed at her furry cheeks.

"Mary?" Emmy called softly.

The girl stilled.

Emmy stepped closer, hands raised. "Your name is Mary, yes?"

Mary nodded, Emmy's face reflected in her ghastly squirrel eyes. If only Emmy could recall Mary's true face well enough to conjure it for her. But instead, she transformed Clara's calling card into one of her own. "Come work for me, and I'll pay you triple your salary."

The card trembled in Mary's hand. "Miss Montgomery wouldn't like that one bit."

"I'm not afraid of Grace Montgomery." The fire in Emmy's voice surprised her.

More surprising still, she meant it.

FOURTEEN

FAR TOO FURIOUS TO BE confined, Emmy leaped from the carriage as soon as it rolled to a stop. Fortunately, Mistfield's staff hadn't expected them back so early, so she did not have to force a smile as she stalked toward the woods, searching every inch of her face for tufts of fur from that wretched mask.

The others trailed behind her, a lantern illuminating her footsteps, though no one dared to speak until they'd reached the cliffs. Only then did Emmy finally flop onto the grass and free her aching feet from their shoes.

"Well," Jimmy's deep voice broke the silence, "that went badly."

The understatement of the century.

Angling away from the others, Emmy ran her fingers along her face. It was hers—Winnie's, rather—but she could not shake the sense that she was still furry.

"We should review." Exhaustion tinged Jack's voice. "Alton?"

"The chancellor mentally recited Society rules and regulations whenever I was nearby." Caleb pinched the bridge of his nose. "Safe to say he doesn't like having a telepath around."

The muscles of Jack's jaw tensed. "Learn anything at all?"

"I had to be careful, since everyone believes I'm a nugat. Oh, but I listened in on Grace's maid after 'Winnie' offered her a job." He glanced at Emmy. "Strangely, she likes you. And she heard we pay well. I think she'll accept, once she speaks to her parents."

It was good news, but it was hard to celebrate a small victory after such a disastrous night. Even Mary's job offer had been shortsighted:

to learn Grace's secrets, Emmy should have tried to win Mary over while she still worked for Grace.

"I heard a few valets talking about how well the staff at Mistfield are being paid." Jimmy clapped Caleb on the shoulder, not bothering to hide his smugness. It had been his idea to overpay the staff as a means of increasing their loyalty. "Other than that, people hardly spoke to me, though they stared quite a bit."

Emmy rubbed her tired eyes. Their old neighborhood had a vibrant Chinese population, but nearly everyone at the Inaugural Ball had been white, including the staff.

"But I heard some whispers," he continued, "about the poker dealer dropping the cards. They spoke of weakening conjury. It's getting worse, they said."

Caleb sighed. "Not surprising, given how crowded New York has become. The immigrant issue was on the chancellor's mind, too."

Emmy waited for him to elaborate, but of course, he didn't. "The 'immigrant issue'?"

Caleb shot Jack a weary look, as if expecting him to explain. Jack, for his part, looked hesitant. "The Society views the influx of newcomers as a security risk. With thousands of immigrants arriving each day, they can't keep tabs on who's charmed and who's ordinary. And sometimes, newcomers are a bit more obvious with their gifts than the Society would like."

"'More obvious'?" Caleb scoffed. "They perform their conjury on street corners for tips!"

Emmy stiffened. "Not once, in sixteen years, did I see conjury on the street."

"It's rare, but some people will do anything for a buck."

"And the Society takes care of that." Jack shrugged. "The best way to protect the charmed is to keep our existence a secret from ordinaries. Most of the time, charmed people everywhere keep a low profile, even if they've never heard of the Society. But occasionally, charmed folks draw too much attention to their conjury, and the Society needs to step in."

"What do you mean, 'step in'?" Emmy could not keep the sharpness from her voice.

Jack hesitated. "They put them in Grimsbane."

Emmy rubbed her face, unable to shake the lingering sensation of fur. The Society and all its bigotry was downright exhausting. They could have been a resource for charmed immigrants, a place for them to find community and perhaps even employment.

But instead, they locked them away.

"What does that have to do with conjury?" There was a rare edge to Jimmy's voice.

Caleb, at least, had the decency to look uneasy. "Because the more charmed people we stuff into New York, the more strain we put on the brume."

"You think the brume is a limited resource?"

"Everything precious is. Diamonds. Clean water. An address on Central Park West."

That was hardly evidence. As Emmy and Jimmy exchanged a look, Caleb shrugged. "Look at the facts. Conjury is weakening, as we saw tonight. Immigration is increasing, as we all know. It has to be straining our resources."

"So Society members have a right to the brume," Emmy said slowly, "but immigrants don't."

He narrowed his eyes. "You're twisting my words."

"There's an obvious answer." Rising to his feet, Jimmy dusted off his trousers. "Ban all the immigrants from the countries you don't like. Oh, that's right; you already have."

With a tight nod to Emmy, Jimmy stalked back to Mistfield.

Frowning, Caleb watched him disappear between the trees. "What did I say?"

"Perhaps he didn't want to 'strain' your resources," Emmy said dryly. "Or he was thinking about the family he might never see again because they're not allowed to set foot here. Or maybe, after a night of being gawked at, he didn't expect to hear prejudice from a friend."

"Well, I didn't mean *him*." The creases in Caleb's brow deepened. "I thought we could talk about these things. After all, I'm Irish, and a few decades ago, *we* weren't exactly welcome here."

"It's not remotely the same thing!" Emmy ought to have kept her voice down, but she'd had enough. "Irish, Italian—they might look down on us, but they can't tell just from one glance. And they didn't feel the need to pass laws to keep us out."

A heavy silence hung over them, one that remained until Caleb rose to his feet, his expression pained. "I really didn't mean to hurt him. I just . . . want him to be careful. The Society loves a scapegoat."

Jack rubbed his temples. "Just apologize."

"Fine." With a long sigh, he shuffled away.

When he was gone, Emmy tried to swallow her anger, but it refused to stay down. She stole a glance at Jack, ready for a fight, but he had fallen quiet. His ascot hung around his neck, one gust of wind away from falling into the Hudson.

"If we manage to pull this off," he finally said, "I'm jumping off this cliff to celebrate."

"Death wish?"

He stared over the edge. If the weather had suited their mood, it would have been storming. But of course it was an infuriatingly lovely night, with a warm breeze rolling off the river and stars twinkling up above, far more than Emmy had ever seen.

Reaching into his pocket, he fetched a playing card. "It changes appearance. Watch." He squeezed his eyes shut. "Ace of spaces, ace of spades . . ."

The ten of hearts shimmered and swayed, replaced by the ace of spades.

Emmy snatched the card from him. Sure enough, it was cold to the touch, a telltale sign of Grace's creations. "So Grace *was* cheating."

"Maybe Grace. Maybe Oliver. Either way, she made this with *your* conjury." He rubbed his jaw. "How much of your gift do you think she's kept?"

It was salt in a stab wound, imagining Grace with a trunk full of items imbued with transformation magic. "I was one of two charmed people she knew. The only way she could practice was with my conjury or my father's."

Grace had infused Emmy's gift in buttons, trinkets, pennies, pebbles—everything and anything was fodder for practice. Emmy had never given much thought to whether Grace had stockpiled her creations. She'd trusted her. Foolishly.

"And the masks. Was that your conjury, too?"

"My father's." It pained her to even utter the words. Papa had never used his conjury for anything but healing. Grace was perverting his magic with such cruel games. Worse, conjuring those masks took tremendous skill, far more than anything Grace had made back home. It hardly seemed possible—unless she had help. "Could Grace's relic be as powerful as Rose's?"

Jack shook his head. "It's the only one of its kind. Grace's is an ordinary one."

It was absurd, given that Emmy had missed so many signs of Grace's deceit, but she couldn't shake the sense that Grace was hiding something. "If Rose's relic gave her the ability to steal your conjury from across the room, she'd be desperate for that power. Maybe she copied the steps Rose—"

"The bone fragment was cut from the amplifying witch's sternum, just above the heart. And it was sealed in silver and gold by Fontaine fire, which only I can wield." He tugged at his hair absentmindedly. "Still, we underestimated the weapons she has at her disposal."

"We shouldn't be worried about just *my* gift," Emmy pointed out. "Grace could be stockpiling conjury from everyone in the Society who lets her bridge something."

The truth of her words hung in the air between them.

Jack threw off his jacket, then attacked his top buttons. Emmy's gaze traced the subtle lines of muscle beneath his skin, disappearing under his shirt. Remnants of the years he'd spent training to be commander.

"Grace might have all the conjury in the world at her fingertips. Oliver seems to have truly quit gambling in pool halls, which ruins my plan for him. The chancellor wants nothing to do with a telepath, which I should have known, given all the vile things that man must be hiding. And Clara was supposed to be the easiest, since all she does is enchant fabric." His molars ground together. "But I underestimated her, and you paid the price."

Did Jack actually feel guilty? Was that why he was refusing to meet her eye?

"What happened with the mask is my own fault." Emmy had been soft. Strike something soft, tear a hole right through it. Strike something rock-solid, break your knuckles upon impact.

To make it in the Society, Winnie Fairchild needed to be knuckle-breaking hard.

"If I ask you a question, will you tell me the truth, with no regard for my feelings?"

"When have I ever regarded your feelings?"

He didn't even crack a smile. "Do you truly believe we can do this? Ruin the lives of four powerful people in as many weeks?"

Emmy tried to imagine Grace in Grimsbane, with Clara and the Strattons wasting away in cells of their own. But it was too far-fetched. "It's . . . hard to picture."

"I planned for this every minute I was in there. I thought of every detail. Every potential hindrance. But I still underestimated them."

He didn't need to say where.

"It was never going to be easy." Her voice was soft, her gaze trained on the dark sky.

"Did you ever hear me?"

He'd been right on the other side of her wall, but she'd never heard a voice, a shout, or even the creak of another pass-through window. The guards hadn't been lying about Grimsbane's impenetrable silence. Shaking her head, Emmy studied her hands. "Did you ever hear *me*?"

"Not once, in eleven months." He swallowed thickly. "But Caleb did, when he got close enough to communicate with me. Jimmy asked him to check on you."

Just when she thought she'd used up all her humiliation for one night. "And let me guess: he told you that I was stark raving mad."

"He said you were in agony."

A humiliating quiet settled over them.

It was too much, thinking of Caleb listening to her thoughts. Of Jack pitying her, and Jimmy being worried sick about her. Jimmy, who showed everyone in the world kindness, yet was being treated like a threat to democracy, simply for his heritage.

She jumped to her feet, ready to burst from her skin. "I can't just sit here doing nothing." After all, Jack hadn't gotten her out simply to placate Jimmy. She was supposed to be their secret weapon, but tonight she'd been nothing but a liability.

"It's a few days before the next event," Jack pointed out. "And we can't exactly go back to the Inaugural Splendor, though it'll keep going until dawn, at least."

She had spent all night playing defense against Clara's whispered attacks. Maybe it was time to quit playing defense. "What if we had a look around Clara's dress shop?"

"A little breaking and entering?" A spark returned to those gray eyes, one that reminded her of his wild expression after he killed the guards. It had frightened her then, but now, it sent a quiet thrill through her.

"Dawn's in two hours." Jumping to his feet, he offered his hand. "Let's hurry."

FIFTEEN

IN THE DIM MOONLIGHT, EMMY studied the locked door in the back of Clara Claremont's dress shop.

"I could melt it," Jack offered.

"No need." Emmy pressed her palm against the heavy wood and, with a deep breath, gathered the brume. The particles arched away from her like ripples from the center of a lake. Slipping her hand through the hole, she turned the handle from inside the shop.

With a loud creak, the door opened.

"I'd say 'ladies first,' but I know you better than that." With a quick glance behind them, Jack slipped into the dress shop. A moment later, Emmy followed.

The hall was darker than the night, nearly pitch black. Like Grimsbane.

"The relic?" Jack's quiet voice wavered nearly imperceptibly.

Emmy removed it from around her neck, and Jack kept his hand on her back as if the night would swallow her. That point of contact anchored her as she fumbled in the dark, searching for his free hand. Their fingers grazed, his unmistakably warm as he plucked the cool coin from her.

His flames unfurled like a beautiful, hellish flower, revealing the dresses around them.

Squinting in the shadowy light, Emmy tiptoed through the back room. Dresses, dresses, and more dresses. As she brushed one, flower petals drifted across the luscious fabric.

"It's not particularly useful conjury." Jack held up a bolt of fabric with lace goldfish swimming across it. "She enchants certain aspects of the pattern into perpetual motion."

Emmy ran her hand along cloud-soft charmeuse. "She claims they'll move forever, but the embroidery on my debutante gown stopped moving fairly quickly."

"Charmlinking is always temporary. They can inject only so much power into ordinary materials."

Charmlinking, Emmy was learning, referred to gifts that connected conjury to something else. Like Grace's bridging. "Maybe Clara has a relic?"

"Her mother has one. It's possible Clara borrows it, but it still isn't enough for all this." He set down the bolt. "Ordinary relics are only a fraction of the strength of Rose's."

Which was why Emmy could never let it out of her sight. Even now, as Jack wore it, she longed to snatch it back.

He never strayed far as they wove through a windowless storage room, where row after row of enchanted gowns hung from satin hangers, order forms dangling from their necklines. The sheer volume of Clara's business made Emmy want to pull out her hair. Seemingly every single Society lady, along with the majority of men, was outfitted by the shop.

The workshop was next. It was an idyllic workspace, with fresh cut flowers in little jars at the centers of the vast tables. Sewing machines were evenly spaced along both sides, accompanied by wicker baskets full of colorful spools of thread.

"Grace runs a charity out of Clara's flagship store in the city." Jack ran his hand along the picturesque table. "She teaches poor children how to sew."

"What an angel." The acid in Emmy's voice brought a dark smile to Jack's lips. It was thrilling, catching one of Jack's roguish expressions in Nathaniel's princely face.

At the end of the hall, Emmy searched for a seam in the wall. "There are doors that appear only when Clara touches the wall with her palm."

Raising his palm, Jack burned an enormous hole in the wall. Dark as his flames were, the sudden burst of fire brightened the room, and Emmy glanced toward the far windows. No movement outside, though it was too dark to be certain.

"An hour until dawn." Jack glanced out the window. "Let's hurry."

The serpentine fabric was still in Clara's top drawer, the snake slithering as soon as Emmy touched it. After studying it in Jack's dim light, she searched through Clara's neat drawers. There were ledgers and receipts and folders bursting with cutouts of French gowns Clara had imitated. Copyright infringement, perhaps, but the Society wouldn't mind, so long as they benefitted.

Returning to the lady's salon was like returning to the scene of a crime. Emmy trailed her fingers along the silks she'd been admiring when she saw Grace for the first time. She meandered down the aisles she'd run through when her resolve had crumbled. She searched in hat boxes and shoe bins and crates of fabric and underneath the rugs.

Nothing was amiss.

In a small workshop, two ornate cloaks and sashes hung on a pair of mannequins. Even in the dim light, they were exquisite: thick ivory velvet with elaborate golden swirls that wound their way to the centers of the cloaks. Emmy ran her fingers along one, but the swirls did not shift. Not yet enchanted.

"'Prince of the Charmed,'" Jack read, his fingers trailing a golden sash. "The triumvirate must have commissioned Clara to design these for the summer pageant. It's our annual contest, a chance for the Society's bachelors and belles to show off their abilities."

"They're rather thick for summer." Emmy picked up the matching sash, with *Princess of the Charmed* splayed across its front in elegant gold lettering.

"The winners wear them only for the victory dance. Clara probably fitted them to Grace's and Oliver's sizes."

No part of Emmy wanted to dance in public—but she'd always hated to lose to Grace, even when they were the best of friends. "You don't think we can win?"

"As much as I'd *love* to dance with you, Vallillo, Oliver always cheats to get what he wants." Letting go of the sash, Jack rummaged through the back shelf. "When we were playing cards with him, I kept thinking about what a pompous ass he is. How the hell didn't I see that before?"

She placed a fabric crown on his head. "Because you were *also* a pompous ass?"

"Possibly." He flipped the crown upon her head. "What about Grace? Did you ever suspect she might turn on you?"

In Grimsbane, Emmy had tortured herself with this very question ad nauseam, turning over each memory like a stone. "There was this one thing, in retrospect. On my birthday."

"January sixteenth."

"Your intimate knowledge of my life is entirely unsettling."

His grin widened. "Not intimate enough."

She flicked a ribbon at him. "Papa always made a big to-do about our birthdays. He'd bring home a little gift from work—a figurine someone had whittled for him, or a twine bracelet. And he'd treat us to our favorite supper."

"Dumplings, from Chatham Square," Jack supplied.

Her hard look did nothing to quell his amusement.

"On my thirteenth birthday, Grace fell down the stairs. My father spent the night healing her broken wrist."

Jack glanced up from a rack of swirling ties. "You think she fell on purpose?"

"Not at first," Emmy said carefully. "But the next year, she burned herself on the stove. And the following year, she had a stomachache so severe, she was doubled over in pain for hours while Papa tried to heal whatever ailed her." Speaking of that night made Emmy feel strangely disloyal. Real tears had fallen down Grace's cheeks. "It was probably a coincidence. Why would she hurt herself on purpose?"

"Because she was competing for your father's attention."

"But he loved her, too." And he'd died without knowing the truth about her.

As Emmy trailed her fingers along a spool of ribbon, sending reeds blowing in a phantom wind, Jack muttered, "I don't understand how she did it."

"Did what?"

His lips twisted as if fighting back his words. "Convinced you that you're inferior to her."

Emmy whirled to face him, snap at him, *something*. "I was better than her at school. And at magic." Emmy had always been able to access the brume quicker—and hold on to it for longer.

"But you watch her dance like she's some sort of savant. And even though you're breathtaking, you laugh at the mere suggestion that Oliver might find you attractive."

He had a way of hurling a compliment like an insult. "Winnie may be beautiful, but I spent the last two years hardly feeling human, let alone *pretty*. It's an adjustment."

"And it isn't for me?"

"This is your world. You're used to lavish parties and palling around with the Stratton heir." She removed the fabric crown, fiddling with its edges. "Did you ever make a servants' bet?"

He froze.

Deny it. It struck her with surprising strength, her need for him to be different from them.

Color rose in his cheeks even as he shrugged. "They were

commonplace. I never questioned them."

"You never questioned cruelty toward the people who looked after your well-being." She could not hold back her ire.

"Don't make the mistake of thinking I'm one of the good ones, Vallillo." His haughty smile was as vexing as ever. "Servants' bets are hardly skimming the surface of the things I've done."

This was precisely why she should not have even asked. They were not friends. They were never going to be friends. "No need to worry about that."

He blocked her path at the end of the aisle. "Then why do you look so furious?"

"Because your casual indifference toward your own life is infuriating!" She ticked a list off on her fingers, one by one. "You speak of your death like a welcome holiday. You were thrown in jail when you might have avoided it because 'Oliver has a face that just *begs* to be punched.' And you humiliated your staff because everyone else was doing it!"

His eyes blazed, his lips twisting with whatever comeback he was considering. But he said nothing. For once, she'd rendered him speechless.

They were, objectively speaking, rather nice lips. Not quite plump, but full nonetheless. A tiny *V* marked the center of the upper one, its plunge endearing, especially while he was pouting. She ought to pat herself on the back for giving him such a nice mouth. Unless these had been his lips all along and she'd never noticed them.

They looked quite soft, too.

Emmy spun on her heel, returning to the cloak she'd already examined.

What had gotten into her? She did not care about lips, especially *his*.

"Would you like me to be more action oriented?" The faint hiss of his flames crackled behind her. "Should I burn down this shop and all the dresses in it?"

"It'd be a start." Fiddling with the cloak, Emmy tried to swallow her anger. Of course Jack had been cruel toward his staff. He was a Society darling. And if they managed to finish what they'd started without him dying, he'd return to being a Society darling. "On second thought, don't burn anything. That'll only make a martyr of her."

The shadowy light dimmed. "What about petty revenge? Is that beneath you?"

Petty revenge had kept her alive in Grimsbane. Like when she'd bitten that guard. "Not at all."

"Then let's do *something* tonight." He flexed and unflexed his still-smoking palms. "What is the worst thing that can happen in a dress shop? Everything shrinks?"

"Spoken like a true rich boy."

"I doubt the poor enjoy ill-fitting clothes, either."

"We don't mind them nearly as much as lice or—" Emmy stilled.

Jack's teasing smile vanished, and he swiftly moved between Emmy and the door.

"It's not that." Emmy waved him off, her mind buzzing with possibility. "I have an idea."

Jimmy would help, of course. Between the two of them, they'd find what they needed.

Jack tore his gaze from the closed door. "Well?"

Excitement raced through Emmy. So many new orders. There had to be one for every mansion in Avalon-on-Hudson, save Mistfield. "We infest the gowns with pests. Tiny ones, like lice or bedbugs. *Lots* of bedbugs."

A slow smile curved Jack's infuriatingly perfect lips. "I'm in."

SIXTEEN

IT TOOK TWO DAYS TO locate infested blankets and clothing, and one night to dust them into every order in Clara Claremont's shop. Bedbugs for the gowns. Lice for the hats. A sprinkle of scabies over everything, courtesy of an outbreak Jimmy had located downtown.

With the bugs in place, all they could do was wait—and attend the next party.

"You're all anyone's talking about," Mary gushed as she tightened the laces on Emmy's corset. "Even the servants heard how you threw that rabbit mask at Miss Montgomery."

The petite maid had arrived two mornings after the Inaugural Splendor, a satchel over her shoulder and a list of demands in her fist. No servants' bets, a stipulation to which Emmy readily agreed. Time off to visit her parents, which the Windsors had rarely permitted. Emmy offered her a part-time schedule, one in which she could return home each evening for the same lofty salary. Caleb had balked at that, but Emmy did not want Mary by her side night and day. It was too easy to slip, to forget to call the others by their aliases, or to forget to act like a millionaire.

"I didn't throw the mask *at* her," Emmy tried to respond, but Mary was astoundingly strong, each tug of the laces stealing Emmy's breath.

"Don't worry, miss." Mary's cheeks were as russet as her hair as she yanked the laces even tighter. "You've given the Society something they covet even more than magic or money."

"And what's that?"

In the mirror, a mischievous smile tugged at Mary's lips. "Drama."

This time, Emmy was ready for the pop of her ears as they crossed the illusion that hid Windfall House, the newly built home of the Villadoms. She tried not to stare at the numerous guards stationed around the perimeter, the embossed ivory of their uniforms whirling in the sunshine. A pity those hadn't been in the dress shop when they'd planted the little critters.

The guards, unfortunately, had no qualms about staring at Emmy.

"To be fair," Caleb murmured, "you threw a mask at Grace Montgomery."

"I didn't throw it *at* her." Emmy glanced over her shoulder at the guards. Still staring.

"Relax, you two." Despite Jack's easy tone, he fidgeted with the sleeve of his pale blue suit. "All we need to do is make friends today—which will be easier if we don't throw things."

Emmy nudged him with her wide gown, but unfortunately, he maintained his balance.

They'd gone over the plan last night. Since Oliver had quit the pool halls, Jack was going to befriend him in the hope of being invited to his private card games. In the meantime, Emmy was supposed to play nice with Grace while also getting under her skin. If Emmy had to choose between cozying up to Grace or the chancellor—Caleb's objective—Emmy would have preferred her father's killer.

Which left Clara Claremont, who, with any luck, had a massive outbreak on her hands.

"That's a lot of colors," Jimmy murmured as they approached the lawn full of partygoers in bright pastels.

"Miss Fairchild!" A streak of lavender cut across the verdant grass, the matching hat so wide, Emmy could not see Mrs. Stratton until she kissed the air on both sides of Emmy's cheeks. An assortment of flowers embellished the bodice of her gown, furling and unfurling in a never-ending loop. Yet another Claremont original. The party was full of them.

Let the scratching begin.

Mrs. Stratton linked their arms and guided Emmy down a path lined with enormous Montauk daisies. "Is Mr. Fontaine your escort for the afternoon? Or is it one of the others in your party?"

"My escort?"

Mrs. Stratton gave her a stern look. "You cannot arrive with *three* fetching young men. Next time, have at least two of them accompany other young ladies. It'll help you secure allies, and in the Society of the Charmed, you need allies." She nodded toward a group of young women standing beside the refreshments. One offered Emmy a soft smile before being elbowed by none other than Clara.

And beside Clara, whispering furiously in her ear, was Grace.

She wore a summer gown so pale, it was nearly white, with gray tufts of dandelion fur drifting over the skirts. The sight of it was a balm for Emmy's soul. Two nights ago, she'd placed bed bugs inside that very gown.

Returning Emmy's smile with a hesitant one, Grace absentmindedly scratched her arm.

"Ladies and gentlemen, gather around!" A young man stood on a small platform, one hand on his wife's back and the other holding a cone to his mouth, amplifying his words. "Welcome to the Enchanted Pursuit!"

"The Villadoms," Mrs. Stratton whispered. "Married last season. Mrs. Windsor believes they're already expecting," she added, her voice tinged with approval.

"The rules are the same as always," continued Mr. Villadom. "Players must stay on the field. If a guard calls you out of bounds, you're disqualified."

"What, exactly, is the Enchanted Pursuit?" Emmy whispered to Mrs. Stratton.

"Hide-and-seek, of course!" Mrs. Stratton beamed like a child. "It's Society tradition."

Emmy glanced at the vast field, which was peppered with the Villadom's waiting staff. Other than a few trees and a small fishing pond, there was almost nowhere to hide.

"Once you're tagged," Mr. Villadom continued, "you join the search party. The last one to be caught wins."

"We thought we'd let one of our newcomers be the seeker." Mrs. Villadom's serene voice held the slightest edge of mischief. "Mr. Fairchild, will you lead this year's Pursuit?"

Surprised, Caleb stepped forward to a polite round of applause. As they fixed a blindfold over his eyes, Mrs. Stratton flashed Emmy a knowing smile. "They're asking him because they think he's a nugat."

So she knew the truth. Her husband must have found Caleb's telepathy interesting enough to discuss with his wife. That was something, at least.

"You have five minutes to hide, starting . . . now! Let the Enchanted Pursuit begin!"

At Mr. Villadom's signal, the staff in the field touched something in their hands.

The landscape shimmered and shifted as illusions burst to life. A dramatic waterfall cascaded into the pond. Cliffs of tall rocks shot from the southern edge of the field. A forest blinked into existence in the east, cloaked in an eerie dark fog. Bonfires and swamps and even a few exotic-looking animals appeared all over the field. Illusions. Dozens of them.

So awed was Emmy, Mrs. Stratton had to nudge her twice. "Hurry!"

Oliver's mother moved with such surprising vigor, Emmy struggled to keep pace with her. The rest of the guests also darted about the field in a flurry of excitement. As they hurried, Emmy nearly fell into a pit in the ground, courtesy of two earth conjurers who were attempting to bury themselves. An elderly couple stepped into the pond, their faces tense under conjury's strain as the water moved from their path like Moses splitting the Red Sea.

Mrs. Stratton frowned at them. "That was my spot last year."

Conspiring together must have forged some sort of bond between Emmy and Jack, because she was perpetually aware of his whereabouts, even across the field. Flanked by two young ladies, he conjured a ring of fire that made the girls scream with delight. Shameless flirt.

A burst of agitation shot through Emmy, and she turned away.

"Be careful, Miss Fairchild." Mrs. Stratton nodded at Oliver sauntering toward them. "The last time my son played a game with you, he was far from a gentleman."

"I'm sure Miss Fairchild has a sense of humor." Oliver's smile wasn't the least bit contrite. Between his pale yellow suit and his golden sunglasses, he ought to have looked ridiculous, but confidence oozed from him as he held out his arm to her. "A quick word?"

Emmy blinked in surprise. She glanced toward Mrs. Stratton, who sighed. "*Very* quick."

"My mother," he murmured as Emmy stepped away with him, "wants me to apologize."

"That's quite an apology."

"Look at it from my perspective. You materialize out of thin air. Your cousin rebuilds Mistfield Manor while no one is looking, and the three of you are granted temporary status by my father without a formal vote." He smiled at a cluster of water conjurers turning a small section of the field into a swamp. "I know when a game is afoot."

It was only their second Society appearance, yet Oliver was already sniffing her out for the fraud that she was. Still, Emmy's face betrayed nothing. "And what game is that?"

"Beautiful. Unattached. Set to inherit five million dollars." He leaned closer and dropped his voice. "Your brother has not been subtle in his desire to see you matched this season."

A laugh slipped from Emmy. Even if he was not far from the truth, she would have died before revealing a thing. "You think I wish to marry you?"

"You've taken quite an interest in my mother."

Emmy freed her arm from his. "You find me so hideous that I must trick your mother—"

"Of course not, it's just—"

"Commander Stratton." Emmy stole a quick glance around, half expecting to see Grace watching. "No matter what my brother has said, I won't be marrying anyone this season. And I certainly won't be scheming to trap the self-absorbed son of the chancellor, no matter how many times his mommy writes his name on my dance card."

Her hands shook something awful as she stormed away. Caleb had laid it on too thick. Pretty girls from wealthy families were old news to the Stratton heir. But she'd seen how he'd looked at Grace while the two of them were dancing. Grace, who'd kissed him while she still lived in Five Points. She was a different sort of challenge. And Oliver Stratton was a chronic gambler who, like the rest of these cursed people, loved to play games.

"Wait."

She kept walking.

"Miss Fairchild, please." He touched the small of her back, and she had to swallow her disgust. "If you tell my mother, she'll never let me hear the end of this."

With a quiet sigh, Emmy made a show of considering his apology, though, like Jack, he had yet to actually apologize. "I'm not one to tattle."

"Let's have a fresh start." He sank into a deep bow. "I'm Oliver Stratton, son of a meddling mother. I am occasionally known to be an ass and often to be a rake."

Honesty, for once. Emmy curtsied. "I'm Winnie Fairchild, sister to a meddling brother. I am occasionally known to throw masks and often to storm away."

Emmy searched his grin for a crooked tooth or a tea stain, but alas, life was not fair.

"It's time!" Mr. Villadom's voice echoed across the field.

Mrs. Stratton pulled Emmy away, flashing her son a peeved look. But underneath her irritation, the meddling mother was clearly all too pleased.

People were shrieking in delight as Caleb began his search. With Emmy in hand, Mrs. Stratton hurried toward the tree on the edge of the pond. "Hold on tight, dear."

Mrs. Stratton shut her eyes and squeezed her necklace. A relic—Emmy hadn't noticed it before. A wind gathered at their ankles, whipping Emmy's hem. Mrs. Stratton's face flushed with effort as the gale surged from the ground, lifting them into the air. With a yelp, Emmy held Mrs. Stratton's arm tighter, but the air conjurer did not break her focus until the wind carried them to the top, where they perched on a branch that bowed underneath their weight.

With a satisfied smile, she settled onto the branch and dabbed her forehead. "Your turn."

Judging by Mrs. Stratton's sly look, this was a test of sorts. Emmy searched the tree for something she could transform. What, exactly, could an earth conjurer do?

Running her hand along the bowed branch beneath them, Emmy made it as strong as the steel beams Jimmy had placed in Mistfield's walls, as thick as the old oaks that greeted her along the trails to the cliffs. Once the branch was sturdy, she swept her fingers over the leaves, making them fuller and wider to hide them from view.

"I *knew* you had powerful blood." Mrs. Stratton grinned appreciatively. "Do leave us a little peephole. We may be here for hours."

Emmy complied, eager for a glimpse at charmed hide-and-seek.

They watched as Caleb managed to catch a few people, including Jimmy, who then joined his hunt. Two seekers disappeared in the fog of the illusory forest while another cried out in pain, holding his arm in front of a fire that was, apparently, real. As Caleb chased a pretty girl in a frilly magenta dress—one with a particularly bold pattern of enchanted cardinals swooping from neck to hem—she leaped, using her air conjury to soar high above his head.

Elemental conjury—air, earth, water, and fire, though only Jack wielded black flames—was certainly the most common gift on display, along with the Villadoms' illusions, which were a type of sensile conjury. But the Villadoms didn't seem to be straining themselves to maintain their faux forests. No, they must have commissioned Grace's bridging conjury, a form of charmlinking. The only type of conjury not on display was alchemical, like hers. And Papa's.

How he would have loved to play such a game.

"Special, isn't it?" Mrs. Stratton's voice softened as they watched seekers splash into the pond, laughing as they chased the couple hiding at the center. "All this conjury out in the open."

"I've never seen anything like it." Emmy could not keep the reverence from her voice.

"Well, you're one of us now, so you'll see it every summer." Mrs. Stratton leaned against the tree bark, her smile content. "It's always a risk, but it's *worth* the risk to remember who we are. That we're different from ordinary people. Though they may outnumber us two hundred to one, we're special. Every last one of us."

Emmy might have been touched by her words had Mrs. Stratton not reached into the back of her dress to scratch her neck. Hiding her smile, Emmy inched away. It was only a matter of time before the Society realized the outbreak on their hands and, with any luck, the source. Soon, Claremont Originals just might be out of business.

Caleb was chasing the girl in the magenta gown again, grasping the air as she jumped out of reach. His smile was real; Emmy could see from here. But as she floated as high as the treetops, he set off in pursuit of a couple who'd peered out from behind the illusory waterfall. Grace and Oliver. They were together, of course, which dimmed Emmy's surprisingly good spirits.

Grace grabbed Oliver's arm, reached for a pocket in her skirts—and disappeared.

Mrs. Stratton's expression soured. "It seems Miss Montgomery still has some of her invisible maid's conjury. Though rumor has it, the girl quit after the mask ordeal." She stole a glance at Emmy. "You wouldn't happen to know where she ended up, would you?"

There was no point denying it. Though Emmy hadn't brought Mary today, lady's maids were expected to be at their employers' beck and call at many events. They'd all know soon. "I couldn't let such exquisite conjury go to waste."

Mrs. Stratton's snicker was nothing short of delighted. "Well, well, well. Miss Fairchild has teeth of her own. Be sure to bring the girl next—"

A shrill scream pierced the air, long and sharp.

Emmy gripped the branches, searching. It almost sounded as if it was above them, but—

The scream ended with an awful thud.

Mrs. Stratton gasped, her hands rushing to her mouth.

Emmy saw her then, the girl with the magenta gown. The one who had leaped out of Caleb's way, her air conjury carrying her far overhead.

She'd fallen.

More screams erupted, and as eager as Emmy was to get out of the tree, Mrs. Stratton hardly looked capable of conjury. But she got them to the ground quickly, and they hurried toward the circle of people that had formed around the poor girl.

Her neck was as crooked as an elbow. Her eyes wide but unblinking.

"This has gone on for far too long!" Mrs. Stratton had pushed her way to the front of the circle, waving her fist at Keeper Windsor.

"Not now, Trudy." He motioned for the guards, his complexion paling.

"They're taking our brume!" Tears flooded Mrs. Stratton's eyes. Oliver was beside her now, but she shook him away. "How many of us must die before you *finally* let my husband do something about it?"

They're taking our brume. Though they were a two-hour train ride from the city, she was blaming the immigrants. The Society's scapegoats.

Numbly, Emmy stared at the dead girl. She couldn't have been older than sixteen.

"Someone cover her," Keeper Windsor said gruffly, "before her parents see her."

Grief tinged his words. He had to be thinking of Elizabeth, his late daughter.

Blood darkened the girl's dark hair. Like Papa, who'd lain on that tile floor, his head framed by a halo of crimson.

The Society grieved this loss. But they hadn't blinked at Papa's. Hadn't given *him* a moment of compassion.

"C'mon." A gentle hand took Emmy's elbow. Jack's. His gaze met hers, and for a moment, she thought she glimpsed tenderness in his unyielding gray eyes. "Everyone's leaving."

As Jack led her away, Emmy stole one last glimpse at the dead girl.

The cardinals on her gown had ceased flying, as if their wings had failed them, too.

SEVENTEEN

TWO DAYS' WORTH OF FESTIVITIES were canceled for the dead girl—Henrietta Chilton, the daughter of a Society lady and her husband, a former protégé. Tragic as her fall was, it also was poorly timed, for Emmy could not tell who was growing itchier from the gown infestation. She mustered the courage to ask Mary if she'd heard anything about an outbreak, and the poor girl had looked positively horrified, swearing that she bathed regularly.

"Clara and Grace were the only ones wearing enchanted gowns today," Jack pointed out after the funeral. He still wore his black silks, and although they looked handsome on the regal Nathaniel, mourning colors would have been far more fitting for Jack himself, with his dark hair and even darker smile.

She needed to stop doing that. Imagining Jack's true face.

Emmy sighed. "That's only because Clara doesn't have a funeral line."

"It's working." Jack yanked off his tie as if it had personally insulted him. "But everyone's too concerned about their reputations to admit they're afflicted with critters."

At least they *had* reputations to protect. Winnie Fairchild, meanwhile, was still a social pariah. Mrs. Stratton was the only person who'd ever visited Mistfield. At her insistence, Emmy had called on a few of the other girls her age, but their butlers had claimed they were not home. Judging by how Clara had nudged any girl who so much as looked in Winnie Fairchild's direction, Emmy knew who was to blame.

"We need to be more aggressive." Emmy paced in front of her

window. "The summer pageant is tomorrow, and we haven't made a lick of progress."

One week in the Society, and Clara still ran a successful business. The chancellor was still in charge. Grace and Oliver were rumored to be close to an engagement, despite Mrs. Stratton's insistence that her son "would never marry beneath him."

They'd hardly gotten started, yet already, they only had three weeks left.

"I have something that'll help." Disappearing back into the hole he'd once again burned between their rooms, Jack reappeared a few moments later with a stack of books. "Here."

Emmy ceased pacing. "Old books?"

"Old books on conjury." He dropped them on her bed, looking all too pleased with himself. "These were from the Fontaine library. The Society finally returned them."

Emmy stared at the books. At Jack. "Is the top one what I think it is?"

"The Fontaine grimoire." He patted it with pride. "Been in my family for centuries."

Emmy could not get her hands on it quickly enough. Settling onto her bed, she unlatched its black leather binding and savored the musty aroma of old parchment. The pages were yellowed and handwritten—everything she'd ever wanted in a book.

Jack perched on the edge of the bed. "Obviously, there are no spells like the ordinaries think. It's more of an account of our family's conjury, with some advice along the way."

"But Rose found instructions on forging her relic in here?"

"Caleb thinks so. She certainly spent a great deal of time with this tome." Jack rubbed the back of his head. "But don't expect to find a step-by-step guide. Our ancestors used to forge enchanted artifacts with our flames quite often, but Rose had to improvise. Other than ordinary relics, it's mostly a lost art. More evidence that we're weakening over time."

Emmy peered at the thick scorch marks on the back cover. "From magical mishaps?"

"Sort of." At her arched brow, he shook his head. "I don't want to tell you."

"Why not?"

"Because I'm not in the mood to make you loathe me even more."

"Not possible." She'd meant it teasingly, but his scowl deepened. "Oh, come on, Jack."

"Fine." He tugged at his shirt collar. "But first, you have to understand just how close Rose and Caleb were. They had a world of their own, with little room for anyone else."

She nodded, but his words struck a bruise. People had described her and Grace like that.

"Rose devoured any book she could get her hands on, but she was most curious about conjury. Like you, I suppose. Anyway," he sighed, the tips of his ears pinkening, "one day, when Caleb wasn't around and she was still refusing to play with me, I . . . set the library on fire."

Emmy gaped at him, a protective hand over the grimoire. "You did what?"

"It was a tiny blaze!" He raised his palms, a few inches apart. "Easily extinguished, with the help of the staff . . . and the fire brigade. We lost only a small section of the library."

"A small section!" And he'd nearly destroyed a centuries-old family heirloom full of secrets and history and knowledge that could have been lost forever. "Were you punished?"

"Of course not." At Emmy's arched brow, he shrugged. "I was the future head of the family, heir to the Fontaine fortune. Besides, I never admitted to it."

"Wasn't it obvious?"

"We illuminated the entire house with our black flames. One candle could have easily fallen over. And . . . I don't think Rose imagined I was capable of doing something so awful. She thought better of me."

Swallowing thickly, he turned away.

It was a positively unhinged thing to do, even for a child. Still, as Jack struggled to hide the blush creeping over his cheeks, Emmy felt a tendril of compassion for him. It was too late for him to come clean to his sister.

Emmy traced the silver lettering of the leather cover. "It's odd, attending a stranger's funeral today, when we missed the ones for those we loved."

"I hate it," he agreed quietly. "It felt disloyal, somehow."

Reluctantly, Emmy set the Fontaine grimoire beside her bed. As curious as she was about Rose's relic, she'd grown accustomed to using it. The research could wait.

When she looked up, Jack was watching her with his usual intensity. "Plotting?" she asked.

He gave his head a small shake, as if coming out of a daze. "The final ball is the thirtieth of June. That's only three weeks away."

It wasn't nearly enough time. "Do we stay the course?"

"For now." He frowned, his lower lip jutting forward. Another quintessential Jack expression on Nathaniel's face, and it assuaged her nerves a smidge. "We go to the pageant tomorrow and we try to get closer, to unlock their secrets."

"And if that doesn't work?"

He glanced at the scorch marks on the grimoire. "Then we get more aggressive."

Oliver was escorting Winnie Fairchild to the summer pageant, likely at his mother's behest. Still, as Emmy entered the Claremonts' residence on his arm, with Mrs. Stratton at her side and Mary dutifully following in their wake, Emmy could not help but feel victorious.

Grace, unfortunately, was not there to witness Winnie's grand entrance, but Clara Claremont greeted Emmy with enough fire in her eyes for the both of them.

"Don't mind her, dear," Mrs. Stratton whispered as they continued into the ballroom. "She's in a foul mood because there's been an outbreak in that shop of hers."

Emmy nearly tripped over her gown. "Oh?"

"Lice *and* bedbugs, if you can believe it. They probably crawled off those ungodly children Miss Montgomery teaches to sew in her back room. But to be safe, steer clear of her shop."

Emmy practically choked on her scoff. They were blaming the poor. Again.

"I'll sign you up to be last," Mrs. Stratton continued, "which is the best position. And Mrs. Claremont used my florist for the centerpieces. You have plenty of plants at your disposal."

Oliver caught her eye. Meddling mother indeed.

The Claremonts' ballroom was already crowded, its temperature climbing by the second. Even the guards stationed on its periphery tugged on their enchanted uniforms.

Emmy glanced about the party. The other ladies wore extravagant gowns, but they weren't enchanted. Luxurious, yes, with statement jewelry that probably cost more than all of Baxter Street, but the patterns did not twist, or flutter, or move at all.

They had hurt Clara's business, but she'd ruined Emmy's life. It wasn't nearly enough.

"These are the winners of years past." Oliver brought her over to the trophies, the same ones she'd glimpsed in the Society's basement weeks ago. "Remove your glove and give them a try."

Trying not to bristle at his imperious tone, Emmy touched the trophy labeled *Stratton, 1868*. It was solid white gold and as frigid as ice. Montgomery bridging conjury, yet again.

"What's it supposed to do?" Emmy tried to say, but—no words passed her lips. She tried to snatch her hand away, but she couldn't move. This was the conjury that had kept her still when she'd tried to reach Papa. That had ruined her vocal cords when she'd tried to scream for him.

Oliver grinned as he shifted the trophy away from her. "Each year, the winners get trophies in their families' honor. We Strattons have the most."

There were at least half a dozen trophies with *Stratton* on them, each one more elaborate than the last. Avoiding those, Emmy mustered the courage to run her fingers along *Villadom, 1880* and an illusory genie hovered above her hand. A wind burst from *Windsor, 1876* and flowers grew out of *Zermatt, 1862*. For a secret society, they were rather fond of flashy magical things.

Oliver yawned, already bored with the trophies. And her. Pretending not to notice, Emmy scanned the room. Mary waited against the wall with the other attendants. Jimmy stood beside Jack, who was chatting with yet another pretty Society girl. Sometimes, it was hard to reconcile the Jack who schemed in her bedroom each night with the one who was at ease in the Society of the Charmed. Still, Rose had drawn him kissing several girls. One of them might be tonight.

The mere thought twisted her gut.

From the stage, Mrs. Claremont clapped her hands. "Welcome, everyone!"

But the excited chatter continued as the hostess tried—and failed—to catch the attention of her guests. If anything, the roar of conversation grew louder.

In a breath, the chatter vanished, snuffed out like the flame of a candle.

Stratton silencing conjury, yet again.

It will pass. Emmy was still breathing, though each inhale grew shallower. The tremendous power this man possessed, to silence an entire ballroom on a whim. No wonder he hadn't been tempted by Caleb's telepathy. He was at the top of the food chain, able to shoot men without consequence, all the while keeping their daughters' screams muted, locking them up—

The chancellor relaxed, dabbing the sweat from his brow with a handkerchief. A quiet murmur flooded the ballroom as the Society hurried to their seats.

"Well, *that* was fun," Jack muttered as he sidled up beside her, that pretty girl nowhere in sight.

Oliver aimed his lazy, arrogant smirk at Jack. "Not a fan of my father's methods?"

"Oh, come on, Stratton. You must admit, your father's a rather fierce man."

Oliver made a noncommittal noise before turning to Emmy as if Jack weren't there. At this rate, Jack would never befriend him. They needed a new plan. And soon.

The pageant began much like the debutante ball. One by one, Mrs. Claremont called the participants to the stage. Two golden stopwatches floated above it, their numbers replaced with diamonds. The first measured how long it took the participant to conjure. The second, how long they held on to their power. Given that she and Jack had a plan to share the relic tonight, they were both at quite the advantage.

"Next, we have Mr. Nathaniel Fontaine," Mrs. Claremont announced.

With an easy smile, Jack sauntered up the stage's stairs as if he neither noticed nor cared about the whispers that still followed the name Fontaine.

"If you're not interested in marriage, you should keep an eye on your cousin."

Emmy turned to Oliver, whose gaze remained fixed on Jack. "I beg your pardon?"

"Your cousin. He's always watching you, even from across the room."

She nearly laughed. Oliver was perceptive enough to notice Nathaniel guarding his secret weapon, though not perceptive enough to realize Nathaniel was Jack.

"I'm only trying to help." He winked. "From one determined singleton to another."

"That's not what I hear. In fact, I hear you're quite unavailable."

"So you've been asking after me?" Oliver leaned closer, eyes alight. "Careful, Miss Fairchild, or I might take that as an invitation to call on you."

"Your mother would enjoy that far too much."

"A problem indeed."

Oliver was as handsome as he was terrible, yet Emmy *liked* when her clever words made him smile like that, even when Grace wasn't here to witness it. Where the hell was she tonight?

Onstage, Jack sent a burst of tar-black flames surging over the heads of the guests. The audience screamed, ducking their heads as the fireball returned to Jack like a boomerang.

Emmy clapped. Oliver did not.

"Tomorrow," Oliver raised his voice over the growing applause, "perhaps we can . . ."

Emmy glanced at him, but something else had stolen his attention—stolen everyone's attention, if the *oohs* and *ahhs* spreading through the ballroom were any indication.

Grace stood in the entranceway. Her blonde hair was woven into the most extravagant braid Emmy had ever seen, with purple blooms and glittering diamonds tucked in her golden twists. The tight bodice of her gown was shaped like two petals, resulting in a deep plunge that revealed the curve of her breasts. A risqué cut, but the real eye-catcher was the voluminous skirt made entirely of petunias. Waves upon waves of the purple flowers cascaded from her waist, flooding the vast doorway and spilling into the ballroom.

The dress wasn't enchanted. That ought to be cause for celebration, but nothing about this dress screamed "crawling with critters." No, Grace had still managed to shine.

"And next," Mrs. Claremont announced, "we have Commander Stratton."

So enchanted was Oliver by the sight of Grace that he did not even hear his name. Swallowing her frustration, Emmy nudged him, and he finally snapped out of his daze, leaping onto the stage. "Mr. Fontaine, care to join me?"

Heads turned to Jack, who shrugged.

"Since you're the one to beat, I have a proposal for you." A mischievous smile spread across Oliver's face. "Fight me."

Unease washed over Emmy, especially as the Society leaned forward in their seats. *This* was the sort of entertainment they craved.

Jack, for his part, laughed. "You want me to—"

Oliver slammed his fist into Jack's cheek.

Jack's head snapped back, and Emmy's breath rushed from her lungs. He'd just—hit him.

Pain erupted across Jack's face, followed by shock as he registered the audience's laughter.

Her teeth grounded together to keep her from screaming at them all.

Spitting blood onto the stage, Jack whipped toward Oliver. "My turn?"

"Whenever you're ready." Oliver squeezed his eyes shut.

Hit him back. She'd seen Jack snap a guard's neck without breaking a sweat. And though he vexed her to no end, seeing Oliver strike him made her positively murderous.

Jack curled his hand into a fist, and—froze.

Oliver gave Jack a little shove, and he tipped over stiffly, slamming his head into the stage. The audience roared with laughter, but Emmy was breathing fire.

What was wrong with her, that she'd enjoyed Oliver's approval, even for a moment?

"What do you say, Fontaine?" Oliver stood over Jack, grinning. "Do you yield?"

Unlike his father, Oliver couldn't silence people with his conjury. But with his lips frozen, Jack could not shape his words, which earned Oliver another wave of laughter.

Jack's hand curled into a fist.

Everyone was still laughing. Even Grace, who never missed a thing, was grinning at Oliver while shaking her head in mock disapproval. But Oliver grimaced. His conjury had failed him, even if he was pretending otherwise.

Burn him. If Emmy had Caleb's telepathy, she would have seared the thought into Jack's skull. *Burn him and show them all what you're made of.*

But Jack remained still. Not striking back. Not giving Oliver what he deserved.

Oliver made a show of letting go of the brume. The gilded stopwatch stopped. Two minutes and fourteen seconds. The longest time yet, but utterly fraudulent. Jack had *let* him win.

Mrs. Claremont beamed at Grace. "Miss Montgomery, dear, it's your turn."

With a prim smile, Grace cut through the ballroom, the crowd parting for her and her train of purple flowers. It was sickening, really, how much they adored her.

Jack, meanwhile, silently took his place beside Emmy. The tanned skin of his right cheek was shiny and crimson, and part of his bottom lip was already hard and discolored.

"Why?" she whispered. She'd seen his hand move. He'd let Oliver win.

"You know why." Bitterness laced his quiet words.

Because, for Nathaniel to befriend Oliver, he needed to let Oliver make a fool out of him.

Jack's fingers tangled with hers, slipping her the relic, and Emmy gave them a comforting squeeze before quickly pulling away, willing herself not to look at him.

"I'm ready," Grace announced, and the golden clock started ticking.

Ignoring Jack's gaze, Emmy watched Mrs. Windsor hand Grace three teacups, each painted with the same flowers as Grace's gown. After setting them on the stage, Grace removed her gloves, one finger at a time. The little cheat should have done so before they'd started the clock.

Grace touched the first teacup—and disappeared.

Mary's conjury, once again. Emmy glanced toward the line of staff, but petite Mary was probably hiding with embarrassment. No one seemed to care that Grace had prepared these items in advance. She was, and had always been, a goddamn cheat.

Grace reappeared as abruptly as she'd disappeared, this time picking up the second teacup. A cloud formed in her free hand, one that began to rain over the stage. Water conjury.

Once she'd collected her round of applause—and wasted more seconds—Grace plucked a petunia from her gown, then dropped it into the third teacup. The delicate flower grew until the petals cascaded over the porcelain rim. Earth conjury. But Grace wasn't done yet. No, she lifted the giant flower, and a swarm of bees blinked into existence, furiously buzzing about it.

Grace tossed the flower to Emmy, sending the bees rushing toward her.

With a yelp, Emmy ducked, flailing to defend herself. Papa had been allergic, but Emmy had never been stung, so she couldn't know for sure—

The crowd laughed, and Grace flashed her a victorious smile. The wretch had tricked her. With an illusion.

As the crowd cheered exuberantly for their darling protégé, Emmy forced herself to clap, her heart still racing. Jack, curse him, had been right. Emmy *did* feel inferior to Grace. How she looked, how she danced, how she carried herself through the world.

But Emmy had always been stronger in conjury. And she had the relic Grace had failed to steal.

"And our last act," Mrs. Claremont announced, "is Miss Winifred Fairchild."

As Emmy climbed the stairs, Clara looked exceedingly pleased with herself.

Ignoring her, Emmy glanced about the ballroom, but—the floral tree centerpieces, the colorful vase arrangements—they were all gone.

Anything Winnie Fairchild could use for earth conjury had disappeared.

EIGHTEEN

EMMY COULD HAVE KICKED HERSELF for taking her eyes off Clara.

"Miss Fairchild?" Mrs. Claremont gave her a funny look. "Are you ready?"

A giggle wafted from beside the stage. Clara.

Emmy rubbed the relic in her sleeve, refreshingly cool against her skin. She hadn't the faintest idea what she was going to do, but she had to do *something*.

Tugging a thread loose, Emmy called to the brume as she unraveled it. A rush of that ethereal fog answered her call, and she envisioned the thread as a delicate vine, the sort that crawled up the trees deep in Mistfield's woods. She laid the ever-shifting vine on the ground, giving it sharp roots to penetrate the wooden stage. Stepping away, she spread her arms to release more, more, more of the vine, transforming its shade until its leaves were as emerald as her eyes.

The crowd gasped. As far as they knew, she had conjured a plant from thin air. Emmy draped it across the judge's table, making the leaves wider, greener. Once they held several yards of vine, she let go of the thread, sweeping her hands over her creation while she made her way back to the stage. Bright flowers bloomed between the verdant leaves. Purple petunias like the ones on Grace's gown, interspersed with blood-red poppies like those on Clara's. Not able to help herself, she peppered those crimson petals with little black spots that gave the illusion of insects. Anything to keep that clock running at least a few seconds longer than Grace's time.

Gripping her knees, Emmy made a show of catching her breath

while the Society rose to their feet, delivering a thunderous applause.

It was a risk; Winnie Fairchild had declared earth conjury, but this plant was far from real. Anyone who looked closely enough might notice its subtle waxiness.

Then again, no one truly knew a thing about Winnie Fairchild's talents.

"Participants," Mrs. Claremont called, cutting Emmy's applause short, "please return to the stage while the judges deliberate."

"How talented you are, Miss Fairchild!" Grace called as she joined Emmy onstage.

Emmy stiffened. Grace still smelled like Grace, somehow, despite the fancy perfumes. Even more unnerving, she looked as pleased as Clara had just before Emmy's turn. Her gaze found Jack's and he lifted his brows, but she did not need him to handle Grace.

"It would be generous of the judges to let one of you elemental conjurers win, for once." Grace's smile was all sharp edges. "Especially since there are so many of you."

Before Emmy could muster a clever response, Mrs. Claremont returned with a small square of paper. Standing in the center of the stage, she made a show of unfolding it. "The Prince of the Charmed of 1882 is . . . Commander Stratton."

The Society cheered exuberantly for their young commander. And though Emmy pretended to clap, she did not allow her hands to make a single sound.

"And for the young ladies"—Mrs. Claremont made a showing of unfolding the next square of paper dramatically—"the Princess of the Charmed is . . . Miss Winifred Fairchild."

Emmy turned up her nose at Grace as she took Oliver's waiting hand.

The winners' garb was brought to the stage, the same cloaks and sashes that had been in Clara's dress shop, only updated. Scarlet gemstones now lined their hems, their glittery shade matching the velvet swirls of flames that covered the cloaks. Curious whispers spread through the crowd, and more than once, Emmy thought she heard the word *infested*.

Cloaks in place, Clara rose from her seat and clapped her hands, just once.

A glittery haze curled around Emmy, rolling in waves off her sash. For a second, she thought Clara might have set her on fire, but she wasn't burning. Instead, minuscule fireworks burst from the fabric, sparking in vibrant pink, purple, and gold. The adoring crowd drew closer, positively enthralled by Clara's latest creation.

They'd hit Clara's pride with the bugs, but she'd punched back by creating something so extravagant, people would be willing to forget that she was the source of their outbreak. By the end of the night, Clara would have dozens of new orders.

Emmy was ready to scream.

"It's customary for the winners to perform an encore," Oliver spoke directly in her ear to be heard over the applause, and Emmy fought the urge to wriggle away. "Better you than me. Unless, of course, you're volunteering to take a punch."

He laughed at his own joke, but Emmy ignored him, raising her arms. After her winning performance, she needed to at least pretend she was almost drained. Reaching for her power, she felt the heavy presence of the brume—but not quite as heavy as usual.

Had she reached the relic's limit? Impossible; she'd only conjured some vines.

Emmy's gaze snapped to Oliver. "Are you suppressing me?" The impact was subtle, and with the relic, hardly a hindrance. But if he was testing her, she had to play along.

He shot her a strange look. "Why would I do that?"

Because he was on Grace's side. Because he wanted her to look like a fool. Because he'd suppressed her conjury when she'd been but a stranger trying to prove her innocence.

The applause slowed to a trickle. Mrs. Stratton nodded encouragingly to Emmy. And from the front row, Clara's grin spread from ear to ear.

"Miss Fairchild? Commander Stratton?" Mrs. Claremont's smile grew impatient.

Emmy caught Caleb's eye and shot him a meaningful look. *Listen to Clara's thoughts.*

Given his confused expression, he could not hear her.

"We'll give you an encore after the winners' waltz." Oliver led Emmy toward the center of the dance floor, where the crowd formed a circle around them. Wonderful, she now had to dance in front of the entire Society.

Listen to Clara's thoughts. Emmy's gaze bore into Caleb.

What is it? Caleb whispered in her mind, and Emmy could have collapsed with relief.

Listen to Clara's thoughts. I think she's trying to limit my power somehow.

"Are you all right?" Oliver asked as he took her hand.

"Just a little weak. I could have sworn I had a bit of conjury left."

If Oliver knew anything about Clara's machinations, his face revealed nothing. "Well, I've stalled them for now, but they're still expecting an encore."

Emmy swallowed her frustration. He had as much empathy as a statue.

You're right, Caleb whispered. *She enchanted the winners' garments to do far too much. They're ten times the strength of her usual gowns, and she's hoping it wipes you out completely.*

Mind racing, Emmy spun away from Oliver. *But what does that have to do with—* Oh.

Clara was a charmlinker like Grace, Jack had said. Their enchantments were temporary, though Clara claimed hers had so much power, they'd "outlast us all."

But the clouds on Emmy's debutante gown had stopped meandering in Grimsbane.

And at the lawn party, the cardinals on the dead girl's gown had ceased flying.

Clara's garments did not work on ordinary people because they *drew power from the charmed*. That was why they never ran out of strength. She was siphoning her customers' access to the brume, unbeknownst to them.

At the first ball, the dealer who had faltered had been wearing an enchanted suit.

And at the lawn party, that poor girl's gown had drained her. It had killed her.

Conjury was growing weaker. And Clara's creations were at the height of their popularity.

You're right. Caleb's internal voice trembled with excitement. *You can ruin her right now. Make an announcement. The Society will be outraged.*

Oliver must have said something to Emmy, for he was looking at her expectantly. She missed a step, and someone giggled rather loudly. Grace.

Would the Society believe Winnie Fairchild when they hadn't believed Emmy Vallillo? Perhaps. Winnie had money. Ties to a respected charmed bloodline. She might be able to convince them . . . but Clara was not their only target.

You tell the chancellor, she said in her mind. *Pull him aside.*

If Caleb demonstrated how useful he could be to the chancellor—if he slipped him important information—then maybe, just maybe, the chancellor would begin to trust him.

As Oliver twirled her, Caleb cut through the crowd to the chancellor, nearly bumping into Jack, who watched the winners' waltz with his arms tightly folded over his chest.

Emmy stopped dancing, wavering on her feet. Time to put on one hell of a performance.

“What is it?” Oliver could hardly hide his annoyance.

“I’m fine, I’m just—I feel so strange.” Pressing the back of her hand to her forehead, Emmy transformed her complexion to a paler shade, a thin sheen of sweat upon her brow. Fluttering her eyes closed, she let her legs give out.

Oliver caught her just in time to soften her fall.

The violins screeched to a halt, and Emmy tried to lie as still as the dead. It was a rather dramatic performance, but she committed to it wholeheartedly. Someone lifted her head. Someone else pressed a glass to her lips. She made a show of fluttering her lashes as she roused.

For a few minutes, Mrs. Stratton fussed over Emmy while nearby onlookers murmured criticisms of Clara’s choice of velvet in the summer. Oliver stood beside his mother, looking inconvenienced. A gentleman indeed.

Jack kept trying to catch Emmy’s eye, looking downright panicked. Good; he was playing his part well. And behind him, Caleb was whispering furiously to the chancellor. By the time Oliver had eased Emmy into a chair, the chancellor climbed the stage and, lifting his arms, commanded everyone’s attention. “Ladies and gentlemen of the Society of the Charmed.”

It was overwhelming, the flood of hope that washed over Emmy.

“Something terrible has been brought to my attention.” He let his words hang over the ballroom, his face grave. “Miss Claremont, please step forward.”

Emmy might actually faint this time.

Clara’s pleased smile froze in place. Whatever she’d been expecting the chancellor to say, it hadn’t involved her.

“Is there a problem, Stratton?” Mr. Claremont pressed a hand on her shoulder.

“I requested your daughter.”

From Clara's other side, Grace took a subtle step back.

"Surely it can wait—"

"It cannot." The chancellor kept his penetrating glare on Clara. "Young lady, if you do not come here, my guards will bring you, and they won't do it kindly."

Whispers followed as she tentatively approached the stage.

"Oliver, bring me your cloak."

Robbed of his usual air of impertinence, Oliver obeyed.

The chancellor examined the cloak, which continued to shoot miniature fireworks—but only when he touched it. When he laid it on the stage, the enchantments ceased.

Satisfied, he called Keeper Windsor to join him and Oliver onstage. As they dipped their heads in hushed whispers, the air surrounding them shimmered like the iridescent surface of a bubble. A wall of air, erected to block listening ears from eavesdropping on the triumvirate. Given the rapt expressions of the other guests, this was no common occurrence.

With a final nod, Chancellor Stratton stepped forward, and the iridescent wall vanished. "Miss Claremont, you are under arrest. Guards?"

Under arrest. It took everything Emmy had not to grin like a madwoman.

Gasps flooded the ballroom, none louder than that of Clara, who tried her best to appear confused. But Emmy saw the fear in her eyes. She knew.

"On what grounds?" Mrs. Claremont demanded.

"She has been siphoning the Society's power, bit by bit, for her own profit." The chancellor pinned Clara with an icy stare. "Everyone who wears her clothing has been forfeiting their strength."

"I have done no such thing!" Clara pointed at Emmy, fury on her face. "She only pretended to faint!"

Emmy lifted a gloved hand to her mouth, the picture of ladylike bewilderment.

"Henrietta Chilton fell to her death conjuring in one of *your* gowns." He stepped toward her, his guards closing in behind him. "You claim that your enchantments last for years. How?"

Clara paled. "I'm quite strong. I've practiced."

"You're nineteen years old. How much practicing could you possibly have done?"

"You think I log every hour?" Her shrill voice echoed through the ballroom.

The chancellor only blinked at her. "Is there anyone else who is familiar with Miss Claremont's conjury? Someone who can speak on her behalf?"

"How dare you sully my daughter's good name!" Mr. Claremont bellowed. "She is of the utmost—"

The chancellor turned away from the silenced father. "A non-relation, perhaps?"

A murmur swept through the crowd, and Jack caught Emmy's eye, his uncertainty a mirror of her own. Clara would not go down without a fight.

Grace stepped forward. "I would like to speak."

The sting of betrayal was swift and unmistakable. So Grace would speak on Clara's behalf. Grace was capable of loyalty. To Clara.

"As a dear friend of Miss Claremont, and as chairwoman of a charity that trains needy children in her sewing rooms, these accusations shake me to my core."

Utter lies.

"But as a humble member of this esteemed Society," Grace continued, "and as a Christian, I feel compelled to speak the truth."

Clara's head snapped toward Grace's.

"Everything Chancellor Stratton said is true." Grace's voice carried across the ballroom, as clear as bells. "Miss Claremont confessed it to me herself, only last week, when she was making these cloaks. The knowledge has been eating away at me, and I am ashamed that I did not come forward sooner."

That clever little liar.

Surely they could not be so easily swindled. The only reason Grace was coming forward was so that Clara did not take her down with her. Maybe her bridging conjury was somehow involved in the nefarious fabrics.

"And why," spat the chancellor, "didn't you approach the triumvirate right away?"

Grace's lower lip wobbled. "Misplaced loyalty, sir. She told me she'd speak to you directly. If I'd known she'd reduce poor Miss Fairchild to a pale, sickly looking creature . . ."

Well, *that* was unnecessary.

Mrs. Windsor rushed forward to comfort her niece. It was enough to make Emmy sick.

"Very well, Miss Montgomery."

Grace curtsied to the chancellor before her aunt guided her away.

Clara watched, her pink mouth agape. If she was truly surprised that Grace Montgomery was capable of betraying her friends, then she hadn't been paying much attention.

"Miss Claremont," the chancellor said sternly, "you will remain in Grimsbane Tower until your trial. Guards, seize her."

"Grace is lying!" Clara screamed. "She's—"

As the chancellor silenced Clara, Emmy offered her a secret little smile of her own.

NINETEEN

THE HUMID BREEZE LICKED EMMY'S cheeks as she stood on Mistfield's cliffs with Jack, Caleb, Jimmy, and a bottle of champagne. When Jack had suggested they celebrate Clara's downfall, Emmy had pictured a quick toast while the staff was asleep, but of course, Jack had more grandiose plans.

Jimmy held out the bottle to Jack. "Liquid courage?"

"No need." With a wary breath, Jack stared at the black river, nearly imperceptible in the dark. "This is not how I die."

"Don't you dare," Caleb warned. "Tonight was a win. Let's not ruin it with your funeral."

"But I said I'd celebrate our first victory by jumping." He shot Emmy a devilish grin. "I'm a man of my word."

Emmy shrugged, not giving him the satisfaction of riling her. "He won't jump." Only a fool would leap into the rocky Hudson in the middle of the night, and Jack was no fool.

"You think you know me that well?"

"First of all, you wouldn't ruin your favorite vest. And second, you're not stu— *No!*"

In three quick strides, Jack sprinted off the edge of the cliff.

For a fleeting moment, the moonlight limned him in ghastly silver—shirttails fluttering, legs kicking, arms outstretched like flightless wings—before gravity plucked him from the night.

Emmy rushed toward the edge, searching for his crushed skull or lifeless body limp in the waves. But there was no sign of either.

Cursing under his breath, Caleb lunged toward the footpath. Emmy hurried after him, but Jimmy let out a wild hoot, one loud enough to wake the sleeping staff.

There, bobbing in the pitch-black waters, was the most reckless cad she'd ever known.

"Come on in!" Jack shouted from far below. "The water's warm!"

With her lungs robbed of air, Emmy couldn't properly berate him.

"I'm going to drown him myself," Caleb muttered, his hands pressed to his chest.

For once, they were in agreement.

Jimmy thrust the champagne into Caleb's hands. "See you at the bottom."

"Jimmy Li," Caleb warned, "I swear to—"

Jimmy's yelp cut through the night as he catapulted himself over the edge, disappearing for several agonizing seconds. He resurfaced with a giddy scream that would have made Emmy laugh, had she not been frozen.

Caleb took a swig of the bottle before offering it to Emmy. "We're walking, right?"

"Absolutely." With a shuddering breath, she followed him between the trees.

The heat of the day clung to the darkness, curling Emmy's baby hairs. But she did not mind the humidity, or the mosquitos swarming the narrow path, or even the spiderwebs. The night was alive, more alive than anything she'd been able to picture back at Grimsbane.

Grimsbane Tower. Hard to believe it was Clara Claremont's new residence.

The path ended along the riverbank, where a large, flat boulder jutted into the river. Caleb began unbuttoning his vest, tossing it atop Jack's and Jimmy's drenched shirts. "The water's deep as long as you stay away from the shore. Rose loved to swim," he added, seeing her surprise. "Especially on nights like these, when it's too bloody hot to sleep."

His smile wilted, and Emmy's heart grew heavy, too. *They had a world of their own,* Jack had said, *with little room for anyone else.*

To Jack's and Jimmy's delight, Caleb joined them for a night swim. Emmy, meanwhile, settled on a dry patch of smooth rock. Surreal, to sit on a private beach, at a home large enough to swallow a city block, with three half-naked boys guzzling champagne in the river. Before tonight, she'd never even tasted champagne.

Grace would have loved such a night.

Why was she thinking of Grace? With another swig, she replaced the bitter taste in her mouth with sweet bubbles.

"So Clara Claremont was taken down by a girl from Five Points." Jimmy motioned for the champagne, and Emmy obliged. "How does it feel, Ems?"

Emmy tried to imagine Clara huddled in Grimsbane, still in her frilly gown. It ought to have made her giddy, but nothing about Grimsbane could bring her joy. "It was a team effort."

Jack grinned. "So you're finally admitting we're a team."

"Don't get ahead of yourself."

"Oh, come on. You must trust us a little by now."

"Do you trust me?" She knew he didn't, not when he still kept plenty of secrets.

"I trust my gut. And my gut says you're all on my side." He winked. "Even you."

"I trust you, too, Fontaine." Jimmy tousled Jack's wet hair. "In fact, I trust all of you."

Caleb rolled his eyes. "You trust everyone."

"Innocent until proven guilty."

"An excellent rule for a jury, but less so for the company you keep." Caleb grabbed the champagne from him. "Trust needs to be earned."

"Have I earned your trust? Or am I still a 'charmless bastard'?"

"Ah, well, the truth hurts."

Jimmy splashed Caleb, who indignantly splashed him back. Soon the two of them were in a full-blown water fight, one that nearly drowned the poor champagne bottle. Emmy managed to pluck it out of the river as they splashed away, racing toward the middle while fervently declaring they were not, in fact, racing.

As she watched them over the champagne bottle's rim, Emmy smiled faintly. There was a lightness to their mood that she envied. But letting go like that, celebrating so freely—it was as if they were speaking a language lost to her. She could not trust tonight's good fortune to last. Two years ago, her greatest victory had ended in her swift demise—and she hadn't seen it coming.

Tilting her head toward the stars, Emmy studied the bluffs lining both sides of the river. It'd be so easy for someone to spy on them. Like Grace, with whatever invisibility she had left from Mary. Or the Society guards, coming to drag them back to Grimsbane.

Jack waded toward her. "Nice touch, fainting in Stratton's arms. He loves to be the hero."

"He was hardly the hero." And though he'd been Winnie's escort, he had practically salivated when Grace had appeared in that gown. "No luck with his card games?"

"He truly quit." Jack sulked. "Inconvenient time for him to clean up his act."

"Maybe Grace made him stop." Grace's perfect life likely did not involve a soon-to-be husband who gambled away the family fortune.

"Doubtful. Especially with how he looks at Winnie."

Emmy rolled her eyes. "He's entertaining Winnie to placate his mother."

"It's more than that. Which is good for us, given that I've made no progress with him." He tossed his wet hair away from his eyes. "Knowing him, he'll try to get you alone soon. We'll have to make sure he can't."

"Why?"

"Because he'll . . . well, he'll make advances."

That, Emmy hadn't expected. Jack watched her intently, perhaps waiting for her to panic. Trying not to blush, she slipped off her shoes and dipped her toes into the cool water. "That would certainly push Grace's buttons."

Jack blinked. Twice. "You'd be willing?"

"If it ruins Grace's chance at an engagement, absolutely." But that wouldn't be enough to drive a wedge between Oliver and Grace. They'd been sneaking around for years. They'd lied together. *Killed* together. As far as Emmy could tell, the only reason they weren't already engaged was Mrs. Stratton's blatant disapproval of Grace's pedigree.

"Well, well, well." Jack's teasing smile didn't quite meet his eyes. "Who's the rake now?"

In the distance, Jimmy and Caleb roared with laughter. For two people who claimed to aggravate each other, they certainly enjoyed each other's company. "Should they be that far from shore? They could be seen."

"Night swims aren't criminal offenses." Jack's head tilted as he assessed her. "Is that why you're not swimming? You're worried?"

Though he said it with unusual softness, Emmy bristled. "I'm on this rock because I don't have swim clothes."

"So transform something."

As if she'd ever owned a bathing suit or knew how they were made. "It's too cold."

"You're dripping in sweat." He gripped her ankle. "You leave me no choice."

Emmy stilled, heat spreading from that point of contact. "Don't you dare."

"Jimmy said you used to love jumping off the pier." He lifted a single brow in challenge. "And I've seen you swim in far colder water."

How he loved to pretend he knew her. She tried to kick at his hand.

"I don't need to prove anything to you."

That reckless smile only grew as he tightened his grip on her ankle.

"Jack Fontaine," she hissed, searching the smooth rock for something to hold, "I swear to God, I'll transform you into a gnat and squash you."

"I don't think you will." Lightning quick, he grabbed her by the waist and tossed her.

For a moment, Emmy was suspended in the air, hardly able to register that he had, in fact, thrown her. And then she plunged into the river, water bubbling past her ears, her eyes, shockingly cool. With a swipe of her hands, she transformed her water-logged gown to a simple slip and kicked her way to the surface.

Jack was laughing as she reappeared, which would not do, so she dunked him until that smirk sank into the water. He had her by the waist a moment later, and though she swatted at his arms, he tossed her again.

She'd never heard this unguarded laugh of his. And she rather liked it, which only infuriated her further, so she grabbed his leg, yanking him until the river swallowed the sound. But he kicked free and grabbed her, dragging them both to the surface.

"Do you yield?" He pinned her against the boulder, grinning victoriously.

She transformed her pointer finger into a knife and pressed it to his neck. "Do *you* yield?"

"Completely." He uttered it as if he'd won, though they were at an impasse: her knife on his neck, her back against the rock. His knees dug into her thighs. His face so close, she could count the water droplets on his lashes. The flecks of silver in his eyes, brighter than she'd ever seen them.

So close, those wicked lips were barely a few inches away.

Oh. She looked away from his mouth, but water cascaded from his wet hair, making it darker, more like Jack's true shade. Her gaze dipped to his bare chest, the *V* of lean muscle carved from his hips disappearing beneath the water. She'd never been pressed against a man like this, never felt the searing heat of someone through wet cotton.

"There's a dirt path in the thicket, only accessible by the river." His voice was husky, his gray eyes unyielding. "If someone came for us from the cliffs, we'd take that path south. And if they came from the river, we'd follow the one you and Caleb took, all the way to the stables, where we'd mount my fastest horse. And if they surrounded us, I'd borrow the relic"—he pressed a hand over her rapidly beating heart, over the coin—"And I'd burn them. I'd burn the whole fucking Society before I'd let them take you again."

This was Jack, who'd laughed at her in Grimsbane. Who'd sent her into an ambush at Clara's shop. Who had freed her from prison only because he needed her conjury. This was Jack, yet Emmy's limbs were liquid now, molding themselves against him. He knew what Grimsbane was like. How minutes morphed to decades, and grief fermented to something lethal. He knew, and yet he'd refused to leave Grimsbane without her, because he was willing to suffer to have what he needed for his revenge.

And he needed *her*. That was why he was protecting her, yet her naive, lonely heart was leaning into his touch. It was maddening, how much she wanted to believe he'd have her back. But she could not put that sort of trust in anyone again.

She also, unfortunately, could not bring herself to swim away.

With a surprisingly gentle touch, Jack pushed a lock of wet hair off her forehead. "I'll threaten violence every day if you'll look at me like that."

"Like what?"

"Like I don't ruin everything I touch." His gaze dropped to her lips, dangerously close. He was a match, and she was tinder, recklessly waiting to burn.

His hand was still pressed to her heart, and she trembled beneath it. He had to feel how quickly her heart was racing.

"You're shivering." Frowning, he turned away, the cool river replacing the heat of him. "C'mon."

A rush of disappointment broke the spell.

It was a blessing, really. Rose had drawn him with countless girls. If Emmy had succumbed to his charm, he'd have teased her relentlessly about it. Perhaps she should make his princely face a bit grotesque to prevent herself from losing focus again.

Focus. That was what she needed. Not distracting touches.

As they pulled themselves onto the boulder, Emmy forced herself to summon the same nonchalance as Jack, which would have been far easier if he'd put on a damn shirt.

Borrowing the relic, he lit a small bonfire, his silver-black flames practically glittering in the night. Emmy leaned closer to the heat, doing her best to pretend being near him had no effect on her at all. "We don't have much time left."

"Eight days down; twenty remaining." His gaze flitted over her wet slip before he averted his eyes. "But we've earned their trust. And we still have three more balls, including the masquerade Mrs. Stratton convinced you to throw here."

So everyone could gawk at Mistfield. But it was a perfect opportunity for Jimmy to showcase his work, so Emmy had agreed. "There's also that fundraiser Grace is throwing." Just thinking of Grace playing the philanthropic hostess made Emmy irrationally angry.

"And a flurry of smaller events, assuming we finally get invited to some." In the silvery shadows of his flames, his face was grim. "Our remaining targets won't be easy."

Like the chancellor. "Can a triumvirate member be removed from power?"

"If the Society calls his leadership into question, they can hold a vote to remove him, yes." He shrugged. "It rarely happens, though. Only another triumvirate member can call for such a vote, and they tend to protect each other."

"I told you they'd be plotting," Caleb sighed as he splashed over to the boulder, hoisting himself atop it. Jimmy followed, spraying Emmy with water as he shook out his hair, grinning.

But all traces of Jack's playfulness were gone now. "We need to start a war," he declared. "Between the chancellor and the keeper. Windsor's even-keeled, but he can't possibly like having two Strattons on the triumvirate."

How easily he returned to their scheming, as if that moment in the river hadn't rattled him in the slightest. Meanwhile, Emmy could still feel every place they'd touched.

"Mrs. Stratton said something at the Enchanted Pursuit." Her voice was still too breathy for her liking, but she continued. "She blamed Keeper Windsor for not letting her husband do more about the weakening conjury. Maybe we can use that?"

"But Clara was responsible for the weakened conjury," Jimmy pointed out. "It shouldn't be a problem anymore."

Emmy stared at the black flames. The pieces were there; she could practically see them snapping together, if only she could figure out *how*. "We only need the chancellor to *think* Windsor is going after him. Then he'll get aggressive, like Jack said."

"And we'll catch him doing something heinous." Jack's gaze cut to Caleb. "You earned points with him tonight. Do you think you can convince him that Keeper Windsor is talking to Society members, seeing who else is against having two Strattons on the triumvirate?"

"It's hard to imagine the chancellor listening to me again. But I can try."

"Make him listen," Jack insisted. "Better yet, we should start rumors about the Strattons attempting to rule over the Society alone. Let Windsor think Stratton is coming after him, so he can have the

Society all to himself. And let Stratton think Windsor is coming after him, for stacking the triumvirate with Strattons."

"It could work," Caleb mused. "He'll have more need of a telepath if he's threatened."

"I can try and befriend their staff to gather secrets," Jimmy offered. "As a 'building design specialist,' no one knows where I stand in the social hierarchy, which works in our favor."

"Not a bad idea." Jack reached into the fire—Fontaine flames don't burn those who wielded them, Emmy had to remind herself—and pulled out a blackened stick to scratch four words onto the rock.

Pride. Power. Greed. Vanity.

"Pride was Clara's weakness. And pride brought her down." He crossed out the word. "If the chancellor believes someone's trying to take his power and influence, it just might be his downfall. Which leaves Oliver and Grace."

Greed and vanity. "What if we get Oliver in trouble first?" Emmy asked. "Caleb can tell the chancellor that Keeper Windsor framed his son."

Caleb held up a finger. "One problem: Oliver quit gambling."

"We can't tempt him?" Emmy had seen enough gamblers back home to know it wasn't so easy to quit. "We keep waiting for him to invite Nathaniel to a card game, but maybe Nathaniel should invite him. There must be one he can't refuse."

"I nearly forgot." Jack grinned at Caleb. "The Bronze Door."

Caleb groaned, and Jimmy raised his brows. "What the hell is the Bronze Door?"

"It's a secret gambling hall for New York's wealthiest," Caleb explained. "Rumor has it that fifty grand changes hands there every night. But another problem, Fontaine: Didn't you and Stratton get banned for life?"

"*Jack's* banned. Not Nathaniel." A taunting smile lit Jack's face. "But if Nathaniel bribes the manager to let Ollie back in, he won't be able to resist. And when he cheats—"

"If," Caleb interrupted. "The Bronze Door is full of politicians and other influential ordinaries. He'd have to be a fool to cheat there."

"He'll cheat." Jack reached into his pocket and thrust something in front of Caleb. The enchanted playing card. "With conjury. And we'll make sure he's caught."

"Would that be reason enough to be voted off the triumvirate?" Emmy asked.

"Using conjury in front of ordinaries? Powerful ordinaries?" Jack leaned against the rock. "They'd throw him in Grimsbane."

His excitement was infectious, but Emmy couldn't trust their plans. Not yet.

"We still have Grace." Emmy pointed to the final word. *Vanity.* "I can't just get under her skin for three weeks. We need something that will ruin her."

"I'm sure she has plenty of secrets," Jack mused. "If only we had an invisible maid on our side, so we could learn what they are."

"Not a chance." As much as Emmy liked Mary, she didn't want her to do their bidding.

"Loath as I am to involve another person," Caleb said, "I've listened to Mary's thoughts. She despises Grace. I'm sure she'd be glad to help."

"C'mon, Ems. The poor girl probably thinks you hate her, with how few hours she works." Jimmy nudged Emmy. "You don't have to tell her everything. Just see if she learned anything useful in the time she worked for Grace."

Ask Grace's former maid about Grace. If Emmy'd had any better ideas, she would have refused. "Fine. I'll at least broach the subject."

"Then it's settled." Jack's glittering eyes found hers, and despite herself, she flushed from head to toe. "Let's have some fun and ruin three more lives."

TWENTY

EMMY HAD INTENDED TO ASK Mary about Grace the very next day, she truly had. Twice, she'd nearly broached the subject while Mary was doing her hair, a daily ritual that wrought bitter memories of Grace doing the same for her, back home. As Mary had chatted amiably about Clara Claremont's demise—which, in her opinion, was well deserved—Jimmy had burst into the room to announce that Winnie had visitors.

With Clara out of the picture, Winnie Fairchild was no longer a social pariah.

For days, Emmy served tea and cake to young ladies who hadn't spoken a word to her in Clara's presence. Nathaniel also had a few guests: charmed folks eager to make relics from the remains of their loved ones, but who needed them forged in Fontaine flames. Keen as Emmy was to witness the process herself, Jimmy needed her help giving their guests tours of Mistfield. By the Zermatts' garden party at the end of the week, Jimmy, as Zhao Rui, had scheduled his first consultation, and Emmy was surrounded by new friends.

Grace, however, had missed the party entirely. She'd caught a cold, according to her aunt.

After days of little progress aside from afternoon teas, a much-needed invitation arrived: a picnic at the Strattons'. With time quickly running out, it was their best chance for Jimmy to try to gather gossip from the Strattons' staff, Caleb to whisper in the chancellor's ear, and Jack, who'd snuck off to the city to bribe the Bronze Door's manager, to tempt Oliver with an invitation.

But there was still Grace. The week had slipped away far too quickly, and they still hadn't uncovered any of her secrets. With only two weeks remaining, it was time to ask her former maid about her.

As Emmy waited for Mary to arrive, she dressed herself in the only layers she could handle alone: a thin chemise, soft underdress, voluminous petticoats, a pocketed slip, even the cornflower-blue skirt of the day gown she'd selected for the picnic. With time to kill, she curled up on the window bench with the Fontaine grimoire.

It was a fascinating text, with detailed accounts about generations of conjury in the Fontaine family. The bulk of it referred to the Fontaine flames, though there were handwritten accounts of the various other gifts of Fontaines, varied by marriage and birth. The earliest pages, unfortunately, were in French. But her eyes caught on a word that required no translation.

Relique.

Emmy's breath caught. She turned the page, but the text was English again, and was discussing methods for tapping into the brume. Flipping back to the French text, she held the binding to the light streaming through her window.

A few pages were torn out. No—not torn, but cut. By scissors.

"That's the Fontaine grimoire, yes?"

With a jump, Emmy nearly dropped the tome as Mary whisked into the room, closing the door behind her. "You've seen it before?"

"Miss Montgomery borrowed it for a while." Mary stopped to select a corset from Emmy's closet. "Excited? A private picnic with the Strattons is a coveted invitation."

Grace had read the Fontaine grimoire. This very book. Had she cut out the pages about relics before she'd returned it?

As she began to lace the corset, Mary met Emmy's gaze in the mirror. "What is it, miss?"

Now was the perfect time to probe about Grace. Especially if she'd managed to make a relic just like Rose's. Still, Emmy couldn't bring herself to put Mary in that position. Instead, she busied herself with her jewelry box, perusing to find appropriate adornments for a picnic. "You truly don't mind coming with me today?"

"I'm glad to go. After all, the Strattons may wish to place bets while you're there." Mischief danced in her eyes as they met Emmy's in the mirror.

Emmy couldn't help but smile, which was precisely the problem. She *liked* Mary. The maid's easy banter reminded her of all the laughs she and Grace had shared while doing their school exercises or sewing for Mrs. Feinstein. She missed it. But befriending anyone, especially during this perilous pursuit, was a risk Emmy could not afford to take.

Fastening a pearl drop earring onto her lobe, Emmy asked, as casually as she dared, "Did you go to the Strattons' often with Miss Montgomery?"

She half expected Mary to scold her for prying, but Mary only tugged on the laces, the corset squeezing tighter. "Not at all. Miss Montgomery would have loved a private picnic."

But the Strattons would not invite Grace because the Strattons did not consider a protégé worthy of their son. Earrings in place, Emmy slid a gold bangle carved with tiny leaves onto her wrist. "Did she ever speak to you about Oliver?"

Mary sighed. "Sometimes, she confided in me as if we were sisters. And sometimes, she snapped at me if I so much as asked about her day." She paused, motioning for Emmy to stand so she could further wrangle her laces. "Are *you* interested in Commander Stratton, miss?"

A laugh burst from Emmy before she could help it.

"Oh, thank goodness." Mary giggled along with Emmy, though her cheeks were turning pink. "I was worried because you're so nice, and you're new to the Society, so I didn't know if you were aware that Oliver Stratton is, well—"

"Terrible." The word slipped from Emmy's mouth, entirely uninhibited.

"So you see for yourself." She gave the laces another tug. "But then why accept this invitation? It encourages him to call on you."

"Because I want to ruin him."

Mary's nimble fingers stilled on Emmy's laces.

No, Emmy did *not* just say that. "What I meant to say is, I pay attention to him because—" She racked her brain for an excuse. *Because the Strattons are a good ally in the Society. Because Mrs. Stratton is a dear friend.* "Because it hurts Grace."

Mary's mouth fell open, though she quickly shut it.

"I don't know why I said that." Emmy jumped to her feet. This was not how she was supposed to ask for Mary's help. She glanced at the maid in the mirror, but—Emmy's own eyes were a little too bright, were they not? And her skin was flushed, despite the chill in the air.

Something was terribly wrong with her. "Please get Jack."

"Jack?"

Emmy had said *Nathaniel*. In her head, she'd *said* Nathaniel. "Nathaniel," she tried to say again, but instead she rasped, "Jack."

All the color drained from Mary's face. "Jack . . . Fontaine?"

Jack's true name, from Mary's lips. A bona fide nightmare. Next the guards would burst through her door and drag her back to hell, or the chancellor would shoot Papa all over again. Emmy pinched her ice-cold cheeks, trying to wake—

Her frigid skin. That chill. How hadn't she recognized that chill?

Mary said something, but Emmy couldn't hear it, not as she searched herself in the mirror for whatever Grace had enchanted with her goddamn bridging conjury. She raked her fingers over her stranger's face, but her reflection morphed, and Emmy was no longer Winnie, but Emmy, hollow and pale from years without sunshine.

Emmy stared at her true reflection. Plain. Weak. Utterly inconsequential.

Someone gasped. Mary.

She was backing away as if Emmy were a ghost, hands twisting over each other—

Mary disappeared.

"No!" Emmy groped the air for the invisible girl who *knew her true identity*. She swung her arms but grabbed nothing but air. Swung again, but Mary remained hidden.

Jack. She had to get Jack. With both palms pressed to the wall, Emmy transformed the plaster into a gaping hole and threw herself through it. Her skirts caught on the edges, and she tripped into Jack's room, her skin tingling with the otherworldliness of Grace's bridging conjury.

Grace had gotten into her room.

Grace had tampered with her things.

Jack and Jimmy stood near the door, their mouths falling open at the sight of Emmy's true face—and her half-laced corset.

"Mary knows everything." Emmy could hardly get the words out fast enough. "She knows everything, and she disappeared, and I can't find what Grace bridged, but it's *on* me."

Her dress. All those goddamn layers. She could not get the corset off quickly enough, not when Mary had pulled the laces so viciously, but she yanked and yanked—

"Li, you find Mary," barked Jack. "And Vallillo, tell me what the hell to do."

"Get me out of this!" Emmy tore at the corset, flailing for those cursed laces. "Grace was in my room. In *Mistfield*." That conniving little backstabber must have known they were to dine at the Strattons' today, and she sought to ruin Winnie in front of them by making her blurt out all her secrets.

Maybe she'd snuck inside, using invisibility conjury she'd bridged from Mary.

Maybe she'd paid off Mary to do it herself.

Maybe Mary was *still* working for her, reporting Emmy's every move, and now Grace would know the truth about Emmy being Winnie. And they'd lock her in Grimsbane again.

"Christ, you're freezing." Jack helped her balance as she stepped out of her skirt, his eyes wild as she pulled off her petticoats. "Stay still so I can find it."

She hissed as Jack ran his palms over her back, the heat of him searing against the chill. "Your hands are on fire."

"Fontaine conjury. Makes the body warmer." He tore at her corset, ripping the laces apart. Once it had fallen to the ground, he asked, his voice hoarse, "Still feel it?"

"Yes." She shivered in her chemise, searching herself for something extra frigid. But Jack's hands were so warm. So surprisingly gentle as they skated across her skin.

A small noise escaped her lips.

"Does it hurt?" he rasped, gray eyes frantic.

No, she tried to say, but she leaned into his warmth, letting her head fall against his searing shoulder.

"Stop, Emmy." He stilled, every muscle in his back going rigid as her hands trailed down it. "You need to stop moving."

"Quit barking orders at me." Emmy tried to push away from him, but her lips were so close to the soft skin between his neck and shoulder, exposed by his half-buttoned shirt. Before she could stop herself, she pressed her mouth to it.

His entire body tensed. "What—what are you doing?"

She hadn't the faintest idea, but she could not bring herself to stop, not when his skin was an inferno. As if possessed, she let her teeth graze his neck.

"Emmy." His rough voice vibrated through his bare chest, and he shivered as Emmy trailed her fingers down the taut muscles. "For all that is holy—*stay still.*"

"You're the most infuriating person." She hated how he was aflame while she was freezing, hated how handsome she'd made him, hated how, even now, she could not stop trying to picture his true face. So she transformed him back to Jack, which was an even bigger mistake, because she was absolutely enraged by the cut of his jaw, the angelic lashes that hid his tortured expression. His teeth wrestled with his bottom lip, and damn it, those *were* his true lips all along. She ran her fingers through his dark hair, and he *finally* ceased talking, letting out a groan—

"The bracelet!" Mary burst into Jack's room with Jimmy, skidding to a halt.

Grabbing her hand, Jack yanked off her bangle, the hard metal catching her knuckle.

It fell to the ground, and the cold ceased.

Emmy glanced down at herself. At the others.

Jimmy's mouth was agape.

Mary, with tear-stained cheeks, was staring at Emmy as if she were a ghost.

Jack—not Nathaniel, but *Jack*—was slowly backing away, as if Emmy might launch herself on him at any moment.

And Emmy stood amid a pile of her discarded clothes, her flushed face entirely her own.

TWENTY-ONE

AS THE CARRIAGE CAREENED TOWARD Pinnacle Bluffs, the Strattons' summer estate, Emmy was careful not to jostle against Jack, who sat as far from her as one might sit from a leper. And of course he did; she'd *mauled* him.

From the opposite bench, Caleb studied the two of them warily. "Jimmy will keep Mary in Emmy's room until we return. In the meantime, we need to focus on the Strattons."

The Strattons, who'd be scrutinizing Emmy's every move as a potential match for Oliver. All the while, she'd be trying *not* to think about how Mary knew her and Jack's identities, and how Jimmy was their only hope to keep Mary contained. Jimmy, who'd trust water if it swore it wasn't wet.

A scream bloomed in Emmy's chest, but she had no choice but to swallow it. "Any picnic etiquette I should know?"

"Let the attendants fill your plate. And, as usual, take only small bites." Caleb stilled, squinting at Jack. "Are those *teeth marks?*"

If only Emmy could have jumped out of the carriage.

"Vallillo bit me." His teasing gaze burned into her as he adjusted his collar to hide the blemish. "I tried to stop her, but she was rather insistent."

"The bracelet *made* me do it." Emmy whirled to glare at him. What she wouldn't give to start today all over. But her mistakes were branded on her brain. Mary's horrified expression. Jack frantically trying to run away from her . . . advances.

Emmy was going to make Grace pay.

"What sort of conjury do you think Grace bridged?" Caleb asked. "Seen it before?"

"No, but the Society keeps records of every gift." Jack fanned himself with the brim of his top hat. "We're lucky you discovered it while we were still at home."

"Lucky?" Emmy spat. "She was able to enter Mistfield. To breech my *bedroom*."

The hour that had passed had done nothing to quell Emmy's horror. They knew Grace had objects bridged with Mary's invisibility, and yet they'd let their guard down. Who knew what other enchanted items she might have left behind?

"Grace had the Fontaine grimoire while you were in Grimsbane," Emmy bit out, still unable to meet Jack's eye. "I think she cut out the pages Rose used to make the relic. We need to consider that she might have made her own."

"Impossible." Jack waved a dismissive hand. "She would have needed my flames."

"And the sternum of someone who possessed amplifying conjury." Caleb shrugged. "Rose was certain she'd found the only one. And she didn't simply follow the steps in the grimoire; she had to experiment."

Jack was watching her now, but she couldn't meet his eye. "When Grace held Rose's relic, she stole my conjury without needing to bridge it to an object. If she could do that now, she'd have used Caleb's telepathy against us, and we'd be dead. Or worse: in Grimsbane."

But Emmy couldn't imagine Grace simply giving up on power that vast. "You shouldn't underestimate her."

The muscles in Jack's jaw twitched. "Can't you just trust me for once?"

"She was in *Mistfield*. In my *room*." Emmy would never let her guard down again.

"It could have been worse. If you hadn't caught it in time, you could have bitten Oliver instead."

"How, exactly, is that worse?"

His nostrils flared. "Then be my guest."

"Perhaps I will."

"Oh, for Christ's sake." Caleb rubbed his temples. "I should be paid for this."

The carriage slowed, filling Emmy with dread. The Strattons' estate was the last place she wanted to be right now.

"Time to focus." Still scowling, Jack rubbed his hands together. "I'll find a way to mention my connection at the Bronze Door to Oliver. Caleb, you stay glued to the chancellor."

Caleb smoothed his lapels as the carriage stopped. "Anything else?"

"Be ready for the chancellor to prattle on about the virility of his horses." Jack pitched his voice like Chancellor Stratton's. "'Gunner here sired six males in as many weeks.'"

"That bad?"

Jack's gaze slid out the window. "Worse."

Chancellor Stratton smacked the rear end of a frighteningly large horse. "Gunner sired six males in as many weeks. Six! Can you believe it?"

Emmy did not trust herself to look at Jack or Caleb, so she kept her gaze fixed on the midnight-black stallion.

"Six!" Jack exclaimed in his Nathaniel accent. "If only it were that easy for the charmed to produce heirs."

"Well, if you boys wouldn't wait so long to marry, there wouldn't be such a terrible dearth of charmed offspring." The chancellor gave Oliver a pointed look.

As they moved to the next horse, Jack attempted to fall into step beside Oliver, who regarded him with his usual disdain.

Emmy joined Mrs. Stratton at the back of the party as the chancellor continued his tour of the stables, which were bigger than most homes and smelled more like roses than manure.

"You'll never believe who called on me this morning," Mrs. Stratton whispered as her husband extolled the virtues of yet another virile horse. "Mrs. Claremont."

Emmy felt as if her tea gown had ignited with flames from hell. "What did you say to her?"

"As if I accepted the visit! After what her daughter put us all through, she's lucky I didn't have the dogs run her off the premises." She dabbed a bead of sweat with her handkerchief, all the while smiling at whatever the chancellor was saying. "Our social standings are rather like stock portfolios: one bad investment, and your overall value plummets."

"What about Miss Montgomery?" Emmy whispered. "She and Clara were close."

"Ah, but Miss Montgomery slithered away just in time." With a careful glance at the men, she lowered her voice. "Forgive my candidness, dear, but I do not care for the girl."

With considerable effort, Emmy managed not to look smug. "Because of Oliver?"

"Young men are no better than these animals before they're properly matched. Just look at the late Mr. Montgomery. Devilishly handsome, but I knew he'd never settle down, even if it meant the end of an old charmed bloodline." She beamed at her husband before dropping her voice. "Oliver knows he cannot marry the illegitimate daughter of a rake and a . . . well, a *harlot*, if I'm being frank. To outright refuse the match puts us in a rather precarious situation, as her uncle is on the triumvirate. But if Oliver had another prospect . . ."

Even without Mrs. Stratton's knowing smile, Emmy would have understood. Before Winnie Fairchild, Oliver had paid attention to but one Society girl, one who did not meet his parents' snobbish standards. And now Winnie needed to convince them that she was up for the job. A high bar, given that Winnie was actually a tenement-raised immigrant's daughter who'd spent the last two years pissing in a bucket.

A picnic waited in the apple orchard, the shade a refuge from the blistering June sun. With the Hudson glistening in the distance, it would have been a lovely afternoon, had it not been for the company—and for the crisis waiting back home.

Mary knew their true identities. If she'd managed to slip past Jimmy, she might have already blurted the truth to someone.

"My grandfather, Arthur Stratton, planted this orchard." The chancellor shooed away his attendant's offer of a fan. "He was killed in the war, and I was elected to take his place as the Society's chancellor. The youngest in Society history: hardly sixteen and not even wed."

Mrs. Stratton patted his hand. "You had your sights on me, dear."

"Your pedigree was the only one that held a candle to mine. And," he added with a smug grin, "you had wide hips, perfect for child-bearing. I knew you'd produce an heir for me."

His gaze slid down Emmy's dress to her own hips, and it took everything she had not to squirm. "How old are you?" he asked abruptly. "Seventeen?"

Emmy swallowed her bitter lemonade. "Eighteen, sir."

"In my time, all the best girls were wed by seventeen. Before their fertility declined."

"Jesus Christ," Oliver muttered. "Must we discuss fertility all day?"

"There are far more important things that should be on my mind," the chancellor snapped, "such as the safety of every charmed soul in New York, or how a teenage dressmaker siphoned the brume from underneath our noses for *years*. But instead, I must contemplate your unfulfilled responsibilities to our family."

Oliver rolled his eyes. "Here we go."

"The longer you wait, the further you risk the Stratton line ending with *you*." He spat the last word with such disdain, even Caleb winced. As if sensing it, the chancellor turned to him. "Is it not your father's desire that your sister find a suitable spouse this summer?"

"Ah, well, of course—"

Oliver rose from the table. "I'll excuse myself."

"But we haven't even had dessert!" Mrs. Stratton called. "The chef made your favorite!"

"Let him go, Trudy." The chancellor tossed his napkin onto the wrought iron table. "Mr. Fairchild, might I have your assistance with a matter indoors? It won't take long."

He was asking Caleb for help. Emmy's and Jack's eyes met, but she quickly looked away.

Caleb rose from his seat. "Certainly."

As they departed, Mrs. Stratton smiled as if her husband hadn't just examined Emmy like one of his breeding horses and her son hadn't stormed off. "Shall we visit my rose garden?"

"I hear it's the best in Avalon-on-Hudson." Jack jumped to help Mrs. Stratton with her chair. He'd already abandoned his pale gray suit jacket, instead wearing only his vest and shirt, the sleeves of which were pushed to his forearms. The same arms that had pinned her in the river, that had desperately tried to push her away after she'd *bitten* him—

"Winnie, darling?"

Emmy turned to hide her blushing cheeks. "I, ah, thought I'd take a view of the water."

"We can do both," Mrs. Stratton offered.

"No need. I'll make my way to the roses afterward."

Mrs. Stratton looked as though she was about to protest, but something caught her eye, and she flashed Emmy a dazzling smile. "Take your time, dear."

Just like that, Emmy was left to explore the manicured property alone.

She hadn't made a fool of herself nibbling tea sandwiches while ravenous, which was a victory of sorts. And the chancellor was considering Emmy to bear his grandchildren, which alone would be enough to drive Grace mad, should she hear of it. But Jack was nowhere near luring Oliver to the Bronze Door. And of course, Mary might be screaming their names to anyone who'd listen.

There were no whimsical woodland trails down to the Hudson like there were at Mistfield, nothing standing between Emmy and the glistening river, save a five-minute walk across the sharply cut grass. A gentle breeze greeted her at the edge of the cliff, carrying a hint of rain. Closing her eyes, Emmy savored the sun burning into her skin, the coolness of Rose's relic against her chest, the babbling of the river far below. Sunshine had a quiet aroma, one that lingered on bare skin. She'd forgotten that when she was in Grimsbane.

Could Mary still be loyal to Grace? And if she was capable of such a betrayal, would Emmy even notice the signs?

It was maddening, never being able to trust a soul. But anyone could turn on her. Even sweet maids. Even old friends. Even if Emmy had never, ever imagined they could.

"My father, if you haven't noticed, has determined we should marry."

Oliver was strolling along the bluffs, taking swigs from a whiskey bottle. With his vest unbuttoned and his hair falling over his forehead, it was easy to envision him and Jack as friends, slipping out of Society events together to get in all sorts of trouble.

"I'm surprised he didn't stick his head between my legs to examine me more closely," Emmy replied evenly.

Whiskey sprayed from Oliver's lips as he choked on a laugh. Wiping his mouth on his sleeve, he appraised her. "Winnie Fairchild has a sense of humor. I hadn't the faintest idea."

Smiling to herself, Emmy turned back to the river, but there was something unsettling about standing on a cliff with Oliver Stratton.

He came to a stop beside her. "Better not let my father hear your smart mouth."

"Afraid I'd ruin his good opinion of me?"

"Unfortunately, he'd like your fighting spirit." Oliver swatted a fly off her puffed sleeve. "He'd say it would make for strong sons, though he'd insist your husband beat it out of you."

Emmy gave him a long, hard look. She was in no mood for his insolence.

But he only leaned closer. "When you look at me with such fire in your eyes, I truly cannot tell if you're thinking of murdering me or dragging me to bed."

Her eyes flashed, but his gaze fell to her lips.

His next ploy will be to get you alone, Jack had said. Mrs. Stratton, curse her, must have seen her son when she abruptly changed her mind about Winnie walking to the cliffs.

"What a gentleman," Emmy replied evenly, though her heart had begun to race.

"I think we both know I'm no gentleman." His fingers trailed her arm before resting on her waist. "Which is why you came out here all alone, in the hope that I'd follow."

"You think rather highly of yourself, to assume I thought of you at all."

He gave her waist a gentle tug, turning her toward him. How she longed to walk away, leaving him staring at the cliffs, but this was a chance to kiss the man Grace loved. To take something from the girl who'd taken *everything* from Emmy.

Emmy lifted her gaze to Oliver's, which was all the invitation he needed.

He lowered his mouth to hers, and Emmy froze. His lips were whiskey spiced, and large enough to nearly swallow hers. A rather amusing thought, but Emmy pushed it from her mind. She needed to focus. Though she hadn't the faintest idea what she was doing, she needed to give him quite the kiss, one that could vie with Grace's. No, she had to kiss *better* than Grace.

Oliver was used to Grace, who was brash and confident. So Emmy kissed him as if she were fearless, too. As if she *wanted* him. Instead of keeping her mouth still, she made her lips mirror his, meeting and parting. His tongue darted into her mouth, and she gasped with surprise. A rumble rose from deep within his chest, and Emmy could not help but feel as if she'd won.

Oliver's lips moved over her warmed skin, trailing kisses across her cheek, her jaw, her neck. She gasped at the burst of sensation, and Oliver pressed harder against the vulnerability of her throat, as if he could rip it out with his teeth. Like she'd done to Jack, his skin so warm, so familiar and new. But Oliver wrought a frenzy of sensations, too much—

Emmy pushed him away. The humid breeze was mercifully cool against her hot cheeks, but it tickled the wet spot on her neck, which made her blush even more.

"Winnie Fairchild," Oliver finally said, his voice thick. "You are full of surprises."

Emmy racked her mind for some sort of clever comeback but—Movement. Behind him.

Emmy put as much distance as she could between them, but it was only Jack. Or, rather, Nathaniel.

"I hope I'm not interrupting anything." There was steel in his gaze as he approached.

"Not at all," Oliver said. "We were just . . ."

"Admiring the view," Emmy supplied, her face burning worse than any sunburn.

"Exactly." Oliver smirked at Jack. "*Such* a lovely view."

Jack studied her for a heartbeat. Then another. What was he doing?

"Well, I'm heading to the city for the evening." He clapped Oliver on the shoulder roughly. "Why don't you join me, Stratton?"

Oliver looked as if Jack had offered him rotting food. "If I abandoned Miss Fairchild at my own home, my mother would have my head."

"Oh, I'm sure Winnie can make up some excuse for your mother. Isn't that right, Winnie dear?" Jack kept his gaze fixed on Oliver. "We are rather good at keeping secrets, as long as they're for our friends."

Jack might as well have said *I saw you. And if you don't play nice with me, I'll tell.*

Oliver's eyes narrowed. He didn't give a damn about Winnie's reputation, but perhaps he did not wish to deal with a scandal, either. Or, more likely, he didn't want Grace to hear of it.

"I suppose a night in the city wouldn't hurt," he finally said.

"Excellent. Let's take your carriage to the train. My cousins will need mine to get home."

Speechless, Emmy watched them cross the lawn together. She had to hand it to Jack; he'd thought quickly on his feet, strong-arming Oliver into leaving with him. Knowing him, he'd probably waited until their kiss was done before he'd made his presence known.

With any luck, they'd be playing cards at the Bronze Door tonight.

Alone on the cliffs, Emmy was hit with a wave of nausea.

Oliver Stratton had stolen her magic. He'd conspired with Grace to ruin her life.

And the taste of him lingered on her lips.

Twenty-Two

"YOU'RE QUIET," CALEB SAID ON the carriage ride back to Mistfield. "Dreading facing Mary?"

Ugh. Mary. Emmy's head pounded from too many hours in the sun, and she could not wipe away the lingering taste of Oliver's mouth. "You assume Jimmy hasn't let her go."

"He wouldn't." Seeing Emmy's look, he sighed. "Okay, fine. He wouldn't *mean* to."

They would know soon enough. "What did the chancellor want with you?"

"To interrogate his staff." Closing his eyes, he pinched the bridge of his nose. "He gathered them and accused someone of stealing. I told him the guilty party."

So the chancellor was beginning to make use of Caleb's magic. "Was he pleased?"

"Exceedingly."

"Then why do you look miserable?"

"Because the guilty party was a scullery maid, the lowest paid of all the kitchen staff, and she was taking stale food the cook had told her to toss. Now she has no income." He opened a tired eye. "And thanks to your constant badgering about the inequities of the lower class, I cannot stop wondering if her family will have enough to eat. I can't even walk through Mistfield without contemplating the value of the Fontaines' things, wondering how many mouths a goddamn gold candlestick might feed."

Emmy couldn't hide her smile. "You sound like a labor rights activist."

"I know," he moaned, burying his head in his palms. "It's disgusting."

She patted his arm. "If you find out her address, we can give her money."

"We could send Mary, now that she knows the truth." He lifted his gaze. "I'll read her mind, but one way or the other, we're going to have to let her out of that room."

Emmy nearly quipped that they could kill her, but Caleb had only recently stopped looking at her like she was feral. "Then let's hope you like what you hear."

Although he looked as though he might press the issue, he fell silent for the rest of the short ride home. It was not until they climbed the grand staircase and were nearly at Emmy's door that he spoke again. "Just let me do the talking, okay?"

He was trying to protect Mary, mistaking Emmy's carefulness for cruelty. But she only nodded and, with her heart in her throat, opened her bedroom door.

To a raucous party.

Mary was clapping and singing while Jimmy was dancing on Emmy's bed. It was a tune the organ grinders had played on their accordions back home, filling the streets with boisterous song all summer long.

"Are you *drunk?*" The disbelief in Caleb's voice echoed Emmy's own.

With a gasp, Mary straightened.

Jimmy stopped dancing, too, though he still grinned like a proud fool. "You were gone six hours. We had to entertain ourselves somehow."

"I don't drink," Mary said hastily. "Oh! But we figured out what the bracelet does!" Before Emmy could protest, Mary picked it off Emmy's vanity and tossed it to her.

Emmy dodged out of the cursed thing's way just in time.

"It's some sort of truth conjury," Jimmy explained. "You can't fib while you're holding it."

Emmy stared at the deceptively pretty bangle at her feet. It hadn't just made her say things; it had made her *do* things.

Her lips. Jack's throat. That traitorous prickling heat crept back up her neck.

Plucking it from the rug, Caleb examined it. "I'll try."

"Call yourself Paxton Fairchild," Jimmy said.

"My name is Caleb Alton. Oh!" He gaped at the bracelet.

"We think it lowers your inhibitions," Mary explained. "It makes the truth come out."

Lowered inhibitions—that was a relief, because it made *sense*. Drunk people had lowered inhibitions. And drunk people threw themselves at other people like cats in heat.

Jimmy nodded toward Caleb. "Try to tell another lie."

"I'm twenty-one years old. Chocolate cream pie is my favorite food." He stared at the bracelet. "My God, I can't lie."

"Do you really hate me?"

"Not at all. In fact, I think you're one of the kindest, most handsome—" Caleb dropped the bracelet and backed away, his face as bright red as his hair.

Well, *that* was interesting. Jimmy stared at Caleb as if he, too, could not believe his ears.

Careful to use a handkerchief, Emmy plucked the bangle off the floor. "The conjury will wear off if we keep using it."

And they needed it strong. Grace might have been full of secrets, but she'd just given them a way to make her reveal them.

A slow smile spread across Emmy's cheeks. Grace's recklessness might be their gain.

"I have something to say." Stepping forward, Mary took the truth bracelet from Emmy and slipped it on her wrist. "You might not remember me, but we debuted at the same ball. We didn't speak—you were glued to Miss Montgomery most of the night—but your pa introduced himself to mine, in the back. He was so proud of you, he practically beamed all night."

Emmy felt Jimmy's concerned stare, but she kept her head high, her face unaffected.

"You made gold." Mary's voice was soft, awestruck. "At first, I was envious, but you were smiling at your pa and no one else. It was so sweet—"

"That's enough." Emmy tried to sound stern, but her voice betrayed her.

"I just need to say this once." Mary chewed her bottom lip. "When they shot him—"

Emmy stalked toward the door, but Jimmy, of all people, blocked her path. "Just hear her out," he murmured.

Traitor. But Emmy could not bring herself to push past him.

"I was right there," Mary continued, her expression pained. "Right behind you. The way you tried to get to him . . . the way you fought them, even though the guards had you outnumbered six to one . . . I have prayed for you so many times, without realizing that it was *you*."

All three of them were watching Emmy like splintered glass about to shatter. She could not crack. But she also, at this moment, did not trust herself to breathe.

Of course she remembered Mary from the debutante ball. Her scarlet hair in pinned braids. Her impressive conjury, and the way Grace had dismissed it.

The quiet, shameful satisfaction Emmy had felt when her own applause had been louder.

Mary's gaze fell to the floor, and she fidgeted with her silver ring. "You were the best one of us, by far. *You* deserved the patronage. But Miss Montgomery took it from you. And the Society let her because she's a Montgomery."

With the bracelet, Mary could not lie, but Emmy's gaze cut to Caleb's, just in case.

His brow creased with effort, he gave her a tight nod.

"If you think we can stop them from hurting more people, I'll help." Mary took Emmy's hands in hers. "I'll use my invisibility to spy on her."

Emmy whipped toward Jimmy, ripping her hands from Mary's. "You *told* her?"

"She's on our side, Ems. This is a good thing, isn't it?" He shrugged. "Think how much better our odds are with an invisible spy."

That headache pounded against her skull. Now there were four people who could betray her. Four too many.

"So can I stay?" Mary asked, wide-eyed. "Will you let me help?"

Never had Emmy needed Jack to be here more than she did now, with the three of them staring at her like she might kick a puppy. At least he grasped that revenge was not some sort of social club, but a matter of life and death.

"If you tell a soul"—Emmy kept her voice as sharp as she could manage—"all our lives are at risk. Including yours."

With a squeal, Mary threw her arms around Emmy, too quickly for Emmy to resist. "I won't let you down, miss."

Emmy wanted to believe her, she truly did. And that was precisely the problem.

Letting Mary return home that night felt like signing her own death sentence, but what choice did Emmy have? If Jack were there, he might have had the gall to insist she stay, or at least sent Caleb after her to ensure she didn't run right to the triumvirate. But Caleb and Jimmy had put their collective feet down: *You have to trust her.*

Working with other people was absurdly difficult. She had to bury her better instincts, again and again.

With a new chink in her armor, Emmy woke throughout the night, her ears attuned to any signs of trouble. When she finally managed to sleep, she dreamed of Grace. How she'd slipped Emmy notes during the most boring lectures. How she'd given her and Papa the most thoughtful gifts at Christmas, though she hadn't a penny to her name. How she'd made Emmy's grudges her grudges, slipping rotten tomatoes into the knapsack of a boy who'd teased Emmy about her too-small shoes. She'd been a fierce and fervent friend. Until she hadn't.

Emmy was in that liminal space between dreams when she heard a distant crash.

Her feet were on the floor in an instant, the knife from under her pillow firmly in her hand. She froze, waiting for Jack to burst into her room like he always did, but her wall remained solid. He was still with Oliver, then.

The hushed voices were louder in the hall. Emmy followed them down the darkened stairs.

Another crashing sound, like someone had thrown the pots and pans in the air. Emmy hurried to the kitchen, then skidded to a halt in front of its swinging doors, where the housekeeper stood with a few other staff members, all in their nightclothes, her face tense with concentration as she erected a wall of air.

"Miss Fairchild!" she exclaimed upon seeing Emmy. "I'm terribly sorry for the noise; I was trying to block it, but— Is that a *knife?*"

Emmy glanced at her hand. "I . . . thought it was an intruder."

"It's Mr. Fontaine. He came home and insisted on making himself something to eat. We tried to help, but . . . he's rather stubborn tonight."

"Stubborn!" exclaimed a younger girl, a kitchen maid, perhaps. "He's drunk!"

Emmy's heart sank. "Let's have a look."

At her nod, they opened the kitchen doors.

A footman was extinguishing black flames on a pan over the stove, while two other staff members were attempting to clean what looked like spilled rice and broken eggs. And on the long butcher block sat Jack, a pile of peanuts beside him. "Ah, Winnie. Hungry?"

"What are you doing?"

"After my *lovely* night with Oliver, I had a craving for eggs. But I didn't wish to wake the staff, so I attempted to make them myself." Glancing around at the mess, he flashed her a crooked grin. "I ran into some hurdles. Peanut?"

His eyes were glassy and bloodshot, his dress shirt untucked and half unbuttoned, and the neat hair she'd conjured for him stood in every direction. Even more unsettling, there was a guardedness to his gaze as it met hers, a closing of whatever door had opened between them.

With a tired sigh, she turned toward the staff. "I'm sorry about this. You can return to bed."

"But the mess!" The footman with water conjury—who, mercifully, had put out the stove fire—was now motioning toward the broken eggs on the floor.

"Mr. Fontaine will clean it up."

Her words only stoked their anxiety further. Emmy followed them into the hall, gently dismissing the cluster of staff. When they were gone, she returned to the kitchen to face Jack.

"He marked you." Jack nodded toward her neck, his expression strange. "On purpose."

Emmy wiped at the cursed spot where the love bite had been. She'd tried to heal it, but her conjury was not Papa's, so she'd transformed the blemish to match her skin. "It didn't go well with Oliver?"

"Oh, it went swimmingly. Just like old times."

"Did you go to the Bronze Door?"

"We played cards there until Oliver lost all the money he had on him. Then, of course, he insisted on taking mine. When that was gone, too, we left, but our night was far from over." He squeezed a peanut shell in his fist. "Oliver insisted I join him on a raid downtown, where someone had been spotted performing air conjury for tips. On Hester Street."

Emmy studied his guarded expression. Hester Street ran parallel to Baxter Street, where she'd lived. "What did you do?"

"Precisely what I was told." He stopped cracking the shell. "I held him down while Oliver conjure-bound him."

Emmy stilled. She had very little memory of Oliver conjure-binding her in the awful moments between Papa bleeding out and her being shoved in the back of a carriage. All she could recall was the feeling of hands on her shoulders. And a coldness spreading over her, much like Grace's bridging conjury.

"He could have used handcuffs," Jack grumbled as he resumed trying—and failing—to free the peanut from its shell. "But what fun would that be?"

"You did what you had to do." She managed to sound gentle, though it made her sick to her stomach. All the more reason why they had to get Oliver thrown in jail, where he couldn't continue to hurt people who broke rules they were never told existed.

Jack let out a humorless laugh. "This is the fundamental difference between you and me: You think, deep down, that I'm good. Like you. And Jimmy. And maybe even Caleb. But I know myself, Vallillo. And I'm far more like Oliver."

"Hush." She whirled, searching underneath the kitchen doors. No shadows of footsteps. "You're drunk. We'll talk in the morning."

She tugged his arm, but he refused to budge from the counter. "You asked me about servants' bets, but you failed to ask me how many raids I've taken part in. Ask me."

He was itching for a fight, but she crossed her arms.

"Dozens," he spat. "I'm the son of a commander, and I did my job well."

She whirled toward the door again, but no sign of the staff. No sign of Jack relenting any time soon, either, not when he was hellbent on getting the tongue-lashing he desperately craved.

He wanted her to hate him, just like, in this moment, he hated himself.

Planting her hands on the counter on either side of him, Emmy leaned closer. He froze. Mere inches separated their mouths, and that reckless part of her nearly closed that distance, like they'd done in the river. "Poor little rich boy."

His bloodshot eyes blazed. "Excuse me?"

"You want me to write you off as being just like Oliver. Because that's easier than trying to do better, to *be* better than him." She paused, letting him see how much she meant her words. "Do better, Jack."

It was a risk, whispering his true name so furiously. Even riskier to remain this close to him, when everything in her ached to be closer. It was maddening, this gravitational pull of his. Maybe she'd smack him over the head, just to satisfy the craving.

"Oliver took me to Grimsbane," he said roughly. "To bring the charmed man there."

And there it was, the secret he did not want her to see: the twin pools of pain in those storm-gray eyes. Though hardly a minute ago, she'd been *this* close to hitting him, now she had to fight the draw to wrap her arms around him. To comfort him.

Much like her, he had no one else to do it.

"You are here now," she whispered. "In Mistfield."

His tired eyes fluttered shut. "I'm so sick of it. Grimsbane. The Society. I want to burn it all down."

And she wanted nothing more than to see it burn. "Then let's finish this. Let's bring them down, clear our names, and end this."

Jack's hand found hers and squeezed, his touch searing. They were bonded, whether she liked it or not.

They stayed like that for a few minutes, the quiet interrupted by the morning birds and their chirpy songs. Dawn was coming, and with it, the staff would return.

"Oliver wants to return to the Bronze Door." Jack pushed away the hair that had fallen over his forehead. "He didn't have a chance to grab his face-changing card yesterday, but maybe he'll bring it next time."

"Then I'm going, too." With only twelve days left, the season was rapidly slipping through their fingers. "And we're going to make sure he's caught."

TWENTY-THREE

DESPITE ITS WEALTHY PATRONS, EMMY had still imagined the Bronze Door as a dilapidated poolroom; she hadn't expected the splendor before her. The poker table at which Jack, Oliver, and four other men were playing was polished oak, and it rested on a plush red carpet that stretched from one richly wallpapered wall to the next. Antique-looking paintings added a touch of opulence. Authentic treasures from the Italian Renaissance, supposedly.

Oliver rearranged the cards fanned out in his hand. Plucking one, he dropped it on the table, along with a wad of cash equal to a few years of her and Papa's rent. From this distance, she couldn't tell whether the card was enchanted. Judging by Jack's frustrated expression at Oliver's side, he wasn't certain, either.

The men sipped their whiskeys and puffed their pipes as their stacks grew smaller, one round at a time. Oliver's, meanwhile, grew larger. Just like last night. And the night before that.

Six damn nights, and not a pinch of progress.

Once Oliver won yet another round, Emmy sealed the peephole and let out a groan.

Oliver Stratton was either an excellent cheater or not a cheater at all.

"This isn't working," Caleb grumbled in a low voice. The walls were so thin, they couldn't risk speaking above a whisper, even after Emmy had sealed the hole. "We need to call it a night. The Society is expecting us at Grace's fundraiser at half past three."

Sinking onto the ground, Emmy rested her head between her hands. All week, she'd snuck off to the city with Jimmy and Caleb, risking the suspicion of their staff. And all week, they'd huddled in the flat adjacent to the ritziest card room at the Bronze Door, which had been occupied by newlyweds who'd been glad to vacate for the week in exchange for a wad of greenbacks. It should have been enough time for the other players to catch Oliver in the act. But for six nights, Oliver had left richer than he'd arrived.

They only had seven days left in the season, yet their three remaining targets walked free. It was enough to make Emmy want to scream.

"It's actually impressive," Jimmy mused. "To avoid getting caught, he has to keep track of all the potential cards in everyone's hand. He's smart."

Oliver did not deserve a single compliment. Especially after spending all week getting Jack mind-numbingly drunk.

They'd wasted too much time waiting for him to get caught. Even if they hadn't trekked to the city all damn week, Emmy wouldn't have slept a wink, not with so little time until the final ball. They still had nothing on Grace, who'd attended hardly any events since the pageant. And although Caleb had been dropping hints to the chancellor about Keeper Windsor's untrustworthiness, the chancellor was far too cautious to strike against a triumvirate member due to rumors.

No, they needed Oliver arrested so they could pin it on Windsor, stoking the chancellor's paranoia. "One more round, then we'll go."

"It's already six in the morning," Caleb groaned. "Mary will be waiting."

"Mary's one of us now, remember?" Emmy could not hide the bitterness in her words. Though, to be fair, Mary had been nothing but helpful these past few days. She'd searched the Society's records for someone with the gift of inhibition lowering or truth telling, but had found no one. She'd also volunteered to search Grace's things at Clarity Hall, though she'd nearly hyperventilated before she'd gone invisible. Emmy and Jimmy had waited for her in the woods, counting the seconds until she returned. But she'd found nothing incriminating there, either.

Grace had to be keeping secrets. And Emmy had very little time to unearth them.

Frowning, Caleb eyed the wall. "Oliver and Jack should have called it quits already, too. We're all expected at the fundraiser."

Ah, yes, an entire afternoon during which Grace would be the benevolent hostess, basking in the Society's adoration. Attending would have been far more tolerable with news of Oliver's arrest.

Still, Grace kept a little office at the church, for her charity. While she was busy hosting the fundraiser on the church lawn, Mary would riffle through her things.

"Fine," Emmy sighed. "We'll try again tomorrow."

Two hours there. Two hours home. The Bronze Door was draining the life out of them.

"Try to rest, Ems," Jimmy said as he settled across from her in the carriage, his lids heavy. Caleb was already snoring quietly, and despite his declarations that Jimmy was taking up too much space, his head was resting rather comfortably on his shoulder. "You don't want to face Grace with circles underneath your eyes."

"Ah, but you forget, I can hide them." Emmy swiped her hand over her face, infusing her skin with a tickle of conjury to lighten the shade. Her gift didn't penetrate as deeply as Papa's had, but surface-level adjustments were still within her wheelhouse.

He chuckled silently. "Still, you gotta take care of yourself, yeah?"

His words pierced something inside her. Jimmy cared for her. That ought to have frightened her, because Grace had certainly pretended to care, right up to the moment Emmy was dragged away. But as Jimmy drifted to sleep, Emmy could not help but feel glad for his loyalty.

"Don't drink *anything*," Mary warned as she and Emmy passed through the illusion hiding the vast church lawn. "God only knows what Miss Montgomery has in store for you." She punctuated her words by touching the cross she wore.

Given that Grace had nearly ruined all of Emmy's schemes with a single bracelet, Emmy would not be drinking a drop today. "You be careful, too." As much as they needed to learn more about Grace, if Mary got caught snooping, they'd lose all the trust they'd built with the Society.

Jimmy squinted at the party sprawled on the lawn before them. "I know I'm not supposed to say this, but does a potions fundraiser strike anyone else as a bit . . . witchy?"

Caleb's mouth twitched. "They're not *real* potions. More like enhanced emotional experiences, ones that last hardly a few seconds. And at the risk of complimenting Miss Montgomery, we're lucky she convinced old Mr. Weatherby to donate them. He's the last known person with the gift of liquid imbuement. These may be the last potions ever."

Emmy studied the lawn party in search of something to criticize, but the decor was, unfortunately, enthralling. Attendants stood behind a long table draped in black, pouring colorful brews into minuscule champagne flutes. Cushioned sofas waited underneath trees, inviting guests to seek respite from the sun as they sampled the rare concoctions.

It was unnerving, entering a Society event without Jack. Although it was well into the afternoon, he still hadn't returned from the Bronze Door. And no matter how much Emmy tried to push the image from her mind, she kept thinking of Rose's prophecy.

For all they knew, Jack was lying in a New York alley, his throat slit.

"Miss Fairchild!" Hurrying toward them, Mrs. Stratton kissed the air besides Emmy's cheeks. "Aren't you thrilled?"

"I suppose. I've never had a potion before."

"Not that." Mrs. Stratton leaned closer, her eyes alight. "Miss Montgomery isn't here."

Emmy glanced around. "But it's *her* fundraiser."

"Which makes it even more scandalous." After pausing to offer Caleb and Jimmy her hand, Mrs. Stratton linked her arm with Emmy's and led her away. "According to my maid, who heard it from Mrs. Windsor's maid, Grace has been sneaking out of Clarity Hall. For weeks! Of course, she's home just in time for whatever party the Windsors are kind enough to allow her to attend, despite her deplorable behavior."

It was an effort not to shoot Mary an alarmed look. For all they knew, Grace could be traipsing about Mistfield right now. "Do you know, precisely, when?"

"Every day, from what I hear!" Mrs. Stratton shook her head. "Imagine the nerve!"

Given that truth bracelet in Emmy's jewelry box, she could more than imagine it. "Any idea where she goes?"

"Oh, she's given them some excuse about completing commissions with her conjury. But I know the truth: she's heartbroken." Emmy's doubts must have shown, for Mrs. Windsor leaned closer and whispered, "After our picnic, Oliver made it clear to her: they will never, ever marry."

How Emmy longed to believe her, but she'd seen how Oliver looked at Grace. Was one kiss with Winnie enough to change his heart?

"Ah, there he is!" Mrs. Stratton brightened as Oliver and Jack strolled down the lawn in last night's suits, their gaits too crooked to be sober. Though Jack wore the smirk that used to vex her, she could read him better now. He was unraveling—and quickly.

"Mother." Oliver embraced Mrs. Stratton, planting a kiss on her cheek that made her positively beam. "And Miss Fairchild. Just the girl I came to see."

With his mother watching, Oliver lifted Emmy's hand to his lips and kissed it chastely.

Jack's smirk sharpened.

"You're late," Mrs. Stratton scolded her son. "Make yourself useful and buy a potion for Miss Fairchild."

Oliver tucked Emmy's hand in the crook of his arm. "Let's see what the fuss is about."

It was hard to glance at Jack while Oliver walked between them, but Oliver had monopolized his time so thoroughly, she'd hardly seen him since the kitchen ordeal. He was in one piece, at least, though he looked exhausted.

Jimmy and Caleb excused themselves to mingle elsewhere—and stoke rumors about the Windsor/Stratton feud. Mary, meanwhile, kept pace with Oliver's valet. But once Emmy's gaze met hers, the maid nodded and slipped into the crowd, quite literally disappearing. With Grace not even here, she ought to be able to search her charity office easily.

Then again, when it came to Grace Montgomery, nothing was ever easy.

"Welcome," a jovial attendant said as they approached one of the black tables. "Would you care to try a brew?"

"How does this work?" Jack lifted one of the tiny flutes, examining its silvery contents.

"Mr. Weatherby has a special form of sensile conjury," the attendant explained. "He can infuse liquids so that they trigger emotional experiences. Care to try?"

He flourished the gilded label, which had but a single word in flowing cursive: *Rhapsody.*

Oliver accepted the tiny flute from the attendant, but when he offered Emmy one, she took a step back. "Oh, no thank you."

"A portion this small will last only a few seconds," promised the attendant. "But if you'd prefer, you can have your lady's maid try it first."

As if experimenting on Mary were any better. But before Oliver could notice that Emmy's invisible maid had gone missing, Jack took the flute and tossed its contents down his throat. With a shock of laughter, Oliver grabbed one off the table and did the same.

Their eyes glazed over, and a slow smile spread across Oliver's face, then Jack's. Not the smirk he wielded like a weapon, but his crooked grin, the one she'd glimpsed in the river, when she'd held her daggered nail to his neck. A giggle burst from him—a literal giggle, which sent Oliver into a bout of hysterics. Nearly falling over, they held on to each other for balance. It was an unsettling glimpse into the bond they might have shared, once.

And then it was over, Jack's genuine smile eroding until only his faux one remained.

Clapping Jack on the back, Oliver grinned at the attendant. "I'll take a bottle."

"That'll be twenty dollars, sir."

"Twenty!" Chuckling darkly, Oliver snapped his fingers at his attendant, who was stationed a safe distance behind him. "Pay the man. It's for charity, after all."

They continued through the party, Oliver dominating the conversation, which seemed only to improve his high spirits. Jack took the lead on making enough remarks to keep him talking, letting Emmy off the hook. She was even able to slip away here and there to chat with a few of the other young ladies. Truth be told, she was beginning to like their company. There was genuine warmth in their gentle teasing about her being too skittish to try a single potion.

When Oliver begged Emmy to try a silver flute, Emmy held it in her hand, tempted. "Just a taste."

"I wouldn't drink that one, if I were you," an airy voice called.

Emmy hardly had a moment to gather her courage before Grace stood before her. With her blonde curls pinned beneath a fashionable floral hat, she looked as elegant as always as she plucked the flute from Emmy's hands.

"It's called Carnality. We don't need you throwing yourself at anyone, now, do we?"

Implied in her words was a taunting *again*.

Grace pressed her fingers to Oliver's forearm. "Would you two give Miss Fairchild and me a moment?"

"If you insist." With a smile that indicated he was enjoying this far too much, Oliver bowed to them, pulling Jack along with him.

Emmy could only stare at Grace. Waiting.

Plucking a strawberry from a bowl on the table, Grace held it to her lips. "How kind of you to support my charity, Miss Fairchild."

"Teaching underprivileged children to sew is a worthy cause." For Emmy, memories of sewing were bound to memories of Grace. Had Grace thought of her even once?

"I'd like to tell you something. Woman to woman."

Emmy stiffened. Waiting.

"In one week, Oliver and I will be engaged." Setting the strawberry down, she patted Emmy's arm. "I only say this to help, of course. If I were in your position, and I was being encouraged to seek out an unavailable man, I'd want someone to tell me."

Emmy jerked away from Grace's touch. Her skin wasn't cold with bridging conjury, but when it came to Grace, Emmy could never be certain. And did she take Winnie for a fool? One who'd take her word on anything, let alone Oliver?

Copying Grace's practiced pleasantness, Emmy popped a berry into her mouth. "Mrs. Stratton doesn't seem to think so."

"Ah, but we both know who holds the real power at Pinnacle Bluffs."

Was she suggesting that the chancellor approved of Oliver and Grace? That was too far-fetched, even for Grace.

"If Oliver were to pick between these two options, which do you think he'd choose?" Grace set another plump strawberry beside the one she'd bitten. "This one, which he is careful to treat with the utmost care? Or this one, which bruises the very first time his mouth grazes it?" Grace sank her fingernails into the bitten berry's delicate flesh, and red juice oozed onto the tablecloth.

Emmy's hand flew to her neck. Grace *knew*. Oliver had told her he'd kissed Winnie—that he'd left a mark on her. He'd told Grace, as if it were entertainment for them both.

Her humiliation was hot and swift. That vile bastard had been toying with her. And although she'd kissed Oliver, Grace had outplayed her. Again.

"Do say hello to your maid for me. Every time I try, the silly girl runs away." With a triumphant smile, Grace sauntered off.

That hateful little wench. She had better stay the hell away from Mary.

With considerable effort, Emmy kept her head high—the gossips were watching—but she was breathing fire. She was done with this party, done with Oliver's haughty airs. Done giving him fodder to laugh at her. With *Grace*.

Emmy kept an eye out for Mary as Grace worked the crowd, smiling demurely as person after person sang her praises. About what a lovely fundraiser, and such a rare opportunity to sip actual potions! And so much money—hundreds, if not *thousands*—for such a worthy cause.

So many little street urchins would learn to sew clothes for the rich.

After an eternity, the crowd began to thin, and Emmy's impatience was quickly turning to dread. Mary still hadn't returned.

"Still no sign of her?" she asked Caleb after the Strattons bid them adieu.

"Not since we arrived." Frowning, Caleb glanced toward the church.

"Well, we can't just sit here," Jack murmured. "Oliver's expecting me in an hour."

"Again?" Emmy's voice pitched. The circles under Jack's eyes couldn't get much darker.

"No rest for the wicked." Rubbing the back of his head, Jack glanced around the empty lawn. "We might as well wait in the carriage. The staff are starting to wonder what we're doing."

Please be in the carriage, Emmy silently prayed, which was odd; she hadn't given God much thought since he'd abandoned her in Grimsbane. But she found herself saying it, over and over, as they made their way to the carriage. But Mary was not there.

They climbed inside, shut the doors, and stared at each other.

"This is not good," Jimmy finally said. "Not good at—"

The carriage door burst open, and Mary threw herself inside, a small, ornate box clutched in her arms. "Go! Tell the driver to go!"

Emmy yanked the door shut as Jack pounded on the window. And they were off, the horses galloping down the driveway as Mary tried to catch her breath.

"I'm sorry," she wheezed, "but when Miss Montgomery arrived so late, I thought to myself, *Just what has she been doing?* So I searched her carriage, but her driver returned while I was still inside!"

Jack's tired eyes were suddenly alert. "Were you seen?"

"I waited until he left, which took *hours*. But I found this." With a triumphant smile, Mary handed Emmy the box. The jostling of the carriage made it difficult to open, but once Emmy flipped the latch, she gasped.

A small treasure glittered in the faint moonlight. Earrings and necklaces and more radiant stones than Emmy had ever seen in one place. "You stole her *jewelry*?"

"Not just any jewelry." Mary's grin widened. "It's her private arsenal of conjury she's bridged."

TWENTY-FOUR

WITH A TIERED PEARL DROP earring in one hand, Jimmy squinted in concentration. Water droplets rained from his other hand, and he grinned. "Water again."

"Pearl earrings: water conjury," Mary repeated, dutifully writing it down.

As Jimmy tossed the earring into the pile of elemental conjury they'd identified thus far, Emmy stifled a yawn. They were next door to the Bronze Door yet again, waiting for Jack and Oliver to arrive. Judging by the time, the two Society boys might not make it out of whatever watering hole Oliver had chosen for the night, and this entire trip would be for naught.

Six days until the season ended, and three of their targets still roamed free. The odds were suffocating.

"They'd be more useful if we knew how much power she put in them," Jimmy mused, "or how much they have left."

"That's the least of our concerns." Emmy nodded toward the growing pile of jewelry with conjury they'd never before seen. A bangle that made auras appear, revealing people's emotions. A necklace that allowed Jimmy to move objects across the room without touching them. Perhaps even more disconcerting, there were at least five pieces that were as frigid to the touch as the others, yet they hadn't been able to figure out what sort of conjury Grace had bridged with them.

Grace had been bridging conjury unbeknownst to the Society. Once she realized her arsenal had been stolen, she was going to be livid.

Jimmy selected a silver ring next, pushing it up his pinkie, then giving it a little twist, like Mary had shown him earlier.

He disappeared.

"I had a feeling that one was me again." With a sigh, Mary added *silver ring: invisibility* to their inventory. "She asked to bridge my conjury all the time."

Jimmy appeared right in front of Emmy, startling her. But his eyes were locked on the jewelry box, his brow creased. "The bottom—there's a lift there."

Emmy tried to look where he was looking. "I don't see anything."

"Let me just . . ." Grabbing the ornate box, Jimmy turned it upside down, sliding his fingers along the seam. He paused. "I feel it."

The bottom of the jewelry box sprang open.

Emmy could not reach the box fast enough. Jimmy was already pulling out its contents. Papers. Some were crisp with relatively fresh ink, while others looked ancient.

Careful not to tear them, Emmy plucked the yellowed ones from the box. Three handwritten pages, all in whirling French. The edges were cut. She could hardly breathe as she scanned them. Over and over again was the same word: *relique*. "She took these from the Fontaine grimoire."

"That conniving sneak." From the couch where he'd been listening for Jack and Oliver, courtesy of his conjury, Caleb's eyes flew open. "She might have tried to replicate Rose's relic, but it's impossible."

"So you and Jack keep saying." Emmy stared at the pages. Neither of them knew Grace like she did. "Jimmy, if Grace had gotten a taste of unfathomable power, allowing her to use the conjury of anyone in her vicinity—do you think she'd give up on it?"

"Never," Jimmy agreed. "We already know she's willing to kill for it."

And if she found out that Winnie Fairchild had Rose's relic, she'd slit Emmy's throat in her sleep—a more difficult feat, now that they had her enchanted jewelry collection.

Jimmy set the other papers on the floor. "Addresses, mostly in Lower Manhattan."

Emmy peered at the list. The handwriting wasn't Grace's. "What is she up to?"

"Later," Caleb whispered, squeezing his eyes shut. "Jack and Oliver just arrived."

In silence, they hurried to their positions: Emmy found the mark she'd left on the wall and, with the relic in hand, transformed a tiny hole in it, where it would be hidden by a colorful painting. Jimmy headed to the door, where he'd listen for trouble. Caleb sat tall on the couch, rubbing his temples as he prepared to conjure once again. And Mary put the jewelry back into its box, watching them all with a bewildered expression. She'd begged to come along tonight, eager to uncover whatever secrets Grace's jewelry held.

They were running out of time. With each passing day, the season drew closer to an end.

Swallowing her frustration, Emmy pressed her forehead against the wall. There was Jack and his perennial Nathaniel smile, but by now, Emmy could read him like a book: He was agitated. And drunk. To his right was Oliver, studying his cards from beneath the rim of his top hat. Emmy watched his sleeves, waiting for an extra card to appear. Ideally, one of the other players at tonight's table would be the one to catch Oliver.

But no one seemed to suspect anything as the Stratton heir won. Again.

A flurry of waitresses arrived with drinks, and Emmy healed the wall before leaning against it, her frustration simmering. "I didn't see him cheat."

"And I couldn't hear a damn thing over your stressful thoughts about time running out." Caleb rubbed his temples. "This isn't working."

After so many nights trekking back and forth to the city, he was tired. They all were.

They could not do this much longer. Oliver *had* to fall tonight. "Tell Jack that he's going to have to be the one to catch him. We can't wait for one of these cads to wise up."

With a dramatic sigh, Caleb closed his eyes, wincing. "He says he needs to stay out of it, to maintain their friendship if it doesn't work."

Now was not the time to hesitate. "Tell him to stop overthinking."

Caleb once again squeezed his eyes shut. "He says that's the pot calling the kettle black."

"Tell him—"

His gaze cut to her. "I'm not wasting the little conjury I have left playing messenger."

A fair point, but Emmy was all out of patience. They'd underestimated Oliver. He was excellent at avoiding detection, keenly attuned to the other players to ascertain whether they had the card he needed before he used his face-changing one.

"I hate to point out the obvious," Caleb said in a low voice, "but we need a new plan."

Jimmy was watching her. Mary, too, as if they could sense that she was ready to explode. As supportive as they were, they didn't *need* to succeed. Only Jack could truly understand, and he was stuck at Oliver's side.

Emmy plucked one of the invisibility rings from the floor. "How does this work? I just twist it?" Back home, Grace hadn't had the skill to create triggers and limits for the things she conjured, but while Emmy was wasting away, Grace had turned into *quite* the student.

"You're going in there?" Mary paled. "What if it loses its strength and they see you?"

"Then they'll see someone else." Focusing on the relic against her sternum, Emmy's modest gray dress morphed into the black aproned uniform of the waitresses. Her hair, she lightened to red, like Mary's, and her face, she conjured using features from two of the waitresses she'd seen in the card room. "Well?"

Jimmy grinned, but Caleb looked wary. "Do I even want to know your plan?"

Emmy hardly knew it herself. Before she could lose her nerve, she twisted the ring, checked her arms to make sure she was actually invisible, and walked out of the flat.

From the outside, the casino blended into the other respectable town houses along West Thirty-Third Street, with no signs in its windows or seedy patrons loitering on the stoop. But it had to have a back door. Turning into the alley, Emmy passed a few men having a pissing contest against a brick wall—even uptown, Manhattan could not be tamed—before she found a rear door guarded by two formidable men in navy uniforms. Cops.

She stood as close as she dared, waiting for someone to enter or exit so she could dart in, undetected. The minutes ticked by, and just as Emmy was reconsidering, the door flew open as two waitresses passed through it.

Emmy slipped inside.

A cacophony of music and laughter greeted her, along with the noxious scent of cigar smoke. Gas lamps flickered along the corridor, and Emmy tried to settle her racing heart as she searched for the stairwell. She found it, finally, and hurried to the third floor.

The hall was as luxuriously decorated as any mansion in Avalon-on-Hudson, though the heady aroma of cigar smoke cheapened it. The left side of the hall seemed quiet, so Emmy turned right, but the stairs had spun her around, and she hadn't the faintest idea which way to go.

Oliver's haughty laugh beckoned from the end of the hall. With a steadying breath, Emmy followed it. As soon as she stood in the doorway, she nearly lost her nerve.

The room was far more crowded than she'd realized, the chairs so close to the walls, there was hardly enough space for anyone to pass. Sucking in a breath, Emmy squeezed along the wall until she stood just over Oliver's shoulder.

She'd need to be quick. If he pushed back from the table, he'd bump right into her.

"Have I told you," Oliver mused as he examined his downturned card, a nine of clubs, "how exquisitely soft your cousin's lips are?"

Emmy nearly choked on her own spit.

"You might have mentioned it." Jack glanced at his own cards, his face hidden beneath his hat.

"That's no way to talk about another man's relations," the man to Oliver's left muttered. He had a thick neck with an even thicker beard, and judging by the way he eyed Oliver, he was not taken by the Stratton heir.

"She's a distant relation." Oliver set the cards down as he gazed about the table, scrutinizing the others. If only Grace had bridged Caleb's magic, so Emmy could know what Oliver was thinking—but if Grace could read minds, they'd all be in Grimsbane. Or dead.

The men went around the table, tossing inordinate stacks of money as if it were meaningless, and Oliver glanced at his down card again. Instead of that nine of clubs, he had a king of spades, giving him two pair with his upturned cards. Emmy had to hand it to him; she hadn't even seen him pull the charmed card from wherever he was hiding it.

She waited for him to play it—but what could she do, even if he did? Unless someone else at the table had the true king of spades, there was no way for them to know he'd cheated.

Worse, Oliver folded, as if he knew better than to risk this hand. He was being infuriatingly careful.

They'd underestimated him. And now she was stuck in the card room, wearing an invisibility ring that might lose its conjury at any moment. But she hadn't spent two years in hell to be bested by a rich prick from the Society of the Charmed. She had rare transformation conjury—the very conjury Grace had used to make Oliver his face-changing cards.

The hands were dealt again, and antes thrown, but this time, Emmy did not wait for Oliver to glimpse his downturned card, instead running her invisible finger along it as she envisioned an ace of hearts. Before the dealer finished, she quickly touched the burly man's card, too, giving him the exact same ace.

Fifty-two cards in the deck. Six men at this table, each with one downturned card—and four upturned cards on the way—for thirty total cards. She couldn't calculate the odds, not when she could hardly breathe, but if anyone was dealt the true ace of hearts, there'd be too many fakes for Oliver alone to take the blame.

The true ace of hearts, mercifully, was not dealt in the upturned cards, though with Emmy's help, both Oliver and the burly man each received another ace. With a killer hand, Oliver bet even more aggressively than usual, but the burly man matched him, dollar for dollar. *Please don't fold*, she wished fervently, over and over. *Don't fold, don't fold . . .*

"All right, gentlemen. Let's see 'em."

With a haughty grin, Oliver flipped his ace of hearts. Murmurs and appreciative whistles spread about the table, and Oliver began to collect his enormous pile of winnings—but his opponent stood abruptly. "He cheated."

About damn time. Making herself small, Emmy began to tiptoe toward the door.

"Now, now." Oliver waggled his finger at the man. "That's a lofty accusation from someone who just lost, fair and square."

"You little bastard—look." The man flipped over his ace of hearts, and the room went so quiet, Emmy had to stop moving.

"Impossible!" Oliver stared at the identical aces. "I was dealt this, I swear!"

The dealer stood up. "Well, one of you's cheating."

"And only one of us has been winning all night."

"All week."

The burly man glanced around the table. "Should we have a look for ourselves?"

One instant, all six men were seated at the table. The next, they were jumping out of their chairs.

She dove under the table, crashing into the chair legs. Someone bumped her feet, and she curled up in a ball as the men shouted at each other.

Oliver was pinned to the wall, his shirt ripped open, his jacket shaken upside down. She began to crawl toward the door, but—she could see her arms. The ring had worn off. And she was trapped under the table.

Panic clawed at her throat. How reckless she'd been, relying on Grace's conjury. If they saw her, or heard her, Oliver just might walk—

"What the hell is going on in here?" someone barked.

"I'm being assaulted!" Oliver cried. "And my honor—"

"The Stratton pup is cheating. Found this in his sleeve."

"I've never even seen that before!" Oliver exclaimed. "You must have planted it on me."

They'd found one of his conjured cards. It had to be.

"Are you calling me a liar, kid?"

"You lettin' cheaters into your club, Farrow?" someone growled.

"Enough." The deep voice from the doorway bellowed. "Take him out back."

"Do you know who I am?" Oliver grabbed the doorway to keep them from carrying him outside. "When my father hears of this—"

Emmy could not risk a peek as they dragged Oliver out. She needed them all to leave, every last one of them, before she made a run for it.

The last boots gone, Emmy darted into the hall. The doorways were full of people who had gathered to watch a cheater punished, but no one gave a second glance to her waitress disguise.

She caught up to Jack in the stairwell, touching his arm, but he yanked away, giving her a scathing look.

"It's me," she whispered, quickly transforming herself back to Winnie.

A slow smile spread across his cheeks. Lightning quick, he kissed her forehead. "I had a feeling you were up to something."

Shocked, Emmy raised her hand to where his lips had just been.

"C'mon. Let's see the bastard get pummeled." With the mob of card players well ahead now, they were alone in the stairwell, taking the steps two at a time, just as they had at Grimsbane. It was dizzying, how much had changed in a matter of months. Now Emmy did not even mind Jack tugging her along, the heat of his skin strangely thrilling against hers.

The mob had already brought Oliver outside, and judging by the cacophony of grunts and jeers, they were exacting their own form of justice. Jack pushed through the back door—

The back alley erupted in screams. Frightened, wordless screams.

Jack ducked back inside, his eyes aflame. "He's suppressing their movements."

"The *ordinaries?*"

"The card players, along with the police who are supposed to be arresting him."

It shouldn't have shocked Emmy as much as it did, that Oliver was willing to risk magic's secret—risk the safety of the entire charmed community—in order to avoid arrest.

"Damnit." Squeezing his eyes shut, Jack leaned against the door.

"We need to break his concentration so he stops conjuring."

Emmy fumbled for the invisibility ring on her finger, turning it in case there were drops of conjury left. But nothing happened. She checked her pockets, but she hadn't anything on her.

"Transform me back." Jack glanced at the empty stairs. "Quick, while we're still alone."

"Have you lost your mind?" she hissed. "You can't let him see you!"

"And we can't let him get away." He ran his hands over his face, as if whatever plan was forming was tearing him apart. "Transform me. I'll catch him by surprise."

She wouldn't. It was reckless and brash—and if he faced Oliver as Jack, Rose's prophecy just might come true.

"For one goddamn time, can you trust me?" Jack's eyes bore into hers, his bottom lip jutting in that infuriating pout. "Please?"

If only she had a better idea, but she could not think straight while he looked at her like that, so she grabbed his face. "If you die, I swear to God, I will never forgive you."

His grin was all too fleeting.

How easily she recalled his likeness, from the strong line of his jaw to the sweep of his dark lashes, even the little scar in his right brow. His hair formed chocolate waves once more, falling over his forehead like they had when he slept. Nathaniel was beautiful in the way that the Strattons' estate was beautiful, manicured and perfectly designed. But Jack's true face was like Mistfield. Like his flames. Dark and lively and entirely unbidden.

Once she was finished, he cupped her chin. "Thank you."

She grabbed his arm as he lunged for the back door. "At least take Rose's—"

"Keep it." Jack flashed her his true grin, the vexing one she hadn't seen in weeks. And then he was gone, sprinting outside before she could retrieve his sister's relic.

All she could do now was follow.

There were nearly a dozen men in the alley—the card players, the manager, and the police officers she'd passed earlier—all of them making strange vowel sounds, for they could not move their lips. Their fists were raised, their postures leaning at impossible angles. One officer was midstride. All of them were watching her, their frozen expressions frightened.

It hurt to look at them, but the only way to help them was to stop Oliver.

She rounded the alley corner just as Jack was hurling himself at Oliver, full speed. At his footsteps, Oliver turned, his eyes widening.

As Jack Fontaine punched him in the jaw.

Oliver slammed into the wall behind him. Before he'd raised a hand, Jack struck him again, this time in the stomach, and Oliver crumpled to the ground.

Jack hovered over him, grinning like the goddamn devil. "Miss me?"

"No," Oliver rasped, all the color draining from his cruel, handsome face.

"You *didn't* miss me?"

"You're dead!" Oliver tried to scurry away, but Jack blocked his path. "They pulled your body from the river."

In Emmy's periphery, the men unfroze, falling over themselves.

Jack's expression was as vicious as it had been in Grimsbane. "You killed my sister."

"That wasn't supposed to happen!" Oliver rubbed at his eyes as if willing Jack to disappear. "You're not real. You're a goddamn ghost."

"You killed Elizabeth Windsor, too."

"I had no choice!" Oliver shouted. "She was going to turn us in!"

Something brushed Emmy's arm, and she let out a little yelp. Jack turned, squinting in the dark, but it was only the police officers, paying her no mind as they ran into the alley.

It happened so quickly. One moment, Jack was looking at her, and the next, Oliver thrust his weight forward, headbutting him.

Jack tumbled back, off-balance.

The officers shuffled closer, guns raised.

Jack fell to his knees, his hands catching the ground.

The cops froze, midstride. Emmy, too.

Jack was still on his knees, unmoving, as Oliver unsheathed a knife from his ankle.

The drawing. One second, Jack had been hovering over Oliver, but now, Oliver stood above him with a knife— This, right here, was Rose's prophecy.

Emmy tried to shout, but the panicked noise that she spewed was utterly useless. She tried to run, but Oliver had frozen everyone in the alley. Hushed, frightened conversation still wafted from the Bronze Door, and Emmy willed those men to help, but she hadn't Caleb's gift.

Jack was going to die. He was going to die, and she was going to watch. And it would be her fault, because she'd transformed him, knowing damn well that he wasn't safe facing Oliver as himself. Even though she knew better, she'd let him talk her out of her instincts, let him run off without taking the relic so he could defend himself. And now he was going to die.

With a wild laugh, Oliver whipped his arm back, readying to swing that knife.

Jack looked stricken, and she wanted to scream. Just like Papa. Just like that night.

In one fell swoop. Oliver brought down his knife.

But it disappeared.

He tripped forward, staring at his empty fist. The knife was gone—evaporated.

As if an invisible hand had stolen it away.

"Mary!" Oliver bellowed, swinging about wildly for the maid, but he'd let go of his conjury, and Jack scrambled to his feet just as the cops flooded the alley, guns raised. Oliver realized his mistake, his eyes narrowing with effort. But not quickly enough.

"Fuck you, Stratton." With a vicious grin, Jack slammed his fist into Oliver's face.

TWENTY-FIVE

"HELP ME MAKE SENSE OF this," Mary whispered to Emmy. "We celebrate by jumping off a *cliff?*"

"*They* celebrate by jumping." Emmy nodded to Jack and Jimmy, who were trying to cajole Caleb into joining them. "We can walk down."

By the time they'd returned from the Bronze Door, it was already midmorning, far too late for a cliff jump. In truth, Emmy was hoping they'd forget all about it. Flirting with death had lost its appeal, given that Jack had barely escaped it a few hours ago.

All day, Emmy had been haunted by that close call. As she'd approved the floral arrangements for tomorrow's masquerade ball, she'd seen Jack on his knees every time she blinked. When the chef had asked her to approve last-minute adjustments to the menu, she'd seen Oliver's knife in every metal surface in the kitchen. Even when she'd been alone in her room, studying Grace's jewelry box for the umpteenth time, she hadn't been able to stop thinking about the inhibition-lowering bracelet she'd worn. How Jack's warm hands had torn open her laces.

How she'd wrapped herself around him while he desperately tried to get away.

The pressure was finally getting to her. They had five days to ruin both the chancellor and Grace. An impossible feat, yet her brain was stuck on a torturous loop of Jack Henrick Fontaine.

As Jimmy opened the champagne, the popped cork echoed across the valley like a shot fired. Once the fizz ceased streaming from the bottle, he thrust it into Caleb's hands.

"I hope you're watching, Rosie." After a long swig, Caleb handed the bottle back to Jimmy and, with a white face and a whispered prayer, sprinted off the edge, letting out a high-pitched shriek that was cut short by his splash far below. Mary gripped Emmy's arm as they inched closer to the edge, waiting for him to resurface.

With a wild yell, he emerged, throwing both hands in the air. He'd hardly had a chance to swim out of the way before Jimmy somersaulted after him, disappearing into the night.

"They're *insane*," Mary hissed, clutching her cross.

A few weeks ago, cliff jumping had seemed reckless, but it hadn't physically hurt to watch them. Now Emmy's hand was fisted against her chest, and she could not release it, not even as Jimmy and Caleb splashed away, having a grand old time.

She'd let down her guard. Although she'd promised herself she wouldn't, she'd begun to care for all of them. And now she could hardly watch them jump.

"Worried about me, Vallillo?" Jack was standing precariously close to the edge, backlit by the wild glow of the overcast night.

"Not at all," she lied. "If you want to jump off a cliff, that's your business."

With a shrug, he began to unbutton his shirt, revealing his broad shoulders. His collarbone. The ripples of lean muscle she hadn't even known might exist between a man's chest and his waistband.

Her skin prickled with a sudden heat, her relic the only spot of coolness.

This was ridiculous. She did not need to watch him undress, and she certainly didn't need to watch him jump to his death. "C'mon, Mary."

They began the trek down the winding path along the cliff. Though jagged trees blocked much of their view of the Hudson, Jack's whoop pierced the quiet of the night, and Emmy stiffened, waiting for the thunderous crash.

It was several seconds before Jimmy and Caleb cheered. Unclenching her fists, Emmy continued down the path. "What is it, Mary? I can feel your gaze burning into me."

"The chain around your neck. It's Rose's relic, isn't it? The one you were talking about at the Bronze Door?"

Yet another consequence of letting her guard down: they'd discussed Rose's relic in front of Mary. Her stomach in knots, Emmy managed a shrug. "My relic is perfectly ordinary."

Mary nearly snorted. "Last night, you transformed your face and dress on a whim. No ordinary relic could make you that strong. But you needn't say anything. As long as you know you *can* talk to me, should you choose. Not just about that, but about anything."

Her tentative smile only worsened the knots in Emmy's stomach. She *liked* Mary. Had Emmy not sworn off friendship, she could almost picture pulling Mary deeper into the trees, out of earshot of the river. Confessing how much Jack exasperated her. How she found herself staring at his lips while he rambled on. How his brush with death had rattled her to the bone and she was furious for caring at all. How she'd do anything to free her mind of thoughts of him.

And she could almost picture how Mary would hound her for details, just like Grace would have done. How they'd bond over such confessions.

Female friendship was a wonderful elixir, one brewed with secrets and laughter and an intimacy that buried itself deep in the marrow. And Emmy missed it. Terribly.

But that elixir could morph to poison without warning. The deeper the bond, the graver the sickness. And Emmy would not survive another dose.

Still, Emmy was racked with guilt for keeping quiet the rest of their hike. As they reached the water's edge, she asked, "Should we jump in together?"

Mary blinked up in surprise, her smile pleased. "As long as you make me a new dress."

Taking Mary's hand, Emmy tried not to think of Grace—and how this was the sort of thing they would have done together—as they jumped.

The cool river separated them the moment they sank beneath its surface, but when Emmy emerged, Mary was already laughing. The boys cheered, and Emmy let herself laugh, too, although it felt like tempting fate.

The five of them were a team. Nothing more, nothing less. So long as Emmy remembered that, she could avoid the mistakes she'd made with Grace.

"Let's race to the middle," Jimmy said, tousling Caleb's hair. "Ems? Mary?"

"I'll join!" How different Mary looked in the water, with her scarlet hair dark and matted, her smile wide and uninhibited.

They waited for Emmy, and part of her longed to go, but her mood still felt leaden while theirs seemed featherlight. "I'll watch."

Jimmy's smile dimmed, but Jack gave him a nudge. "Go ahead. Vallillo and I will catch up."

She gave Jack a look, one he pointedly ignored as he counted down for their race. And then the others were off, splashing toward the middle, nearly drowning each other to get ahead.

"All right, Vallillo." Jack followed her as she waded over to the thick branch of a weeping willow jutting over the riverbank. "You first."

"What are you talking about?"

"You're in a mood. Don't try to deny it," he added over her protests. "There's been a cloud hovering over you since Oliver was dragged away in handcuffs."

"I'm just . . . preoccupied. Tomorrow night, we're supposed to throw a ball *and* ensure the chancellor snaps in a very public matter."

They'd planted the seeds all day. While Emmy had been bogged down by last-minute masquerade preparations, Caleb had visited the Strattons, telling them that Nathaniel had seen Keeper Windsor at the Bronze Door while Oliver was arrested. He'd also offered to go to the Tombs with them, to communicate with Oliver through the prison's walls, even though Oliver wasn't permitted visitors. But Caleb would only pretend to contact Oliver, instead feeding the chancellor a tall tale about Keeper Windsor framing him.

Jack, meanwhile, had told the Windsors the truth about what had transpired: that Oliver used his conjury on a dozen ordinaries, including police officers—and that he'd drunkenly confessed to killing their daughter. Keeper Windsor had headed straight for the city to speak with the police.

They were playing both sides of the war they'd started. And Mistfield's ball needed to be the final battlefield. Tomorrow night.

"You're lying." His gray eyes narrowed. "I know you well enough to know that."

You almost died, she nearly screamed at him, but of course, she kept it to herself. Danger was par for the course. Emmy giving a damn was the problem.

"Is this about Oliver?"

"What about him?"

"Are you upset that he's in jail?"

She could only blink for a moment, absorbing his impossible words. "Are you *drunk*?"

"For your information, I didn't have a lick of alcohol between our dress shop break-in and my first gambling escapade with Oliver. And now that he's gone, I won't have a sip again."

Emmy was about to protest that he'd had champagne in the river a few weeks ago, but—had Jack taken a turn? Each night at dinner, he'd accepted the wine the steward poured for him, but she couldn't recall him touching his glass. "Why?"

"Because someone pointed out to me that I make poor choices." He waved a dismissive hand. "But back to Oliver."

Shocked as she was that her words had impacted him, she still couldn't make sense of what he'd said. "Why would I give a damn about Oliver?"

"Because you've been in a sour mood all day." Jack shrugged, water cascading down his bare shoulders. "And from what I saw, he was *quite* the kisser."

Her jaw nearly unhinged. "Have you gone *mad*?"

"So you didn't enjoy it?" His teeth practically pierced his bottom lip. "Help me make sense of what I saw."

"I owe you *no* explanation." She punctuated her words by splashing him, but that wasn't enough, so she slid off the branch, swimming away.

But he caught her by the arm. "I'm sorry, all right? I just . . ." His words trailed off, his expression tortured. "Put yourself in my shoes: Would it bother you if I kissed Grace?"

She jerked back as if he'd struck her. "You want to kiss her?"

"Of course not." His lips curled. "But imagine you watched me do it. That her lips trailed down my neck, and you saw me lean in for more. That you replayed it in your mind every time you closed your eyes."

She glared at him, but his terrible words had already infected her. Grace in Jack's arms. Grace pressing onto her tippy-toes, Jack's hands tangled in her blonde curls—

"You don't like it, either." Jack leaned closer, his eyes downright wild as they pinned her in place. "Now tell me: Why is that? Why does it torture us both?"

"Because I hate her," Emmy hissed, that fire in her chest scalding. "And you hate him."

But that wasn't all, was it? Jack kissing Grace would cut like a betrayal. It would wreck Emmy, wreck the alliance they'd formed. Their lives were linked, whether she liked it or not.

Jack's eyes grew so dark, they were nearly black. "And now you know how I feel."

They were far too close. Emmy's heart was ready to beat right out of her body. He was still shirtless, curse him, his chest rising and falling as if he was fighting that treacherous pull to be nearer. And there was a pull. Loath as Emmy was to admit it, her body was attuned to Jack's. He leaned toward her, and her skin crackled with anticipation. His gaze dropped to her lips, and she was on fire.

"Fuck it," he murmured. "You're already mad at me."

He kissed her.

For a long moment, she could hardly believe his lips were on hers. They were as soft as she'd imagined, and warm in the way Jack was always warm, and he was *kissing* her. Although common sense dictated that she swim away, she wrapped her arms around his shoulders. His hands found her waist, bursts of heat in the cool water. He was a flame, burning away her prudence, her very bones, her sense of time and space and everything outside of Jack Fontaine.

But he turned away abruptly, letting her go.

She gaped at him, her fingers brushing her mouth. "Why did you do that?" The words hardly made it past her lips.

He ran his hands over his face, his expression tortured. "Like you said: I make poor choices." Without looking at her, he swam away, the muscles in his back straining to put distance between them.

Humiliation burned her eyes. Was this some sort of game to him? Jack had kissed plenty of girls and was prophesied to kiss plenty more. But that was the first time she'd kissed anyone, except Oliver, although that hardly counted.

She hardly knew what to do with herself. If she returned to her room, he'd think her heartbroken, but if she stayed, he might see just how much he'd rattled her.

For a little while, she let the cool water quell her burning cheeks. It hadn't meant anything. Kissing someone back was an instinct, much like returning a smile. And if they managed to pull this off, she could forget all about Jack and his "poor choices."

The solitude she desperately needed was coming to an end, for Caleb, Jimmy, and Mary were making a beeline toward her, dragging Jack along with them. Jack, who'd been swimming away from her as fast as possible.

She dipped under the water again and, far beneath the surface, let out a scream.

". . . thunder in the distance," Caleb was saying as she resurfaced, giving her a peculiar look far too suspicious for her liking. "Should we go in?"

"A little rain never hurt anyone." Somehow, Jack managed to sound perfectly normal. "Unless you're worried about ruining your hair."

"My hair is just fine, thank you very much." Caleb glanced at Jimmy. "Tell her."

Emmy ceased her treading. "Tell me what?"

"The addresses in Grace's jewelry box." Jimmy's face was grim. "I think I know what they are."

Between Jack nearly dying last night and then *kissing* her, she hadn't given enough thought to Grace's jewelry arsenal. Yet more evidence that, with five days left, she needed to keep her focus on what mattered. "Tell me."

"While I was at the Windsors' with Fontaine, I overheard a debate in the kitchen." Jimmy's mouth thinned. "Some of their staff were saying that, even with Clara out of the picture, conjury still isn't as strong as it should be. That too many people are sharing the brume."

It shouldn't have surprised her as much as it did. Even if conjury were as healthy as ever, people would still find a way to blame immigrants. "What does this have to do with that list?"

"Apparently," Jack began, the easiness of his tone infuriating when he'd just *kissed* her, "while we were in Grimsbane, the chancellor put forth a proposal to limit brume access to Society members. But Keeper Windsor vehemently opposed it."

They're taking our brume, Mrs. Stratton had screamed at Keeper Windsor when Henrietta had died. *How many of us must die before you* finally *let my husband do something about it?*

"How could he even limit the brume? And what does this have to do with . . . oh no."

Grace had a list of addresses, alongside jewelry bridged with conjury that no one in the Society possessed.

"She might be helping the chancellor," Caleb said grimly. "Maybe she bridged something with Oliver's gift so that it binds the conjury of anyone who touches it. And now she's going door to door in the city, conjure-binding every poor soul on the chancellor's list."

Bile rose in Emmy's throat. "And she keeps any useful conjury for her collection." No wonder Grace had been sneaking out of Clarity Hall all summer. Her uncle would be furious that she was doing the chancellor's hateful bidding. But Grace would risk his ire to gain Chancellor Stratton's approval.

We all know who holds the real power at Pinnacle Bluffs, Grace had gloated when she'd claimed she and Oliver would soon be married. At least they'd ruined that plan of hers.

"If we tell her uncle the truth at the masquerade ball," Jimmy said slowly, "maybe we can bring down both the chancellor *and* Grace. We can end this. Tomorrow."

Grace and the chancellor both ruined in a matter of hours. *Tomorrow.* "She could simply deny it," Emmy pointed out. "As could he. We need proof."

"We don't have time for proof," Jack grumbled. "There's only five days left."

Mary cleared her throat. "Didn't she give us exactly what we need to make her tell the truth?"

The inhibition-lowering bracelet. Emmy could not help it: she looked at Jack, who was finally looking at her. "It could work," he admitted. "Maybe if I melt the bangle into something that she won't recognize, like a hairpin or a chain for her mask . . . we could time it just right."

"Will the conjury still work, if you melt it?" Emmy's voice, mercifully, was cool and unaffected as she looked at him.

Jack shrugged. "It should, but there's no guarantee."

Another risk. Too many risks and Grace would slither away unscathed, once again.

"It's time, Ems." Jimmy clapped her on the back. "Time to clear your name, come back from the dead, and move on with your life. Have you considered what you want to do next?"

What life? she nearly shot back, but that would only make Jimmy worry. He wanted her to go back to being the naive girl who took for granted a life with books and dreams and a father who was alive and a best friend who loved her. But that girl was gone. And Emmy could not picture life after the Society. She couldn't even picture besting the Society. Not yet.

"Have you?" she asked instead.

He shrugged. "As Zhao Rui, I've got two potential projects in the city for the fall. We're talking million-dollar jobs. If I can find some way to merge Zhao Rui with Jimmy Li, then I can hire the best workers I know for my own construction company. And, hopefully, be your neighbor again. All of yours," he added with a grin.

"You assume I'm not already sick of you," Caleb sighed, though Emmy glimpsed the smile he was trying to hide.

"So we take down Grace and the chancellor tomorrow." Mulling it over, Jack nodded to himself. "Speeding things up might be for the best, given that Oliver saw me."

It was no small problem. As soon as Oliver was permitted visitors, he'd cry to his parents about Jack Fontaine framing him. If they believed him—a big if, given just what a mess Oliver had gotten himself into—the chancellor would raise hell at Mistfield.

No, time was not on their side.

Mary cleared her throat. "I don't know if my vote counts, but I'm in."

"You saved my life yesterday, so yours counts extra." Jack flashed her one of his easy smiles, but it didn't meet his eyes. Oliver had come too close to fulfilling Rose's prophecy.

"The sooner we're done, the better," Caleb agreed. "Let's finish this."

Jimmy grinned. "It was my idea, so I'm definitely in."

They all looked to Emmy.

It was a flawed plan, to say the least. The bracelet could run out of its enchantment. Or Grace might recognize her own conjury and remove it before revealing the truth. They had to time it perfectly, in front of the right people.

Still, there was something enticing about Grace being brought down by her own words. And if it worked, and Emmy's name was cleared alongside Jack's, Grace would know that Emmy lived. She'd know that Emmy was the one who had ruined her life.

She'd know, once and for all, that Emmy had bested *her* in the end.

"Tomorrow night," Emmy agreed.

TWENTY-SIX

ALREADY FULLY DRESSED FOR THE evening, Emmy perched on the edge of her bed and waited for Mary, who'd insisted that Emmy, as hostess, make a dramatic entrance. A steady hum of activity whispered underneath the door. Guests arriving? The Windsors and Strattons, already beginning their showdown?

Jack, coming to speak to her after avoiding her all day?

With an exasperated huff, Emmy flopped onto her pillows. The dangers they were facing tonight were too numerous to be counted on one hand, yet time and time again, Jack slipped into her mind, entirely unwelcome. That kiss. The way his eyes had darkened, his mouth falling over hers as if he could not help himself.

The remorse on his face when he'd turned away. Which was maddening, really, because *she* should have come to her senses first, as *he* was the one with a mile-long list of flaws. He lied—often. He used people to suit his needs, including Emmy. He smirked. Constantly. He was too good at keeping secrets, especially his own. He was terrible at apologizing. He was far too handsome, which made it too easy for him to get away with things. He was entitled. And spoiled. He got a kick out of making her angry. And he never knocked, instead burning holes in her walls. He courted death like a challenge to be bested. Even with the prophecy averted, it would be a miracle if he lived past twenty—

"Ready?"

Emmy startled. She hadn't even heard Mary knock. But, with a calming breath, she rose from her bed. It was time.

"Caleb's not back yet," Mary said in a low voice as Emmy gave herself a final glance in the vanity mirror.

Damnit. Caleb had gone with the chancellor to "communicate" with Oliver through the jail walls, but he should have returned hours ago. "Any sign of the Strattons?"

"Not yet. But the Windsors' carriage just arrived . . . and Grace isn't with them."

With a groan, Emmy buried her head in her hands. She'd known Grace would be upset about Oliver's arrest, especially after declaring that they'd be engaged within a week. But Grace was a survivor. She ought to have been here, batting her lashes at her new marriage prospect.

Unless Grace wasn't licking her wounds, but was out doing the chancellor's bidding.

By the time Mary had fastened Emmy's mask and hurried her into the hall, a few dozen guests had already arrived, gaping at the black flames that crackled along every surface. Without Grace's conjury, Emmy had worried the masquerade ball would be bereft of the enchanted touches of the other Society events, but Jack had dug up the Fontaine decor of years past: flammable ropes and table liners, an enormous flammable archway for the front doors, even special candles the staff had fastened to the ballroom's vast ceiling. Now Mistfield was as decorated with dark flames as Grace was with her cursed jewelry.

As Emmy descended the stairs, the guests turned to stare at her.

Red was a risky color, Grace had always said, but tonight was all about risks. And Mary was right, the bold shade complimented Winnie Fairchild exceedingly well, making the mahogany strands of her hair shinier, her emerald eyes brighter. Emmy kept her head high as the guests smiled serenely up at her, taking in the golden skin of her collarbone, the hint of cleavage from her dreadfully tight corset. She descended each step slowly, peering out at the party through her black feathered mask, the perfect match to the slash of black feathers that wove its way from her chest to the bottom of her dramatic train.

And there were the Windsors, standing along the edge of the foyer. Their royal-blue masks hid the top halves of their faces, but Mrs. Windsor's smile was fragile. Tonight was already hard for her, given the rumors swirling about her daughter's death. If their plan worked, it was only going to get harder for the grieving mother.

Swallowing her sympathy, Emmy continued to scan the room. The Society in masks of any sort was too reminiscent of her debutante ball, but at least now she knew their faces. The Villadoms. The Zermatts. And, waiting at the bottom of the stairs, Jack.

Of course he'd gone with a raven-black mask, with a simple silver embellishment looping around one eye. Everything else he wore was also black, from his polished shoes to his tailcoats; even his dress shirt and ascot. He was watching her descend, his lips parted—not that she was looking at his lips. No, tonight Emmy was focused on the only thing that mattered. Revenge.

He offered his arm. "Your brother's late, so it's up to us to greet the guests."

It was vexing, having to be near him, but she nodded, slipping her arm through his.

Despite her better instincts, there was something exhilarating about cutting through the crowd with Jack. That single point of contact—through her glove and the sleeve of his tuxedo jacket—was a drug in her veins. Still, she kept her face neutral, greeting their guests with the enthusiasm of a benevolent hostess. If he expected her to pine after him, he'd be sorely disappointed.

Soon the cocktail hour was in full swing, and Jimmy had quite the crowd of admirers, extolling the quality of his work, and how they could hardly tell such a tragedy had occurred here. Emmy, meanwhile, slipped away from Jack but was caught by a swarm of Mrs. Stratton's friends, who gave their opinions on everything from Oliver ("I've always said he was a crook") to the magnificent woods that sprawled beyond the ballroom windows ("Imagine how glorious this view would be without all those trees blocking the way"). But Emmy endured it all with a polite smile. Winnie Fairchild was no trueborn lady, but she played one well.

"May I present Mrs. Louis Arthur Stratton," the butler announced.

A crackling silence fell over the guests, one that turned Mrs. Stratton's smile to ice as she tiptoed into the reception. Alone. The chancellor and Caleb were nowhere in sight.

As everyone stared at Mrs. Stratton, her eyes began to water.

Excusing herself, Emmy cut through the crowd. Mrs. Stratton had taken Winnie under her wing this summer, and although Oliver's current predicament was, technically speaking, Emmy's doing, Winnie Fairchild would not snub his mother.

"Why Miss Fairchild, how lovely you look!" Mrs. Stratton embraced Emmy, kissing both of her cheeks. "How I wish Oliver could see you in this gorgeous gown."

Her voice caught on her son's name, and Emmy squeezed her hands, confused by the genuine sympathy she felt. "How are you holding up?"

"I'll feel better when Louis gets here." Adjusting her canary-yellow mask, she glanced around. "I'm assuming he and your brother did not come straight from the city?"

So they *had* gone to the city. But Emmy's relief was fleeting. If Caleb didn't get the chancellor to the ball, they'd miss their chance. "I'm sure they'll be here soon."

"Hopefully, he'll have Oliver with him and this whole misunderstanding can be put behind us." Mrs. Stratton waved to her friends, who quickly averted their eyes. Her proud smile morphed to steel.

"And the rest of these turncoats will rue the day they snubbed me."

Emmy was saved by the butler, who gave her a subtle nod. Time to bring the guests to the ballroom. Excusing herself, she made the announcement, and the eager guests filed into the ballroom.

Underneath the dim light of one thousand black-flamed candles, the ballroom was a sight to beholden. Emmy could not help but smile as she gazed at the glittering flames dripping from the ceiling, the chandelier, even the railing of the patio beyond the vast windows. But Jack took her arm once again, his fingers brushing the bare skin above her glove. If he was trying to rile her, to trigger that maddening awareness of his presence, she'd ensure he failed.

"Looks like it's you and me for the first dance."

Caleb was supposed to open the dance with her, while Jack was supposed to dance with Grace, so he could be ready to hide the inhibition-lowering conjury on her at a moment's notice. "I should wait for Paxton." Her tone, mercifully, was as cool as his.

"He's late. We don't have a choice."

"Fine." Accepting his arm, she let Jack lead her to the center of the dance floor and lay his right hand on her shoulder. With her head high, Emmy laid her left hand on his shoulder and let him clasp her other one. It was only a dance. Of all the obstacles they faced tonight, she could handle a dance.

The waltz began.

Jack, unfortunately, was an excellent dancer, leading her through the elegant box steps with a graceful ease. For once, her body's attunement to his worked in her favor, for they moved as one, seamlessly gliding over the dance floor. Emmy was aware of the appreciative glances of the onlookers, of the other couples moving in perfect unison, but she kept her eyes locked with Jack's in a staring contest she was determined to win.

"So you're not cross with me?" With his gray eyes lightning bright, it could have been his true face hiding underneath that masquerade mask. "About last night?"

Was he really choosing to discuss that kiss now, on a crowded dance floor surrounded by their enemies? "Not at all. We all make poor choices."

The dance floor was growing more crowded with couples by the second. Emmy searched the masked faces, looking for a hint of Grace's golden locks, or the chancellor's scowl, but they were both woefully missing.

"They'll be here," Jack murmured. Then, after a pause, he added, "Is it a poor choice to tell you how beautiful you look tonight?"

She whipped toward him, expecting his usual smirk, but there was a note of sincerity in the way his gaze held hers. First, that kiss. Now, a rare compliment.

But Winnie Fairchild *was* beautiful. Emmy had designed her to be flawless.

It hit her then: Last night, in the river, it wasn't Emmy's lips he had looked at with such longing. It wasn't her face he'd gripped, or even her waist he'd kept afloat. He'd kissed *Winnie*. And his horrified expression afterward was likely his remembering that she was really Emmy.

Her heart sank, which was silly, for she was guilty of the same. She'd given him a face she found irresistible, and now she was struggling to resist it. Even now, her body was mapping out every place his hands grazed her back, leaving invisible fingerprints in their wake. But perhaps that was to be expected. An unintended side effect of their beguiling disguises.

She must have relaxed, for he arched a brow.

"It's nothing." It felt good to be at ease with him again. She'd gotten herself all tied up in knots over nothing. And that was what was between them: nothing, save their shared vendetta.

The waltz ended, and he gave her hand a subtle squeeze before they both searched for their next partners.

As the hostess, Emmy had made sure that she knew all of tonight's dances. It was freeing, not having to dread what the orchestra might play next, or to worry about Clara whispering about her. Emmy might have enjoyed herself, had their lives not been hanging in the balance.

During the third dance, she spotted Grace and nearly collapsed with relief.

As Emmy danced with some man in his late twenties who prattled on about stocks, she studied her former friend. Grace was dancing with Richard Hamilton, the boy who'd been Emmy's first dance partner at the inaugural ball, nearly a month ago. Her mask was a glittering silver, much like her ball gown. If Grace was affected by Oliver's arrest—and by the rumors swirling about Elizabeth's death—her face revealed none of it. Rather than appear humbled by the ordeal, she laughed airily as she spun with Richard, her sky-blue eyes bright, her cheeks pink beneath her mask. She was beautiful, Emmy would give her that.

Their eyes met, and Grace's smile faltered, just a smidge. A small victory, yet it didn't bring a smile to Emmy's face. It was as if her loyalties were all twisted, as if some part of her still couldn't take joy in Grace's discomfort. She'd need to squash that part of her—and quickly.

The dance ended, and Jack caught her eye, his face tense as he slipped from the ballroom.

She followed, politely excusing herself from the many guests who tried to engage her in conversation along the way.

"Where the hell are they?" she whispered as he pulled her into the empty parlor and quietly closed the door behind them.

"They should have returned hours ago." Jack rubbed at his jaw, his knuckles brushing his mask. "Don't let the Windsors leave before the chancellor and Paxton arrive."

Keeper Windsor and his wife were certainly not enjoying themselves, but the night was still young, and if Grace was having fun, they'd stay. With a curt nod, Emmy nearly opened the door, but—voices. Angry ones in hushed tones, heading down the hall.

"You have some nerve, showing up tonight," a deep voice bellowed from the hallway.

"I could say the same to you," a second voice snarled. The chancellor.

The breath rushed from Emmy's lungs. It was happening.

A door slammed down the hall, muffling the angry voices, and Jack crept out of the parlor. Once it was safe, he nodded to Emmy, his expression tight.

This was all wrong. Caleb was probably looking for them. Without speaking to him first, they didn't have the slightest idea what had transpired at the jail.

Jack's gray eyes were steel as he glanced toward the ballroom. "Find him. I'll watch—"

Shouting stole the rest of his words, and Jack took off toward it, Emmy on his heels. It was coming from the library. Reaching the doors first, Jack threw them open.

Chancellor Stratton held a gun pointed at Keeper Windsor.

And Keeper Windsor, mask removed, held a gun pointed at the chancellor.

Neither man took their eyes off the other as Jack tucked Emmy behind him, exclaiming, "What is the meaning of this?" Quietly, he added, "Get the guards. And . . . her."

Grace. Of course.

She did not want to leave him with two armed men, but she slipped out of the library, breaking into a sprint in the hall, her gorgeous train a liability. For once, she was glad to find the white-uniformed guards. "Come quick! The chancellor and the keeper—hurry!"

They sprinted ahead of her, but Emmy paused in the ballroom

doorway. No one seemed aware of the crisis unfolding, save Jimmy, who left his post as soon as he saw Emmy.

She pointed toward the library, and Jimmy took off, catching up to the guards.

"What's going on?" Grace demanded, and for once, Emmy was thrilled to see her.

But Emmy didn't need to answer, for the shouting grew louder. Gathering her skirts, Grace hurried toward the racket, Emmy on her heels.

They reached the library doors at the same time—and froze.

The two Society leaders still had their weapons cocked at each other. The guards, meanwhile, remained near the doorway, out of the line of fire and utterly confused.

". . . framed my son!" the chancellor shouted, his fury stopping Emmy in her tracks.

Keeper Windsor's face and neck were as red as Emmy's gown. "Your son confessed to murder of his own volition. A murder *you* investigated!"

Emmy took a minuscule step backward, keeping as close to the door as possible. In her periphery, Grace did the same. Their eyes met, and Grace quickly looked away.

"'Of his own volition,'" the chancellor snarled. "Your niece bewitched him, making him say outlandish things while you bribed the police. You're a disgrace to the Society!"

At Emmy's side, Grace froze.

The guards exchanged a glance and drew their revolvers.

"Where's Caleb?" Jimmy whispered, and Emmy jumped. With Grace so near, he shouldn't have uttered Caleb's true name aloud, but his face was creased with worry. With a small shake of her head, Emmy quickly averted her eyes.

"I'm a disgrace to the Society?" Keeper Windsor laughed bitterly.

"*You* are the one who has been twisted by power, making a mockery of our ways. Letting your own son flaunt his conjury *in public*. Shooting anyone you perceive as a threat on a whim, even the parents of debutantes. Look at you now, making accusations with a gun in your hand!"

Emmy blinked, and there was Papa, on the tiles, framed in crimson. Blinked again, and he was gone.

Jack was on Grace's other side now, and Emmy had to force herself to stare straight ahead instead of watch him slide the charmed hairpin onto her glove. It had to touch her skin in order to work, but if she felt its chill . . .

Grace flinched, glancing at her arm, but—

"Take off that mask, girl." The chancellor was looking directly at her.

She pulled off her silver mask, her face paler than Emmy had ever seen it.

"You were there that night," he growled, "when Lizzie Windsor perished. Now tell the truth: Did Oliver have anything to do with her death?"

Emmy's heart was ready to beat out of her chest. If the truth bracelet—truth *pin*—was touching her, she'd have no choice but to answer honestly.

At Emmy's side, Grace's eyes were impossibly wide. She was practically chewing on her lips to silence her involuntary response.

"Tell the truth." The chancellor's voice grew gentler. "The Society of the Charmed values the truth. I value the truth, and if you speak it now, I will remember how you helped my son."

He was practically offering her Oliver's hand in exchange for her lying about that night.

"I'll ask one more time: Did Oliver have anything to do with Lizzie Windsor's death?"

Emmy held her breath, her heart in her throat as Grace's mouth flew open.

"Yes," Grace rasped, her eyes tearful. "Yes, he did."

The truth, at last. Emmy could have collapsed from relief—had she not seen the look that overtook the chancellor's face.

It was a look she'd seen in Five Points plenty of times, a collision of desperation and ego. Grace might have recognized it herself, had she not been yanking the hairpin off her glove.

The chancellor swung the gun toward Grace.

Shots rang out, and Emmy did not think, did not hesitate as she threw herself at Grace, crashing them both to the ground.

Grace screamed as Emmy crushed her against the hardwood floor.

They stared at each other, inches apart.

Shock. Pure shock widened Grace's eyes, loosened her jaw.

Strong arms pulled Emmy off Grace, searching her frantically. "Are you hurt?"

Jack. The hands flitting over her were Jack's, his expression so crazed, a strange laugh bubbled in her throat.

She blinked. Shock could hide furious pain, but Emmy felt nothing. She blinked, her ears ringing. Blinked again and shook her head.

She'd saved Grace.

Why the hell had she saved Grace?

The cacophony of shouts flooded her ears. People were pouring into the library, guards and guests, craning their necks to see. As Jack helped Emmy to her feet, Keeper Windsor helped Grace to hers, anxiously pressing his tuxedo jacket to the harsh red streak on her arm. She'd been wounded. It was hardly a comfort.

Keeper Windsor was alive.

And Chancellor Stratton was lying on the floor, his cold eyes unblinking. Dead.

A guard was emptying casings next to him. Another was checking the chancellor's vitals, but Emmy had seen enough death to recognize when it looked her in the eyes.

"Are you absolutely certain you're all right?"

A third guard lifted an ornate knife from a strap around Chancellor Stratton's ankle and held it in the light. Blood glinted on the blade, as red as her gown.

Emmy blinked. Jack grabbed her cheeks, saying something she could not hear. Just over his shoulder, Grace stared at Emmy from her uncle's arms.

Someone let out an ear-piercing, soul-crushing scream. Mrs. Stratton.

Blood on the blade.

All the air rushed from Emmy's lungs.

"Where are you going?" Jack followed her as she burst into the hall, pushing past the surge of partygoers heading toward, not away from, the gunshots. Emmy elbowed past them, her gaze snagging Jimmy, a head above the rest as he searched the crowd, worry still etched across his face. Their eyes met, and he made his way toward her and Jack, following them through the foyer and out the front door.

"Have you seen my brother?" she called to the footmen stationed by the entrance, but they shook their heads. The remaining Society guards watched her impassively.

The chancellor could have left him in New York, in some back alley—

"What's going on?" Jack kept pace with her as she hurried across the lawn.

"The chancellor returned without Caleb." Jimmy looked pained.

"He's all right. We'll find him." Jack sounded as confident as always—but he hadn't seen the blood on the knife.

Emmy hurried her step, the knot in her throat growing by the second.

The stable boy met them by the door, looking alarmed to see Winnie

Fairchild in full ballroom regalia. "Have you seen my brother?"

"Saw 'im when the carriage pulled up with the chancellor, miss. But he ain't been out 'ere since."

With her hands on her knees, Emmy tried to catch her breath, tried to hold it together. If Caleb wasn't inside, where the hell was he? She searched the driveway, but nothing. Searched the woods beyond the stable, but it was dark, Jack's flame their only light—

Jimmy let out a strangled noise. Before Emmy followed his gaze, she knew. She *knew.*

Only Caleb's shoes jutted out from between the trees, toes pointed at the ground. As they cut through the thicket, the rest of him came into sight: face-first in the twigs and dirt, the dead leaves caught in his crumpled hair, some sort of bug crawling over his jacket, which was dark and sticky and—

She did not remember hitting the ground, did not remember pulling his jacket off him, sliding her hand underneath his shirt so that her palm was against his skin, sticky with blood—

Oh God, so much blood.

He could not be dead. He hadn't even wanted to do any of this, but he'd done it for Jack. For Rose. And he'd wanted to stop, but Jack had kept pushing. *She'd* kept pushing . . .

He could not be dead. She screamed it at him, over and over, as her trembling hands traveled over his back, envisioning his skin its usual healthy pink, the tissues underneath whole once again. She'd never healed anyone in her life, but if she had even a smidge of Papa's gift . . .

His skin pinkened beneath her trembling fingers, but dark pools of blood continued to gather deeper in his flesh.

"Heal him!" Jimmy's hands were on Caleb now, his eyes wild as he begged her, over and over. Squeezing her eyes shut, Emmy called to the brume, a torrent of that ethereal mist rushing over her. The relic hummed against her chest, but she could not penetrate beneath his pale skin, no matter how much she tried to picture the muscles and organs pristine and healthy. Jack and Jimmy flipped him, and his front was somehow worse than his back, for his face was puffy and white and all wrong. Four, five, six, seven bloody stains, old enough to stick his shirt to his skin. She ran her trembling hands over them, screaming for the skin to close, to *heal*, like Papa could have done. But her conjury kept skirting over the surface, making superficial transformations. It was as if she were trying to speak a tongue she'd never heard, trying to flap her arms and fly without wings. She was not San Rocco. And whatever morsels of his conjury she'd inherited, it wasn't enough.

But she was his daughter. She'd witnessed him heal plenty of knife injuries.

"Get the carriage!" Emmy tore at her crimson gown, willing it to be thick cotton bandages, which she wrapped around his abdomen. Blood darkened the cotton over his stab wounds, but still, Emmy kept adding bandages. Jimmy held Caleb's torso as she circled it with more, more bandages. She had to stop the bleeding. Had to make everything tight enough to keep his blood in his veins, enough to keep his heart pumping—if it hadn't already stopped.

Only when Jack returned with the footmen did she press her bloodied fingers to Caleb's neck, praying like hell for a pulse to thrum through—there *was* a pulse. A faint one.

And then he was gone, Jack and Jimmy loading him into the carriage, Jack reaching back for her to join, but Emmy shook her head, unable to find her voice. She couldn't go to the hospital—someone had to stay at Mistfield.

And she was too selfish to witness another person die.

Twenty-Seven

THE HOURS PASSED IN A blur of frantic guests and rapidly emptying halls. The guards inspected Mistfield for any signs of overt conjury before giving approval for the local ordinance to be called. Emmy gave her statement to the police, using the talking points Keeper Windsor had dictated. Soon the authorities would realize that their stabbing victim, a key witness, and the estate's young owner were all using pseudonyms.

The chancellor was dead. And Grace was alive, courtesy of Emmy's conscience, which had chosen the most unfortunate time to resurrect itself.

From the opposite side of the library, Emmy felt Grace's vigilant gaze burning into her. Grace's gloves were long gone, along with the truth conjury that had nearly forced a confession from her. The graze wound on her arm had miraculously disappeared, too. That little wench must have had one of the bandages imbued with Papa's conjury hidden in her skirts.

The staff were beyond shaken, especially once word spread that the chancellor had stabbed Paxton before entering the ball. They were eager to fuss over Winnie, but after accepting a glass of warm milk in lieu of breakfast, Emmy insisted she needed to lie down while she waited for news. Once in her room, she promptly grabbed one of Grace's many invisibility rings from the stolen jewelry box and made her way to the end of Mistfield's long driveway to wait.

Whatever news came about Caleb, Emmy could not trust herself to receive it with an audience.

The sun had reached its apex when a carriage finally appeared down the road. On stiff legs, she stood and waited, her heart in her throat.

The driver saw her as he passed and brought the horses to a halt a little ahead of her. Her stomach was in knots as the carriage door flew open. Out jumped Jack, his expression haggard as his eyes found her.

"He's all right," he called as he strode toward her. "Lost a lot of blood but he's alive."

Emmy tried to nod as stoically as she could, but her facade must have cracked, because Jack threw his arms around her.

Caleb was alive. She tried to let that sink into her bones, but they'd skirted death twice in the last three nights. She could not trust that they'd continue to have such luck.

Jack smoothed her hair, and she could not summon the will to pull away. Worse, she burrowed deeper against him. The long night had hollowed her out, and she had nothing left. No words. No tears. No reasons not to be soothed by Jack, by the steady *thump thump thump* of his heart.

"This isn't how he dies," Jack murmured in her ear, his hands still caressing her hair.

But that was no comfort, not when Rose's prophecy had been wrong only two nights ago.

"I need to see all of Rose's prophetic drawings. Every last one of them."

He hesitated. "Ask Caleb. When he's better." The driver must have said something, because Jack raised his voice. "Miss Fairchild and I will walk back when we're ready."

Reluctantly, Emmy let go of Jack, bracing herself for the awkwardness that would inevitably follow. But it didn't come.

As the horses trotted away, Jack rubbed his tired eyes. "He needed surgery as soon as we arrived, but he was awake when I left."

"So he's alive." She needed to hear it again, to be sure.

"Thanks to you." He turned to her. "The physicians said they never saw a tourniquet like the one you made. They said if we had found him any later . . ."

Neither of them finished his sentence. It had been much too close.

Emmy sat on the edge of the road, pulling her legs toward her. "I couldn't heal him."

"Even your conjury has limits." He settled beside her, wrapping an arm around her shoulders, and no part of Emmy could resist such comfort. "Jimmy was beating himself up for asking you to do it."

Emmy winced. With Caleb hurt, Jimmy didn't need to invent new reasons to be upset. "With the relic, even I thought it might be possible."

"When conjury evolves, it loses some ability as it gains new ones. Your conjury, while similar to your father's, is not the same. Same with Oliver and the chancellor. While they can both suppress movements, Oliver can also suppress conjury. But he can't silence people, like his father."

It made sense, of course, but with the relic, Emmy had begun to feel as if her conjury were limitless. Already, she'd transformed far more than she'd ever dreamed. "I think, deep down, I knew it wouldn't work. I've never been able to heal anyone."

"You say that as if you've tried," he said gently.

Emmy's nerves were so frayed, she didn't fight the words. "My mother."

"When you were eight."

He remembered. Emmy studied a fleck of dried blood beneath her fingernail. "My father had only just begun to teach me magic, and we thought mine was like his. That I was a healer. By the time he got home, I'd been trying to make her heart beat for over an hour."

Time had eroded so much of the memory, Emmy recalled very little, save her mother's sudden bout of abdominal pain. Her lying down to rest. The tepid temperature of her skin when Emmy had crawled into bed with her.

"Sometimes I forget how much you've lost. How much we've both lost, I suppose." With a long exhale, Jack rested against his hands. "My mother died giving birth to me. I'm pretty sure my father blamed me for it."

"What makes you say that?"

"He used to say, 'You killed your mother.'"

Emmy snorted, then quickly covered her mouth, but Jack was smiling, too, though his faded far too quickly. "When you tried to heal her . . . were you all alone?"

Emmy shook her head. She'd never forget Grace's sky-blue eyes tearfully watching as Emmy tried to fix her dead mother for hours. Never leaving her side. Never raising her voice above a soft whisper: *It's all right, let her go, it's all right.*

Those memories, the good ones, were the worst sort of betrayal.

"About Grace." His teeth scraped his bottom lip. "Last night, when the chancellor shot—"

"It was a moment of weakness." If Emmy had just let the chancellor's bullet do its job, their vendetta would have been complete. They could have come forward with the truth, clearing their names while shedding light on the chancellor's conjure-blocking scheme—and Grace's role in it.

"It was a kindness." His brow wrinkled at whatever face she made. "You're not a monster, Emmy."

"A pity."

"Do you still want to ruin her?"

"Of course I do." She nearly climbed to her feet. "I don't care if I have to do it myself—"

"I'm with you. I'm with you," he repeated more fervently, lowering his forehead to hers.

Here they were, once again in dangerous territory. A current was always crackling between them, and this close, it risked catching fire. But she couldn't muster the energy to care. She wanted to fold herself into him, to lose the boundaries of where she ended and he began.

That was precisely the sort of softness that had led her to *save* Grace, rather than let that bullet exact its own revenge.

Emmy forced herself to stand. They'd lingered but a few minutes, and she was already losing her focus. Time to return to the anxious staff—and to Mary, who, in the chaos of the night, she hadn't seen since the ball began. The poor girl was probably worried sick, given that Emmy had quite literally disappeared without telling her.

Falling into step with her, Jack slid his hand over hers. *Don't be soft*, she pleaded with herself, but two years in Grimsbane had left her starving for company in the throes of her grief. Perhaps it was the same for him.

"Was Caleb able to say what happened?" she asked, keeping her eyes on Mistfield.

With a quiet sigh, he rubbed his forehead. "The chancellor knew all along that Oliver had started the fire that killed Rose and Lizzie. Given Caleb's conjury, he assumed Caleb knew the truth, too. And he didn't want any loose ends."

Of course not. Emmy's temper rose, despite her exhaustion. "We should have seen this coming. The chancellor wasn't going to let a telepath walk free. Not with all his secrets."

"You're right." He glanced at her. "He's truly dead, not just badly wounded?"

She nodded. Death had certainly not been their goal, but he'd killed Papa. And now he was dead.

It was oddly comforting how little she cared.

Jack lowered his voice. "We have only four days left, including today, which is halfway over. If we do this—"

"We *have* to do this," she interrupted. "But we can't ask the others to help. It's too dangerous." After nearly confessing to murder last night, Grace would be far more suspicious. "We can't use her own bridged jewelry against her again, either. She'll be ready."

"So we go to the city first thing tomorrow. We find the person with truth conjury and bribe them to return to Avalon-on-Hudson with us. Then we bring them to the Windsors' for the final event, confronting Grace with the truth once and for all." He nodded to himself, standing taller as the plan took form.

How she longed for his confidence, but all the things that could go wrong were clawing at her throat. "What makes you think there will still be a final ball?"

"The Golden Gala is a long-standing tradition." With a small shrug, Jack shifted his hand over hers, sending delicious tingles dancing over her skin. "I can't picture the Windsors canceling it. Especially since they'll need to hold a vote to fill the empty positions on the triumvirate."

She nearly asked Jack if, with his name cleared, he'd like to be commander, but she didn't want to picture him as an upstanding Society officer. Or worse: wearing one of those ivory uniforms, hunting down people who'd risked magic's secret to make ends meet.

"There are too many things that can go wrong," she finally said. "The person with truth conjury might not be at one of the addresses on Grace's list. And even if I transform them beyond recognition, Grace might refuse to cooperate. There's also still a chance she's made her own relic, like Rose's." She hated even uttering it aloud, but—Grace had the pages tucked in her jewelry box. She'd been willing to hurt people for it—to kill for it. She would not simply accept that it was forever lost at the bottom of the Hudson.

But Jack shook his head. "I've told you; relics are made with a specific bone fragment."

"From the sternum, right above the heart. And with your flames." Emmy lifted her shoulders. "But we can't afford to underestimate her again."

"So we don't rely on just *her* telling the truth." Jack stopped walking, his face solemn. "We tell ours, too. As Jack and Emmy."

She waited for him to laugh, but he looked so grave, her heart sank. Underneath all that anger—all that hurt that drove him toward revenge—was an optimist.

"For better or for worse, I've known these people since I was born. They're not all bad. Most of them are just—like I used to be. Not questioning things enough. Besides, the pieces are all there. Oliver implicated himself in the fire, and last night, Grace confirmed it. The chancellor's the one who threw me in Grimsbane, and his word is ruined." He paused, chewing his lip. "Is it so far-fetched that they might realize I didn't kill my own sister?"

It was the hope in his expression that hurt worst of all. But his heart was set on this plan of his, and with no time left, she didn't have a better one. "Then let's find the truth conjurer. Today, not tomorrow."

For a fleeting moment, he looked as if he might kiss her again. But instead, he blew out his breath. "You need sleep. We both do. And we still have three more days."

"Fine. First thing tomorrow." Summoning her courage, Emmy finally let go of Jack's hand. To take down Grace Montgomery, she couldn't afford another moment of weakness.

Twenty-Eight

FOR THE FIRST TIME SINCE that carriage had whisked her and Grace away, Emmy stood in front of a tenement house in lower Manhattan, her hands fisted at her sides. Not *her* tenement house, but from the outside, there was hardly any difference.

There was little light in the corridor, save the sun streaming between the wrought iron bars on the door. There was little air, too, and Jack kept his nose scrunched at the stench. Though she'd transformed his face to a wildly unattractive one—an effective deterrent during the long trek to the city—his discomfort was evident from the moment they'd entered the dingy building.

"There's no railing," Jack murmured as they made their way up the stairwell. "Or lamps."

"Why don't you file a complaint with the landlord? He's probably a friend of yours."

Jack was wise enough to hold his tongue, but he still walked stiffly, as if he'd contract a venereal disease by bumping into a wall. She should have come alone. But it was too late. They were here, and they needed to find the truth wielder.

Emmy had mapped their route, working clockwise from the Hudson River toward Little Germany before finishing in her old neighborhood. Part of her longed to walk those familiar roads, to stand where she'd stood when her life was right side up instead of upside down. But with fifty-seven addresses to cover, she couldn't afford any distractions.

Jack knocked on the door at the first address, but no one answered. "Should we wait?"

"We'll come back later, if we don't have any luck elsewhere." Swallowing her sigh, Emmy drew a question mark next to the address before turning away.

Emmy led the way through the crowded streets, Jack falling into step beside her. The passersby kept their distance, as if they sensed his silent judgment. Or perhaps the face Emmy had conjured for him was a tad too grotesque, with his eyes different sizes and his nose and chin much too large. More than once, she glimpsed children pointing and whispering.

It mattered not; Emmy did the talking, holding up a replica of the inhibition-lowering bracelet to whomever answered the door—usually mothers with curious children peering behind them—and gauged their truthfulness when they said it didn't look familiar.

"This may be a wild-goose chase," Emmy muttered as they made their way through the bustling streets, trekking to the next address.

"If you have a better idea, I'm all ears."

But a better idea required time, and with the final ball in two days, they were nearly out of it.

Dark had fallen by the time Emmy admitted that visiting fifty-seven addresses was a tad too ambitious for one day. With a gnawing sense of foreboding, she followed Jack to the ferry dock, careful not to lean against him, though her tired limbs ached to do so.

"We'll take the first train in the morning." Jack's confidence was undercut by the exhaustion in his voice. "That'll give us all day to get through the rest."

Emmy could have screamed in frustration. It was too risky, leaving Avalon-on-Hudson for two straight days, especially when the Society had to be reeling from the chancellor's death. They ought to have been receiving visitors—or at the hospital with Caleb. But abandoning their search meant forfeiting their chance at having a truth conjurer present when they confronted Grace. And as much as

Emmy longed to see Caleb in one piece, she had to stay focused on the ultimate goal.

Revenge.

The next morning, they continued their search from flat to flat. How Emmy longed to ask the people who lived at these addresses if they possessed magic—or if a pretty blonde girl had taken it away.

"After tomorrow's ball," Jack murmured, "we'll figure out some way to unblock these people's conjury, assuming Grace and the Strattons have already gotten to them. But first, we find the truth conjurer."

Emmy did not point out that the Strattons might have already conjure-bound the truth wielder, and their search might be for naught.

By midafternoon, the only addresses left were in Five Points, where the streets bent and twisted in open rebellion of any semblance of organization. The buildings leaned in every direction, clotheslines and telegraph wires scratching out the punishing summer sun. Crowds of people hurried past Emmy, speaking Yiddish and German and Italian and a dozen tongues she couldn't place. She stole a glance at Jack, then wished she hadn't, for even in his unsightly disguise, he was completely alert, reacting to the inherent threat of the only home she'd known.

Swallowing her frustration, Emmy led the way to the second-story flat and knocked.

The door cracked open, and a hollow-faced teenage girl peered out at them from behind the chain. "What do you want?"

"We were hoping you'd seen this before." Emmy held the replica of the bangle in her palm.

The girl's eyes widened almost imperceptibly before darting back to Emmy's, then narrowed. "Where did you get that?"

Hope trickled through Emmy's veins. "If you let us in, I'll tell you all about it and pay you for your time."

The door slammed shut. Jack let out a groan, but Emmy kept her gaze trained on the door. That girl had been frighteningly thin. She would not turn away money so easily.

The door swung open, this time without the chain, and a little boy with a cherub's smile took Emmy by the hand and led her inside.

"Have a seat." The girl motioned to the round kitchen table, big enough for two chairs. As Emmy slid into one, Jack held out the other for the girl, who shot him a look so scathing, he retreated to Emmy's side, his gray eyes darting about the small space.

And small it was. The setup was nearly identical to her old home: the charcoal stove next to a counter with the dish basin to its right, and the kitchen table just beside the stove. In the only other room, Emmy knew she'd find a small fireplace and maybe a sofa, or a bed, depending on how many people lived here. And Emmy had a feeling that if she opened the closet behind her, she'd find a cot, one that stayed nice and warm all winter long, courtesy of the stove.

It had felt so grand, having a cozy space all to herself. But now such quarters felt terribly cramped. And Emmy hated it, because the typical flat layout hadn't changed. *She* had.

"Oh!" Emmy went stiff as the little boy climbed into her lap, then turned to face his sister.

"Well?" Now that they were in better lighting, his sister looked older, perhaps even the same age as Emmy, though with her rail-thin figure, it was hard to tell.

Jack cleared his throat. "My name is Michael—"

"Not you." She pointed to Emmy. "Only she talks."

Jack exchanged a look with Emmy. At her nod, he leaned against the wall.

"My name is Bernadette Higgins," Emmy tried to begin, just as they'd rehearsed earlier this morning, but instead of her pseudonym, she uttered, "Emilia Vallillo."

She stiffened. The girl's flat mouth curved into the slightest smile.

"You have truth conjury." Of course, the girl's face revealed nothing, but Emmy was all too familiar with this particular gift and its strange loosening of her thoughts.

Her conjury was not cold, like Grace's, but a tingling sensation settled over Emmy as the girl studied her. "Tell me why you've come here."

"Because I need your help." Emmy tried to slow the stream of words racing from her lips, but she was powerless against them. "Because Grace Montgomery ruined my life. She does terrible thing after terrible thing, but she always gets away with it."

"And you want me to make her tell the truth."

"Yes." It was an effort not to wrestle against the strange urge to speak the truth. As if sensing her discomfort, the little boy nestled against her.

"And why should I?"

"Because it's the right thing to do."

"They're taking away magic, you know. Following any rumors of people with out-of-the-ordinary abilities, then hunting us down." With narrowed eyes, the girl studied Emmy. "Miss Montgomery has worked out a deal so I can keep mine."

"As long as you let her bridge some of it." Emmy could not keep her frustration from her voice. The girl didn't deny it, at least. "She isn't helping you; she's helping the people who are doing the hunting. We found a list of people whose magic she's already taken away. The only reason she hasn't done it to you is because she wants your gift. She's *using* you."

"What does it matter to me?" The truth conjurer shrugged. "I get to keep my magic, and the people she works for are none the wiser."

"The people she works for are dead." Jack's jaw was set. "A recent development."

"Can you guarantee that no one will take their place? That I'll truly be left alone? Not you," she added sharply as Jack tried to answer. "Only her."

"No." Emmy's stomach sank as the truth continued to spill from her. "There's a lot of prejudice in the Society, and they'll likely elect more people who will come after you and other people like you. They're afraid of magic's secret getting out and causing another witch hunt."

"So they're hunting down witches themselves," the truth conjurer said bitterly. She must have seen something in her brother's face, for hers softened as she smiled at him. "We're plenty safe, muffin. These two were just leaving."

Jack groaned. "Please. We're trying to do the right thing here."

"No." The girl stalked to the door and opened it, her expression tense. "Now go."

Emmy and Jack exchanged a look. Emmy hadn't the faintest idea if this girl would see Grace again in a day or a year, but—she knew Emmy's true name. And perhaps even more pressing, they could not leave without her help.

As Emmy rose, she grabbed an old newspaper off the ground. By now, she'd conjured so much money, she hardly had to focus, instead keeping her eyes on the girl. One moment, Emmy held the yellowing paper, and the next, fifty-dollar bills rained from Emmy's hand. "If you help us, I'll transform your face to protect your identity. And then I'll make you so much money, you can live as far away from the Society of the Charmed as you like."

With a gasp, the little boy gathered greenbacks in his fists and hurried to his sister, who had wisely shut the door. Her eyes bulged as she examined the money, and Emmy could not help but think of herself and what she might have done for this sort of sum only a few years ago.

She kept that thought to herself. The money, apparently, was distracting enough for the truth wielder to let go of her conjury.

"I need to think this over." Tucking the money into her apron, the girl opened the door once more. "Give me three hours. Then you'll have my answer."

Three hours was enough time for her to send word to Grace.

Jack dragged his feet toward the door. "We really don't have time."

"If you don't leave now, then my answer is no." She forced them into the hall—

But Emmy held on to the door frame. "Should we come back?"

"Stay local and I'll find you."

"How?"

The door slammed in their faces.

Jack scratched his head. "I can't tell if that went well or not."

"I'm not sure." Emmy leaned against the opposite wall. "Maybe we should wait here."

"I don't think she'd like that very much." With a sigh, he stared at the door. "Well, we found her. And she took the money. That ought to count for something."

The walls were too thin for them to continue this conversation. Emmy nodded to the stairwell, and Jack followed.

The sun blinded them as soon as they stepped outside. With nothing to do but wait, Emmy leaned against the wall for a bit of shade. Heated by the pounding sun, the stench of the waste that littered the street turned her stomach.

Jack smiled at a pair of older ladies walking past, who quickly hurried away. "Why does it feel like everyone is staring at me?"

She could not look at the asymmetrical face she'd given him once again. "No reason."

With a sigh, he settled beside her. "If I have to sit here for three hours, I'll lose my mind."

"What else can we do?"

"You heard the girl. She said she'd find us." He watched the pedestrians weaving between the carriages. "I was thinking . . . I know where your father—"

"No." She could not spit the word out quickly enough.

"The cemetery's not far from here."

As if Emmy did not know that herself. Pushing off the wall, she glanced back at the tenement house. Everything felt wrong. Being here while Caleb was in a hospital in Westchester: wrong. Waiting for that girl while she might be running to Grace: wrong. Sitting in that flat, its layout nearly identical to her home's, yet far too small, as if the haven of her childhood had shrunk: wrong, wrong, wrong.

And being in Five Points without Papa? Infuriatingly, mind-numbingly wrong.

Jack rose, too, loosening the top buttons of his shirt. "What about that dumpling place?"

"I don't want to see you cringe at all the places I loved."

"Hey. *Hey*," he said more urgently as she turned away. "I'm not cringing. I'm just—"

"Disgusted." She pinned him with a hard look. "I can read your face like a book."

"All right, fine. I didn't know . . . I thought tenement houses were just small apartments. But that flat?" He lowered his voice, his expression pained. "It had to be a hundred degrees in there. They didn't even have a window. And the whole time, I kept thinking, *Does my family own this building? Am I the landlord who didn't put up a railing?* Yet another part of my life I never questioned. And that makes me sick."

He turned away, and Emmy felt a stab of unwanted sympathy for him. As worldly as he seemed, this was likely his first time ever setting foot in a home smaller than a mansion.

"I'm not cross with you," she finally said. "It's just, it all used to feel so wondrously vast and unruly, but now . . ." She could not bring herself to say what it looked like to her now. How dingy. How bleak. "I suppose a few months at Mistfield have changed my perspective of 'big.'"

The hint of a smile teased his lips. "Emilia Vallillo, have I turned you into a snob?"

"Stop."

"I have, haven't I?" Straightening his posture, he offered her his arm. "Let's get something to eat while we wait. Unless it's only lobster and caviar for you now."

"You really are terrible."

"I've heard that my whole life." He leaned closer, as if he might touch her face. But her plain blonde disguise was far from Winnie's beauty, and he turned away.

Reluctantly, Emmy brought him to Chatham Square, where the elderly gentleman who made the Cantonese dumplings hadn't aged a day. Two orders came to twenty cents, a price that would have cost her sorely the last time she was here, but now Emmy handed him a five-dollar bill. "Keep it."

The man dabbed at his sweaty forehead. "You want more dumplings?"

"Just . . . consider it a gift."

He beamed, and something stirred in Emmy. It was an irrationally large tip, but Emmy had an irrationally large wad of money stashed in her dress. Maybe that extra four dollars would buy much-needed medicine. Maybe it was the difference between making rent and eviction.

There wasn't an inch of shade available, so they sat against a sun-soaked brick wall, dumplings in their laps. "You have to blow on them," Emmy warned, "or else you'll—"

Jack hissed, midbite, pain erupting over his face.

"—burn your mouth," Emmy finished.

"Worth it. God, that's delicious." Jack lifted the next dumpling, lips pursed to blow on it. Damnit, she'd forgotten to transform that distracting mouth of his.

Averting her eyes, she blew on her own dumplings as she watched the crowds. Everyone was heading in the same direction, the children bouncing and skipping ahead. Their giddiness soothed her mood, just a smidge. She was not misremembering everything about Five Points. For most of her life, she'd been happy, too.

"How much money have you got in those secret pockets of yours?" Jack asked.

"About eighty dollars. Need more dumplings?"

But Jack was digging his leather wallet from his pocket. "I've got about three hundred—"

"Put that away," Emmy gasped, pushing the wallet out of sight. "Are you trying to get robbed?"

"Why not? We don't need it." Seeing Emmy's frown, he shrugged. "It just feels like we should do something good with our money. You made that man's day."

"That man is a dime a dozen in this city."

"I'm not trying to eliminate poverty in an afternoon; I'm trying not to lose my mind while we wait. C'mon." He hauled her to her feet. "If you don't want to be mugged, let's spend it."

She could not argue with that. And with their fates in limbo, a distraction couldn't hurt.

Spending hundreds of dollars was surprisingly challenging. They bought lemonades and ice cream, tipping the vendors enough to make them suspicious. Following the flow of foot traffic, they came across a street festival, one with music and dancing and dozens of vendors hawking goods at their carts. From cart to cart, Emmy bought Neapolitan cakes and gelato and paper cones bursting with popcorn, handing them to any child in sight. Even after that, they had much more to spend.

With his absurdly asymmetrical face, Jack's frown made him even more unsightly. "I keep trying to give sweets away, but no one will go near me."

She tried—and failed—to bury her smile behind her ice cream, and Jack eyed her suspiciously. "You did something to my face, didn't you?"

Before he could glimpse his reflection somewhere, she pulled him deeper into the festival. A stage had been erected, upon which four organ grinders were playing in unison, for once. Italian folk songs. To her shame, she couldn't name a single one. As they moved through the crowd, Emmy slipped greenbacks into ladies' aprons, stuffed them in the fists of wide-eyed children. "For the festival," she told them. "Enjoy yourself."

It didn't take long before a crowd gathered around her, and Emmy emptied every secret pocket she had, doling out quarters and dollars, change and greenbacks. But it wasn't enough. This money could change these people's lives, and it cost her nothing. It could keep their children healthy, or pay for a doctor, or fill hungry bellies, or allow for a much-needed day of rest from work.

And it cost Emmy nothing.

She was dizzy with the need to give it out, drunk with their exclamations of gratitude. The music thrummed and swelled with the crowd, and Emmy slipped dollars into unexpected pockets. She paid for every street vendor's supply so that everyone could eat and drink their fill.

And how they thanked her. How they hugged her and pinched her cheeks and made her feel more alive than she had felt in a long time. Why hadn't she done this the moment she first grasped the relic? That was what Papa would have done.

Have you considered what you want to do next? Jimmy had asked her a few nights ago, and Emmy hadn't been able to see past the masquerade ball. But maybe she'd return to Five Points with Rose's relic. Maybe she'd use it to help people. She could transform all the greenbacks and gold they needed to feed their families, could teach the other charmed folks about the brume, about grimoires and bone fragments and all the wondrous gifts people like them wielded in this very city. A school, perhaps. One that welcomed immigrants and outsiders.

It was hardly the seed of an idea, but already she was protective of it, burying it deep in her chest. If they managed to ruin Grace, she'd let herself dream of such things.

Still, as she found Jack at the edge of the festival, she felt lighter, somehow, though Jack looked far from it. "Did she come back?" Emmy asked.

"Haven't seen her." His cavalier smile might have fooled her a few months ago, but by now, she could see it for the mask that it was.

"Is it Caleb?" Even just saying his name racked her with guilt that he was in the hospital while she was here. *Enjoying* herself.

"No, it's just . . . this is really nice." The strangely uneven eyes she'd given him were full of sadness. "But in my experience, happiness is a prelude to disaster."

He was right. Enjoying themselves was like juggling with knives. At any moment, a sharp end was bound to cut them.

Giving him such a ridiculous face felt cruel all of a sudden, so she led him into the mouth of an empty alley. "Stay still."

He obliged, and she pressed her hands to his heat-flushed cheeks. It should have been quick, but her cursed mind kept picturing Jack's face instead of Nathaniel's. As she completed the transformation, he watched her intently. He'd been Nathaniel for hardly a few seconds, and already, she was drawn to him.

Although she knew better, she let her thumb brush his bottom lip as she took it away.

"Emmy." He uttered her name as if it pained him to say it. A curse and a prayer. His hands captured hers, and he looked as though he might bring it to his lips. He had to feel it, too, this current thrumming between them—between Winnie and Nathaniel. But she didn't even look like Winnie right now, and he was still gazing at her as if she was someone to be desired.

She tried not to succumb to his gravity, she truly did. As his hands found her waist, she meant to push away, but instead, her hands settled on his arms. As he leaned closer, she swore she'd turn away, but she met him in the middle. Wings beat wildly in her stomach as he bowed his neck, bringing those cursed lips closer. Only a lunatic would kiss him again after he'd called her a "poor choice," but Emmy, apparently, was destined for a sanatorium. She lifted onto her toes as he cradled her cheek, the need in those gray eyes sending a thrill down her spine.

Their noses brushed, a delicate dance.

Their mouths touched.

If the last kiss had been a furious shout, this one was a silent promise. Those cursed lips moved with agonizing tenderness, flooding Emmy with the dizzying sensation of being cherished. Utterly foolish, given that he was kissing her blonde persona. As his hand cupped her face, she leaned into his touch, greedy for more. At this rate, she was going to die in this alley, because she was never coming up for air.

He broke the kiss to search her face, and she felt a twinge of disappointment that it was Nathaniel, not Jack, looking at her with such longing. But she was already waist deep in bad decisions, so she changed him back to his true self.

Oh, this was the epitome of foolishness, kissing Jack Fontaine. Their kisses grew hungrier, and she backed him against the alley wall as he gathered her in his arms. His hands trailed her shoulders, her back, setting her aflame. She swore she'd stop, over and over, but she was kiss drunk and deliciously dazed. *Last time*, she promised herself with each pass of his lips. *Last time.*

Finally she broke the kiss, letting her head fall against his chest as he folded her against him. It was as fragile as a snowflake, this moment. She could already feel reality melting it, could once again hear the ruckus of the street fair. But she squeezed her eyes shut and tried to drown it out, listening to the racing *thump thump thump* within his chest.

"I have one more question."

For once, Emmy moved quicker than Jack, spinning to face the person at the edge of the alley. The truth conjurer. Her little brother skipped to Emmy, taking her hand.

"What is it?" Jack called back—and damn it, his face was truly Jack's.

For the first time, the girl seemed uncertain. "How can you guarantee my safety?"

"I can't." The truth rushed from Emmy. "All I can do is transform your face like I did his, and give you a carriage to leave as soon as you're done."

"Grace Montgomery doesn't ask me to risk my life for revenge."

"Justice," Jack interrupted. "It's *justice* we seek. And it is dangerous, but you wouldn't be the target. Oh, hello there." Jack patted the little boy on the head as he took Jack's hand.

The truth conjurer watched her sweet brother closely. Too closely.

Emmy glanced back and forth between the teenage girl and her brother, wishing it to not be true. "*You* don't have truth conjury."

The girl's gaze snapped to hers, that protective fire unmistakable.

The little boy was clever, climbing into her lap earlier. Cleverer still for doing it so playfully, she hadn't realized their act.

Emmy pointed to the little boy, her heart sinking. "*He's* the truth wielder."

TWENTY-NINE

THOUGH EMMY HAD EXPECTED TO surprise Mary with a pair of siblings from Five Points, Mary had an even bigger surprise for them: Caleb was home.

They burst into Caleb's quarters, where Jimmy had already made himself comfortable in an armchair beside the bed. "How is this possible?" Jack exclaimed.

"The hospital had no private rooms." Caleb's weak voice carried a hint of arrogance that brought a smile to Emmy's lips. "And if I had to spend another night in that crowded ward, I was going to rip out my own stitches."

"He's supposed to stay in bed." Jimmy shot Caleb an ominous look. "If he does anything strenuous, the wounds could reopen and he'll bleed to death."

Caleb huffed. "The giant won't let me so much as blink."

"And you better get used to it." Jimmy folded his arms over his broad chest. "Because this giant is going to be watching you, night and day."

Mary's gaze shifted between Jack and Emmy. "Any luck?"

In hushed voices, they told the others about the truth conjurer, and how the little boy and his sister would accompany them to tomorrow's Golden Gala. Once the Society understood how the truth conjury worked, Jack, as Nathaniel, would confront Grace about her role in Mistfield's fire. If—and only if—Grace was ruined, Emmy and Jack would reveal themselves, clearing their names once and for all.

It was a risk, to say the least. Even if the Society believed him, they might not look kindly on their duplicitous quest for vengeance. Even more discomfiting, they'd know of Rose's relic. Jack swore he would not let them so much as touch it, but Jack was not invincible.

But if it worked, Emmy would see the look on Grace's face when she realized that her perfect life was aflame—and Emmy Vallillo was holding the match.

"So let me get this straight," Caleb said once they'd finished. "You kidnapped a little boy and his sister?"

"Their names are Tobias and Agnes," Jack replied smoothly, "and they came willingly."

Willingly, with new faces and the promise of enough money to buy their own city block.

Jimmy sighed. "It doesn't feel right, dragging a little kid into it."

Emmy exchanged a look with Jack. Neither of them was proud to involve a six-year-old. "We understand if you want out, but we're finishing this. Tomorrow."

"I'll help," Mary said softly. "The Windsors deserve to know the truth."

Emmy couldn't help but hug her. With Mary, they'd have invisible eyes on Grace all night.

Jimmy sighed. "For the first time in my life, I wish I had magic, so I could help keep you all safe."

"You help plenty," Emmy said gently. "You keep us *sane*."

"And charmed or not, you know how to handle yourself if everything goes to hell." Jack's steady gaze met Jimmy's. "You know what needs to be done."

A heavy look passed between them. "Fine. I'm in. Unless Alton needs me here."

"Why would I need you here? I'm going, too."

Almost instantly, the four of them replied with a quick and resounding no.

Caleb was affronted. "I'm sure we can scrounge up a wheelchair from somewhere!"

"If you so much as *blink* without a doctor's approval," Jimmy growled, "I will carry you back to the hospital myself."

Caleb and Jimmy stared at each other for a long beat. Finally Caleb gave a reluctant nod, his ears pinkening as he turned away.

"Enough plotting, everyone." Jimmy nodded toward the door. "Alton needs his rest."

Jack's gaze met Emmy's. She gave him a small nod, ignoring how her pulse ratcheted from a single glance, or how, without uttering a word, she knew he'd burn a hole in her wall tonight. Two months of conspiring together had tightened this bond between them, but she could not confuse it for something more. Especially on the eve of their final takedown.

"Emmy?" Caleb called, his voice faint. "Do you mind staying back for a moment?"

Just her. That was a first. She glanced at Jimmy, who looked equally surprised, but he shut the door quietly, leaving them alone.

"I was going to thank you," Caleb began, "for saving my life—"

"You don't need to do that." Emmy could not even look at him without seeing his feet protruding from the woods, his skin sallow and gray.

"I knew you'd say that. So I thought I'd show my gratitude a different way." He nodded toward his desk. "Can you fetch that brown leather book?"

"Another ancient magical text? You know me too . . . Oh." It was no ordinary book; it was Rose's portfolio.

Accepting it from her, Caleb set it on the bed between them. "I assume Jack has shown you these?"

Emmy nodded, trying not to think of Jack on his knees, Oliver looming over him.

"You've asked me, maybe a dozen times, about Rose's prophecy for my own death. So . . . here." He flipped open the portfolio, his fingers deftly turning to the proper page.

The thick ink lines possessed the same cursory sharpness as the other morbid drawings, but there was no fire. No knives in throats. Only two lovers in bed, fast asleep, with deep crinkles around their eyes from decades of smiling.

Emmy had forgotten such a death existed. A peaceful one. And Rose was quite the artist, because even though he was half a century older, one lover was unmistakably Caleb. And the other—

Sweet relief washed over Emmy. "The other person, that's—"

"Yes, that's a man." Caleb sighed. "And now you're the second person I've told my secret. Third, if you count Jack, who happened to be present when Rose drew this."

He was trusting her with something precious to him. "I'm honored," she said softly. "But what I was going to say is . . . that's Jimmy, isn't it?"

"What?" Caleb squinted at the picture. "No it isn't!"

Emmy traced the handsome face of the elderly Chinese man curled around Caleb. "Look how tall he is. And look at that half smile."

Pink blossomed across Caleb's cheeks. "How could you possibly tell? This is sixty years down the road, at least!"

"I know my friend," she said simply. "And I think you do, too."

She saw it then, in his frantic expression as he looked at her. Hiding beneath his panic, beneath every dismissive jab he'd slung at Jimmy.

He was in love with him.

"You can't tell him," Caleb rasped. "I don't think he feels the same. I don't even know if he *likes* men. Even suggesting that— Oh God. I think I might be sick."

It was wrong, really, to feel so delighted while Caleb was so flustered. But the more she studied the drawing, the lighter she felt.

Jimmy and Caleb just might live long enough to have decades etched into their faces. Together.

"I think," she said gently, "you should have more faith in Rose."

He lifted his gaze, and a quiet smile blossomed over his face, revealed itself slowly. And Emmy was absurdly glad that he had survived the chancellor's attack.

"You and Rose would have gotten along swimmingly." He chuckled. "In fact, she was almost as desperate to meet you as Jack was."

"But she'd never even heard of me."

"Of course she had." Grief weighed on his smile. "We called you 'woodland girl.' Rose and I teased him to no end about that prophecy."

Emmy stilled. "What prophecy?"

Caleb opened his mouth. Shut it. His eyes darted to the portfolio.

They lunged for it at the same time, but Emmy reached it first, swinging it off his bed. Caleb hissed, his hands flying to his stitches. A better person would have stopped to check on him, but Emmy raced from his room. "Emmy, don't you dare," he called after her. "*Don't you dare!*"

Ignoring his irate yells, she shut the door and dropped to her knees in the hallway, spreading the portfolio in front of her.

The hall was dimly lit, making the charcoal drawing of Jimmy and Caleb seem more ominous than it had a few minutes ago, though not nearly as morbid as the ones of Rose and Elizabeth burning in black flames. She flipped past those quickly, flipped past Jack on his knees, not letting her eyes linger.

The next few drawings contained color, though they were rudimentary. Almost childlike, but with enough skill for Emmy to recognize a young Rose and Caleb laughing in an empty ballroom. An elderly woman playing a grand piano. With each turn of a page, Rose's skill improved until the drawings possessed an ethereal quality, dreamy but clear.

A moonlit night swim, Caleb's smile freer than Emmy had ever seen it.

A dark-haired man with eyes just like Jack's, only older. He stood on Mistfield's balcony in the Society's uniform, a letter crinkled in his fist.

Jack slumped in Mistfield's cemetery, eyes red rimmed, empty bottles littering the overgrown grass.

She flipped to the next drawing—and stilled.

Jack was lying on his back in the woods, grinning at a girl leaning over him. No, at *Emmy*.

With trembling hands, she angled the drawing toward the dim light. It was, unmistakably, her true face. Thin and hollowed out, courtesy of Grimsbane, but with a wild smile, as if she was mid-laugh. Branches and leaves were caught in the long skirt of her gray wool dress, dirtied and torn from running through the trees. There were even twigs caught in her loose braid, making her look downright savage.

Woodland girl.

It was the moment after they'd narrowly escaped the Society headquarters. After she'd transformed Jack back to himself, instead of her horrid rendition of Oliver Stratton. That was why she was touching his face. Why their cheeks were flushed. A perfectly reasonable explanation, yet in Rose's hand, their expressions were downright amorous.

No wonder Caleb had gaped at her when he'd come across them that night.

As if in a daze, Emmy hugged the portfolio to her chest and walked back to her room.

Jack was waiting for her, a tendril of smoke rising from the fresh hole between their rooms. He grinned—until he spotted the portfolio.

She'd seen him escape a heavily fortified prison. And on his knees, frozen in front of Oliver Stratton. In neither of those instances did he look as frightened as he did now.

With surprisingly steady hands, she laid the drawing in front of him. "Tell me there's some reasonable explanation why your sister—your sister who was dead an entire *year* before I met you—drew me."

"Define 'reasonable.'" He tried to flash her his cheeky grin, but he could not hide the wild panic in his eyes. It was the look of someone caught in a lie.

A big, terrible lie.

"I want to know the truth."

"I don't think you do."

"Jack."

"Okay. We're doing this." He dragged his hands over his face. "Rose drew that a long time ago."

"How long?"

"Very long." His throat bobbed. "As in 1875."

Seven years ago. Not trusting her legs, Emmy lowered herself onto the edge of the bed. In 1875 she'd been eleven years old. "I don't understand. Why would she draw this?"

"Her conjury was no crystal ball. She couldn't ask questions of it, or even find reason to what she drew most of the time. Except when she held the relic. And we all know how well *that* turned out. Though I've always wondered, if she'd tried it again, knowing what to expect—"

"Jack."

"Right. Okay." He blew out his breath. "Rose called her prophecies 'little pivots.' She thought she drew moments when the course of our lives would shift. Maybe we would receive crucial news. Maybe we would make up our mind about something. Either way, our lives would pivot."

"But there's nothing important about this moment. We were just laughing because we'd nearly died, and you looked so ridiculous—"

She saw it then, layered between his wince and his nervous smile.

The same caught expression Caleb had made, only moments earlier, when she'd brought up Jimmy.

"Don't," Emmy warned, rising to her feet.

"You said you wanted the truth."

"Don't."

He cut off her path to the door. "I know you don't want to hear this, but I think I might be . . . a little bit in love with you?"

She squeezed her eyes shut, blocking out the uncharacteristic hope in his face.

"And my nosy sister drew the exact moment I realized it."

"You hardly even knew me!" Her heart beat erratically against its cage, the sudden burst of oxygen dizzying. "When this happened, I'd been living at Mistfield for what—two weeks? Three? And other than your harassing me about my magic, we rarely spoke!"

"I was thirteen when she drew you. Thirteen," he repeated, following her as she escaped toward the hearth, "with a mother I'd killed at birth and a father who held it against me. Rose and Caleb were in their own world, with no space for me. Most of the time, I was with Oliver, who hardly even tolerated me. But there was a girl out there who would one day touch my face like I wasn't bad luck personified. Like I mattered."

She heard the gentle rustling of paper as he lifted the drawing from the portfolio, but Emmy kept her back turned. He did not love her. He couldn't.

"I was desperate to meet you. As soon as I came of age, I attended every single ball, charmed and ordinary, searching every stranger's face. Rose and Caleb teased me to no end, but I couldn't find you. Not until you climbed onstage at the debutante ball, five years later."

"Don't," she rasped, ignoring his gentle hand on her shoulder. It was hard enough keeping her strength without thinking of that cursed ball.

"You were so beautiful," he whispered. "So earnest in your pursuit of conjury. And so fiery, too, tossing your gold at the triumvirate's feet—at my father's feet, as if you cared little for his pomp and circumstance. And the way you searched the crowd for *your* father . . ."

Emmy stayed very still, lest her chest crack open.

"But they accused you of fraud."

She blinked, long and slow.

"I hated myself for it later, that I didn't fight for you when they dragged you away."

As he fell quiet, Emmy tried to recall a boy with gray eyes that awful night. It was too much.

"You said to me once that I did not question things, and you were right." Shame laced his quiet words. "My father said you'd have due process, and I believed him. It was Rose who insisted we do more to help you. She was the one who thought to attend your father's funeral."

Emmy could bear it no longer; she whipped toward him. "If I was so important to you, why didn't you tell me? Why did you aggravate me every chance you had?"

"Because I was supposed to die, and you were never supposed to find out any of this!"

"How honorable," she said dryly.

"That's not what I meant." Eyes closed, he dug his fingertips into his forehead. "I found you on the worst night of your life. And I was thrown into the penitentiary on the worst night of *my* life. Finally, I was near you, but I couldn't see you, or hear you, or help either of us. . . . My sister was dead. Her morbid prophecies were coming true, and quickly."

He opened his eyes, his expression pained. "Unlike you, I had hope. I had Rose's drawings. But believing in them also meant accepting I was going to die soon."

She was back at Grimsbane now. Alone in her cell, while he was alone in his.

"You did not need to fall in love," he said quietly, "only to grieve again. But you needed your conjury back. You needed to stoke that self-righteous fury that burns in your heart, the one that compels you to fight against injustice. For your father. For yourself. In those first few weeks at Mistfield, the only time you looked alive was when you were angry. So, yes. I stoked the embers of your fury. And it worked."

They stared at each other, and Emmy tried to absorb this new Jack. One who had known about her for seven years. "So while you were in Grimsbane, you knew we would both be free one day in order for that"—she nodded toward the drawing—"to come true."

"I didn't know if it'd be days or weeks or years. It all depended on my getting my conjury back, and Caleb and Jimmy making arrangements. But I spoke to you through the walls." He turned away, crimson flooding his cheeks. "I yelled for you to hold on. And when my conjury started to return, I ignited the walls with my pitiful flame, pretending I was keeping you warm. My obsession became my madness: taking care of you, pretending you could hear me."

Her favorite wall, the one that was slightly warmer than the rest. The voice she'd thought she hallucinated: *Hold on, just a little longer, hold on . . .*

"This isn't how I wanted to tell you." He raked his fingers through his hair. "I had a whole speech planned, but I can't remember a damn word."

She saw his pain. Felt his need. It was tragic, really, because if they'd met before the debutante ball—when she was naive enough to believe in love—she would have been swept off her feet by Jack. A prophesied romance between a girl from Five Points and the son of a rich, magical family? Grace would have swooned over it, too.

But Grace had taught Emmy an important lesson, one she could not afford to forget: love was a lie.

"I think I understand." She kept her voice gentle. "At a time when you were very alone, your sister predicted you'd meet a girl. And that girl became a fantasy—"

"No." He shook his head adamantly, coming closer. "No, that's not what I meant—"

"You don't love me, Jack. It takes *years* to fall in love. Not months."

"Then I'll tell you again in as many years as you'd like." He grinned. "Two? Three?"

"You love the girl from the drawing." Emmy could hardly stand that laughing, carefree version of herself. It was too much of a tease, a glimpse at what life might have been. "And I think you know it, deep down. That's why you kept this from me."

"I was afraid you'd run for the hills! Especially when you saw all the other girls she'd drawn me with." Seeing her confusion, he added, "You didn't see the other girls?"

She'd already known that Rose had drawn him with several lovers, so it should not have hurt. It should not have twisted like a fucking knife that someone else was destined to matter to him. But by now, Emmy was well-versed in choking down her feelings.

With renewed vigor, he turned the pages of the portfolio, thumbing through prophecy after prophecy. "This is another reason I stayed away from you in those first few weeks. Well, this and the fact that my family was dead and I was searching for the antidote to grief in the bottom of a wine bottle."

"Maybe your future is with one of these other girls," she forced herself to say.

"Unlikely." He kept thumbing through his sister's prophecies.

"Maybe one of them is destined to be your wife," Emmy continued, her voice strained. "Someone who loves the Society, and the fuss and frill of balls, and—"

"Here she is." With a triumphant smile, Jack set the portfolio in front of her.

Hesitantly, Emmy glanced down at the drawing.

It was her. Not *her*, but Winnie Fairchild, her wide emerald eyes locked on Jack's. He cupped her chin, his face full of determination. Adoration.

The room began to spin.

It was just before he'd confronted Oliver. When she'd transformed him to Jack.

No wonder she'd rendered him speechless when he'd returned from the city, seeing her Winnie face for the first time. It wasn't that he was awestruck; he'd *recognized* her.

She gripped the bedpost to keep herself upright.

"Ready for the next one?"

There was Jack, with a half-dressed brunette buried against his neck. His shirt was only half buttoned, his eyes squeezed shut. Though her face was hidden against him, it was her, when she'd been wearing that inhibition-lowering bangle.

He flipped to the next, and Jack was locked in a passionate embrace with a blonde girl. His back was against a brick wall, her hands tangled in his hair as they kissed with a tenderness that made Emmy want to strangle him for making her look at this terrible—

Her hand flew to her mouth. The lovers were in an alleyway, just as she and Jack had been earlier today. The blonde girl—that was the disguise she'd used.

She must have made a pained noise, for he pulled her against him.

How weak she was, letting him hold her. How weak, burying her head against his chest, listening to the reassuring *thump thump thump* of his heart.

"You have transformed me more than you intended," he breathed against her hair. "I'm still not worthy of you, but I'm trying, Emmy, I swear it."

She shook her head against his chest, refusing to look at him while he was so earnest.

"You've called me obsessed, but it's worse than that. It frightens me, the things I'd do to keep you safe. I'd kill for you, Emmy." His thumb trailed her lips, his gaze so piercing, her eyes fluttered closed. "I'd set the world on fire just to keep you warm. And I'll never let anything bad happen to you again. I swear it."

His nose grazed hers, and she could have melted from longing. All she had to do was turn mere millimeters, and his waiting lips would find hers. Never before had she been so torn. He was the only person who understood what it was like to hurt the way she hurt. To lose the way she'd lost. She'd begun to rely on him so slowly, so thoroughly, she hadn't realized what she was doing until it was too late.

He meant his words now. But if she lost him—if he turned against her like Grace had—she'd never piece herself back together. She *needed* him. And that was precisely the problem.

Gently, she untangled herself from his embrace. "I'm sorry, Jack, but I just—can't."

"No more cliff jumping, I swear it." He took her hands, those gray eyes pleading. "No more burning holes in your walls, and making jokes at inopportune times, and—"

"Whoever gets your heart will be one lucky girl." She gave his hands a final squeeze. "But that girl isn't me."

He flinched as if she'd struck him. "You mean that."

"I'm saving you a lot of trouble." Her voice was calm now, her resolve growing as she let go of him.

Jack absorbed her words as he searched her face. She hated seeing him so devastated, but what choice did she have?

"Tomorrow, we'll face Grace." Her name alone made Emmy feel

more certain that she was, in fact, doing the right thing. "And if we ruin her, you'll go back to being Jack Fontaine, with no prophecies hanging over your head. You'll fall in love with someone new, and she'll move into Mistfield, and you'll forget all about those drawings." *And me*, she nearly added.

"I'd rather go to hell than share Mistfield with someone else."

"Jack—"

"I'd rather rot in Grimsbane. It'd be a picnic in comparison." Pushing up his sleeves, he glanced around the room, looking unsteady for once.

And she hated it.

He walked stiffly back to the hole he'd burned, and Emmy racked her brain for the words to set things right between them. "About tomorrow . . ."

"Don't worry, Vallillo. You've just given me a whole new reason to hate Grace Montgomery." His smile was forced, his eyes once again shuttered. "Sleep well. It all ends tomorrow, one way or the other."

There was so much more to say, wasn't there? But Emmy only nodded and, once he was safely on the other side, healed the wall for what felt like the last time.

THIRTY

IT WAS DOWNRIGHT FRIGHTENING, HOW thoroughly Jack wore his mask of nonchalance. As the carriage pulled up to Clarity Hall with their strange party of six, Jack's gray eyes were clear and alert, without any dark circles beneath them. No sign of any special regard for Emmy, either, as he grinned at them with a polished bravado that made her chest ache. "Ready?"

Before anyone could answer, the Windsors' footmen swung open the carriage door and they were surrounded by the Society of the Charmed wearing head-to-toe gold. Golden suits and gowns, golden top hats, golden gloves stretching past the women's elbows. Glittering gold bracelets and chokers and pins and rings. Several ladies even had sparkling golden paint in their hair, giving the illusion of dozens of Graces, which was more than a little unsettling.

Jack had insisted their outfits go all out, too, and Emmy hadn't resisted. By now, she knew how seriously the Society took their themed events—and she did not want to disagree with Jack while things between them felt like they might shatter at any moment. So she'd transformed their garb to gold, including Mary's uniform. She'd even conjured Agnes's and Tobias's clothing so that they looked like gilded court jesters: pointed hats and shoes, ruffled golden collars, even a thin layer of gold paint to their skin, making them look like walking statues.

The guards stationed by the front door took one glance at the gilded strangers and stopped them immediately.

"They're performers, approved by the chancellor himself." Jack curved his lips. "Before his death, of course."

The guards bristled, studying Agnes and Tobias suspiciously. Before she'd painted their skin golden, Emmy had altered their faces, but Agnes still glared at them.

After deliberating among themselves, the guards waved them inside, and Jimmy took Emmy's arm. The knots in her stomach loosened a smidge.

"Be careful," Mary whispered, squeezing Emmy's elbow before slipping behind a column—and disappearing entirely, using her invisibility to weave through Clarity Hall undetected. She'd have to use it sparingly—a minute, here and there—but Mary knew how to blend into the crowd, remaining undetected as she shadowed Grace. In a half hour, she'd check back in with a full report.

The first ball of the summer had been along Clarity Hall's sweeping pavilion, but the last was in the neighboring ballroom, with the translucent glass wall that overlooked the Hudson. Tonight, a jaw-dropping golden waterfall stood in its place. Molten gold cascaded from the ceiling, tumbling in mesmerizing waves that caught the candlelight.

"An illusion," Jack said in a low voice as he joined her and Jimmy in the doorway.

Of course. Grace must have bridged the glass with Villadom conjury. "I'd be more impressed if it *sounded* like a waterfall." The rushing water was eerily silent.

Jack tried to smile, which was far worse than if he'd simply ignored her. Their eyes met, and he looked away.

Swallowing her sigh, Emmy followed him deeper into the Golden Gala, passing an enormous gold-frosted cake that was taller than even Jimmy, who was now shaking hands with Mr. Zermatt, another potential millionaire client. As Tobias and Agnes gawked at the cake, the other Society members pointed to them, whispering behind their golden gloves about the strange interlopers dressed as pint-size entertainers. Emmy, meanwhile, searched the sea of golden curls for Grace.

"She'll be here," Jack murmured. "After all, this is her palace."

His words were laced with bitterness, but his smile snapped into place, and he was off, making his rounds among the Society of the Charmed. It felt wrong not to follow—not to take his hand and offer some sort of comfort—but that was precisely the problem.

"Miss Fairchild!" Mrs. Windsor touched Emmy's elbow, greeting her with a tentative smile. "How lovely you look! And your brother is expected to make a full recovery, I hear?"

"He is." As Emmy returned Mrs. Windsor's smile, she searched her face for any resemblance to her niece. Their pale blue eyes, perhaps. Her button nose. "And what about Miss Montgomery? She was struck in the arm, yes?"

"The bullet missed, fortunately." Her eyes watered as she squeezed Emmy's hands. "We owe you tremendous gratitude for that."

For Papa's conjury, more like. "I did what anyone would do."

"Most people would have thought only of protecting themselves, but you thought of Grace. Which, if I may be frank, Miss Fairchild, is even more impressive given that there was little warmth between my niece and you this summer. But perhaps, with Oliver Stratton out of the picture, that might change?"

There was a note of desperation in her voice, one that surprised Emmy. "I'd like that," Emmy said carefully. "Perhaps Grace and I could have a word?" After Grace had skipped or been tardy to so many events this summer, Emmy would breathe easier once she had eyes on her.

Mrs. Windsor's smile faltered. "I'd like that very much, but—I'm afraid Grace might miss tonight's festivities."

Her words were sandpaper over Emmy's nerves. Their entire plan hinged upon Grace being here. "Is she all right?"

"Oh, Miss Fairchild. This has been a difficult summer, indeed. She cries herself to sleep most nights. And in the morning, she locks herself in her room all day. She did that this morning, and a few hours ago, I had the footmen break down the door, but she was *gone*." Mrs. Windsor glanced around, her expression pained. "It's unfair of me to ask for your help, but—you saved her life. Perhaps that could be a new beginning for the two of you. She could really use a friend."

Good lord. Emmy hardly knew what to say. Part of her longed to tell Mrs. Windsor the truth—that Grace had spent the summer sneaking off to do the chancellor's bidding—but they needed to reveal a far more personal crime tonight: that Grace, whom her aunt loved, had a hand in her daughter's death. Either way, Mrs. Windsor would be devastated.

Emmy offered a shaky smile. "I'd be glad to."

"Good." With a final squeeze, she let go of Emmy's hands. "Ah, there's my maid. Perhaps Grace has been found."

Emmy watched Mrs. Windsor cut through the crowd, disappearing from the ballroom. From his circle of potential clients, Jimmy raised his brows, but Emmy gave her head a small shake.

Tobias slipped his hand into Emmy's gloved one and showed no signs of letting go. With him in tow, and his sister glaring from a few steps behind, Emmy made her way to the other young women, exchanging air kisses and answering their questions about the gilded court jesters with a mischievous "You'll see." She greeted Mrs. Stratton's friends, who were still picking through the bones of the Strattons' ruin, reviewing all the times they had found the new widow's temperament unbecoming.

"Excuse me, everyone." Keeper Windsor stood in the entrance to the ballroom, tapping his champagne glass with a spoon. "I have a few announcements to make. Grace, dear? Join me."

Emmy could have collapsed with relief as Grace finally glided into the ballroom. Scanning the party, Emmy looked for Jack, but he was nowhere to be seen. Neither was Mary, though Emmy was dying for a report on Grace's whereabouts at the start of the ball.

Like all the other ladies' gowns, Grace's was golden, though hers was several shades darker, nearly bronze. A diamond-encrusted gold tiara was perched upon her shiny blonde curls. Her fingers were adorned with delicate gold rings, and her wrists with gold bracelets, though her only necklace was the relic she claimed was her father's.

All that jewelry. A new arsenal, waiting at her fingertips.

Keeper Windsor motioned for Grace to stand beside him, and she obliged, Mrs. Windsor flanking her other side.

"This year's Golden Gala marks the end of what has been a rather dramatic season, to say the least," Keeper Windsor said, and nervous laughter rumbled through the crowd. "Deceptions were revealed. Loyalties have been called into question. And tomorrow, we leave Avalon-on-Hudson with a pressing duty hanging over us: the election of two new members of the triumvirate. I will pass along information about the nomination process later this evening."

"Once he's done speaking, it's our turn," Jack whispered, and Emmy flinched. He was beside her now, his hand on Tobias's shoulder, his steely gaze on Grace.

You've just given me a whole new reason to hate Grace Montgomery.

It was the perfect time to address the crowd, with the Windsors and Grace front and center and the Society already gathered around, but dread pooled in Emmy's core. There was so much that could still go wrong.

"Now, on a personal note, Mrs. Windsor and I would like to share some special news."

Jack's eyes met Emmy's, his confusion a mirror of her own.

Hand in hand, the Windsors stood before Grace. "My sweet niece, you have been a part of our family since the day you were born."

A lie. Until she was accepted into the Society, they'd ignored her.

"You treated Elizabeth like a sister." His voice cracked. "And you shepherded us through the dark days that followed her passing."

A murmur swept through the guests. They hadn't forgotten Oliver's confession, and with it, the uncertainties of what, exactly, had happened the night Elizabeth had died.

"To end this eventful season on a celebratory note, we'd like to formalize your place in our family. You'll become Grace Windsor, if you'll have us."

A gasp passed through the crowd. Parents eyed their eligible sons, who stood taller. For her part, Grace managed to look perfectly surprised. She wrapped one arm around her uncle, and the other around her aunt, and applause spread through the ballroom.

For a long time, Emmy had wanted the Windsors to acknowledge Grace, if not to sweep in and save her from her neglectful mother. How strange it was now to watch an even vaster dream come true. Grace was now the wealthiest young woman in the room.

Grace got what she wanted. Time and time again. Grace used, and she hurt, and she tiptoed away from the trouble she caused. With each deceit, she soared higher and higher.

"I am at a loss for words," Grace said breathlessly once her applause quieted. "Lizzie was more than a cousin to me. She was the first true friend I ever made."

A bitter laugh fell from Emmy's lips. Their friendship had never been real to Grace. Not once, in the decade they'd spent inseparable, had she mattered to Grace.

"Ready?" Jack stared at Grace, his jaw set.

Emmy was more than ready. She glanced at Tobias, but Agnes took her elbow.

"Nothing happens to him." Agnes uttered it like a threat, but her voice warbled.

"Nothing happens to him." Emmy squeezed Tobias's small hand and, with her heart in her throat, followed Jack toward the front of the crowd.

Keeper Windsor clapped his hands. "Now that all that's out of the way, let's celebrate—"

"Actually, Keeper Windsor," Jack interrupted, stepping forward, "might I have the floor for a moment?"

Keeper Windsor blinked in surprise. "I don't see why not. We're all rather curious about your entourage this evening."

Emmy's gaze found Jimmy, who made his way through the crowd to join her.

"The Windsors' announcement is well-timed, because I have a gift for their new heiress." Jack flashed a smirk at the guests, who leaned closer, delighted. "Miss Montgomery, do you have any burning questions for anyone present? Perhaps a handsome young man?"

Grace blinked innocently at him. "Are you gifting me a suitable husband?"

Everyone laughed, and Emmy had to hand it to Grace; she was adept at charming a crowd. Jack motioned for Tobias, and with impressive bravery, the little boy let go of Emmy and walked into the half circle of strangers.

"Ask a question of anyone here," Jack said, "and this handsome little court jester will give them no choice but to answer truthfully."

Emmy did not miss the brief surprise that crossed Grace's face. As familiar as she was with Tobias's gift, she hadn't recognized him in disguise.

As Grace's eyes flitted about the crowd, Emmy could nearly picture their plan working. Grace would have no choice but to confess her role in Mistfield's fire, and she and Jack could reveal their true identities. The Society would be horrified by their duplicitousness all summer long—but they'd also know that they'd been wrongfully imprisoned.

And Emmy would see the look on Grace's face when she realized the dead friend she'd backstabbed had been Winnie all along.

Grace cleared her throat. "I'd like to know why the young Mr. Whitmore has never asked me to dance."

More laughter. Grace's smile grew. They were eating out of her hands, and she knew it.

Paul Whitmore stepped forward, his cheeks a bit pink. Tobias took his hand, and Paul gave him a strange look before replying, "Because I feared Stratton would pound me if I danced with you." His hand flew to his mouth, the laughter of the crowd nearly drowning out his raspy voice. "Why did I say that?"

"This boy's conjury brings the truth." Jack grinned. "It's unavoidable."

"What a delightful gift!" Grace pasted a smile to her pink cheeks as she clapped, the other guests following suit. "Perhaps we can set up a station for him by the refreshments."

Clever, to try to move their game along, but fortunately, Jack was cleverer. "Ah, but we have a question for *you*."

This was it. Emmy could not breathe as Tobias wrapped his fingers around Grace's bicep, just above the edge of her golden glove.

All the color drained from Grace's rosy cheeks.

"Miss Montgomery." Nathaniel's perennially amused smile was still firmly in place. "Do you have secrets of your own?"

Grace's eyes went wide. "Yes."

"That's enough." Keeper Windsor shot Jack a scathing look.

But Jack raised his voice. "And do your secrets pertain to your cousin's death?"

Emmy could not suck in a single breath.

"Yes," Grace rasped. She tried to break free of Tobias's fingers, but his hold remained firm.

"How *dare* you." Keeper Windsor stalked toward Jack, grabbing him by his golden collar. "Grace has already told us everything about that awful night."

But Jack shook him off, his gaze locked on Grace's. "Does your uncle know the truth? Or have you kept secrets from him, too?"

"I haven't told him everything." Grace's eyes were wild as she shook off Tobias, nearly tripping over her train as she backed away from the little boy. "Uncle, I—"

But Keeper Windsor had gone ashen. "Take the boy's hand."

"But I—"

"Now."

Grace glanced at her aunt for help, but Mrs. Windsor looked as if she was about to collapse. Still, Grace kept her distance as she searched the crowd as if some solution would present itself, but the audience stared back at her, their attention rapt.

Emmy leaned forward as Tobias's fingers circled Grace's arm once again.

Jack's gray eyes were unrelenting as he stared at Grace. "How did Lizzie die?"

Grace tried to fight the words, covering her mouth with her free hand. If the ballroom hadn't been utterly silent, Emmy might not have heard her whisper, "She was murdered."

This was it. Emmy did not even trust herself to blink, lest she jinx it.

"By who?" Keeper Windsor shouted, his voice anguished.

The ballroom was as quiet as church. No one moved. No one breathed.

With her sky-blue eyes wide, Grace lifted her free hand and pointed.

To Jack.

"By him." Grace's finger trembled. "That's Jack Fontaine. *He* killed our Lizzie, and he's come for me, too!"

THIRTY-ONE

EMMY WAITED FOR JACK TO spew some clever response, but he only stared at Grace.

"She's lying!" Emmy blurted. She could not stand idly by while Grace wriggled out of trouble yet again. "She must be wearing something to suppress the truth."

Of course. Oliver's suppression conjury. As Grace shifted one of her golden bracelets, Emmy could have kicked herself. Grace had probably bridged his gift countless times. She never would have agreed to answer a single question unless she knew she could control her responses, especially after they'd nearly gotten her to confess at the masquerade ball.

What fools they'd been, thinking they could trap her with her own words.

The crowd whispered furiously. The Windsors looked as if they might keel over. And Grace's delicate finger still pointed at Jack.

Smoothing his jacket, Jack strode to where Emmy stood at the front of the crowd. "Do it. It's now or never."

He wanted her to change him, but Emmy shook her head. Convincing the Society of the Charmed to trust him was a long shot, especially since Grace had been touching Tobias when she made her accusations. Transforming him back to Jack would only confirm she was telling the truth.

Grace gripped her aunt's arm for support. "He's been lying to us all summer. He had Oliver arrested and convinced his father that my uncle was conspiring against him, making the poor chancellor lose his mind. And now he's come for me!"

Damn her. She knew—somehow, she knew everything.

"She's lying!" Emmy cried out again. "If he were Jack Fontaine, I'd know it!"

But Emmy had never had Grace's gift of persuasion, and wary looks were cast her way.

"Please," Jack pleaded. "I can convince them. *Please.*"

There was no time for debate, for brainstorming better plans. As quickly as she could, Emmy let her pinkie graze Jack's, pouring her relic-infused conjury into him. His hair darkened to chocolate, and his features lost the marbled flawlessness of Nathaniel, instead returning to the rugged handsomeness of Jack. The faint scar in his brow. The slight crookedness in his nose. The faint dimple in his left cheek as he realized Emmy had obliged, for once.

Someone gasped. And before Emmy could pull away, Jack gripped her face on both sides. "Finish this."

He kissed her. On the mouth. So shocked was Emmy, she was frozen until he staggered back, pretending she'd pushed him. Laughing, he faced the crowd. "You have no idea how long I've wanted to do that."

Jack Fontaine bowed to the Society of the Charmed, his smirk as devilish as ever. "Took you all long enough to figure me out."

Emmy could hardly hear the crowd's shock as she stared at Jack. This was not their plan. He was supposed to tell them the truth, not prove Grace *right*.

Finish this, he'd whispered. Instructions. Because he knew their plan would no longer work. He was sacrificing himself.

All the air rushed from Emmy's lungs. Of all the brash, impulsive things Jack had done—

The guards circled the ballroom, gathering toward the exits. Jimmy shot her a look, but she shook her head. To have even the slightest chance of proving that Grace was lying—and that *she* was responsible for Mistfield's fire—they needed to let Jack play this foolish hand.

"The body you found in the river? Not me. And that charred corpse you found in my cell? Also not me." Jack ignited a flame in his palm, and everyone gasped, though he'd been doing it all summer. "I don't burn."

"How did—" Keeper Windsor stammered, gripping his wife's arm. "How did you get here?"

"Chancellor Stratton was more than happy to vouch for another Fontaine, once he saw the pretty young heiress I'd brought for his son." Jack grinned. "Fortunately for me, Winnie Fairchild is as dim-witted as she is beautiful."

He was maintaining their covers. But Jack hadn't thought this out. They'd take him back to Grimsbane Tower—or they'd kill him.

It frightens me, the things I'd do to keep you safe.

The room began to spin.

"Arrest him!" roared Keeper Windsor.

A half dozen guards surrounded Jack. He dug into his conjury, but without Rose's relic, he was slow, his brow scrunching as his black flames grew. A guard lunged for him, but Jack threw a ball of black fire at him, missing. The guards scurried back, arms raised. Screaming guests scattered, caught between protecting themselves and watching the drama unfold.

Nausea rolled through Emmy as Jack threw another black flame. And another. How long might his magic last without the relic? A minute? Two?

"We have to help him." Jimmy was beside her, rolling up his sleeves.

"Don't." Emmy grabbed his arm. "This is what he wants."

A guard unleashed a torrent of water over Jack's flames, extinguishing his left palm quickly, and Emmy winced. She knew too well the bruises water conjury could leave.

But Jack still had a ball of black fire in his right hand, and he tossed it at the water wielder. He missed, singing the coat of a man standing beside him, and the screams grew louder.

Jack's flame sputtered, then went out. Emmy's hand flew to her mouth as the guards surged toward him.

Two of them threw him to the ground, and Jack wrestled free, but a third guard delivered a hard blow to his side. A fourth joined, then a fifth, and bile burned in Emmy's throat, but she refused to look away. Watching was the least she could do.

"We can't just do nothing!" The accusation in Jimmy's voice cut right through Emmy, but she kept staring at Jack. This was his choice. He'd told her to finish their revenge.

I'd set the world on fire just to keep you warm.

They had him pinned down by air conjury now, Jack gasping like a fish out of water.

I'll never let anything bad happen to you again. I swear it.

The water conjurers aimed at Jack's face now, a furious frenzy that shocked Emmy in its cruelness, even from the guards. With his arms pinned to his sides, Jack could not so much as lift an arm to protect himself. Even from ten yards away, Emmy heard the unmistakable crack of his nose. All the while, the air conjurers kept him restrained with an unyielding gust of wind.

They were torturing him.

Without his flames soaring about the ballroom, the onlookers were growing bolder, pointing and laughing as Jack struggled against the guards.

Jimmy snapped.

With a blood-curdling yell, he launched himself at the guards before Emmy could stop him. Surprise alone had given him an advantage, and Jimmy threw them off Jack, their concentration breaking, and Jack gasped as he sucked in much-needed air—

A sudden gale tore through the ballroom, loosening Emmy's hair from Mary's extravagant handiwork. Champagne flutes flew from hands, shattering on the floor.

More guards had arrived.

The gust hit Jimmy with enough force to toss him against the golden waterfall. Emmy clutched her chest, ready for the glass hidden by the illusion to break, but the wind relented, and he slumped to the ground, his head lolling. The guards were upon him a moment later, kicking him as if he were a rabid animal, not a brave soul defending his friend.

Jimmy, who'd left his own life behind to find her. To help her.

A pair of guards dragged him from the ballroom while the rest pinned Jack once again.

She could bear it no longer.

Emmy charged. The water wielder tried to push her back, but Emmy lifted her skirt, deflecting the deluge with a transformed shield. A second guard cocked a rifle, but Emmy grabbed it before he could pull the trigger, transforming it to stone.

She heard Grace scream, heard Keeper Windsor call for them to catch her as another powerful wind tore through the ballroom. Jack was struggling against the guards as they dragged him to the exit. She sprinted toward him—

Sand filled the air, pelting her like needles against her skin.

It was everywhere, the sand, blown into every orifice in Emmy's face. She fell to her knees, trying to heal the stinging in her eyes, but as soon as she opened them, she was assaulted once again. Someone grabbed her roughly, and she bit them. Hard. Stumbling to her feet, Emmy tried to lift her skirt shield, but the sand accosted her from every angle. She had to get out of this ballroom before they dragged her back to Grimsbane—

A gun exploded behind her, the bullet whizzing just past Emmy's ear. It struck the golden waterfall, piercing the glass underneath the illusion before disappearing into the night.

The glass wall.

Emmy ran to it, tripping over God only knew what as she stumbled through the sand-swept ballroom. Pressing her palms to the ice-cold glass within the waterfall, she imagined it as broken as their plans, as broken as her heart if she did not rescue her friends.

It shattered beneath her hands, shards of molten gold raining down with a deafening crash. Screams erupted, and Emmy ran directly into it, the glass cutting into her arms, her shoulders, even her scalp. Once she was through, she tried to squint to find the others, but the sand was relentless, and another bullet surged past her, close enough to nip her gown.

She had to run.

Emmy flung herself across the patio, the screams echoing over the river. She ran up the same stairs she'd taken at the start of the summer, when the Society had laughed at her. The screams were quieter here, but more guests were pouring onto the patio by the second.

The front of Clarity Hall was a commotion of guests and their attendants, debating whether to leave or stay to witness the melee. Transforming her ruined ball gown into a dark slip, Emmy hid in the shadow of the trees and struggled to catch her breath.

Failure's crushing weight was too much to bear. Their covers were blown. And once again, Grace had outsmarted Emmy.

But Emmy could not think of Grace now. She had to find the others.

With any luck, Mary had slipped out undetected. The last glimpse she'd had of Jack was of him being dragged toward the exit, just like Jimmy.

And—Tobias and Agnes. Oh, God, what had she done? She'd

promised them safety, yet bullets were flying, and Tobias had been at the center of it all.

They were her responsibility. And she'd failed them.

A commotion by the front doors. The guests were backing away and pointing, and Emmy risked a glimpse around the tree.

All the air rushed from her lungs.

A pair of guards was lugging something heavy between them. Jack.

His face was so bloodied, Emmy had to bite her knuckles to keep from making a noise. His hands were bound behind his back, but he was conscious, still trying to wriggle free. All the while, his gaze swept through the crowd in front of Clarity Hall. Searching. For her.

Seeing him in pain brought her to the edge of sanity. She was going to transform the guards into twigs, then snap them in her hands before burning them alive.

They brought Jimmy next. Also handcuffed. Also bloodied beyond forgiveness. And Emmy could not muster a single goddamn breath as the guards shoved them into a carriage with bars on its windows, the same sort that had delivered her to Grimsbane.

Someone appeared between the trees, and Emmy lifted her hands, ready to conjure, but—

"Oh, thank God." She nearly collapsed at the sight of Tobias and his sister, who looked ready to throttle her. But there was no time for apologies. Reaching into the hidden pockets of her slip, Emmy found the wad of cash she'd promised them, along with every other dollar she had on her. Then she pressed her palms to each of their faces, transforming them back to their original selves. "Find somewhere safe to wash off that paint. Then get as far from here as you can."

With a murderous glare, Agnes grabbed the cash and shoved it into her pockets before taking her brother's hand and disappearing in the darkness.

"There she is! In the trees!"

Arms trembling, Emmy pressed herself against the thick trunk, but bullets whizzed by her, and she gasped. They could hit Agnes and Tobias.

"I'm over here!" Sprinting in the opposite direction, Emmy waved her hands as she envisioned each and every drop of dew in the riverside breeze, multiplying the droplets over and over until a thick fog spread between the trunks, cloaking her. Bullets continued to pierce the air, along with shouts, so she hid deeper in the woods, deep enough to lose sight of the mansion—and the jailer's carriage in front of it. She needed to loop back around without being spotted.

The brume waited, its power surrounding her as she racked her brain. What could she transform to get Jack and Jimmy out unseen?

A twig snapped, far too close. Emmy stumbled back—

"It's me," Mary whispered as she stepped through the fog, her cheeks pink and damp.

Mary. In one piece. Emmy threw her arms around her, burying her face in her hair.

"We need to hurry." Pulling away from Emmy's embrace, she took Emmy's hand—

And they both disappeared.

Emmy could not see her arms, her legs, her dress, any of it. Mary's invisibility, apparently, could cover them both. But there was no time for wonder, not when the jailer's carriage might leave at any moment.

In silence, they tiptoed between the trees. Too slow, they were too—

They flickered back into existence. Dropping Emmy's hands, Mary gripped her knees, struggling to catch her breath. "I'm sorry! It's much harder with two."

They were so painfully close. Another thirty seconds of invisibility, and they'd reach the jailer's carriage.

"What do we do?" Mary whispered.

In the distance, a whip snapped. The horses whinnied.

Emmy nearly broke the relic's chain as she pulled off the necklace and pressed it into Mary's palm. "Keep the coin touching your skin and call to the brume again. Hurry!"

With a quick nod, Mary disappeared, and Emmy searched the darkness for her. There she was—her hand cool as it slipped into Emmy's once more.

Hand in hand, they were off, moving faster now, looping farther around the mansion. Emmy longed to protest as their distance from the carriage grew, but Mary had worked at Clarity Hall. She had to trust the maid knew a different way to intercept its path.

In the darkness, Emmy tripped on a root, and she stumbled onto her knees, cutting her palm on something sharp in the dirt. Worse, she was visible again.

"Mary?" she whispered.

No response.

"Mary?"

Breathless, Mary reappeared through the trees, a few yards away. Emmy reached for her.

But the maid stepped back, her hand flying to her cross.

"What are you doing?" Emmy hissed. "We need—"

Mary yanked the cross's silver chain, dropping it into the dirt.

And Emmy stumbled back.

"No," she tried to say, but her voice was a broken, pitiful thing.

In Mary's place stood Grace, Rose's relic clutched tightly in her hand.

"Oh, Emmy." She sighed. "You always were so trusting."

THIRTY-TWO

EMMY TRIED TO RUB HER sand-battered eyes, tried to clear the impossible vision of Grace Eloise Montgomery in a moonlit maid's uniform. But there Grace stood, passing the chain of Rose's relic over her head with a triumphant smile.

And she'd called her Emmy, not Winnie Fairchild. She *knew*.

"What did you do to Mary?" She was wearing Mary's clothes, right down to her cross. Mary never would have parted with it willingly.

Grace patted the relic against her sternum. "You still haven't figured it out, have you?"

"Where is she?" No blood underneath Grace's fingernails. No cuts or signs of a struggle.

"And you're supposed to be the smart one." Grace waved her hands over her body. "Don't you see now? I *am* Mary. I have always been Mary."

"That's ridiculous," Emmy spat. "I've seen you together."

"Ah, yes, you met the real Mary at my aunt and uncle's ball." Grace could hardly contain her delight. "But ever since that night, it's been me."

Emmy must have made a face, for Grace laughed, a titter as delicate as bells.

Caleb had read Mary's thoughts. He'd vetted her, making sure her intentions were good.

"You're lying," Emmy heard herself say. Mary had been nothing but kind since Emmy hired her. Mary had jumped in the river, celebrating the Strattons' downfall. They'd picked out Emmy's gowns together, sorted through Grace's enchanted jewelry together—

Mary, who worked only part-time.

Mary, who dutifully did Emmy's hair, just as Grace had done for most of their lives.

Grace, who'd been disappearing from Clarity Hall all summer.

Humming to herself, Grace procured a ring from a pocket hidden in her skirt. As soon as she slipped it on her finger, she disappeared.

Emmy's legs shook precariously as she threw out her hands, meager protection from the invisible backstabber. Without the relic, Emmy was almost defenseless.

"I have had to bridge so many of these little rings." Grace's voice echoed through the trees. "I've had to pay the real Mary quite handsomely to keep making them. Though not as much as the small fortune you've paid me to be your part-time maid."

The real Mary.

Because Emmy hadn't hired the real Mary; she'd hired *Grace*.

Tears burned behind Emmy's eyes, and she fought like hell to keep them at bay.

But of course, Grace saw right through her as soon as she reappeared. "When I learned of your offer to my maid, I knew I couldn't pass up an opportunity to find out what the pretty new girl was hiding. Mrs. Stratton might have been taken by Winnie Fairchild, but I've always been an impeccable judge of character."

Emmy stared at her, each breath growing more ragged. "It's not possible."

"Ah, but with Papa's gift, it is." Grace grinned proudly. "Using conjury I'd bridged from him over the years. I transformed my face, but I modulated my bridging so that the transformation takes effect only while I'm touching this cross. When I'm not wearing it, it's undone."

"Your conjury can't do that," Emmy growled.

"You're so arrogant, you truly believe you know my conjury better than me. Even now." Grace shot her a scathing look. "I was a Society protégé for two whole years. Watch."

She plucked the silver cross from the ground, her face rearranging to Mary's. She pitched her voice so that it was higher and breathier. "Why hello, miss! How can I help you, miss?"

Grace's face changed back to her real one as she returned the cross to her pocket. The ease of the transformation made Emmy's stomach twist, and for a horrifying moment, she thought she might be sick all over the ground between them.

"You put the truth bracelet in my jewelry box," Emmy rasped.

"And imagine my surprise when Winnie Fairchild turned into *you*." Raw hurt shone in Grace's eyes. "I thought you were dead. I *grieved* for you."

"Grieved for me?" Emmy choked. "You left me in Grimsbane to rot. You framed me!"

"I had no choice," Grace hissed. "I wanted us both to become protégés, I truly did. But if they were taking only one, it had to be me. My life was hell compared to yours."

No remorse. Not even a drop. Emmy glared at her. "Papa is dead because of you."

"I couldn't possibly have known that he'd go after the chancellor like that!" She had the audacity to look wounded. "I loved Papa. You know I did."

"Just like you loved me?" Emmy scoffed.

"I did love you, Emmy." Grace gave a small shrug. "But it was going to be either you or me."

They stared at each other. Six paces away.

"I know you're thinking about how to get this back." Grace patted the relic's chain. "But it's mine now, which is fitting, given that Rose was able to make it only with my help."

"Liar." But Grace looked so smug, Emmy could not help but consider it.

Grace and Oliver had known of the relic's existence, though no one had breathed a word of it.

Rose's relic did not work like an ordinary relic. It was made from the bone of someone with amplifying conjury. Touch activated that conjury . . . much like Grace's creations.

Had Rose needed bridging conjury to complete the relic? And if so, wouldn't she have told Caleb?

Reaching into her skirts, Grace removed her other relic and slipped it onto her neck. "Rose's is *much* stronger, but two is better than one."

"That's why you went through all this trouble?" Emmy was so angry, she could hardly get the words out. "You were after Rose's relic the whole time?"

"*Think*, Emmy." Grace's fingers tapped her temple. "If I only wanted the relic, I would have ripped it off you the first time I tied your corset. But by ensuring you succeeded against the Strattons, I gave myself the perfect opportunity to win over Oliver's mother. How can she refuse me as a daughter-in-law now that I've cleared Ollie's name?"

Emmy was going to rot in hell after today, because she was going to murder Grace, to squeeze her skinny neck until her face was as blue as her eyes.

"You may not believe me," Grace said quietly, "but it was nice to be your friend again, if only for a little while. Those first few months without you were so hard."

"You poor thing," Emmy snarled. Her anger was a living, breathing monster in her chest, and the longer she stared at Grace, the more it clawed its way out. But she needed that relic. She could not get Jack, or Jimmy, or anyone back without the powerful amplifier.

"Oh, quit with the sarcasm. It's unbecoming." Smoothing her skirts, Grace lifted her chin. "I believe I have a fair compromise for us: if you leave right now and never return, you have my word that Jack and Jimmy will both live."

She must have thought Emmy a bumbling fool. "Your word means *nothing*."

"This is rather generous of me, Ems. *I'm* the one who must convince my aunt and uncle not to seek the death sentence for their own daughter's killer. And I must convince Mrs. Stratton, too, which will certainly put a damper on my engagement to Oliver."

"Fuck you." She stepped closer to Grace. Five paces now.

"Such language is unbecoming of a lady." With a knowing smile, Grace tilted her head. "Oh, come on, Ems, don't you want to live? You still have your conjury. Make yourself rich! Find a nice man far away from here. One who doesn't lie to you all the time."

Four steps.

Grace tilted her head. "Oh, I see. You're so obsessed with me, you cannot bear to leave."

Three steps would have to do.

Emmy launched herself at Grace. Screaming, Grace fell to the dirt, and Emmy clawed at her neck, searching for the relic's chain, the one Jack made for *her*—

Something sharp slashed at Emmy, cutting her across the jaw. She rolled away before lunging for the relic again, but Grace grabbed a stick, transforming it into a crude-looking sword.

They both stilled.

"My word," Grace breathed. Examining her clawed hand, she grinned. "I don't even need to touch you to bridge your conjury. Evidence that my gift trumps yours."

Grace lifted her palm, and Emmy felt the icy caress of bridging conjury on her face. She tried to turn away, but it was useless. Tried to gather the brume, but it hardly rustled in response.

That otherworldly chill rattled her teeth, but Emmy pushed herself to her feet, her limbs aflame. Still, a frigid cold prickled over her face.

"Much better." Grace grinned. "Now you look like yourself."

The gash on Emmy's face stung as she stared at Grace, who was using Emmy's conjury. And Emmy's relic. And she'd already taken Emmy's patronage, and her freedom, and everything good she'd had in the world.

With a wild yell, Emmy lunged for her again.

"Help!" Grace screamed as Emmy dragged her to the ground. "She's attacking me!"

Emmy had always been scrappier than Grace, and she pinned her with a frightening fury. But Grace wriggled an arm free and swung the stick-sword wildly, all the while screaming as Emmy yanked at her skirts, sending jewelry raining down from Grace's secret pockets.

A guard burst into the clearing, palm raised, and Emmy was tossed from Grace. As the guard's face creased in concentration, Emmy struggled to her knees, but another burst of wind knocked her back to the dirt.

"Got her!" the guard called, but still, Emmy struggled against the crushing wind. They'd take her back to Grimsbane—but she would not go back, she could never go back. Flattened against the ground, she searched the dirt for something, anything she could use as a weapon.

Something cold dug into her palm, and she disappeared.

The wind ceased. "Where did she go?"

Too stunned to move, Emmy focused on the frigid metal in her palm. One of Grace's invisibility rings.

"She's still here!" Grace shrieked. "Find her!"

Painstakingly slowly, Emmy slid the ring onto her finger and pushed to her feet, careful not to shift the dead leaves beneath her. Grace was swinging the sword with reckless abandon, but if Emmy timed it just right, the relic—

"Shield your eyes," the guard commanded.

Dirt rose from the ground, and the wind picked up, scattering it in Emmy's eyes, her nostrils, everywhere.

"There! I see her!"

Emmy took off between the trees. Her ballroom slippers were no match for the guards' boots, but without the relic, Emmy could not transform better shoes for herself. She couldn't outrun them, but she didn't slow down, not even when her lungs were ready to burst. Only when she was certain she'd collapse did she pin herself against a tree trunk and try to make herself as small as possible, squeezing her eyes shut as the guards ran past, unseeing. Without the relic, she was utterly defenseless.

Without the relic, Jack could not burn his way out of Grimsbane. He was trapped. Jimmy too.

And Emmy, once again, had trusted the wrong person.

THIRTY-THREE

BY THE TIME THE GUARDS' shouting quieted, the damp night air had seeped into Emmy's bones. Shivers coursed through her as she crept from tree to tree, slowly making her way from Clarity Hall. Her muscles ached, especially in her chest, which felt as if it'd been cleaved in two.

The body cannot distinguish between physical and emotional hurts.

Grace had fooled Emmy. Again. Emmy was so full of self-loathing, she wanted to claw out her own heart, but she could not cry, could not scream, could not do a goddamn thing until she was certain the guards had given up their search. As she hurried through the dark with the invisibility ring, she stumbled often, the thicket slapping her in the face as if punishing her for her stupidity. Thorns and twigs lodged themselves in her skirts just like the night she and Jack had run from the Society's headquarters. Like Rose's drawing.

I think I might be . . . a little bit in love with you?

Clarity Hall was far behind her before she removed the invisibility ring. The woods rustled with life, but Emmy was too furious to be afraid of whatever animals lurked in the impenetrable dark. Bile burned the back of her throat but she swallowed it down, alongside the blood-curdling scream she longed to let out.

It was all her fault. Once again, she had been a trusting, blundering fool.

And Grace was right; Emmy *had* underestimated her conjury. She must have found a way to modulate Oliver's gift so that it activated when she triggered it. Like when she'd been able to lie to them at Mistfield while she'd held that truth bracelet. While she'd revisited the horrors of the debutante ball, saying exactly what Emmy longed to hear. *You were the best one of us, by far.* You *deserved the patronage.* And perhaps she'd even used Oliver's gift to prevent Caleb from reading her mind. Unless Caleb had betrayed them, too.

With a strangled noise, Emmy slumped against a tree trunk, burying her head in her hands. Jack was either headed to Grimsbane or dead. Would they lock Jimmy there, too, even though he had no magic? Or had they shot him like they did Papa?

And Mary was Grace. Mary had always been Grace.

Betrayal had a venomous bite, more lethal each time it struck. Even though Emmy had promised herself she would not let her guard down, she'd done it. Again and again. Even though she'd known, right from the start, that the only way to avoid another bullet through her heart was to never let anyone within shooting distance.

If she survived this mess, she'd never trust another soul to so much as speak to her. No, she'd get Rose's relic back, right her wrongs by freeing the others, then leave New York. Leave civilization entirely.

But first, she needed a plan.

The Hudson churned quietly in the darkness, and Emmy followed it downstream, slipping the invisibility ring on her finger to pass through the smaller estates that peppered the woods between Clarity Hall and Mistfield. Cutting right through the backyards of those hunting her, her only protection a jagged rock clutched in her fist. She had not made the conscious decision to return to Mistfield, but before she knew it, the woods grew more familiar.

Mistfield was a start. Caleb was inside—unless the guards had come for him, too. She could not even think about them dragging him from his bed. But she still had Grace's jewelry arsenal hidden in her room. With it, she'd have a dozen conjuries at her disposal.

The golden sun rose slowly, chasing away the last remnants of the cursed night. Birds sang. Deer pranced. And Emmy dragged her blistered, aching feet to Mistfield.

After an eternity, the manor appeared through the trees. Wrapped in the solemn gray haze of its signature morning mist, Mistfield was almost too much to bear, especially while it was infested by guards. They were ransacking it, dragging its contents onto the front lawn.

"Emmy?"

She whirled, rock raised, as someone stepped between the trees. Caleb.

Relief struck her like a punch to the gut. Never had she seen him so disheveled, with deep circles under his eyes and blood staining his nightshirt. He looked ready to collapse, and Emmy ran to him before quickly drawing back. Hadn't she learned?

Caleb had assured her, time and time again, that Mary was on their side. How could a mind reader be wrong?

"What the hell happened?" He glanced at Mistfield. "The guards are tearing the house apart. I had to sneak out the servants' stairwell."

Caleb, as badly wounded as he was, had managed to slip past the guards. She tightened her grip on the rock.

But he was so shaken, he hardly noticed. "The guards were thinking about how they'd captured Jack Fontaine and his Chinese friend. They're going to execute them."

His words took the wind out of her, and she staggered to the ground and leaned against one of the towering oaks. "When?"

"Not sure." He grimaced. "They took them to Society headquarters."

Emmy tried to let the words quell her crushing panic. Headquarters was closer, and much easier to breach, than Grimsbane. But without the relic, Emmy's transformations were far too slow to be of much use.

No, she needed the relic. And to get the relic, she needed to beat Grace, once and for all.

"Where are you going?" Caleb whisper-shouted as she rose to her feet.

"To get Grace's jewelry box." And then, to Clarity Hall, to strangle her with her bare hands.

Finish this, Jack had said, but she could hardly stand to remember how he'd whispered those last words, how he'd kissed her—

"It's gone, Emmy." Caleb looked pained. "Grace and Mrs. Stratton came with the first round of guards. They had the jewelry box with them when they left."

The need to scream nearly toppled Emmy. Was she destined to always be one step behind Grace? Or was Caleb lying to her, because he'd been working with Grace all along? "I need to search for it myself."

He limped in front of her, wincing in pain. "We don't have time for your cynicism. Any minute now, they're going to kill our friends. We need to free them *now*."

But she could not free anyone. Not without Rose's relic. And she could not trust anyone, either. Especially when Caleb had urged her to trust Mary, over and over.

She studied him carefully. "How often did you read Mary's mind?"

"Mary's?" He shot her a strange look. "I don't make a habit of spying on my friends."

"You claimed you read it when I hired her."

His eyes narrowed. "Of course I did. And I heard how much she hated Grace. Why, did they arrest her, too?"

That conversation had been Emmy's only one with the real Mary. Rather convenient.

"Will you tell me what the hell is going on?"

"Grace was Mary. For as long as Mary worked here."

"Horseshit," he snapped.

"She was pretending to be Mary all along. That's why Grace was missing so often this summer. Why she was late to so many events. Why 'Mary' requested a part-time schedule."

"That's impossible! I would have known if she were Grace."

"An excellent point."

Caleb glared at her. "I talked with her. Laughed with her. Hell, I *liked* her."

"You liked Grace."

He shook his head, his gaze unfocused. "Horseshit," he muttered again.

A mind reader who'd failed to notice the imposter living among them. Who'd encouraged Emmy to bring Mary into the fold. Not Mary; *Grace.*

"I don't understand how you didn't hear one revealing thought of hers." Emmy did not take her eyes off Caleb, not even for a second. "She couldn't have been suppressing your conjury the whole time."

You're so arrogant, Grace had said, *you truly believe you know conjury better than me.*

"I use my gift only when it's absolutely necessary." He scrubbed at his face, growing paler by the minute. "Come to think of it, I don't remember ever hearing her thoughts by accident. If I was listening to someone else's thoughts, hers never interfered."

It was torturous, not knowing truth from lie. Grace might have had some way to block Caleb's conjury, like she'd blocked Tobias's. If it was something she had on her, Caleb would not have felt its coldness.

Or, a simpler explanation: Caleb was a goddamn liar. "Did Grace help Rose make the relic?"

Caleb froze. She didn't need him to say a word; his guilt was plain on his face.

It hurt more than she'd expected, which was her own fault, really. But it made it far easier to walk away from Caleb. If the guards were still here, she could slip past them with the invisibility ring. Then, if she found Grace's jewelry, she'd do whatever it took to retrieve the relic from her.

"It was Rose's secret, okay?" Caleb whispered as he followed her.

"She needed a tiny bit of bridging conjury to complete the relic, but she knew how much Jack despised Grace for what she'd done to you. But she didn't make Grace an amplifier; I swear it."

"It doesn't matter." Emmy hated uttering the words aloud. "Because I gave her Rose's."

"You *what?*"

"I handed it to her," Emmy snapped. "I handed her unfathomable power like a goddamn fool. Without a moment's hesitation. Because *you* said I could trust her."

With a groan, Caleb leaned against a tree. His distress seemed genuine, but it no longer mattered if he'd betrayed her or not. That was the benefit of working alone: she did not have to torture herself trying to separate friend from foe, when so often they were one and the same.

He grabbed her arm as she turned away. "It's over, Emmy. Grace won. But if we hurry, we still have a chance to save our friends."

The thought of Jack or Jimmy suffering made Emmy want to tear out her own heart. And if they died—no, she would *not* let herself imagine such things. Especially when she was powerless to help them.

Grace's haughty smile was burned into Emmy's retinas. It would hang over her for the rest of her life—a life in hiding, thanks to Grace. The injustice was maddening, but Emmy welcomed its burn. Because when she was on fire, she was not a naive little pushover who let herself be bested by Grace Montgomery again and again.

Grace had framed her—and gotten away with it.

She had taken Emmy's place in the Society of the Charmed—and gotten away with it.

She had framed Jack for the death of two innocent girls—and gotten away with it.

She had posed as Mary, weaseling her way into Mistfield to use Emmy's schemes for her own selfish purposes—and gotten away with it.

And now she had stolen the one thing that made Emmy powerful enough to make a damn difference in this bleak world. And Emmy could not let her get away with it.

"Do you know the last thing Jack said to me?" Emmy's traitorous voice warbled. "'Finish this.' He still wants Grace to pay. That's why he sacrificed himself."

Caleb scoffed. "You and I both know that's not it."

"Then why?"

"Because he'd do anything for you!" He practically screamed it at her, and they both glanced through the trees. Lowering his voice, he added, "He already went to jail for you once, and now he's gone and done it again."

"That's not true." She shook him off her arm, hating how he grimaced in pain. "I didn't even know him the first time he was arrested."

"You didn't know him, but he knew *you*." Glaring at her, Caleb shook his head. "Jimmy filled his head with stories of this big-hearted girl who lived on the fifth floor. Who swam in the East River in her knickers in the summer and read books so late, her father had to hide the spare candles so she'd go to bed. Who looked after everyone, no matter their station."

"Quiet." She could not listen to this romanticized version of herself, not when she needed to be ruthless.

Clutching his abdomen, Caleb hobbled into her path yet again. "Every day for a year, Jimmy reminded us that this wonderful girl—Jack's precious woodland girl—was wrongfully imprisoned. And every day, Jack harassed his father to do something about it. But Mr. Fontaine died, and Oliver and Grace set Mistfield on fire."

His voice wavered, as it always did for Rose, and Emmy swallowed her bitter retort.

"Jack should have laid his sister to rest." Disgust tinged Caleb's bitter words. "He should have been there, but instead, he got himself arrested on purpose. To free *you*."

Emmy shook her head. "That had nothing to do with me."

"The chancellor could not arrest Jack with only Oliver's testimony. But Jack punched Oliver in the face, nearly knocking him off the cliffs. Why do you think he did that?"

The woods began to spin, and Emmy gripped her knees.

Oliver has a face that just begs to be punched, Jack had said.

"He wouldn't," she rasped.

"As he proved last night, he most certainly would."

Jack needed to be alive so she could scream at his beautiful face. How could he have gone to Grimsbane for her, a stranger?

Those haughty smirks had been hiding a shockingly tender soul, one that had suffered for her. Starved for her. "Of all the reckless, stupid things he could do . . ."

"For once, we agree." There was a protective edge to Caleb's glare as he assessed her. "You have to make a choice. Either you give up on getting back at Grace, or you give up on the person you love—Don't you dare make that face, Emilia Vallillo. You're falling in love with him, whether you like him or not."

"Jack said it himself," she hissed. "Nothing matters more than revenge."

"So you'll let him die? Jack, who traded his freedom for yours, twice?"

She backed away, pinning him with a murderous look.

"You'll let Jimmy die? Jimmy, who upended his life to find you, throwing himself into a cutthroat magical world so he could watch over you—"

"Stop." She almost shoved him as she stalked away.

But Caleb grabbed her arm. "Then Grace has already won. She wins when you become as heartless as she is. She wins when they execute Jack—"

"Stop."

"Just like they executed your father—"

"STOP!"

"Because that's the worst betrayal of all, isn't it?" Understanding glistened in Caleb's eyes. "When we can't imagine being apart from someone, but they go and die."

He had let go of her, but her feet remained rooted to the ground. Each inhale was a jagged stone, tearing the strength she desperately needed.

And there was Mama, her skin tepid and blue as Emmy tried to heal her.

There was Papa, lying on that pristine marble tile as Emmy tried to reach him.

There was Emmy herself, curled against the warmest wall of the coldest cell. Cursed to live. Cursed to yearn for her oldest friend in the world, who had deemed her expendable.

"I hate her," Emmy rasped, her face suddenly wet. "She needs to pay for what she's done."

"She turned on you. She left you alone when you needed her more than ever." His words were infuriatingly gentle. "But Jack would never do that to you. Jimmy will never do that to you. Even I wouldn't do that to you, and you're my third favorite of all of them."

She had promised herself she'd never let another soul within striking distance. But she'd failed, because it was tearing her to pieces, knowing Jack was hurting, or in danger, or worse. That reckless boy had snuck behind her walls, close enough to devastate her.

And they always devastated her. In the end, everyone she'd ever loved had either died or betrayed her.

But not Jimmy. No, he'd made it his mission to look after her.

And not Jack. Before they'd even met, he'd been loyal to the mere idea of her. And no matter how hard she tried, she could not cure herself of her infernal connection to him. It was as if a dark, broken shard of her heart had found its twin in the dark, broken shards of his.

But Jack was far too cavalier with his own mortality. He burned too brightly, daring fate to snuff him out. Too many times, he'd risked his life for her. Because he loved her, damn him. And that made him foolish. Reckless.

Brave.

"I can't do it again." She didn't have the courage to face Caleb as the words fell from her. "I mean it, Caleb. If they die . . ."

Because Emmy was the furthest thing from brave. She could not add Jack and Jimmy to the list of loved ones she mourned, could not be cursed to live while everyone died.

"I know." Caleb was on the ground now. Knee to knee. Forehead to forehead. "Believe me, Emmy, I *know*."

He offered no solution. Not even a glimmer of hope. In fact, the devastation in his eyes was a mirror of her own.

But somehow, Emmy sucked in a breath. Her first in ages.

Grace deserved to die for everything she'd done. But Jack and Jimmy . . .

"They're at headquarters?" she whispered. "You're certain?"

Caleb nodded. "Unless we're too late."

Emmy wiped her face on her dress sleeve, then forced herself to stand.

Grace Montgomery could keep her perfect little life. She could even keep Rose's relic, though the loss of it burned deep in Emmy's chest.

For a chance to save Jack and Jimmy, Emmy had to let Grace win.

Thirty-Four

THE LAST BREATHS OF DAYLIGHT made monsters of their shadows as Emmy and Caleb huddled in the clearing. Headquarters had revealed itself once they'd passed through the illusion, but the formidable white building was far too quiet. In twenty minutes, they had seen only two guards, the same number they'd seen during the Society's offseason.

They were too late. Emmy knew it. Caleb knew it, too, though neither said it aloud.

"We should at least have a look around," Caleb finally said. "Maybe there's some indication of where they took them, or . . ."

His voice trailed off, but Emmy's torturous mind gladly filled in the blanks.

Or they're already dead.

"Can you listen to their thoughts?"

"I'm tapped." He blew his breath out through his teeth. "But I can keep watch. If someone's coming, listen for a bird squawking that sounds an awful lot like someone panicking."

Emmy studied the long gravel driveway. Deep grooves crisscrossed the length of it. Several carriage wheels had passed through here. And inside headquarters, candlelight glowed through a single window on the first floor.

Please be alive, she pleaded. *Be alive, be alive, be alive . . .*

"The guard's making rounds again." Caleb pointed to the smear of white in the twilight. That same pristine uniform that had been taunting her for years now. As soon as it disappeared around the corner,

Emmy slipped the ring onto her finger, letting the iciness of Grace's cursed conjury wash over her.

It better not fail her now.

The grass over which she ran was the same path she and Jack had taken several weeks earlier, when they'd broken into the basement. The same locked window. She pressed her hand against it, remembering how Jack had taunted her: *Must you overthink even the smallest of tasks?* Always riling her, always trying to keep the fire in her eyes.

Squeezing her eyes shut, she reached for her conjury, but it was not there. So unaccustomed was she to having to work for it, she hardly remembered how.

She called to it again, readying herself for the heaviness, the ache of power. Still nothing.

How the hell had she done this before the relic? With constant practice, she'd steadily increased how quickly she could conjure so that she could impress the Society. Yet now she could hardly feel the brume without an amplifier.

The brume. Closing her eyes once more, Emmy sucked in a deep breath, picturing that ethereal fog surrounding her, filling her lungs.

There—a tendril of mist. She latched on to it, muscles already straining, and envisioned the glass as soft as water through her fingers, as thin as Caleb's smile as he'd tried to quip about their odds. Sweat trickled down her temple, and exhaustion shook her muscles, but she held on to the brume as if Jack's and Jimmy's lives depended on it.

The window relented. Emmy peeled away the fragile remnants and shimmied inside.

Twilight did not reach the basement. And without Jack, Emmy had no flame. Worse, nothing in the darkness spoke of other people. No breathing, no fidgeting. No sound at all, save the guards' footsteps upstairs.

After a few minutes, her eyes adjusted well enough to rummage through the basement, which looked the same as it had weeks ago, save the summer pageant's trophies, which sat atop a table, freshly polished. Grace had never bothered to make a Fairchild trophy to celebrate Winnie's victory.

Losing that night might have been what pushed Grace to plant that truth bracelet.

Emmy could not think of how she'd draped herself over Jack, the tortured sound he'd made—because he'd *wanted* her. It was maddening, how wrong she'd been.

She needed him to be alive so she could be brave enough to admit it.

Ancient books spilled from shelf after shelf. No sign of a struggle, and certainly no sign of prisoners.

Upstairs was far too quiet, but the walls might have been enchanted to silence any noise, like in Grimsbane. Perhaps that, too, had been Grace's conjury.

Careful to stick to the sides of the stairs to reduce their creaking, Emmy tiptoed upstairs.

The hinges on the first door groaned as she pressed against it, and Emmy hesitated.

Several candles were lit on the main floor, the warm light a strange contrast to her cold sweat as she crept through the room, hoping like hell the floorboards would stay silent. Both guards were nearby, the walls muffling their conversation.

Slipping into an office, she moved about the desk, the gentle breeze of her passing disturbed the stack of papers atop it, and one fluttered to the ground. Watching the doorway, Emmy picked it up—and froze.

Your Presence Is Requested
at Stratton Mansion on Sunday,
the Second of July
at Nine O'Clock in the Evening
for the Trial of Jack Fontaine,
Who Is Charged with the Following Crimes:
The Murder of Elizabeth Windsor;
The Murder of Laurel Foster, guard;
The Murder of Nicholas Razzette, guard;
The Murder of Louis Arthur Stratton,
chancellor;
The Attempted Murder of Oliver
Stratton, commander;
The Attempted Murder of Grace Windsor;
Manslaughter, in the first degree, of
Rose Fontaine;
Revealing conjury's Secret to
Unauthorized Parties;
and Conspiring Against the Society of
the Charmed

Justice to Be Delivered On-Site, per
Societal Laws and Regulations

With trembling hands, Emmy slipped the notice into her pocket. Thank goodness Jack was alive—at least until tomorrow evening. She could not panic. Not yet.

Though she already knew it'd be empty, she checked the rest of the main floor before slipping back out the basement window. Night had finished its descent while she'd been indoors, but she kept the invisibility ring on until she reached where Caleb waited in the woods.

His face fell when she appeared alone. "Nothing?"

Emmy handed him the notice and slumped on the ground beside him.

They were throwing the book at Jack. Perhaps even more ominous, there was no mention of Jimmy. For once, Rose's prophecy offered some comfort. Jimmy was supposed to live.

Unless Rose was proven wrong. Again.

"'On-site, per societal laws and regulations.'" Caleb chuckled darkly as he folded the paper. "That means they plan to kill him on the spot, giving the honor to the most aggrieved party."

"And they think the poor are barbaric." Emmy took the invitation back from Caleb. "If they find him innocent, will they let him go?"

Even the night could not hide his devastation. "The trial is a farce. This is a death sentence."

Emmy could not let his words sink in, not without unraveling completely. "It's at Stratton Mansion."

"Which means Mrs. Stratton is back in the Society's good graces." Caleb crumpled the paper in his hands. "I haven't the faintest idea what to do, and I want to scream."

"Not yet." Emmy gripped her pounding head. "There must be a way for us to get them out."

A heavy silence fell over them, save for the leaves whispering in the July breeze. That it was such a lovely summer evening was yet another betrayal.

Holding his abdomen, Caleb slowly lowered himself to the ground beside her. "Be careful," she warned. "If you burst those stitches, Jimmy will never forgive me."

"What I wouldn't give for that giant to yell at me again." Closing his eyes, Caleb rubbed his temples. "We need to think this through. After all, you and I have always been the brains of this operation, no matter what Fontaine thought."

Emmy snorted, then instantly regretted it, because there was nothing funny about the utter hopelessness of their current predicament.

"No panicking," Caleb warned. "Let's . . . review what we're up against."

"The entire Society." Emmy blew air out through her teeth. "Oh, and with Rose's relic, Grace can bridge conjury from a distance. She can take anyone's gift on a whim."

"Like we'd suspected, after the fire." Caleb whistled under his breath. "So if I get too close to her, she'll hear our thoughts."

Emmy laid her head in her hands. Months of sleep deprivation were finally catching up to her, and she didn't have the relic, or coffee, or Jack to keep her sharp. "I'm terribly out of practice without the relic."

"And I'm thoroughly depleted." Closing his eyes, he stared at the sky. "We have no relic. No allies. I have about fifty stitches barely keeping my insides from falling out of me." He paused. "Anything else?"

Emmy patted her skirt pocket. "An invisibility ring that might run out at any second."

"Lovely," Caleb said dryly. "So we're doomed."

Emmy tried to picture Jack's frenetic energy whenever he explained his elaborate plans. "Jack's schemes focused on people's deepest desires. If we figure out what matters most to them, they'll do anything to protect that."

"Like Clara and her pride. Or the chancellor and his quest for power." He rubbed his jaw. "In a way, that's how Grace got you to give her the relic. She figured out what mattered most to you, maybe before you did."

Jack. Emmy had lost it while trying to get Jack.

But Emmy could not succumb to her fury now, not when she needed to keep her wits about her. She was smarter than Grace Montgomery, damnit. Her mind was the one advantage Grace couldn't steal.

"What does the Society of the Charmed desire most? Power? Money? Status?"

"Believe it or not, what they want most of all is safety." Caleb tried to shrug, but he looked ready to keel over. "They got off course somewhere along the line, but their ultimate goal is to protect charmed people in a world in which they are greatly outnumbered."

"Not all charmed people. Only the ones who are rich like them, or who work for them." Emmy rubbed at her temples. She was so tired of the Society and its twisted virtues. "Part of me wants to burn it all down."

"Burn Stratton Mansion, right on Fifth Avenue?" The corner of Caleb's mouth lifted. "That would certainly attract unwanted attention."

"Especially if the flames were black."

"Jack would survive, but not Jimmy." With a groan, Caleb rested his head in his hands. "I applaud your passion, but arson on a massive scale may go a bit too far for my conscience."

"I don't want to kill them; I only want to hit them where it hurts. Their pride."

Emmy stilled. The Society had plenty of pride. In fact, they had a trophy case full of it.

"How are you at corralling wild animals?" Caleb asked. "If we break into the zoo—"

Emmy surged to her feet. Hope was thrashing inside her, painfully sharp.

"How quickly can we get to the city?"

THIRTY-FIVE

IN MANHATTAN, THE SOCIETY COULD not flaunt their conjury like they did in Avalon-on-Hudson. Instead, they slipped into the back entrance of Stratton Mansion, the same one they'd used the night of Emmy's debutante ball. Hidden from Fifth Avenue by greenery and an illusory dead end, each guest stepped through the bricks and disappeared.

Emmy had to use the invisibility ring sparingly, so she kept to the shadows, wearing a simple homespun dress Caleb had bought from one of the girls hawking goods by the ferry port. He had also changed, wearing a newsboy cap and trousers that he clearly thought beneath him, but he'd held his tongue.

No one had so much as glanced their way as they'd ridden the el uptown.

Caleb's eyes were squeezed shut, his mouth tight. "It's time. They've started."

Emmy glanced at the door. "You know what to do?"

Letting go of his conjury, he opened his eyes, his expression pained. "I really don't like that we're splitting up."

"It's the only way." They had no idea just how large of a web Grace's conjury could cast with the relic, but without the element of surprise, they were doomed. Caleb could not be nearby. Which was for the best, given that he looked as if he was about to pass out.

He gripped her shoulders. She gripped his.

"If you die," he said softly, "I'll be stuck as Paxton Fairchild forever, and I'll never forgive you."

But without Rose's relic, he was already stuck forever.

Emmy buried the bitter truth as she hugged Caleb. "If you start feeling worse, get yourself to Bellevue. I'll look there if you're not at the ferries."

Before she could lose her nerve, she let go of him, slipped the invisibility ring onto her finger, and left the safety of the alley. After crossing Fifth Avenue, Emmy tiptoed along Stratton Mansion until she stood just opposite the back entrance, before the illusory brick wall.

She stepped through it, coming to a stop in front of a door with a Society guard.

Her throat squeezed, but she could not clear it as he stared through her.

There had to be a late guest. There were always a few stragglers. But as the seconds ticked past, each one longer than the last, Emmy racked her brain for some other way inside.

Finally, a tardy couple arrived.

The guard opened the door, and Emmy slipped in front of them, hurrying down the narrow hall.

This was the long corridor that she'd walked with Grace and Papa, their usual banter falling silent as they'd taken in the austere mansion.

This was the back stairwell where the guards had separated her and Grace from Papa, where he'd blown a kiss over his shoulder as they led him toward the servants' entrance and the girls toward the main one. The last place they'd been together. Happy and full of hope.

And this turn, here, was where she and Grace had glimpsed inside the Stratton ballroom, the orchestra's greeting notes luring them like a siren's song. Where Grace had squeezed her hand and whispered, *Is it possible to die from happiness?*

Tonight, there was no music, only Keeper Windsor's commanding voice.

". . . witnesses have completed their testimony. Are there any additional persons who wish to speak against the accused?"

Still cloaked in invisibility, Emmy entered the Stratton ballroom once again.

The guests stood in a wide semicircle, too packed together for Emmy to pass between them. Their faces were familiar by now, even though their attire was far more muted than it had been all summer.

"Ah, yes, Mrs. Stratton. Please come forward."

Emmy slid along the wall. She hadn't noticed the guards at the debutante ball—had not yet known to look for them. But now, she stepped gingerly around the ones stationed at the exits, careful not to brush into the backs of the guests who stared straight ahead.

"From the moment this vile boy was born," Mrs. Stratton's airy voice carried over the silent crowd, "I knew he was bursting with wickedness. He clawed his way out of his mother. Killing her was the first thing he ever did in this world."

Finally, Emmy reached the far edge of the crowd. Slipping around the guards, she glimpsed Mrs. Stratton, her arm supported by none other than Grace Montgomery.

They both wore mourning black. Grace's golden hair glowed against the dark shade.

Emmy tensed, but she was still invisible. And Grace was far too busy patting Mrs. Stratton's arm with gentle sympathy as she bemoaned the cursed life of Jack Fontaine, who had been hellbent on corrupting Oliver since they were in diapers.

Any guilt Emmy had felt about widowing Mrs. Stratton disintegrated.

Careful not to scrape her ballroom slippers along the tile, Emmy tiptoed around the edge of the crowd for a better look.

There, propped against an ornate column, was Jimmy.

His hands were bound around the column. A scab cut through his eyebrow, and a few bruises marred his cheeks, his knuckles. But he was alive, peering over his shoulder at—

Jack. Emmy's heart leaped to her throat. He was also bound, arms stretched around the column at a terrible angle. How she longed to run her fingers across his beautiful face, bruised but still impossibly alluring, because it was his. Jack's.

How had she ever convinced herself that she could walk away from him? Remaining across the ballroom now required all her self-control, especially as Mrs. Stratton continued to describe Jack's wickedness, uttering all his worst fears about himself. That he was vile to his core. That he ruined everyone and everything he touched.

All the while, Jack rested his head against the column, resigned.

For three long seconds, Emmy allowed her fury to flood her before she clamped it down.

"Thank you, Mrs. Stratton, for your testimony." Keeper Windsor returned to the center of the stage as Grace helped Mrs. Stratton descend the stairs. Her worth in the eyes of Oliver's mother had gone up tremendously. Just as she'd planned.

In one week, Oliver and I will be engaged, Grace had said at the potion fundraiser. It was infuriating, all the ways Emmy had played right into Grace's hands.

"Would anyone else like to bear witness in the case against Mr. Fontaine?"

A quiet murmur passed through the crowd. They were growing restless having to wait when, in their eyes, his fate had been determined long ago.

"Very well. Are there any witnesses in defense of Mr. Fontaine?"

Someone snickered. With a gulp of air, Emmy slid between the guests. Now or never.

"In that case—"

She removed the ring. "I would like to speak."

Confusion spread through hushed whispers as Emmy stepped forward. No one remembered her true face, save Grace, but Emmy was not looking at her. No, she was looking at Jack, who was staring at her as if she were a ghost.

She offered him a tentative smile, but he only grew paler.

"That's her!" Mrs. Stratton shrieked, pointing at Emmy. "That's the escaped prisoner who infiltrated us!"

"Emmy, behind you!"

At Jimmy's warning, Emmy whirled as the guards made a beeline toward her.

"Are you so afraid of the truth?" Emmy planted her feet, her voice carrying above the uproar. "You won't even hear my story before you kill another innocent soul?"

"He is far from innocent," someone snapped.

Three guards broke through the crowd, guns raised. They did not know Emmy. They would not pause to conjure their gifts, but instead jump right to lethal force.

"How did you get in here?" Keeper Windsor demanded.

She shuffled back, but the guards were quicker, seizing her roughly by the arms. "This is justice with you at the helm?" Her gaze locked on Keeper Windsor's. "Witnesses dragged away before they're allowed to speak?"

But the guards did not wait for his answer. They carried her through the glaring crowd, and it took everything Emmy had not to fight back. Not yet.

"You're no better than Chancellor Stratton!" she yelled. "You're just as corrupt as he was!"

She had one card left, but she had hoped to save it until the very last minute.

"Wait."

The guards halted at the command from Keeper Windsor.

"Bring her here," he ordered.

She could have collapsed with relief, had the guards not been shoving her toward the stage. As she passed Grace, her former friend glared at her with pure, unadulterated hatred.

Emmy had surprised *her* for once.

With her head high, Emmy climbed the stairs just as she'd done two years earlier.

"According to our bylaws, witnesses for the accused are permitted to say their piece. No matter the obvious guilt of the accused." Keeper Windsor's words hardly made it past his tight lips.

Breathe. Emmy's heart thrashed as she faced the crowd. Jimmy strained his neck to see past the guards, his face full of concern. Jack gaped at her, clearly alarmed that she was here.

"My name is Emilia Vallillo." Emmy's raspy voice carried across the ballroom. "I attended my debutante ball here two years ago. I arrived with Miss Montgomery, my neighbor and my oldest friend."

"Liar!" someone yelled, but Keeper Windsor silenced the heckler with a stern look.

With her aunt on one side and Mrs. Stratton on the other, Grace curled her lips.

"After I demonstrated my transformation conjury, I was accused of fraud by Grace Montgomery, who had convinced Clara Claremont to sew fool's gold into my hem." She let her gaze slide around the crowd. She might have been forgettable, but surely they remembered her gift. "I was arrested, right here in this ballroom."

Still blank faces.

Anger stirred, a bone-deep boiling that laced its way into her voice. "My father was shot by Chancellor Stratton for attempting to come to my aid. He died over there while all of you watched."

That, they remembered. Emmy could not help it: she stole a look at Grace to see if there'd be any remorse, any grief in her face. But Grace remained as impassive as a porcelain doll.

"I spent two years, three months, and seven days in Grimsbane," Emmy continued. "With no blanket to keep me warm, no books to occupy my mind, nothing but my grief."

It was a new form of torment, bearing her soul to an indifferent audience. If she hadn't promised Caleb she'd try, she would have quit already.

But she kept going. She spoke of Jack's escape, how he'd freed her, too, leaving out Jimmy's and Caleb's help. She described Jack's own injustices. How Grace had enchanted blankets with Stratton conjury so that Rose and Elizabeth could not move while Mistfield burned. How Emmy had transformed their appearances so they could pursue their own form of justice because they did not trust that the Society, under the Strattons, would be impartial.

And perhaps it was because she'd left out Rose's relic—she refused to trust the Society with the knowledge of that sort of power—or perhaps it was because they'd never been interested in the truth, but before she was finished, she could see her fate in their hateful eyes. The only person not casting a venomous stare her way was Mrs. Windsor, who watched Emmy from beside the stage, her face full of pity, as if Emmy belonged in a sanitorium.

No one believed her. With every sentence, they grew more impatient for blood to be shed.

Jack rested his head against the column. For so long, he'd thought they'd believe him. That they'd welcome him back. But they did not deserve his loyalty.

At least now she could tell Caleb that she'd tried.

"I can see you do not care for the truth." Emmy was unable to keep the bite from her voice. "But perhaps you care for your reputations."

Still, they stared at her impatiently. In their eyes, she was a nobody. A nuisance.

She heaved a breath. This was it. "Last night, I snuck into the headquarters of the Society of the Charmed and I stole your trophies. The ones from the summer pageants."

Surprise erupted through the ballroom—that she'd admitted to such a crime, that she'd dare touch their beloved displays of wealth and conjury.

"Arrest her!" someone yelled, and Emmy reached into the folds of her dress, producing a trophy engraved *Windsor, 1879*. With a saccharine smile, she held it high.

"At my signal," Emmy continued, satisfaction surging through her as panic began to spread, "my friend outside will deliver them to Manhattan's most respected newspapers, along with detailed descriptions of what sort of conjury each of your families has used to obtain your wealth. By morning, the entire city will know not only of magic's existence, but who wields it."

Emmy could not help it; she stole a glance at Grace, who was seething, her perfect mask cracking.

Guards moved in Emmy's periphery, climbing the stage, and Emmy planted her feet. "Don't you dare touch me. If I don't walk out of here in three minutes with both of my friends, everyone in New York will know that you're all lying, cheating witches."

When Emmy had described the crimes committed against her and Jack, no one had batted an eye. But now that their secret might be released? A goddamn uproar.

People yelled over one another. Plenty moved toward the exits, while others clutched their diamonds, gaping at the stage. Keeper Windsor stalked toward her, his eyes aflame. "Do you realize what you've done? The lives you're putting at stake?"

"The lives that matter to me are already at stake."

"This affects you, too! They'll carve us all up like science experiments."

"Not all of us." Emmy smiled innocently at him. "Only the most *elite* Society members compete for trophies. The staff, the nonmembers—we'll be perfectly safe."

"Wait!" Grace yelled as people streamed from the ballroom. "She's bluffing!"

"I suppose they'll freeze your assets, too," Emmy mused. "People won't take kindly to doing business with bona fide witches. Two minutes now."

Keeper Windsor glared at her, his chest rising and falling in quick, angry breaths.

"Don't believe her, Uncle. She's lying!"

But Keeper Windsor's gaze remained fixed on Emmy. "Unbind them," he ordered the guards. "Do it quickly."

"Uncle, no!"

Two guards began to untie Jimmy. Another pair still flocked Emmy, but she tucked the trophy underneath her arm and strode ahead of them, stopping in front of Mrs. Windsor. Taking the frightened woman's gloved hands before she could yank them away, Emmy pressed Grace's invisibility ring into her palm. "If you don't believe me, see for yourself what your niece does when you're not around. You owe that to Elizabeth."

It was the only way Grace would ever be caught. But Mrs. Windsor staggered back. "Don't you *dare* speak of my daughter."

How maddening, that they all believed Grace's lies so thoroughly, even after Emmy had told them the truth. But Emmy was going to have to learn not to care.

As Emmy turned around, familiar arms lifted her into a bear hug. "You're out of your damn mind," Jimmy breathed against her hair, "you know that?"

She allowed herself to smile for a moment as she squeezed him—but only for a moment. They still needed to get the hell out of this ballroom.

"Nicely done, Vallillo." Jack stood before them, rubbing at his wrists. Their eyes met, and he glanced about the ballroom. Of course he couldn't look at her, after what she'd said.

But now was not the time to find the right words.

"Out of the way, out of the way," Jimmy called as he cleared a path.

Even the guards did not react as Jack plucked a pistol from a man's holster. "I'll be taking this."

Grace stood by the door, her hand pressed nervously against her father's relic, but the more powerful one remained hidden. And Emmy ought to have let it go—she'd promised Caleb that she'd let it go—but she locked eyes with Grace. "Keeper Windsor, there's one more condition."

"You're lucky we have not shot you on the spot," Keeper Windsor snapped. "Now *leave*."

But Emmy did not look away from Grace. "Your niece stole my relic."

A vase burst off a table, heading straight toward them. With a grunt, Jimmy pulled Jack and Emmy to the ground, and it sailed over their heads, shattering against the ballroom wall.

The guards glanced at each other, but none of them had broken Windsor's order not to attack. No, that was Grace's doing. She could steal anyone's conjury in the ballroom, perhaps even farther. They would never be safe as long as she had it.

As long as she had it, she'd won.

"Are you strong enough to conjure?" Emmy murmured to Jack. Reaching into her hidden pocket, she removed the long, thin stick, the other item they'd purchased in good old Five Points.

A firework.

"Just leave," Keeper Windsor ordered.

"Not without my relic." Emmy stared at Grace as Jack's flame flickered in his palm, igniting the wick. Grace was practically seething.

"Leave us!" Keeper Windsor bellowed.

Not taking her eyes off Grace, Emmy handed the trophy to Keeper Windsor and shrugged. "I don't bluff."

The firework exploded across the ballroom, its high-pitched shriek drowning out the Society's screams.

THIRTY-SIX

GRACE SLIPPED OUT THE DOOR just as the crowd crushed against it. Unless Emmy wanted to be stampeded, she had to let her go.

"We need to get out of here." With one hand firmly in Emmy's, Jack pushed his way through the fleeing crowd, flourishing the gun at anyone who got in their way. For the most part, the guests were far too busy rushing the exits to give a damn about them.

"Is Caleb all right?" Jimmy ducked as a powerful wind whipped another flower arrangement dangerously close to their heads.

"With any luck, he's already down by the ferries, resting." As much as she wanted him to deliver the trophies to the newspapers like she'd claimed, Caleb was far too weak. And loath as she was to care for anyone in the Society, Emmy did not want to trigger another witch hunt.

But they'd stolen the trophies. The Society didn't need to know the rest.

A guard stormed toward them, gun cocked, but Jack slide tackled him, sending the gun spinning across the dance floor. "I know a back exit. Follow me."

As if she'd leave his side.

Hurrying along the perimeter of the ballroom, they passed a pair of curtains being consumed by Fontaine flames. Jack slowed, staring at the black fire. "From the firework?"

A dark fireball whirred past them, nearly singeing Emmy.

"Grace." Emmy searched through the smoke. "She has the relic, and she can—"

"Steal conjury," he finished. "I see she isn't done smearing my name."

Another ball of black fire streamed across the ballroom, thick smoke trailing in its wake. Motioning for Jimmy to follow, Jack kicked open a servants' entrance.

"I'd say 'ladies first,' but by now, I know better." Jack turned to Jimmy. "You take the front. We'll follow."

With a quick nod, Jimmy disappeared into the pitch-black stairwell. Emmy gripped Jack's hand, and he gave hers a returning squeeze as he began the dark descent. How relieved she was, how blissfully euphoric, that he was alive and holding her hand—

Strong arms plucked her from the stairwell. Kicking wildly, she tried to get her feet on the ground, to strike whoever had—

A cool blade pressed against her throat.

"You have caused me to suffer quite the ordeal," Oliver growled in her ear.

Jack surged from the stairwell. Eyes wide, he cocked his gun, flipping the safety.

"Put that down," Oliver snarled, "or I'll slit her throat from her chin to her chest."

"Shoot him!" Emmy screeched. "Before—"

She froze in Oliver's arms. His goddamn suppression conjury. With the knife still against her throat, she was a stiff porcelain doll, completely defenseless.

Jack knew it, too. His face was tortured, and he kept the gun pointed at them as if searching for an angle that would not hurt Emmy. With infuriating resolve, he set the gun on the floor. "C'mon, Ollie. It's me you want."

Don't you dare, she tried to scream, tried to tell him with the intensity of her glare.

"Get on your knees," Oliver growled.

Don't you dare, she tried to say, but all she managed was a pathetic whimper.

Jack hesitated.

Oliver pressed the knife deeper into her neck. Pain burst from the wound, and a warm rivulet of blood oozed down her collarbone, her dress. But Emmy could not wince, could not even put on a brave face.

Jack watched her as he lowered himself to his knees. She could practically see his heart racing in his chest: *Thump thump thump.*

"Don't hate me." He managed to smile sheepishly. Still trying to take care of her.

I'll never let anything bad happen to you again. I swear it.

He was a liar, because this was far worse than Oliver slitting her throat. Emmy tried to summon the brume, but Oliver's hold was too strong. She should have chased Grace down for the relic, should never have let it out of her sight.

Oliver dumped Emmy on the floor and lifted his knife above Jack, just as he had in the alley.

But this time, when he brought it down, the blade tore through Jack's throat.

Emmy tried to scream, tried to scream, tried to scream—

A riot of red splashed from Jack's neck, an infuriatingly pretty shade, spilling over the same pristine marble floors as Papa's. Jack's hands flailed to his throat, shock widening his eyes—

Thump thump.

Her scream made it past her lips. She struggled to her feet, her limbs as heavy as iron.

Thump thump.

Emmy staggered to him. Wide-eyed, he tried to speak, but a terrible choking sound escaped his perfect mouth.

Thump thump.

Emmy pressed her hands over the horrible wound. Crimson poured between her fingers, warm and slick and pulsing with every beat of his heart. She tore at her skirts to make a tourniquet, just as she'd done for Caleb, and she wrapped the fabric around Jack's neck, but she could not squeeze it tight enough without further choking him, could not keep the blood from spilling into his airways—

There had to be something she could do to help him, but she couldn't think past that awful spluttering sound. He was hurting, and frightened, and *drowning* in his own blood.

"Don't you dare die," she rasped. Squeezing her eyes shut, she called to her conjury.

Thump.

After relying on the relic for so long, Emmy could hardly feel the brume without it. Still she dug, but her magic only whispered in response, and there was so much blood. Too much—

Thump.

Jack's hands jerked forward, searching as if he could no longer see, and she yanked at the brume, finally filling her lungs with a heavy wisp of power. She was San Rocco's daughter. She had survived her mother's death, and her father's, and two years alone in a barren cell. She was more powerful than she knew—even without an amplifier. She had to be.

Digging deeper, she imagined Jack's throat stitching back together, just as he'd stitched her back together. He'd ignited her fury when the fire in her had nearly gone out, had propelled her to be strong when she was collapsing. And she would not fail him now, not when he needed *her* for once.

But blood still leaked from his neck like water through a sieve. He was so pale, so frightened, just like Papa had been, and what the hell could she do? She couldn't stop the bleeding, couldn't lose him, too—

His choking sounds worsened, his desperation cleaving her heart in two. He was dying, and scared, and she couldn't stop it, couldn't do a damn thing, just like Papa—

Later, she'd hate herself for letting go of the brume—and his wound. For quitting, when there might have been some fractional bit of healing conjury buried in her.

Her hand was slick with blood as she slipped it into Jack's.

"You're a good man, Jack Fontaine," she whispered in his ear, and he ceased flailing. An awful wetness accompanied each of his breaths, but he squeezed her hand, and what was left of her heart shattered into a million worthless pieces. "You're selfless, and you're brave, and you're *good*. And you were right about us. You hear me, Jack? You were right."

Blood no longer seeped from his neck. Had she slowed the bleeding? Not daring to breathe, Emmy pressed her ear to his chest, listening for that *thump thump thump*.

Silence.

"Jack," Emmy whispered. With trembling fingers, she caressed his cheek, but what should have been hot skin was quickly losing its warmth. She stared at those beautiful gray eyes, waiting for them to find her, like they always did. But they remained empty.

"He's dead," Oliver informed her coolly, still twirling that knife.

The truth of his taunt buried itself in her chest like an arrow. She could not pull it out.

Because Jack Fontaine was dead.

The world narrowed around Oliver, and something raw snapped within Emmy. She thrust herself at the pistol, still right where Jack had laid it at Oliver's feet. She did not know how to use it, but she knew to press it to his chest. She knew to squeeze the trigger.

As it fired, the kickback knocked her onto the marble floor.

Oliver stumbled backward, crashing to the ground, too. Smoke burned her eyes, her throat, but Emmy made herself climb to her feet to watch him writhe and twitch.

The sight of Jack, lifeless beside Oliver, pulverized the last pieces of Emmy.

She would never be the same.

She was no longer human as she climbed to her feet and screamed, with all her might, for Grace.

THIRTY-SEVEN

"GRACE!" EMMY'S SCREAM WAS A vendetta and a lament, so full of anguish, she hardly recognized it herself. "Grace Eloise Montgomery!"

Emmy stalked through the thick smoke, narrowly avoiding the ever-growing black flames, but every cursed soul had already fled Stratton Mansion, Grace included.

Emmy could not feel the night air on her skin, could not hear the wailing fire bells, the screams of the ordinary folks as they fell to their knees at the sight of the devil's fire on Fifth Avenue. She searched the staring faces until she found the Windsors. Her gaze locked with Grace's aunt's, and Emmy did not bother to hide her devastation. Let Mrs. Windsor see what her niece had wrought. Let her watch as Emmy evened the score.

But Grace was not beside her. Grace was a rat. And rats scurried from disaster. Rats hid in corners, waiting for chaos to pass. Far enough to avoid detection. Close enough to return to gather the spoils of the fallen.

She found Grace in an alley.

Upon seeing Emmy, Grace lifted her hands just as she had when she'd hurled Jack's flames at Emmy, using the relic to bridge his gift from a distance. But no flames erupted.

Because Jack Fontaine was dead.

Confused, Grace stared at her flameless hands before her gaze snapped to Emmy. To the knife she was holding. "That's Oliver's," her voice wavered.

Emmy hadn't even realized she'd grabbed the knife. Jack's blood still stained it. "He's dead."

"*What?*" Grace knew Emmy well enough to know she spoke the truth. She staggered back, tears lending her blue eyes an air of innocence. "You ruin *everything!*"

"Give me the relic." Emmy hardly recognized her own voice, the unnatural calm in it. Grace had taken and taken and taken. But the relic had been Jack's. He'd given it to Emmy.

"Or you'll stab me, too?" Grace screeched. "Do you see how insane you are?"

Emmy lunged for her. She managed to slash Grace's arm with Oliver's knife, leaving a thick red trail down her bicep. Grace screamed as she ducked away, pressing her hand to the bleeding wound.

Emmy lunged again, but the red slash on Grace's arm was knitting itself together. Papa's gift—protecting Grace once again.

With an inhuman scream, Emmy swung the knife. But Grace dodged it with ease. Scooping a loose brick off the floor, she transformed it to a knife of her own.

She was using Emmy's own gift against her. Papa's gift against her. And Emmy would rather die than let her have them. "My father would be ashamed of what you've become."

"He was practically my father, too." Grace kept her head high. "And he'd be proud of how strong I've grown. How hard I've worked."

They stared at each other. Each holding a knife they did not know how to wield.

Each with a dead lover in the burning ballroom behind them.

"Don't think I won't do it." The knife in Grace's hand elongated, turning a brilliant silver that glittered in the unnatural glow of the hellish flames.

"Go ahead." Emmy kept her own knife firm in her hand. "You've already taken everything else from me."

Because Jack was dead. Their plan had failed. *Everything* had failed.

"As if this is my fault? *You're* the one who couldn't just let me have a patronage, even though I needed it much more than you!"

"A patronage?" Emmy could hardly believe her ears. "You're justifying everything you did—because you think you deserved a patronage?"

"I *did* deserve it," Grace snapped. "Look how the Society needs my conjury. My gift makes their lives more convenient. It makes their illusions last longer, their existence safer."

"If you're so sure, then why go through the trouble of sabotaging me?"

"Because I knew you would try to take it from me, just like you're doing now! You can't *stand* not being the best!"

"What are you talking about?" Emmy exclaimed. "I always rooted for you, just as hard as I rooted for myself."

"You rooted for me as long as I was behind you." Grace swung the knife, keeping Emmy back just as she tried to sneak closer. "Teachers gave you higher marks. You made sewing for Mrs. Feinstein a competition, then rubbed it in my face when you finished more pieces. You had to make sure everyone back home *liked* you more."

Emmy gaped at her. "And that gave you the right to ruin my life?"

"You had the doting father. The bigger flat. The adoration of the whole damn building. But the Society was *mine*. And you *knew* they were going to pick me. That's why you had to try to outdo me, figuring out a way to make gold at the last minute." Grace blew a stray hair out of her face. "Well, guess what, Ems: for once in our lives, I won."

Like hell she did. With a wild cry, Emmy lunged again, but Grace turned her wrist, and the weeds at Emmy's feet grew, tripping her. Earth conjury. An earth conjurer was near.

Emmy's pulse quickened as she scurried to her feet.

"I wanted a patronage just as much as you did." She could not best Grace physically, but she could try to keep her talking. "I worked my entire life for it."

"But you didn't *need* it. You had everything you wanted already, and I had nothing."

"What are you talking about?" Emmy exclaimed. "You know my roots. You *are* my roots!"

"There's poor, and there's daughter-of-a-whore poor." There were real tears in Grace's eyes now. "Your mother took better care of you in the eight years you had together than mine did my whole life."

Emmy stared at Grace. That, at least, was the truth.

"And Papa—that man would have done *anything* for you."

"And you too." Emmy's voice shook tremulously. Now was not the time for her anger to abandon her. Not when she was hanging on by a thread.

"I outdid *you*, for once. I had the guts to do whatever it took to get into the Society. And now look at me." A smile broke over Grace's tear-stained cheeks. "I am a *Windsor* now. You never could have accomplished what I did."

"You did *nothing*," Emmy snapped. She had to goad her, had to keep her talking. "If I'd been born a Montgomery, I would have climbed even higher."

"You think you could have sacrificed *me* to ensure you'd get picked?" Grace barked a laugh. "You think you could have watched Papa get shot and not let a single tear fall? Or convince rule-abiding Lizzie Windsor to sneak into Mistfield in the middle of the night, ensuring she'd be there when it went up in flames? Spreading those flames yourself to make sure she never told a soul?" The long knife in Grace's hands morphed to a rifle. "And you wouldn't have the guts to finish this. Once and for all."

Emmy stilled as Grace lifted the rifle, hands trembling.

She'd do it. And perhaps that was fitting. Jack had died by Oliver's hand. Now Emmy would die by Grace's.

Grace's gaze snapped behind Emmy, her expression so horrified, Emmy risked a glance.

Mrs. Windsor stood at the mouth of the alley, the invisibility ring in her palm. Just as Emmy had hoped.

So stunned was Grace, she didn't see Emmy charge, knife poised to strike. She didn't take her eyes off her aunt until Emmy drove it into her forearm.

They both tumbled to the ground, along with the rifle. Grace managed to fire it, and blinding pain tore through Emmy's stomach. Shot—she'd been shot.

With a scream, she tore at Grace's neck, yanking the two chains that hung from it. The wrong relic came free. She yanked again, but the chain Jack had made her did not relent. Grace tried to roll away, but as soon as Emmy's finger grazed the coin's cool surface, she envisioned its chain as thin as a strand of hair.

It snapped free.

"Give it back!" Grace shrieked, but Emmy scurried away with both relics. Grace tried to throw herself at Emmy, but the weeds grabbed her by the ankle, laying her flat.

Mrs. Windsor still stood at the mouth of the alley, palms raised, tears streaming down her cheeks.

"Auntie, please! She *stabbed* me!" Sure enough, blood was seeping out of her forearm. It was an impressively deep cut. Emmy would savor that, at least.

"Emmy!" Jimmy sprinted into the alley, not giving Grace a second glance. "You're bleeding!"

Jack's dead, she tried to say, but she choked on the words.

Jimmy's hands fluttered over her stomach, and Emmy tensed, waiting for the pain.

"We need to get you to a hospital," Jimmy was saying, but Emmy was too dazed to hear him. One hand still grasped both relics, but with the other, Emmy hugged her abdomen. Her dress was torn, and blood coated her fingers as she prodded her skin, but there was no wound. Not even a slight one.

Papa's conjury. It had healed her, somehow, but Emmy couldn't feel the coldness of a bandage bridged with his gift. Come to think of it, Grace hadn't put anything on her wounds, either. Nor had she turned one of her rings or touched a bracelet.

And Grace was still bleeding from where Emmy had cut her. But Emmy was healed.

Rose was able to make it only with my help, Grace had boasted outside Clarity Hall.

Grace, who had stolen the pages from the Fontaine grimoire after Rose's death.

"Your father didn't gift you a relic when he died." Emmy was shaking now, her entire body trembling as she stared at Grace, who was still struggling against the weeds. "You made it from *my* father's bones."

Through her tears, Grace still managed to snarl at her. "He was *my* father, too."

Emmy blinked, hardly registering the Society guards gathering in the mouth of the alley. Mrs. Windsor waving them over to Grace. Jimmy's gentle tug on her elbow. More insistent now.

Rose's relic gave amplifying conjury to whoever touched it. And Grace's—no, *Papa's* relic—gave healing conjury to whoever touched it.

Emmy took off toward the burning mansion.

Jimmy was yelling after her, but Emmy was already throwing the door open, hurtling herself back through the hidden entrance. Smoke burned her eyes, coated her throat, but Papa's conjury healed her instantly. Waving her hands, Emmy transformed the air around her, courtesy of the other relic. Rose's.

And despite everything, it felt *good*, the power coursing through her once again.

She climbed the stairs two at a time, tripping over her skirts. The smoke was deathly thick in the ballroom, but Emmy waved wildly, searching the floor, her conjury clearing the air a few feet at a time.

She tripped over legs, black flames licking through charred skin, and let out an aggravated scream. It had to be Oliver. Fontaine flames did not burn the wielder.

Digging deeper into the brume, Emmy swung her arms about, willing the smoke to thin.

And there was Jack, beside Oliver. How long had he been gone? Five minutes? Fifteen?

Emmy removed her pathetic attempt at bandaging his throat and pressed the relic with her father's remains atop the gory wound.

"Come back," she pleaded, squeezing her hands against both sides of the wound, willing Papa's gift to thread it back together.

Jimmy was beside her now, too devastated for Emmy to bear. "Ems . . ."

"I know it seems impossible, but if there's *any* chance . . ."

The bruises on Jack's beautiful face were fading now, as if an invisible eraser had dabbed them away. But his throat was still torn open, and as the seconds ticked by, nothing changed.

Papa had made a dead heart beat again once, after two minutes. But it had been much longer than that, and whatever fragment of his magic the relic contained wasn't strong enough. Not unless—

Grabbing the relic off Jack, Emmy lunged for the nearest flames. She cupped her hands around both relics and, squeezing her eyes shut, dipped her hands inside the black fire.

The pain was incredible, unbearable, but Emmy refused to remove her hands, no matter how much Jimmy screamed, no matter how much *she* screamed. Fontaine flames forged relics—and maybe, just maybe, it combined them, too.

When she could bear it no longer, Emmy pulled her hands from the flames. The metal still seared her palms, but the two coins were now one dripping, glinting amalgamation.

By the time she laid it on Jack, her burnt hands had already healed.

"Please come back. *Please.*" He needed to be as alive as he was when he launched himself off the cliffs. As alive as he was before he revealed something conniving, or when he purposely made her mad. As alive as he'd been when he was trying to be brave: *You have transformed me more than you intended.*

Jimmy gasped.

Jack's throat—it was knitting back together, and Emmy knew better than to hope, but—color was returning to his cheeks. With her pulse thundering through her veins, Emmy pressed her ear to his chest, but it was still silent. So she begged God. Papa. Rose. Whoever else might be listening from wherever came next, to let Jack return to her.

They'd had so little time together. And there was so much she hadn't told him.

Jack's lashes fluttered against his cheeks.

Thump.

Thirty-Eight

"JACK?" EMMY'S HOPE WAS TERRIFYING, far worse than it had been when they'd run from Grimsbane. She'd been half dead then, but now, she was so very alive.

Eyes still closed, Jack coughed, and Emmy nearly collapsed against him. She kissed his knuckles. Dragged her hands through his hair, across the smooth skin of his neck. No bruises, no cuts. Pressed her hand to his heart and—*thump thump thump*.

"Vallillo?" Jack rasped. "What the hell happened?"

She hadn't the faintest idea how to answer.

"We need to get out of here." Jimmy helped Emmy pull Jack to his feet, passing the conglomerate relic over his neck so that it bulged beneath his shirt.

The flames had engulfed the ballroom, and the heat was overwhelming, but Jack insisted on calling to his conjury to extinguish them. It took him several minutes to tame the fire, reducing it until all that remained were black plumes of smoke.

Outside, the ordinary onlookers were shouting that God had answered their prayers and extinguished the devil's flames. The Society was gone, Grace included. Perhaps she'd used her silver tongue to talk her way out of whatever Mrs. Windsor had heard.

Emmy no longer cared.

"We need to get to the ferries." Jimmy was practically dragging them across the street. Although the Society was nowhere in sight, Emmy knew he would not breathe easy until Caleb was nearby.

Caleb needed to tell him about that one last prophecy.

Jack, for his part, did not make a sound. Block after block, he remained silent, though he kept pace with surprising ease. He was deep in his thoughts; Emmy could practically hear his gears spinning.

"Does your throat feel all right?" She squinted in the dark, but there was no trace of the lethal gash. "Does it hurt to speak, or breathe, or—"

Jack slowed, turning to face her. "You don't owe me anything, you know."

She stopped walking, brow raised.

"I know you feel guilty because I almost died back there—"

"Definitely died," Jimmy interrupted. "You were very, very dead."

Jack paled. "How?"

How, indeed, could she possibly explain what had just happened? "Grace never had a relic made from Mr. Montgomery. She had one made from my father, using the same method Rose used to make the amplifying relic." All the bitterness surrounding that particular deceit had evaporated. "I tried to heal you with that, but . . ."

"So you combined both relics." Jack lifted the oddly shaped metallic mess that Emmy had made. "How long was I . . . ?"

"Too long," she whispered, trying to blink away the threat of tears. He was alive.

His face fell as he reached for her, but he dropped his hand, looking away.

"Jimmy?" Emmy gave him a meaningful look. "Can we catch up with you in a moment?"

"I'll find Caleb." He offered her a tight smile. "Meet you at the ferries."

As Emmy watched Jimmy jog across the street, she tried to gather her courage.

Her turn to be brave.

Jack was already studying her with his usual intensity. She had been delusional, trying to convince herself that she preferred him as Nathaniel. It was such a bald-faced lie, she nearly laughed. How she'd missed this mess of chocolate hair, the devastating cut of his jaw, the dark lashes framing eyes that could not help but seem mischievous.

"Jack," she began, but all the bravery she'd mustered abandoned her. How could she possibly put into words what she was feeling? How she already knew his death would haunt her for the rest of her life? She could hardly stand the thought of leaving his side. Even the few feet that separated them on the sidewalk made her chest ache something awful.

Jack studied his feet. "Let me do us both a favor. You don't need to feel guilty. I may have poured my heart out, but you made it clear—"

She reached for his hands, but he pulled away.

"I don't need your pity." His voice was hoarse, those gray eyes full of words he was not saying. "Tonight was . . . a lot. And I know how your mind works, Vallillo. You hate that I put that gun down. And you're relieved that I'm alive, but—I'm not going to let you confuse whatever you're feeling right now for whatever I feel for you all the damn time."

"Oh?" She folded her arms across her chest. "You're not going to *let* me?"

His eyes narrowed. "I'm doing the right thing. If you're trying to make me feel better because I almost died, or did die, I suppose, I'm not going to let you. Either way—"

Lifting onto her toes, she pressed a finger against his infuriating lips. "Why are you still talking?"

His eyes widened, the hope in his expression too much to bear.

She'd meant to make him smile, but they were too close now, the gravity between them too powerful. She wrapped her arms around his shoulders. He tangled his hands in the smoke-filled hair that had come loose, spilling over her back. Their noses grazed, sending delicious chills skittering all over her skin. Like the first notes of a beautiful song. Like coming home after a long time away.

This time, she kissed him.

Epilogue

TWO GIRLS ATTENDED A MAGICAL ball, but one burned it to the ground.

Then built it anew.

A week after Stratton Mansion burned, the remaining triumvirate member returned to Avalon-on-Hudson with his hat in his hand. Cautiously, they let him inside Mistfield's bare and damaged halls, courtesy of the guards' ruthless search. Jimmy had already begun repairs, and Emmy was eager to help, but the strange new relic was far weaker at amplifying her conjury. It'd taken her a long time to transform Caleb's and Jimmy's faces back to their own.

Jack had offered to separate the two relics, but the four friends were in agreement: they were not ready to tamper with something powerful enough to bring back the recently deceased.

With grief-tinged eyes, Keeper Windsor disclosed his two orders of business.

First, he issued formal apologies to Emmy and Jack for their wrongful imprisonments. Though they gripped each other's hands, they managed to remain blank faced as Keeper Windsor walked them through the consequences against those who had framed them.

Grace and Clara were in Grimsbane. Oliver and his father were dead.

And second, Keeper Windsor offered Jack his father's position as commander of the guard. The four of them stared at the man before Jack laughed uproariously. But as Keeper Windsor described the need to rebuild the Society from the ground up, Emmy knew that a tendril of hope still flickered inside Jack, a stubborn candle that refused to be extinguished.

It flickered inside her, too.

The Society could be a place for all charmed folks, they whispered to each other that night, after Jimmy and Caleb were fast asleep. Not as a social club, but as a place for people of all social classes to learn. To help each other. To use their gifts for good, in a city full of people who desperately needed a bit of goodness.

And so, leaving the tranquil isolation of Mistfield, they returned to the city.

Each day, Jack and Emmy left for work early in the morning, sharing a too-brief kiss on the stoop before he made his way uptown, and she, downtown. Jack held meetings with what remained of the Society's old guard. More times than not, he came home burning with indignity at whatever snobbishness stood in his way.

It wasn't supposed to be easy, Emmy reminded him.

With Caleb's help, Jack began taking the Society's old guard to meet the charmed families Emmy had found downtown. He showed them the wonderful, untapped power that existed within the city limits, gifts that were being wasted while charmed folks worked sixteen-hour shifts at menial jobs, simply to eat. He brought them to Grimsbane, forcing them to sit in the same cell he'd languished in for nearly a year, to taste the same paltry food served to all prisoners. He walked them through his plans for reworking the system, for laws that were fair and trials that gave due process. With Jimmy's gentle guidance, he learned to listen past their cries about change, their moans about the Society becoming a charity. He learned to hear their unspoken fears. About their families' security in this new system. About change itself.

By the time the first snow fell, Jack was coming home reenergized more often than he was grumbling. He even, Emmy dared to say, *liked* his position. Which was a gift, really, because Emmy loved everything about her own project: a school for children from the poorest tenements, one in which they could learn to read, and write, and dream of something more.

And if that embroidered snake on Clara Claremont's fabric shifted when a child held it, they'd learn conjury, too.

Her growing student body never went hungry, not with Emmy's seemingly endless supply of treats and meals to take home. And the students loved when their beloved headmistress stopped by their flats, bringing gifts for the whole family. A visit from her brought good providence, the students believed, for afterward, they often had a stroke of luck: torn boots mended themselves, lost coins suddenly appeared on the mantelpiece, and sweets found their way into the cupboard. Practicing her conjury each night, she made so much currency Jack teased that she alone would be responsible if the dollar crashed. But it was not enough. The machine of greed still devoured New York's poorest inhabitants. No one could better their circumstances when they were starved and worked to the bone.

Jimmy was the one who first began researching labor unions. By Christmas, he'd attended his first meeting, then implemented a forty-hour work week within his flourishing construction company, which was quickly becoming a favorite among charmed families, even without Zhao Rui. Within the year, Caleb had declared, he'd have more new builds than Cornelius Vanderbilt.

With any luck, Jimmy would have enough clout—and money of his own—to lead the charge against the Chinese Exclusion Act.

It was Jimmy's success they were toasting one blistering February night, crammed into the room Emmy insisted on calling a library, though it held hardly fifty books. Jack kept offering to flood the shelves with tomes from Mistfield's vast collection, but Emmy wanted to hand select each and every one.

As Jack clinked his mug to hers, his free arm pulled her deeper into his lap. She'd never grow accustomed to touching him like this, wherever and whenever she pleased. How she longed for Caleb and Jimmy to experience such joy. But Caleb and Jimmy were thigh to thigh on the couch, and Jimmy's hand rested on Caleb's knee. A small victory, but progress.

One of these days, Caleb would *finally* tell Jimmy about their own prophecy.

On evenings as lovely as this one, Mary's absence could still strike Emmy like a stone to her chest, one that sank her good spirits. It was maddening, to miss someone she'd never actually known. To realize that it had been Grace who had done Emmy's hair, who had clasped Emmy's hand as they jumped in the river. Who had quietly encouraged their schemes to meet her own selfish needs. But Emmy was determined to bury the life they'd shared before the Society, the moments they'd had while Grace was pretending to be Mary, anything and everything Grace.

Jack, curse him, wouldn't let her.

It was his incessant pestering that convinced Emmy to return to Grimsbane Tower with him. For closure, he said, though Emmy wasn't sure such a thing existed.

There had been no visiting room when Emmy had been prisoner here, but as Jack spoke to the warden he'd appointed, the guards led Emmy to a cell with doors on both sides. Folding her hands in her lap, she took a seat at the long table in the center and, with her stomach in knots, faced Grace.

In the wool uniform, with her blonde hair in a long braid down her back, Grace appeared younger than she had in her ornate ball gowns. More like the Grace from the tenement house. Still annoyingly pretty, just . . . fragile.

Once the guards left, her blue eyes shifted to Emmy. "Did you come here to gloat?"

"No."

Silence. Grace's eyes flitted about the room, taking in every detail. "I can hear the guards talking, so I know Jack Fontaine is the new commander. You lied about his death."

Emmy said nothing, only stared at her former friend.

Grace slammed her cuffed hands against the desk. "You think you can assuage your guilt by visiting me? By improving the conditions of this hell on earth? As if a bed and a book are all it takes to forget that I am not free. But I will be," she added, her lips curving as she reclined.

Still taunting. When Emmy didn't take her bait, Grace's eyes wandered about the room again, marking every stone, every detail.

It hit Emmy then. She was Grace's first visitor. Her *only* visitor.

Because Grace had no one left in this world who cared for her.

How wrong Emmy had been about Grace's motivation. She'd thought vanity was her weakness, that she'd do anything to make the Society love her. But Grace did not seek the Society's adoration because she wanted to be loved; she sought it to *survive*. So desperate was she to not be poor and powerless that she'd betrayed the closest thing she'd had to family.

Survival drove her to pursue someone like Oliver. To not be satisfied by the love of her aunt and uncle. To burn Lizzie Windsor for daring to stand between Grace and what she deemed hers.

Survival drove her to forge a relic with Papa's remains. To protect herself.

Grace watched her warily. "Why are you looking at me like that?"

It was not an excuse. It did not justify a single thing she'd done, but still, Emmy felt a smidgen of relief. It had never been about her.

Grace had done terrible, unforgivable things.

Grace had also suffered. She had been neglected. This was true, too.

As Emmy rose from her chair, she studied Grace one final time. She'd loved her; she truly had. And though Grace would never admit it, she, too, had to miss what they'd shared. Their friendship had been real, even if it had ended in so much pain.

Emmy would see if there was anything they could do for the prisoners without visitors. A priest, perhaps. Or maybe Grace could have time with Clara, who was serving her sentence for a few more months.

"Ems?" Grace called.

Emmy turned slowly.

"Whoever did your hair did it all wrong. When you part it that way, you look like a man."

Of fucking course. It was a gift, really, to end on such a note. "Goodbye, Grace."

With surprising lightness, Emmy slipped out of the cell. Out of Grimsbane.

As she walked with Jack back to the dock, their breath pluming in the winter air, Jack nudged her with his hip. "Would you like to swim back? Or is it not cold enough for you?"

Emmy gave him a playful shove, but he righted himself easily, sliding his arm over her shoulders. Leaning against him, Emmy let herself shed this place for good.

The ferry approached the dock lazily, its lanterns illuminating the swirls of fog displaced by the bow. There was a sharpness to the brisk air, an ethereal quiet that always came when snow was approaching, as if New York was holding its breath.

Time was passing, as it always did.

"So what's next?" Jack wrapped his arms around her waist, tugging her closer. "Any other secret elitist societies you'd like to dismantle?"

"Perhaps." She lifted onto her tiptoes, brushing her lips against her favorite smile of his, the one tinged with mischief. "After all, there's always Wall Street."

ACKNOWLEDGMENTS

SOPHOMORE NOVEL COMPLETE! THERE IS little more humbling than setting out to write a book—a fully outlined, carefully planned, already contracted book—only to rewrite it. Repeatedly. If I didn't have such wonderful people supporting me, I might still be drafting this novel.

First and foremost, to the readers: You truly know how to make an author's dreams come true. Your enthusiasm, from DMs to social media posts to book signings, keeps writing fun. Whether you've been on this journey with me since *Revelle*, or you've just discovered *Gilded in Vengeance*, I'm so grateful you're here.

An enormous thank-you to my editor, Kristin Daly Rens, for reading the embarrassing first drafts of this story and not running for the hills! Thank you for your patience as I kept digging for the right way to tell Emmy's tale, for the brilliant (albeit intimidating) idea of beginning in what used to be the middle, and for your unyielding kindness and dedication to quality.

Thank you to my agent, Lauren Spieller, for always being in my corner. You pushed me to brainstorm until the idea for this story was born, and you kept me sane with reminders that "some books need more time." Extra thanks to Hannah Teachout for all the support. You two are a dream team. Shout-out to the rest of Folio Literary Management for championing *Gilded in Vengeance*, especially in foreign markets.

The HarperCollins team! Thank you, Christian Vega, for all you do behind the scenes. When I realized you'd read and discussed those early drafts with Kristin, I cringed for a whole year. Thank you to designers Chris Kwon and Jenna Stempel-Lobell for making this book so beautiful, inside and out, and to Zoë van Dijk for the stunning cover illustration. Thank you to senior production editor Caitlin Lonning, with the help of Emily Adrukaitis and Lana Barnes, for ensuring that the story is smooth, polished, and internally consistent. Thank you to Annabelle Sinoff and Melissa Cicchitelli for production, to Lisa Calcasola and Audrey Diestelkamp for marketing, and to Kelly Haberstroh for publicity. Extra thanks to Patty Rosati, Mimi Rankin, and the rest of the school and library marketing team. And to the sales team, especially Monica Shah, Kathy Faber, Jennifer Wygand, and Jessica Abel, for your hard work getting my words into stores.

I am particularly grateful to the authenticity readers who helped shape the representation in this story.

All my gratitude to my lovely friends and critique partners who (eventually) read this story in its entirety: Tauri Cox, the angel who read repeatedly; Anna Mercier, the cheerleader and craft expert who kept me sane; Emily Taylor, the world-building guru who challenged me to level up; and Ashley Winstead, the thriller queen who made sure the revenge packed a punch. Alexa Martin and Meg Long, thank you both for talking through this revenge idea with me, and for always being willing to read a tricky scene. Emily Thiede, your discerning eye and generous squeals gave me the confidence to move past the midpoint. And to the Slackers: I can't imagine surviving publishing without you all.

So many author friends read a version of my prologue or (many) first chapters: Allison Saft, Rochelle Hassan, Ruby Barrett, Angela Montoya, Jill Tew, Brian Kennedy, Clare Osongco, and Erinn Salge: I'm indebted to you all.

And now, closer to home: Jessica Watson, thank you not only for your fresh eyes (and ears) on this one, but for knocking on my window with late-night treats while I'm having a deadline meltdown. Eternal thanks to my parents and in-laws for their endless support, both for the kiddos and for me personally. And to Poppy, my grandfather who traced our family's roots from Italy to the tenement houses of Brooklyn: your research helped inspire the setting, and our talks about writing and perseverance will live in my heart forever.

Bodhi and Luca, my (not so) little muffins: You kept me humble by trolling me about how long I worked on this book. Luca, thank you for suggesting magical hide-and-seek, which is now in Chapter 16. And Bodhi, thank you for always waiting patiently for your good-night kiss while I finished one more page.

Alex, my love: Quite simply, I couldn't write a thing without you. Thank you for holding down the fort and prioritizing my writing time and time again. And no, you're still not Jamison, and you are absolutely not Jack Fontaine.